"You're the man who married me, Noah Buchanan, and I command you to treat me with respect!"

"If I'm the man you married, Isobel, then you'd better do as I say. That means no taking matters into your own hands and getting somebody killed. If I'm your husband, I'm the boss. You hear?"

Simmering, Isobel stared at the towering cowboy who presumed to rule over her by his bartered title of "husband." His blue eyes fairly crackled as he met her gaze.

"You know nothing," she managed.

"I know that right now you're starting to look like a blushing bride."

"Oh, yes, my strong, brave husband," she responded, batting her eyes for effect. "I will stitch and bake—and weep for joy when I hear your footsteps on the porch."

"You do that, sweetheart." Chuckling, Noah tucked Isobel close and strolled with her toward the adobe home.

At the warmth of his arm around her shoulders and the graze of his unshaven jaw against her cheek, it occurred to Isobel that perhaps she wouldn't mind being a wife who would sew and bake and wait for her husband to come home at night. What a curious thought.

Catherine Palmer
and
Renee Ryan

The Outlaw's Bride
&
Dangerous Allies

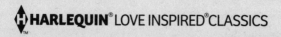
HARLEQUIN® LOVE INSPIRED®CLASSICS

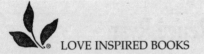 LOVE INSPIRED BOOKS

ISBN-13: 978-1-335-45470-6

The Outlaw's Bride & Dangerous Allies

Copyright © 2020 by Harlequin Books S.A.

The Outlaw's Bride
First published in 2010. This edition published in 2020.
Copyright © 2010 by Catherine Palmer

Dangerous Allies
First published in 2010. This edition published in 2020.
Copyright © 2010 by Renee Halverson

CONTENTS

THE OUTLAW'S BRIDE   7
Catherine Palmer

DANGEROUS ALLIES   261
Renee Ryan

Catherine Palmer is a bestselling author and winner of the Christy Award for her outstanding Christian romance. She also received the Career Achievement Award for Inspirational Fiction from *RT Book Reviews*. Raised in Kenya, she lives in Atlanta with her husband. They have two grown sons. A graduate of Southwest Baptist University, she also holds a master's degree from Baylor University.

Books by Catherine Palmer

Love Inspired Historical

The Briton
The Maverick's Bride
The Outlaw's Bride
The Gunman's Bride

Steeple Hill Single Title

That Christmas Feeling
Love's Haven
Leaves of Hope
A Merry Little Christmas
The Heart's Treasure
Thread of Deceit
Fatal Harvest
Stranger in the Night

Visit the Author Profile page at Harlequin.com.

THE OUTLAW'S BRIDE

Catherine Palmer

Never take your own revenge, beloved, but leave room for the wrath of God, for it is written, "Vengeance is mine, I will repay," says the Lord.
—*Romans* 12:19

To Sharon Buchanan-McClure,
who introduced me to the real Belle Buchanan

Chapter One

February 18, 1878
Lincoln County, New Mexico Territory

Isobel stood, her crimson boots side by side like drops of bright blood on the snow. She stared at her feet for a moment, thinking how far they had come from the sprawling pasturelands of her beloved Spanish Catalonia to this slushy trail in the New World. Weeks aboard a wave-tossed ship, days across the Texas prairie to Fort Belknap, miles along the Goodnight-Loving cattle trail toward Santa Fe... and for what?

Sighing, she pulled her lace mantilla closer around her face, lifted her chin and walked on through the scrubby, wind-whipped trees. Her emerald hem swept across fallen, brown pine needles, the ruffle on her skirt rippling along behind.

It had happened here, she thought, near this very place. A shiver of apprehension coursed through her as she looked in the twilight at the secluded forest. Five years earlier, her father—the powerful Don Alberto Matas—had been jerked from his buckboard wagon and shot.

Isobel tightened her knotted fingers inside her muff

and squeezed her eyes shut against the sting of tears. As a child, she had believed her father invincible.

Forcing away the fear that haunted her—transforming it to the more comfortable heat of anger—she gritted her teeth. Why had the lawless Americans done nothing to find her father's murderer? Not only a murderer but a thief. The killer had stolen the packet of land-grant titles and jewels that had been her inheritance—the dowry to secure her marriage to Don Guillermo Pascal of Santa Fe.

She inhaled a deep breath of crisp, pine-scented air. Five years had passed, yet the anger and betrayal still burned brightly in her heart. Despite the pain, the five years spent managing her father's vast estates in Spain had been good ones. She had overseen lands, governed workers and carved a faith that could not be shaken. And then she had traveled to America.

Though at twenty-three she knew her hopes of marriage might appear dim, she still was betrothed to Don Guillermo. She would see to it that he married her. She would recover her stolen inheritance as well. Isobel Matas was not one to cower when faced with a challenge. Glancing behind, she scanned the scrub oak and twisted-pine woods. The small party of travelers who had accompanied her from Texas to New Mexico—an itinerant preacher, a missionary doctor and his family, a schoolteacher—rested from the journey. Their horses grazed, tethered a safe distance from the trail.

The delay would put them in Lincoln Town after dark, too late for her to speak to the sheriff. She chose not to tarry and drink coffee. Instead she walked alone through the forest and thought about her father. If he hadn't come to the New Mexico Territory, he would still be alive, his golden hair shining in the sunlight, his deep laughter echoing over the rolling hills of Catalonia.

Hoofbeats thudded across the damp snow. Her eyes darted toward the trail. Highwaymen? Banditos, like the men who had murdered her father?

Alarm froze her breath. Her traveling companions were too far away to be of help, and she had left her pistol in her saddlebag. Clutching her mantilla at her throat, she melted into the shadows of a large juniper. Leaning against the rough trunk, she peered through the lace in the direction of the sound.

"Things are unhappy indeed in Lincoln Town, Noah." A young voice. English—not American.

"We're glad you're back from the trail. Mr. Chisum is wise to let you run his cattle. South Spring River Ranch profits under your management."

Isobel counted three riders, one dapper in a brown tweed coat, the others roughly dressed, their faces obscured by hats and heavy beards. Livestock behind. More men at the rear.

The man called Noah rode tall on his black horse. He wore a long coat of black leather and was massively built, with broad shoulders and lean, hardened legs. With skin the color of sunbaked adobe, his face was grim beneath the wide brim of his black felt hat. His blue eyes flashed back and forth…alert, missing nothing. This man—and not the dandy—knew a dangerous life.

"Do you suppose Mr. Chisum would take my side against Dolan?" The young Englishman's voice held a note of hope. He could not be more than thirty years old.

Noah shrugged. "Chisum stays out of a fight until it reaches his own back door."

"Don't worry, Mr. Tunstall," the third rider put in. "He'll come out of that jail fightin' mad against Dolan."

"I expect so—" the Englishman began. A raucous squawk shattered the stillness in the canyon. Isobel stiffened.

"Turkeys." Noah Buchanan rose in his stirrups and searched the gathering dusk. "How about it, boys? Let's bag one."

"Sure!" The slender man slid his rifle from his saddle scabbard. "Coming, Mr. Tunstall?"

"No, thank you." The Englishman beckoned the three riders behind the packhorses. "But go on—all of you. Perhaps Mrs. McSween will cook it for us when we get to Lincoln."

The men set off toward the nearby ridge. Noah glanced to one side, and his eyes fell on Isobel. He frowned. Reining his horse, he let his companions ride on.

"What have you there, Buchanan?" the Englishman cried out.

The American looked at Isobel an instant longer, as if to confirm the strange apparition in the woods. "Some kind of bird," he called back.

She squared her shoulders and lifted her chin. *Bird?* She knew the man might do anything. Yet there was something gentle in his manner. Perhaps it was the way he held the reins…as if he were an *artista*. She had seen the hands of a poet and she felt sure this man's hands, though large and strong, held no malice.

Glancing at her one more time, his eyes flashed with—what was it—warning? Then he flicked the reins and his horse vanished into the woods.

Isobel licked her wind-parched lips. Looking up, she saw suddenly what the others had not. Forty or fifty armed horsemen guided their mounts down onto the trail from the ridge.

"Tunstall!" A shout rang out from halfway up the slope. "That you, Tunstall?"

The Englishman reined his horse. "Who's there?"

"Jesse Evans. I'm with Rattlesnake Jim Jackson and

a posse Jimmie Dolan sent to round you up. He made us deputies." The riders advanced to within twenty yards of Tunstall, and Isobel calculated they would meet directly in front of the juniper tree.

"Come ahead, Tunstall," a second man commanded. The blue light of the setting sun coated his heavy jaw and wide nose. "We ain't gonna hurt you."

"What is it you want, Jackson?" Tunstall kept riding as the men facing him lifted their rifles so the stocks rested on their knees. Isobel tensed, willing the Englishman to draw his own weapon. Could he not see these men meant to harm him?

Jackson urged his horse forward.

"Not yet," he muttered to Evans. "Wait till he gets nearer."

Isobel's mantilla buffeted her face, and she struggled to push it aside. She must warn the Englishman. But at that moment, his companions burst through the trees onto the trail.

"Take cover, Tunstall!" Buchanan shouted. "Head for the woods!"

"Now!" Jackson raised his rifle and fired. Tunstall jerked backward and dropped from his horse to the frozen ground.

Evans dismounted and ran to where Tunstall lay face down. He pulled Tunstall's revolver from its holster and shot the fallen man in the back of the head. Then he turned the gun on the horse and pulled the trigger.

Isobel swallowed in revulsion. She realized that Tunstall's friends had been too late to help him. They dispersed into the woods as the posse crowded forward, a mixture of triumph and horror written on their faces.

"With two empty chambers in Tunstall's gun," Evans crowed, "the judge'll think he fired first. Let's round up the rest of his men and give 'em the same medicine!"

Trembling, Isobel watched Evans remount and ride away. Jackson and three others remained. They stretched out the Englishman's body and wrapped it in blankets. Chuckling, Jackson pillowed Tunstall's head on a folded overcoat. Then he laid the horse's head on the Englishman's hat.

"This is abominable," Isobel muttered, icy fear melting before crackling rage. And suddenly she saw her father—lying just as Tunstall now lay—murdered, with no one to defend him.

As she stepped from behind the juniper, the wind caught her lace mantilla, tugged it from its comb and whipped it across the trail like a dancing butterfly. She caught her breath. Jackson glanced up and snatched it midair. Frowning, he spat, and stepped over Tunstall's body.

"Don't move, *señorita*." His voice dripped with contempt. "Hey, fellers. Looks like we got us a Mexican."

Isobel swallowed the last of her fear and remembered the raw wound of her father's death. A familiar anger flowed. If she must die, she would die bravely. Lifting her chin, she stepped onto the trail.

"You…" She stopped before the men. Forcing herself to think in English, she spoke. "I have seen your murder. I curse you—*asesinos*—assassins!"

"You ain't seen nothing yet, honey." Jackson whisked his rifle to his shoulder. But before he could fire, a horse thundered across the trail. Its rider leaned down and swept Isobel from the path of a bullet.

"You're dead, you little Mexican!" Jackson's voice rang out behind her. "I swear I'll kill you!"

"Keep your head down, lady." Noah rode through the trees, one arm around the woman's waist, the other controlling his horse. "They got Tunstall, didn't they?"

"The man called Rattlesnake killed him," she cried. "Give me your rifle and horse. I shall make them pay."

"Whoa, now." Noah reined his horse to a halt beneath an overhanging sandstone ledge. As he lowered his bandanna, he looked the woman up and down. Emerald gown, red ruffles, crimson boots. "Give you *what?*" he asked.

"Your horse. Your rifle. For revenge."

Around them, all had calmed—the wind, the horse, the trees, Noah's pounding heart. He studied her eyes, her nose, the high curve of her Spanish cheekbones and her lips.

"My father," she choked out. "My father was…" Covering her face with her hands, she folded inward. Her shoulders convulsed as a sob welled from her throat.

Noah set a gentle hand on her back. "Now then, little lady, don't you know revenge never did a lick of good? The Good Lord's in charge of that. One way or another, He'll see that those men pay. You put everything you saw right out of your head, hear?"

She nodded, dabbing her eyes. "They even killed his horse."

Noah shook his head, then spoke. "The woods are clear. The posse's gone to Lincoln to tell Dolan they've done his dirty work. I'll take you back to your people. I passed them on the trail. They'll keep you safe."

He turned his horse, and the rhythmic gait eased the tension in his shoulders. Darkness like velvet silk enfolded them. Noah knew he must weigh the implications of Tunstall's murder. But for now, he drank in the stillness, the quiet.

The woman had draped against him, her cheek resting on his chest. He recognized this was an improper, even dangerous, situation for a man in his position—single, bound to a mission and lonely. He had rescued her, and now, by all that was moral, he should move his arm from around her.

But she had closed her eyes. Her breath stirred the hair in his beard. Her hand…each individual finger…warmed the skin on his arm.

The horse picked its way up a hill. Noah watched the moon rise above the pines on a ridge, his heart heavy. John Tunstall had been a good man. And young, maybe in his early twenties. Now a powder keg had been lit. Though Alexander McSween was a citified lawyer, he would go after Tunstall's killers.

Noah shifted in the saddle, and his thoughts swung away, too. The woman intrigued him. Her accent was Spanish, and she looked the part of a rich Mexican doña— green dress ruffled with red lace, red boots, jeweled comb. All this, yet her hair gleamed golden in the moonlight.

He gazed at the silken ringlet that curled down her back. If he took out her comb, the whole mass of hair would come tumbling down. Its mysterious, spicy scent would waft out into the air and—

"There is my party, vaquero," she said suddenly. "And your amigos, too. You see the fire?"

Caught by surprise, Noah shook off his wayward thoughts. He had been on the trail with Chisum's cattle many months. What else could be expected of a man who found his arms wrapped around a fine-smelling lady? He sent up a quick prayer to help him stay on task.

Tunstall's men were standing with the other travelers around the fire. There was Dick Brewer—Noah's closest friend and Tunstall's foreman—along with Billy Bonney and several others.

"Miss Matas!" A young, spectacled gentleman hurried forward as Noah guided his horse into the clearing. "We've been worried. Thank you, sir. I'm sure Miss Matas's family will reward you for saving her."

"Not necessary," Noah said. "Glad to help."

"Oh, Isobel, are you all right?" A pale woman rushed to her side. "When we heard the shots, I was terrified for you!"

Isobel's expression softened. "I'm all right, Susan. I was walking in the forest."

"Did you see what happened, ma'am?" Dick asked her. "A man was shot and killed."

Noah dismounted and lifted his hands. Isobel slipped into his arms, but when her feet touched the ground, he set her aside. He had been distracted by the woman long enough.

As Tunstall's men gathered around, she lifted her chin. "The one called Rattlesnake shot first. Then Evans. The killers must be brought to justice."

"Yep, and you belong with your friends," Noah spoke up. "Leave justice to these fellows."

"But, Noah," Dick argued, "she's a witness. She could help us. She could testify."

"Dolan's men saw her," Noah told them. "Snake swore he'd kill her. She needs to get out of the territory fast. Where are you headed, ma'am?"

"To Lincoln Town," she replied. "To speak with the sheriff."

"Someone murdered Isobel's father here five years ago," the pale woman, Susan, explained in a soft voice. "Isobel is determined to find out who did it."

Noah shook his head. "Bad idea. If you're going to Lincoln, *señorita*, you can bet Snake will find you."

"If one of us could protect her," Dick said, "we could use her testimony."

"How about you?" Noah suggested. "Your place isn't far. She could lie low there until the trouble blows over."

Dick looked away, his gray eyes troubled. "Noah, they killed John. It's not that I wouldn't protect a woman, you know that. But I was Tunstall's foreman and his friend. I'm going after them."

"We're all going after them!" Billy Bonney stepped up. "C'mon, Buchanan, you can't expect one of us to babysit the *señorita*. You're not a Tunstall man, and Chisum's in jail. Why don't you take the job?"

Noah held up a hand. "Not me, kid. I've got papers to deliver to Chisum and my own business to see to."

"But you told us John Chisum ain't gonna sell you no land unless you can prove you're willing to settle down and knock off that reputation you carry around. Now, say you come along with this pretty *señorita*—hey, what say you marry her? Chisum would sell you the land quick if you did that. You know how sentimental he is about families."

"*Marry* her?" Noah felt the blood siphon from his face. "Billy Bonney, you're a fool. There's no way—"

"Can you be serious?" Isobel interrupted. "Never would I marry this…this dusty vaquero! I am betrothed to Don Guillermo Pascal of Santa Fe. Nor do I need a protector. I am a better marksman than most of the men in Catalonia and I ride like the wind. I shall go with you on this journey of revenge."

"You can't come with us," Billy exclaimed, eyeing Isobel as if she were possessed. "The men who killed our boss have the law on their side. And the law in Lincoln County is as crooked as this trail. You'd best get on up to Santa Fe and marry your rich muchacho."

"Not until I find my father's murderer."

"Isobel," Susan broke in, "please consider what these

men are saying. The murderers have threatened to kill you, and you have no protectors. Why not take on Mr.—"

"Buchanan," Billy put in. "His name is Noah Buchanan."

Lest the conversation erupt into a shouting match, Isobel had agreed to walk a short distance from the men to discuss the situation with Susan.

"Isobel," her friend said softly. "Can you trust me?"

Nodding, Isobel acknowledged the truth. Though she had not planned to get close to the others on the journey, they had won her friendship after all.

"This is a lawless land," Susan said. "If you insist on finding your father's killer and getting your inheritance back, you must have protection. I know you ride and shoot well, but you'll never survive against fifty armed men. If you won't go to Santa Fe and get married like you should, let Mr. Buchanan watch over you."

Isobel glanced at the huddled group of men. Billy Bonney and Dick Brewer clearly were exhorting Noah to action. "Don Guillermo may not accept me now, anyway," she murmured, finally admitting aloud her fear. "Without my dowry, I cannot push for marriage. By law he should marry me, but his family is powerful."

"Then you *must* get your rightful land. And to do that, you must let Mr. Buchanan look after you."

Isobel knew it was the right decision—the only possible conclusion. She gave her friend a quick hug and hurried across the slushy snow to the men.

"Very well, Señor Buchanan," she informed him. "If you agree to protect me, I shall bear witness to the authorities about the murder."

"Sure, I'll take you on," Noah said. "If you'll marry me."

She gasped. "Marry you? *Borrachón*! What have you been drinking?"

"Not a thing." He studied her for a moment, then gave a nod. "We'll get the preacher over there to hitch us up. I'll tell folks you're the wife I brought in from the trail. That's true enough."

She stared at the blue-eyed man. "But I am already engaged."

"And the last thing I want is to get married." He glanced at Dr. Ealy, a missionary who was standing quietly in the background. "We'll get it annulled later. Extreme circumstances…marriage without parents' consent…lack of consummation…we'll think of something. Once I convince Chisum to sell me the land I've been after and you settle your business in Lincoln, you can go to Santa Fe and marry your don. Meantime, I won't lay a hand on you."

"Whoa, Buchanan!" Billy laughed. "Don't get carried away."

"Naw, kid. It'll all be on the up-and-up."

Again Isobel assessed the bearded, brawny trail boss. Did she really need his protection? Probably. Her father had been murdered despite his armed guard.

Could she delay marrying Don Guillermo? Certainly. Her fiancé had never even responded to her letter of intent to journey to America.

Retrieving the stolen land-grant titles was her primary goal. More than anything, she ached to possess those rich pastures on which to graze cattle of her own.

"Very well, Mr. Buchanan," she declared. "If you will protect me while I search for my father's killer and recover my family's stolen land, I shall marry you and prove to Mr. Chisum that you are very settled. And I shall be your witness in the law courts."

"Then I reckon we've got a deal."

Dick Brewer spoke up. "Stay at my place tonight, Noah, and head for Chisum's ranch in the morning. We've got to get Tunstall's body to Lincoln, and we can see the others safely into town."

The two conferred a moment before Dr. Ealy cleared his throat. Accustomed to unexpected weddings, funerals and the like, he had agreed to perform the ceremony and wanted to get on with it.

Isobel barely heard his words. Instead she stared down at the pointed toes of her red boots. What had she done? Minutes ago she had been planning to marry Don Guillermo of Santa Fe. Now this leather-clad cowboy who owned nothing but his horse and gun would be her husband.

The ceremony ended, and Susan presented her friend with a bundle of folded garments. "Not much of a wedding gift, Isobel. But wear them, please. Those killers will recognize you right away if you stay as you are."

As the shaken group set off down the moonlit trail in one party, Noah explained to Isobel the situation in Lincoln Town.

Jimmie Dolan had profited from his store and vast acreage by keeping the small landowners financially strapped, until the young Englishman John Tunstall had moved to the area. On the advice of his business partner, Alexander McSween, Tunstall had started his own store and ranch.

Dr. Ealy added that he, along with his wife, two young daughters and Susan Gates, had been summoned to Lincoln by McSween. "It looks as if we're already in McSween's war," he observed, "and we haven't even arrived in Lincoln."

"Just keep quiet about tonight's business," Noah instructed the group. "We'll do the same."

As Isobel watched her companions head north in the darkness, she and Noah turned their horses east. Less than an hour later, they arrived at an old cabin with a sagging front porch. With some trepidation, she followed this man who was no more than a stranger up the steps.

Without speaking, he lit two oil lamps and began to build a fire. She watched him work, appraising biceps that bunched as he placed logs on crackling kindling, brown fingers that set an iron pot he had filled with water on a hook above the blaze. Broad back. Shaggy brown hair and beard. Muddy boots. Leather chaps. Such a common man, this Noah Buchanan.

"Like to wash up?" He asked the question so abruptly that she took a step backward.

He dusted his hands on his thighs before pushing open a door and carrying her bag into a small bedroom. She followed, surveying with some dismay the narrow iron bed, the washstand with its chipped white crockery, the window fitted with paper. Noah filled a cracked bowl with heated water, then shut the door behind him.

Isobel walked to the door and listened to him whistling in the other room. Dare she trust the man? She slid her revolver from her bag and set it on a table near the tub. With another glance at the door, she changed into a nightgown. Then she removed her comb, dipped her hands into the water and finally began to relax.

Curling onto the narrow bed, she sighed deeply. But as sleep crept over her, a movement rippled behind her eyelids. Horses cantering up a trail. Men shouting. Gunshots.

Noah sat on a three-legged stool before the fire and warmed his hands. A second pot of water had begun to steam. The woman in the next room would be asleep by now. No matter how hotheaded, she must be exhausted.

He smiled and shook his head as he filled a large basin with hot water and set to shaving his whiskers off with Dick Brewer's straight razor.

Good old Dick. As Tunstall's foreman, he was bound to get into the thick of the trouble. Noah peered into a mirror hung by the iron cookstove. If Dick got hurt, he couldn't stand by, no matter what he'd promised the *señorita*.

Of course, the way she'd acted today, he'd probably have trouble keeping her out of it.

He dipped his head into a second bowl of fresh water and scrubbed his scalp. She was crazy to come after her father's killer all by herself. Of course he was just as loco to have married her. John Chisum would take some fancy convincing to swallow that one.

Trail dust was getting a little old. Noah looked forward to settling down and fixing up his own cabin. Then he could really begin to make his dreams come true.

He stared for a long time at the flames, thinking of the small packet he had brought in his saddlebag from Arizona, filled with pens and ink bottles. Soon he would start to put down the thoughts he had been having for years. Stories about trail rides, roundups, cowboys. Images and memories he didn't want to forget.

The thought of writing sent him searching Dick's cabin for paper. Maybe he would start right now—the tale of the *señorita* and the Dolan gang. He wished he had a blank notebook with him, but they were back at his cabin.

Dick never kept paper. He searched the first room and hesitated at the bedroom door, then knocked. When he got no answer, he wondered if the woman had left. He leaned closer, peered into the room, caught his breath.

She lay curled on the bed, asleep. A fan of dark lashes rested on each pale cheek. Her chin was tucked against her arm. Long, golden hair draped around her shoulders and down her side.

Noah took a hesitant step toward the bed. She wore a silky white gown but her feet were bare. He was staring at her slender ankles when she turned. A soft moan escaped her lips as she lifted her head.

Rising up on one elbow, she whispered, *"¿Mamá? ¿Dónde está?"*

She lifted her hand to her eyes.

"Who…who are you?" Her voice was husky in the night air.

"I'm Noah Buchanan," he answered. "I'm your husband."

Chapter Two

"Noah Buchanan?" With a gasp, Isobel scrambled out of bed. What on earth was the vaquero doing in her room?

"That blanket," she ordered, pointing. "Now!"

As he fetched a faded homespun coverlet from a nearby chair, she sorted through images of this so-called protector. Shaggy black beard, dusty denims, travel-worn leather.

Outlined in lamplight, his strong, clean jaw was squared with tension. His hair shone a damp blue-black.

"You look different, *señor*," she said, glancing at her pistol on the table.

"I shaved." His blue eyes sparkled as they flicked down to her ankles.

Before he could speak again, she snatched the gun and leveled it at his heart. "Take your hungry eyes away from me!" she commanded, cocking the gun for emphasis. "Stand back, Buchanan."

"Whoa, now." He held up his hands. "I didn't mean any harm. I was looking for paper."

"Paper? Why paper?"

He didn't answer.

"Why paper?" Her fingers tensed on the pistol handle.

"I wanted to write." Swifter than the strike of a rattlesnake, his hand shot out and knocked the pistol from her grip. A blast of flame and smoke erupted from the barrel. The hanging glass lamp shattered. The gun clattered across the wooden floor. As the light died, he grabbed her shoulder and stared hard into her eyes.

"Don't ever pull a gun on me again, woman," he growled. "You hear?"

"Let me go!" she cried out, the nearness of the man plunging fear like a knife into her heart.

Relaxing his shoulders, he stepped back. "I won't hurt you, Isobel. I made a vow."

She swallowed in confusion at the change in him. "I must trust you to take me to Lincoln Town. Yet I know nothing about you."

"You know me real well. John Chisum says if you want to know a man, find out what makes him mad. If you draw a gun on me again, you can say adios to the best shot west of the Pecos."

"The best shot west of the Pecos?" She laughed. "I will have to see that to believe it, *señor.*"

The moon kindled a silver flame in his eyes as he spoke. "Stick around Lincoln County and you'll see it. I can outdraw any man in the territory. But that's not what I aim to do with myself from here on."

She lifted the blanket to her chin. "And what is your aim?"

"The minute John Chisum gets out of jail, I'll introduce you as Isobel...no, Belle. Belle Buchanan, a slip of a lady I met and married on the trail."

"My name is Isobel Matas."

"You'd better be Belle Buchanan if you don't want Snake Jackson after your hide. And Belle is just the shiest, quietest little thing Lincoln Town has ever seen."

"If I'm to be Belle Buchanan, quiet and shy for your

John Chisum, you had better be the fastest gun west of the Pecos—or your little wife will change swiftly into Isobel Matas, the fastest gun in Catalonia."

Noah chuckled. "I've tangled with a few women in my time, but never one as sure talking, high strung and mule stubborn as you."

"Nor as pretty," she added.

"Ornery is more like it," he said with a grin. "You put on a shy smile, and I'll keep my trigger finger ready. We'll settle the matter of my land first. Then we'll check into this question of your father."

"My father first. Then your land."

"The trouble over Tunstall's death needs to die down before we start poking around in Lincoln. We'll go see Chisum first."

"I have waited five years," she told him. "I have traveled many miles. I will wait no longer. Now, leave me to sleep, Buchanan. I must speak to the sheriff tomorrow."

"Sheriff Brady deputized that posse you saw today. He gave Snake Jackson a lawman's badge. Brady's a Dolan man. You ride into Lincoln tomorrow and you'll be eating hot lead for supper."

He headed for the open door, but he paused with his hand on the latch. "And it's Noah… Noah to you…not Buchanan. Don't forget I'm your husband."

As he shut the door behind him, Isobel sagged against the bed frame. How could she forget? The man would be with her every moment, ordering her around, insisting on his own way. He was a bull. Rough and unrefined. Headstrong and stubborn. So powerful he frightened her.

Sinking onto the lumpy mattress, she closed her eyes. But instantly she saw him. Noah Buchanan. She felt the grip of his hand on her shoulder. He was a brute—nothing like Don Guillermo Pascal of Santa Fe.

At that thought, she left the bed again and searched through her saddlebag until her fingers closed on an oval locket. Holding the pendant up to catch the moonlight, she studied the tiny painting of her intended. His jutting chin, firm mouth, deep-set brooding eyes and shock of black hair made her proud. Here was the splendid Spaniard who could outwit the roughshod cowboy. This was the torero who could defeat the bull.

For ten years Isobel had known that Guillermo Pascal would become her husband. He owned a sprawling hacienda, a fine stable, countless cattle, land that stretched many miles across the New Mexico Territory. He was wealthy, noble, Spanish. And he was hers.

She snapped the locket clasp and slipped the golden chain back into her bag. As she crossed to the bed, she noticed the shards of glass from the shattered lamp. She ought to sweep them up.

But Isobel Matas had never touched a broom in her life. She was to be served—not to be a servant. Someone else would have to sweep the glass, someone meant for menial tasks. Shrugging, she found the fallen pistol, pushed it beneath her pillow and climbed back into bed.

The first rays of sunlight were slipping over the pine trees when Isobel waded from the shallows of slumber. She fought to catch the remnants of her dream—of that magnificent man who strode through the purple-ribboned depths, his chest broad, his shoulders strong, his eyes so blue. Blue?

Isobel frowned. Guillermo Pascal's eyes were not blue.

At a tinkling sound in the room, she eased onto one elbow. In the gray light she made out a tall figure.

Noah Buchanan.

His black hat tilted toward the back of his head. His

shirtsleeves were rolled to his elbows. He wore a leather belt with a silver buckle. In his hand he held a stick. A rifle?

No…a broom.

Humming, he swept the broken glass. Unaware of her watchful eye, he raked it into a tin dustpan and stepped out of the room. She shook her head. This vaquero who could knock a loaded gun from her hand, who could guide his horse through darkness, who had walked through her dreams all night…this cattleman of the plains was sweeping!

As she rose from the bed, she caught the smell of frying bacon. He sweeps, he cooks, what else? Mystified, she peered around the door frame.

His worn brown boots thudding on the floor, the bull stalked across the room. His shoulder grazed a hanging pot, one knee knocked a rickety chair aside. But as he leaned over the fire, Noah Buchanan might have been a *cocinero* in a nobleman's kitchen. As he broke six eggs into sizzling grease in a frying pan, he hummed.

Bemused, Isobel eased the bedroom door shut and propped a chair beneath the handle. She wanted no intrusions this time. As she took a petticoat and faded skirt from the bundle Susan Gates had given her, she smiled. Noah Buchanan was rugged and earthy, but he was gentle and unpretentious, too. Perhaps they would do well together for the few days of their marriage.

A wash of guilt crept over Isobel as she slipped on Susan's petticoat. She had married Noah Buchanan under God's eyes. For as long as she could remember, she had faithfully attended church and said her prayers. She knew this marriage was a sin worthy of the harshest punishment.

As she fastened the row of buttons lining the bodice of the blue gown, she wondered what she would suffer. Would she lose her chance to wed Guillermo Pascal? Would she never learn the truth behind her father's death? Or something worse?

"Dear God," she whispered in prayer. "Forgive me, please." She knew God was harsh, vengeful, given to anger. His sacraments were not to be treated lightly. Yet she had done just that.

Struggling with the shadow such thoughts cast across the morning's bright sunlight, she slipped on a pair of boots and laced them. She would make the best of the situation, she decided. She would see to it that the contrived marriage lasted no longer than necessary. Noah Buchanan would remain the stranger he had been from the beginning. For a few days Isobel would become Belle Buchanan—a soft-spoken, common woman, like Susan Gates, the schoolteacher.

Setting her shoulders, Isobel wound her hair into a tight chignon and buried her tortoiseshell comb deep in the saddlebag. Facing the world without her mantilla was uncomfortable. To be bareheaded in public was a disgrace.

Sighing, she thought of the trunks making their way by mule train to Lincoln Town for transfer to Santa Fe. Gowns of silk, ivory linen, satin and taffeta. Lace mantillas, velvet jackets, cloaks, stockings of every hue. She had packed ebony combs, gold pendants, pearl earrings.

But an uneven hem, sagging petticoats and a limp cotton dress were the lot of Belle Buchanan. Drawing a shawl around her shoulders, she recalled the hours she and her mother had spent choosing the perfect gowns for a dance or a visit with friends.

What would Noah think of her transformation? Cautious, she opened the bedroom door. He stood beside a rough-hewn pine table, setting out chipped white plates and spoons. Her heart softening to this strangely gentle man, she stepped out.

* * *

At a sound from the door, Noah glanced up, straightened, and let his gaze trail down the slender figure approaching. Like some Madonna of the prairie, the woman wore a gown of soft blue with a white cotton shawl around her shoulders. Sunlight from the front window framed her, backlighting her golden hair.

"Well, I'll be." He shook his head to clear the surprise and let out a low chuckle. "You sure have changed. You look regular now."

The light in her eyes dimmed as she glanced at the fire. "Susan Gates gave me the dress."

"It looks fine." He wanted to rectify his careless comment, but the words came hard. "You look pretty, ma'am. Like you belong here."

"But I do not belong here." She crossed the room and seated herself. "I belong at the Hacienda Pascal in Santa Fe. I have been trained as a *marquesa*—to oversee many servants, host officials of the government, plan fiestas and bear sons and daughters for my husband in accordance with our Spanish tradition."

"Sounds like a real humdinger of a life." He sat down opposite her. "Care for some scrambled eggs, *marquesa?*"

She bristled until he held the frying pan under her nose. "*Sí.* I suppose I should eat."

Noah set a spoonful of fluffy yellow eggs on her plate and a slab of crisp bacon beside them. He reached into an iron kettle, pulled out two steaming biscuits and tossed them onto her plate.

Bowing his head, he spoke in a low voice. "God, thanks for this new day and Dick Brewer's grub. Amen. Whew! Good thing Dick had his chickens penned up. Otherwise, we'd have been scrounging for breakfast."

At her silence, he glanced up to find her staring at him. "Was that a prayer?"

"Sure. Talking to God like always." He spread butter on a biscuit. "Tunstall did right making Dick foreman. He's got education. He can read and keep record books."

"And you? Have you an education, Buchanan?"

"Name's Noah." He took a sip of coffee. "I can read and write. Mrs. Allison taught me."

"Who is Mrs. Allison?"

"Richard and Jane Allison. He owns land around Fort Worth. English folks." He smiled, remembering. "Mrs. Allison took a liking to me. She didn't have children of her own, see. She used to invite me into the library—books from floor to ceiling. She read me all kinds of stories, mostly from the Bible. Taught me to read, too. I reckon I read nearly every book in that library."

"But where were your mother and aunties to care for you? Why did you live with Señora Allison?

"I didn't live in the big house. Mr. Allison put me in with the other hired hands when I was six or seven. I worked in the stables. What about you? Are you educated?"

"Of course," Isobel replied. "I had a tutor. Later, my father sent me to a finishing school in France. I speak six languages, and I am accomplished in painting and embroidery. Arranging homes is my pleasure."

"Arranging homes?" Noah looked up from his plate and glanced around the cabin with its tin utensils, rickety furnishings and worn rag rug. "What's to arrange?"

"Chairs, tables, pictures. My fine furniture will arrive with my trunks. You would never understand such things, Buchanan. Yet we are alike in some ways."

"How's that?"

"Books. Horses." She sat back in the chair and studied the fire. "I was away at school when news came of my father's murder. I wanted to go to America immediately and avenge his death. But my mother was devastated, and she knew nothing of my father's businesses. So I stayed with her, preparing the books, paying debts, managing the hacienda. Five years passed, and I learned that my greatest love was the land. The cattle. The horses."

"Then you're a vaquero yourself."

"Oh, no!" She laughed. "I am a lady."

"And the land in Spain? Will you go back one day?"

Her smile faded. "My mother has remarried, and my brother is grown. Now he and my stepfather fight. In Catalonia, we follow the tradition of the *hereu-pubilla*. Only a firstborn son can inherit. My brother is the *hereu,* the heir. He will win the legal battle against my mother's new husband."

"And what about you, Isobel? What about all that work you did while your little brother was growing up? You ought to get something out of it."

One eyebrow lifted. "I'm not considered worthy to own land. Nothing is left for me in Spain. I cannot marry there, because my father betrothed me to Don Guillermo of Santa Fe. I'm old now, a *soltera,* a spinster. So I came here to avenge my father's death and find the man who stole my land titles."

"It's the land, then." Noah poured himself another mug of coffee. "You want your land a lot more than you want to marry that don in Santa Fe."

"I do wish to marry Guillermo Pascal, of course. But by law the land is mine. I intend to have it."

"You won't have it long if you marry him. The Pascal family is ruthless. They'll take your property and set you to planning fiestas."

"That is not how it will be!" She pushed back from the table and stood up. "I shall manage my own land. Those grants have belonged to the *familia* Matas from the earliest days of Spanish exploration. Don't presume to predict my future, Buchanan. You are a vaquero. You know nothing. Now, saddle my horse while I prepare for the journey to Lincoln Town."

"Hold on a minute there." Noah got to his feet and caught her arm. "A cowboy is as worthy of respect as any land-grubbing don. And I didn't take an oath to be a servant to the grand *marquesa*. I'll see to your horse while you wash dishes, but we're not going to Lincoln today. We're headed for Chisum's South Spring River Ranch until the trouble dies down."

Nostrils flared, she peeled his hand from her arm. "You may go to the Chisum ranch, Buchanan, but today I speak to Sheriff Brady." Starting for the bedroom door, she paused and looked back. "And Isobel Matas does not wash dishes."

Biting back a retort he would regret, Noah banked the fire and set off for the barn. He tried to pray his way through the silence as he saddled his horse, and he had just about calmed down when he heard the woman step outside.

"You finished with those dishes?" he called.

She lifted her chin. "I am not a servant, *señor*."

He was silent a moment, his jaw rigid. Then he left the horse and strode to the porch.

"Listen, *señorita*. We have a rule out here in the West. It's called, 'I cook, you clean.' Dick let us use his cabin, and we'll leave it the way we found it. Got that?"

Her pretty lips tightened. "And in Spain we have a rule also. 'A woman of property does not wash dishes.'"

"But you don't have any property, remember? So you'd better—"

Noah stopped speaking when the haughtiness suddenly

drained from her face. Her brow furrowed as she focused on the distant ridge, and her lips trembled.

At that moment he saw her as she saw herself: fallen from social class, power, wealth. Linked with a mule-headed cowboy who sassed her and ordered her around. Threatened by a cold-blooded killer. Unsure of her future, maybe even afraid.

"I... I don't know how to wash dishes." Her voice was low, soft. "It was never taught to me."

At her confession, he took off his hat and tossed it onto a stool. "Come on, Isobel. I'm an old hand at this. I'll teach you how to wash dishes."

Chapter Three

The sun painted the New Mexico sky a brilliant orange as Noah Buchanan and his bride, Belle, rode into Lincoln.

She had not expected this victory.

While up to her elbows in soapy water, Isobel had told Noah about the letter informing her family that someone in Santa Fe had begun proceedings of land transfer. Unable to learn the name of the man who possessed the Spanish land-grant titles—no doubt the same man who had killed her father and stolen them—Isobel had departed for America.

As she dried dishes at Noah's side, he suddenly relented. They would go to Lincoln instead of Chisum's ranch. But the town would be up in arms over Tunstall's murder, he warned. Rattlesnake Jackson, Jesse Evans and the rest of the posse would be there, along with Alexander McSween and Tunstall's men. It would be a powder keg waiting for a match.

"You'd better get to know New Mexico if you want to run cattle here." Noah spoke in a low voice as they entered the town. "That plant with the spiky leaves is a yucca. The cactus over there is a prickly pear."

Riding a horse borrowed from Dick Brewer, she pointed to a twisted vine. "That's a *sandía,* a watermelon."

Noah shook his head. "We call it a *mala mujer*."

"A bad woman?"

"Looks like a watermelon vine. Promises a man relief from his hard life on the trail. But the *mala mujer* grows only cockleburs."

"And so it's a bad woman—promising much but delivering only pain?"

"Yep." He straightened in the saddle. "There's Sheriff Brady's place. His neighbor is my friend Juan Patrón. We'll stay with him."

A lump formed in Isobel's throat. She was here at last, in the town of her father's burial. And no doubt a place well known to his killer. A dozen flat-roofed adobe houses lined the road. Where it curved, she saw a few finer homes and a couple of stores.

"Listen, Isobel." Noah slowed his horse. "I brought you to Lincoln, but while we're here, you'll do as I say. Got that?"

"*Sí*. But if we disagree, you may go your way. Isobel Matas makes her own decisions."

"You're not Isobel Matas anymore, sweetheart. You're Belle Buchanan—and you'd best not forget it."

He reined in outside a small house with two front doors. "Patrón's store. He used to be a schoolteacher and a court clerk. When his father was killed in seventy-three, he took on the family business."

"Seventy-three?" She slid from her horse into Noah's arms. "My father was killed in seventy-three."

For an instant she was drawn into a dark cocoon that smelled of worn leather and dust. Resting her cheek against Noah's flannel shirt, she relaxed in its warmth. But at the sound of his throbbing heartbeat, she caught her breath and stepped away.

"Seventy-three," she mumbled. "My father—"

"Old Patrón was murdered by a gang," Noah cut in. "The Horrell Gang went on a rampage, killing Mexicans."

"But my father was from Spain."

"Wouldn't matter. If you speak Spanish around here, you're a Mexican." He absently brushed a strand of loose hair from her cheek. "And remember, *you're* an American. You don't understand a word the Patróns are saying. Your name is Belle Buchanan. You're my wife."

She nodded, aware of his fingertips resting lightly on her shoulder. His face had grown gentle again, with that soft blue glow in his eyes, that subtle curve to his mouth. He was too close, his great shoulders a fortress against trouble, his warm hand moving down her arm.

Her eyes flicked to his. She opened her mouth to speak, but before she could form words, he bent his head and pressed his lips to hers. Gentle, tender, his mouth moved over the moist curves as if searching, seeking something long buried.

She softened. This male kiss, the first of her life, held a delight she had never imagined from the perfunctory pecks of mother and aunts. But it was over as quickly as it had begun. Noah lifted his head and focused somewhere behind her.

"*Buenas noches,* Juan," he said. "Put down your six-shooter. It's me."

"Noah?" The stout young man started across the darkened porch, walking with a limp. He was sturdy yet trim in a tailored Prince Albert coat. "*¡Bienvenidos!* You've been away too long. Come in, come in!"

"Juan, I want you to meet someone." Noah set his hand behind Isobel's waist. "My wife, Belle Buchanan."

"Your wife?" The snapping black eyes widened. "So pleased to meet you, Señora Buchanan."

"And I you," Isobel said softly.

"Noah, you are the last man on earth I would guess to take a wife. But come inside! You must meet my family."

As they started up the steps, Isobel caught Noah's hand and raised on tiptoe to his ear. "The murder! You must ask him about the murder."

He nodded and gave her hand a squeeze. She struggled to dismiss his easy intimacy. The man at her side was only pretending, after all. The kiss had been nothing more than a signal of the role each must play as man and wife.

She brushed at her dusty skirts and tucked the strand of hair into her chignon. But the burning on her lips remained as she watched Noah's shoulders disappear through a door leading from the porch.

"Please meet my wife, Beatriz!" Juan held the door for Isobel. "She is of the family Labadie, from Spain. But they have lived in New Mexico many generations. Beatriz, can you believe Noah has brought a bride?"

"Señora Buchanan, welcome." Beatriz, surrounded by children of various sizes, curtsied in greeting.

At the sight of the woman's lace mantilla and comb, it was all Isobel could do to keep from hugging her. She managed a whispered, "Thank you."

"Sit—Noah, *señora*." Juan gestured toward the fire. "How long will you stay with us? A week or more?"

Noah chuckled as he settled on a bench. Playing the dutiful wife, Isobel took her place at his side. He stretched an arm along the bench back. "We're just passing through, Juan. I need to settle up with Chisum and then—"

"But do you not know?" Juan sat forward on the edge of his chair. "Chisum is in jail! Lincoln is in a terrible state. I believe it will soon be war."

Noah's arm moved to Isobel's shoulders. "What's going on, Juan?"

"It is difficult to speak of." He lowered his voice. "John

Tunstall was ambushed and killed yesterday. Shot twice. Most believe it was Jimmie Dolan's posse."

"Dolan. No surprise there."

"Tunstall's men brought his body here. The judge took affidavits from Dick Brewer and Billy Bonney and issued arrest warrants for the men in the posse. A coroner's jury is taking testimony even now."

"Who's named in the warrants?"

"Jim Jackson, the one they call Rattlesnake. Jesse Evans. Others. Maybe up to forty men."

"How's McSween taking it?"

Juan shook his head. "You know Alexander McSween. A lawyer—so mild, always thinking of law and justice. I saw the shock on his face when they told him about Tunstall. But he is busy. His house is full of guests. A doctor and his wife, their children, a schoolteacher."

Isobel bit her lip to keep from asking about Susan. Noah inquired about his boss as Beatriz set a bowl of steaming posole on a nearby table.

"Chisum won't get involved," Juan predicted, watching his wife ladle out the spicy pork and hominy stew. "But come. I shall tell of Chisum's predicament at dinner."

Isobel followed Noah and hoped she was creating the right impression. But she might as well have been invisible for all the attention paid her.

"McSween told me the story of Chisum's jailing," Juan said after he had asked a blessing on the meal. "Just after Christmas, John Chisum, together with Alexander and Sue McSween, left for St. Louis. McSween was to settle some legal problems for a client. Chisum wanted to see a doctor. He has poor health, *no?*"

Noah nodded. "Off and on."

"When they reached Las Vegas, the sheriff and a gang of ruffians assaulted them. They knocked Chisum to the ground, and left Mrs. McSween crying in the buggy. She was taken to a hotel, but the men were thrown in jail."

"On what charges?" Noah demanded.

"McSween was accused of trying to steal money from his own clients. Chisum was charged with debt, if you can imagine that. The sheriff wanted him to reveal all his properties, you see, as debtors must."

"Dolan's behind this."

"It is bigger than Dolan, my friend. Never forget the ring in Santa Fe."

"What ring in Santa Fe?" Isobel could no longer hold her tongue at this mention of her future home.

Juan leaned across the table. "Men in high places have united in a ring of corruption, *señor*a. They take bribes, arrest innocent men, steal land titles."

"Who's in the group, Juan?" Noah caught Isobel's hand and pressed it to silence her. "Do you have names?"

"Governor Axtell, of course. But even more dangerous is the United States district attorney. Thomas Catron is a friend to Jimmie Dolan. The two are working together to take the whole territory. Your boss will be lucky ever to get out of jail."

"But McSween's here in Lincoln," Noah said. "How did he get out of jail?"

"McSween was set free to settle his business. But Chisum refused to reveal his properties."

"So he's still in jail." Noah looked at Isobel. "We may want to have you go on up to Santa Fe."

"Santa Fe?" Juan frowned. "But why?"

"Belle has relatives up there." Noah glanced at Isobel. "Juan, would you send her people a telegram? I may need to send her up there right away if things get worse."

"Of course." Juan stood. "I was planning to pay Mc-

Sween a visit anyway. We'll rouse Mr. Paxton to open the telegraph office. Will you come?"

"Glad to." Noah rose and patted Isobel's shoulder. "You stay and visit with Señora Patrón, honey. I'll be right back."

"I'll go with you, *honey*," Isobel sputtered as she leapt to her feet and nearly upset her chair. Hot anger radiated from the place where Noah had patted her as if she were no more than a dog. "If you send a telegram on my behalf, I must know what it says."

Juan chuckled. "Your new wife has a strong will. You must mend your stubborn ways, Noah—or break her spirit as you break the wild horses."

Noah was silent a moment before speaking again. "Stay here, Belle. I'll take care of this."

Isobel clenched her jaw as the two men walked to the door. The *señor*a and her children eyed their guest as she stepped to an open window.

"You did the right thing, Buchanan." Juan Patrón's words carried across the night. "A woman should stay at home. If your new wife isn't happy with that now, she will be soon. You'll see."

Battling fury at Noah, Isobel shifted her attention to the bustling Patrón family. The table was spotless now, its rough pine top scrubbed clean and its mismatched chairs pushed beneath. A clamor of giggles and pleas arose from the kitchen, where Beatriz, surrounded by reaching arms and grasping hands, was doling out portions of yellow custard.

"Flan?" she asked Isobel, holding out the dish.

Isobel shook her head. "Where is Alexander McSween's house?"

"*¡No, señora—por favor!*" The woman's eyes were wide with pleading. "You must stay here! There is much trouble in Lincoln. *¡Violencia!*"

As the children swarmed their mother again, Isobel turned away. A cramped home, rough-hewn furniture, hungry children, corn to grind, clothes to mend. This was the life of a woman in Lincoln.

Thanking God that she would be leaving Noah Buchanan soon, Isobel sank into a chair. Even now he was sending a telegram to Guillermo Pascal, alerting her betrothed in case she needed a quick escape from Lincoln.

But if Guillermo came here, he would take Noah's place as her protector, as the one to help solve her father's murder. Noah would be free of her. And she of him.

Isobel closed her eyes, imagining the life she had always dreamed of having. A vast hacienda. Countless cattle. A home filled with beautiful furniture. Gracious parties attended by dignitaries.

Her eyes snapped open. There would be no visits by members of the Santa Fe Ring if she had any say. And she would have no hacienda to manage if Guillermo had his say. Noah had been right on that account. The Pascal family would swallow up her land. She would be mistress of a prison more than a house. There would be small mouths to feed, meals to plan, stitching to fill her days. How different would that life be from the difficult lot of Señora Patrón?

A gentle tugging at her skirt caught Isobel's attention. A bright-eyed little girl with shiny black braids smiled up at her. "*La casa* McSween is very close. It is just past Tunstall's store."

Isobel shook the girl's hand. *"Gracias, mi hijita."*

The child scampered away to join her brother in a chasing game. Their mother leaned against the kitchen door, watching her children. As her son ran by, she swept him into her arms and kissed him.

Amid the laughter and fun, Isobel took her pistol from her saddlebag, drew her shawl around her shoulders and slipped outside. But a glance back at the flat-roofed house revealed a subtle transformation in what she had termed a prison. In the window, mother and child made a picture of happiness. The whitewashed adobe walls glowed almost translucent in the moonlight. The home was swept and scrubbed, the children well fed and cheerful, the mother content.

Turning away, Isobel wondered if she would find such peace with Guillermo Pascal. Passing a saloon, she saw several men leaning against a crude wooden bar and lifting mugs of beer. They were the likely compadres of a man like Noah Buchanan—common, obstinate, inconsiderate.

So why did her lips still burn from his kiss? Why did her breath catch in her throat at the memory of his hands around her waist? Worse, far worse, was the persistent image of his gentle smile. She could see that smile even as she hurried down the road, her leather boots stumbling over frozen wagon ruts. There it was as he poured steaming water into her basin, as he offered her a spoonful of scrambled eggs, when he plunged his arms into the dishwater to teach his new wife the mysteries of housekeeping.

Men were not supposed to be gentle. They were matadors, toreros—vanquishing life as if it were a bull that might rip open their hearts. Brave, strong, intelligent, bold. Fighting the sense that Noah Buchanan might be all these things as well, she hurried past the courthouse, a corral, a small shop.

As she pulled the shawl over her head, she heard the thunder of hoofbeats on the road. There! A band of men— five or six—riding at a gallop toward her. Clutching the pistol, she crossed the road toward a tumble of stones that had been cemented with mud to form a knobby tower. She crouched down into spiky, frozen grass and watched the riders approach. As they neared the tower, their leader reined his horse.

"You see that, Evans?" His breath formed a cloud of white vapor.

"See what?" Another rider edged forward. "We got an ambush?"

The first man was silent for a moment, listening. Isobel studied the low-slung jaw, the wide, flat nose, the narrow eyes searching the darkness. "I seen something run across the road just as we rounded the curve. It was her."

"Confound it, Snake, if you don't stop seein' that Mexican gal in every crick and holler, one of us is gonna have to give you what fer."

"I ain't seein' things this time, Evans." Snake drew his gun and leveled it at the tower. "She's over near the *torreón*. She had somethin' white on her head, just like that Mexican that seen us level Tunstall."

"So what if she's here? Who'd believe a no-account Mexican over us? We're deputies of the law, remember?"

Snake reached into his saddlebag and jerked out a handful of delicate fabric. Isobel caught her breath. Her mantilla! He draped it over the barrel of his gun and waved it in the air.

"Listen up, *señorita*," he called. "I got your veil—and I'm gonna get you."

"Aw, come on, Snake." Evans spat onto the road. "What is it with you and Mexicans? They ain't worth half the heed you pay 'em."

Snake flipped the mantilla into his open hand and shoved it into his bag. "Let's go, boys. Dolan's waitin'."

But when the other men spurred their horses down the road, Snake circled around and approached the tower. Isobel shrank into the shadow, her hand trembling as she gripped her gun.

"I know you're there, *chiquita*," he growled. "One of these days I'll make you wish you had never laid eyes on Jim Jackson."

His horse whinnied as he dug in his spurs. Hooves clattered across the frozen track. With difficulty, Isobel got to her feet.

"Just try to kill me, *asesino!*" she ground out as she shook her gun at the retreating form. "Murderer!"

Her blood pulsing in her temples, she lifted her skirts and began to run, her heels pounding out her anger. The shawl slipped to her elbows, catching the frigid wind like a sail. She passed an empty lot and then came to a low-slung building. Its painted sign creaked as it swung in the crisp air.

"Tunstall Mercantile," she read aloud. "Dry goods. Bank."

Tunstall. Isobel saw again his young face, blue eyes wide with an innocence rarely found in men. The hat, the tweed coat, the brown kidskin gloves. So young, so naive. With a shiver, she set off again, knowing she must find Noah and tell him that Snake Jackson was back in town.

Grabbing up her skirts, she made for a large adobe house a few yards beyond the Tunstall store. She knocked on McSween's door. When no one answered, she turned the handle and stepped inside.

All talking at once, a crowd of men sat around a table. Isobel picked out Dick Brewer, Tunstall's foreman and Noah's friend, bent over a sheaf of papers on the table. Billy Bonney had pointed his gun to the ceiling and looked as if he might fire it at any moment. Juan Patrón was shouting at Dr. Ealy, who was arguing back.

But where was Noah? She scanned the room again until her focus came to a window. On its deep sill Noah sat watching her, his blue eyes soft.

Isobel approached, her shawl sliding unnoticed to the

floor. Her heart thundered as she came to a halt before him. Fingering a loose button at her throat, she shrugged. "I came."

He nodded. "I was waiting for you."

Chapter Four

Hand over her mouth, Isobel sagged against the wall. The men around the table turned to look, then resumed arguing. Noah took in the woman's damp hem, muddy boots, fallen shawl. Her hair had scattered across her shoulders, a golden cape.

"If you knew I would come," she murmured, "why did you tell me to stay at Patrón's house?"

"I'm supposed to protect you, remember?" he said. Though color was slowly returning to her face, she was breathing as if she had seen a ghost. Noah battled the urge to take her in his arms. "Did Snake Jackson and his boys see you?"

"Only Snake. Do the others know they're in town?"

"Not yet." He jutted his chin at the boisterous group. "They're squabbling over how to counter Dolan's latest move. Sheriff Brady appointed Dr. Appel from Fort Stanton to perform a postmortem on Tunstall's body. Appel's a Dolan man. He'll support the posse's claim that Tunstall fired first."

She frowned. "Then I must give my testimony now."

"No." He caught her hand, drawing her closer. "Don't say anything, Isobel. Stay out of it."

"Did you send a telegram to Santa Fe?"

"Yes."

"You know I won't go until I find my father's killer."

"If things blow here, you'll need a place to run. Tunstall's men are bent on revenge. Dolan's gang will do anything for him."

Noah made a place for her on the sill. He couldn't tell if the woman was terrified or exhilarated by her second brush with danger. Her hazel eyes had gone green in the firelit room. Strands of hair brushed the arch of her brows. That button she was fooling with had dropped off, and he could see the creamy curve of her throat.

Looking away quickly, he ran his thumb and forefinger around the brim of his hat. Isobel could get herself shot by Snake Jackson. The man had a reputation for killing—he and Billy the Kid over there.

Isobel was staring at her knotted fingers, and he remembered how they had felt sliding tentatively up his back when he was kissing her. That kiss was a big mistake.

Noah shut his eyes, recalling the transformation of Isobel's face from anger to hesitation to pleasure as she had rolled up her sleeves and dipped her arms into warm, soapy water. She had chattered the whole time—something about a horse she'd owned back in Spain. She'd talked on and on, unaware of the tingle that shot up his arm every time she handed him a dish and her wet fingers touched his.

The kiss had come from that, from the way she had gotten inside his mind. And now here she was beside him, her lips still beckoning. Even worse, he was beginning to care what happened to the *señorita*.

"Salir de Málaga para entrar en Malagón," she said with a sudden smile. "It's like when you say, 'Out of the frying pan and into the fire.' My father used to shake his

finger and call me *la alborotadora,* the troublemaker, of my family."

"Now you tell me." Noah shook his head. "Well, Miss Troublemaker, Snake Jackson's in town, which means the constable hasn't been able to serve the warrant. He'll be at Jimmie Dolan's house cooking up a plan. If we're smart, we'll lie low the next few days and then head for Chisum's place."

"Will you ask Señor Patrón about his father's murder?"

Noah stood and took her arm. "Let's head back to the house. Patrón will go with us. I'll ask him then."

They started across the room, and Noah lifted her shawl from the floor where she had dropped it. As he drew it over her shoulders, she leaned against him. It was all he could do to keep from catching her up in his arms right then and there. A kiss…just one more…and surely his craving would be satisfied.

As they passed the throng of arguing men, he realized Patrón had gotten into the thick of the debate, his face red above his collar and his shouts adding to the chaos in the room. Noah was about to suggest they talk to him later when Isobel slipped away from him and pushed through the crowd.

At the appearance of a woman in their midst, the men around the table fell silent.

"Excuse me," she began. "My husband and I wish to return to the home of our host. Mr. Patrón?"

"Señora Buchanan," Patrón spoke up, "forgive my rudeness. Mr. McSween has been kind enough to let us gather in his home to discuss the situation."

Noah studied Alexander McSween. No older than thirty-five, the lawyer wore a drooping mustache that hung even with his chin. His tailored suit, polished boots and pocket watch set him apart from his colleagues. Noah had little doubt he was unarmed.

"A doctor has been bribed to perform the postmortem," Patrón continued. "We must find a way to avert this injustice. Dick Brewer and Billy Bonney do not agree. Dr. Ealy and I—"

"Dr. Ealy?" Isobel lifted her eyebrows as if she had never seen the man who had ridden across half the New Mexico Territory with her. "Are you a medical doctor, sir?"

Dr. Ealy gave an uncomfortable cough. "I am."

"Then two doctors must perform the postmortem," she declared. "Or Dr. Ealy might help with the embalming. It cannot be difficult to record the truth."

The men gawked in silence until Dick Brewer finally spoke up. "She's right, fellers. Doc Ealy, we'll make sure you help with the postmortem—if you don't mind. Thank you, Mrs. Buchanan."

Isobel tilted her head. "You may call me Belle."

As the sea of men parted to let Isobel through, Billy Bonney called to Noah. "Hey, Buchanan, you bringin' your pretty wife to McSween's fandango Saturday night?"

Noah's blue eyes flicked toward Isobel. "We'll see. I want to get on over to Chisum's place."

"Come on, Buchanan! I deserve at least one dance with the lovely lady. You may be faster on the draw than me, but I guarantee I'm the best dancer in town."

"You've got the biggest mouth in Lincoln County, that's for sure." Noah shifted his attention as Juan and Isobel joined him. "Hey, Dick. Come here a minute."

The young foreman detached himself from the group. As he neared, Susan Gates emerged from the shadows of a back room. Clutching her skirts in her hands, she rushed toward Isobel.

"Susan!" Isobel caught her friend. "Susan, what's wrong?"

"You know this woman?" Patrón asked, his brow drawn into a furrow.

"I'll explain later," Noah said. "Miss Gates, meet Juan Patrón. Looks like you already know Dick."

Susan gave Juan a polite nod, but when she looked into Dick Brewer's eyes, a pink flush spread across her cheeks. Noah's friend and the schoolteacher had met only the day before, Isobel realized, but there was an obvious attraction between them.

She wondered if anyone saw such a spark between Noah and herself. Surely not. After all, Noah was just her protector. He cared nothing for her. And she had no more feeling for him than she might for a loyal stable-hand at her family's hacienda.

While he informed the men that Snake Jackson and the posse were in town, Isobel and her friend stepped aside.

"You've lost a button," Susan said. "My dress doesn't fit you well. Why don't we buy some fabric at Tunstall's store? I'll sew a new dress for you. Isobel?"

"That cowboy is looking at you, Susan." She maneuvered her friend away from Dick Brewer's line of focus. "Stay away from him. He is in the midst of the trouble."

Susan glanced over her shoulder. "Don't you think he's terribly handsome?"

Isobel shrugged. She preferred a man with a stronger frame, with broad shoulders and hands that could bring down a steer. She preferred a man whose face bore the weathering of life, who had seen good and evil—and who knew to choose the good. She preferred—

"Noah!" she gasped as he caught her around the waist.

"Let's get out of here," he growled against her ear. "This place is a powder keg."

As he led them away, Isobel turned and caught her

friend's hands. "Don't let any man capture your heart, Susan," she said softly. "Never let anyone take away your dreams."

"Oh, Isobel, I…"

"I'll come tomorrow. We'll go to the shops."

Susan waved as Isobel, Noah and Patrón stepped outside. As the three started down the moonlit road, Noah spoke. "I see Dick's taken a fancy to your friend."

"Susan's red hair charms everyone," Isobel replied. "She is lovely."

"She's skinny," Noah pronounced.

"Dick was never a man to take after women," Patrón added. "Is that not so, Noah?"

"Yeah, he's like me. Prefers the company of a few good cowboys around a campfire to the meaningless chatter of women."

Isobel bristled. "What do you know about women, anyway?"

"Not enough," Patrón interjected. "I am surprised my friend chose a wife. The rumor in Lincoln says these men—Noah, Dick, Chisum and more—were all wounded by love."

Noah grunted. "Chisum told me he proposed marriage years ago. The gal wanted to carry on being the belle of the ball a bit longer. Chisum got impatient. Told her it was now or never. She chose never."

"And he's been a bachelor ever since," Patrón concluded. "Too bad for him. But what about you, Noah? You always had a reputation as a man to leave alone. Women have given their hearts to you, but you never kept them long."

"Settling down with a wife is the farthest thing from my thoughts," Noah said. "God didn't make me the marrying kind."

"But now you're married!" Patrón exclaimed. "And you

found a beautiful wife. She's smart, too. Smart enough to capture you."

Isobel held her breath in anticipation of Noah's reply, but he changed the topic. "How's your leg these days, Juan? Looks like you're walking pretty good."

Patrón patted his leg. "It is not the leg, my friend. It is my back."

"Did the Horrell Gang peg you the night they killed your father?"

"No, no. My father died in seventy-three. John Riley shot me two years later—but for the same reason. Hatred of Mexicans. Riley accused several Mexicans of stealing, and shot them dead. I demanded an investigation. When we went to arrest Riley, he shot me in the back."

"In the back?" Isobel stopped on the frozen road. "Did he face trial?"

Patrón shook his head. "Riley is allied with Jimmie Dolan. He was never even arrested."

Isobel was beginning to piece together a picture of Jimmie Dolan. The man held great power and he used it for evil.

"Did Dolan have anything to do with your father's murder?" Noah asked Juan.

"No, the Horrell Gang was just a group of worthless men." Patrón's voice held a note of bitterness. "Outlaws, renegades. In early December, the gang rode into Lincoln, shot up the town and got into a tangle with the Mexican constable. Several men were killed on both sides. A couple of weeks later, the Horrells returned for *revancha*—revenge. The Mexican community was having a Christmas dance at Squire Wilson's hall. The Horrells stormed into the room and began shooting. That night, my father was shot and killed."

Isobel walked in silence, imagining the horror of a celebration transformed into a bloodbath.

"Did you go after the Horrells?" she asked.

"Killing and more killing?" Patrón shook his head. "That is futile, *señora*. My father was dead. Another man's death could never bring him back. You understand?"

She nodded, but she didn't truly understand. Where was the *venganza*—a man's proud avenging of his father's spilled blood? By all that was right, Patrón should have gone after the killers.

"The Horrells made a pact to kill every Mexican in Lincoln County," he was saying. "For a month, they rode through the countryside slaughtering Mexicans. Finally they went to Texas, stealing mules and horses, murdering both Mexicans and gringos along the way. Eventually, the Seven Rivers Gang ambushed and killed some of them, but the rest made it safely to Texas. They were indicted, of course, but none was ever taken into custody."

He paused. "I've heard that some of the gang—not the Horrell brothers, but others who rode with them—returned to Lincoln. But we don't talk of this. It's better left alone."

Isobel studied the tower of stones as they passed it in the moonlight. If the Horrell Gang had ridden through the countryside in 1873 killing every Mexican in sight, might they have murdered her father? His golden hair would have distinguished him from the Mexicans of the territory, but his native tongue was Spanish. Perhaps he had encountered the Horrell Gang on their journey to Texas. Perhaps they had heard him speak and gunned him down.

"These men," she said softly. "Which of them returned to Lincoln? What are their names?"

Before he could answer, Noah spoke up. "Juan, I need to tell you that my wife's father was killed near Lincoln about the same time your father was shot down. We're looking for his murderer."

"I guessed there was more to this marriage than met the eye. So you wonder if the Horrells may be involved? What else? This woman knows more than she says."

"I witnessed Tunstall's murder," Isobel admitted. "Snake Jackson has vowed to kill me."

"Noah, you must take your wife to Santa Fe," Patrón said. "To her relatives. In Lincoln County, no one is far from violence. Look at Billy Bonney. John Tunstall gave him a clean slate, taught him to read, paid him well. Now I fear the boy's past will catch up with his present."

"Billy's always hot for blood," Noah said. "The kid would rather pull the trigger than talk things over."

Patrón gave a wry chuckle. "How many men is Billy claiming to have killed now? Seventeen? Or is it twenty-one? Señora Buchanan, the men of the West will tell you many things. Do not believe one tenth of what they say, and you will have no trouble here."

Glancing at Noah, Isobel lifted her damp skirts and stepped into the warm Patrón house. If Juan was right, she should not trust her own protector. Nor could she be sure that the Tunstall-McSween faction was nobler than the Dolan gang. After all, Jimmie Dolan had the law on his side, and he was allied with the powers in Santa Fe.

Doubt slinking through her stomach, she drew her shawl tightly over her shoulders as Juan placated his agitated wife in Spanish. Isobel understood every word, of course, and had to work at maintaining a look of innocence. Once Juan had assured Beatriz she was not to blame for Isobel's disappearance, she led them down the hall to a bedroom. After unlocking the door with one of the keys at her waist, she lit a pair of candles on an ornate bureau.

Awash in a yellow glow, the guest room held a bed, a

washstand, a chair. A small crucifix hung over the bed, and a cross of woven palm leaves topped the washstand. Beatriz pointed out logs and kindling, then nodded, smiled and left.

Noah knelt and began building a fire. "What was Juan telling Beatriz?"

"He said I followed you because I'm so devoted to you. And that you're in love with me."

Noah's hand halted. He glanced across at Isobel. She was looking out the window. "Juan is going to talk to you tomorrow," she continued. "To tell you the correct way to treat your wife."

Striking a match, Noah held it to the tinder. Was Juan really fooled about the marriage? Did he see something that neither he nor Isobel could admit? Sitting back on his heels, Noah spread his hands over the crackling flames. He didn't trust himself with the woman. Maybe she didn't feel anything, but he sure did.

"My parents had two bedrooms at our hacienda in Catalonia," Isobel said as she joined him by the fire. "With a door to connect them. Where will you sleep?"

Noah looked up, read the trepidation in her eyes and stood. "I said I wouldn't touch you."

"And Juan told me not to trust any man in the West."

"Do you have a choice?" At her nervous expression, he pulled a chair to the fire. "Relax, Isobel. Sit here. I want to talk about your father."

She perched on the edge of the chair. "What about him?"

Noah pushed a log with the poker, and a spray of sparks shot into the air. "Do you know which day your father was killed?"

"No. Only that it was late December. He had spent

Christmas with my uncle at Fort Belknap, then he followed the Goodnight Trail north."

"Is your father buried here? In Lincoln?"

"At the cemetery. I promised my mother I would go there." Her lips trembled, and she stopped speaking.

Noah knelt again, reached out and covered her hand with his. "I'll go with you."

Isobel was cold, shivering. She clutched the ragged shawl close around her in one white-knuckled fist. How vulnerable she was, Noah realized. She was scared, too, though she would never admit it. Without her land titles, Isobel had nothing. She insisted she could shoot well enough to protect herself, but a cold-blooded murderer had threatened to gun her down.

"We'll visit the courthouse tomorrow," he told her. "They'll have the record of your father's burial. We can check the date and look for someone who remembers where the Horrell Gang was that day. But, Isobel, you'll never be able to track down the killer. You should go to Santa Fe and try to stop the transfer of the titles."

"You're asking me to forget my father's murder? Do you really think I can stop a land transfer without any documents or proof?" She shook her head. "Impossible without the titles. And without the land, I cannot marry Don Guillermo."

At the mention of her intended husband, Noah stood and slapped the wood dust from his thighs. "Who cares about ol' Don when you've got me? I mean, what more could a lady want?" He couldn't hold back a grin as her eyes went wide. "Why, there's a gal right here in Lincoln who'd be mad as a peeled rattler if she knew about this arrangement."

"What arrangement?" Isobel stood. "Your woman has no cause to feel jealous. We have a *contrato*, a contract."

Edging past Noah, she walked to the washstand, drew her shawl from her shoulders and draped it on the bed. After pouring water into the bowl, she splashed her face and rinsed her hands. Dabbing an embroidered linen towel on her cheek, she turned back toward Noah.

"For that matter," she said softly, "there are many men who would gladly trade places with you, vaquero."

Noah took a step toward her. "I don't doubt that. For a woman who's fretting over land titles and a Spanish dandy, you have a lot more assets than you know."

"What do I have? My father left me nothing but empty land in a bloodthirsty country where no man can be trusted. And Don Guillermo—"

"Don Guillermo doesn't know what he's missing." He caught her hand and pulled her close. "You've got everything you'll ever need right now. You're smart, Isobel. Gritty, too."

"Gritty? What is that?"

"Brave. You'd take on Snake Jackson and the whole Dolan gang if you had to. You know how to ride and shoot. And you're pretty. Real pretty."

She removed her hand from his and turned her shoulder. "I have gowns and jewels, but here I dress as a peasant."

"You don't need fancy gowns to be beautiful, Isobel." He lifted a hand and brushed a lock of hair from her shoulder. "You've got those eyes—green, brown, gray—what color are they?"

"My brother used to say they matched the mud in a pig's pond."

"What do brothers know?" He placed one finger under her chin and tilted her face toward the candlelight. "There's a wild cat that hangs around Chisum's bunkhouse. We call her La Diabla, and she's a devil, all right. Always in trouble, always getting into things she shouldn't. If you can catch her long enough to get a good look, you'll see the fire in her eyes—a green fire that makes them glow like emeralds. Your eyes are like that, Isobel."

For a moment she didn't speak, and Noah stood transfixed by the scent of her hair and skin. He could almost feel the velvet touch of her cheek against his fingertips. Trying to breathe, he knew if one of them didn't talk soon, he would lose himself.

"You should write a book, Buchanan," Isobel suggested, her voice husky. "Any man who sees emeralds in my mud-pond eyes has lost his senses."

"I will write a book," he told her. "And my senses never let me down."

Noah's finger now traced the line of her jaw. He knew she was unaware of how her full, damp lips entranced him. His throat tightened, and his breath went ragged with just one stroke of her skin. She was soft, silky, dangerous. Like the barnyard cat, she was elusive. He knew he shouldn't try to catch her. One look in those eyes, and all of his careful plans could go up in smoke.

"I trust my senses, also," she was saying. "And I sense you are not keeping our contract."

"I'll keep the contract, Isobel. I'm a man of my word. But your lips are telling me one thing, while your eyes are telling me something else."

"No. You're wrong."

She tried to step aside, but he caught her shoulders and drew her close. His hands slipped up and cupped her head. His fingers weaving through her silky hair, he pressed his lips against hers.

Her breath was sweet, fragrant, coming in shallow gasps as she stood rigid in his arms. Puzzled, he studied her face. Surely this gun-toting, haughty, gutsy woman had been kissed many a time. But she trembled against him, her eyes deepening to pools as she gazed into his.

"Isobel," he whispered, uncertain what to do next.

"Kiss me one more time," she murmured, her eyelids drifting shut. "Just once, and never again."

Chapter Five

Moonlight wafted through the iron fretwork on the window to drape a lacy shadow over the room. Unaware, she drifted toward him as his lips brushed hers. She slid her arms around his chest. Reveling in the rich scent of leather and soft flannel, in the rough graze of his chin against her skin, she ran her fingers down his back, which was solid, as hard as steel.

The sense that he was someone she must keep at a distance evaporated in yet another crush of heated lips.

"Isobel," Noah murmured. His blue eyes had gone inky in the flicker of the candles. "I promised not to touch you. I made a vow."

Even as he spoke, she read his plea to be released from that oath. How should she respond to the unbearable tumult he had provoked inside her? She must think of who he was—a mere acquaintance, an American, a common cattleman.

But why did his words sound like poetry in her ears and his kisses feel like music? Perhaps it was the moonlight or the crackling fire. Maybe it was the turmoil that spun through her heart. Or simply the magic of a man's touch.

"I don't know what you've done to me," she whis-pered.

"The same thing you've done to me. But it's not right. For either of us."

She wanted to argue, but the words didn't come. For endless minutes, they gazed at each other. Then with a deep sigh, Noah shook his head, grabbed his saddlebag and bedroll and left the room.

"Isobel." A cool hand rested on her arm. "Isobel, wake up. The morning is half gone!"

Her eyes flicked open. But instead of the man with blue eyes who had walked through her dreams, she looked into the face of her sweet friend. "Susan? Where is…what time is it?"

"After eight. Noah sent me to look in on you."

Isobel struggled to one elbow. "Where is he?"

"At Alexander McSween's house. He and Dick have been talking since dawn."

"About what?"

"I don't know. I was in the kitchen helping Mrs. Mc-Sween. Here's your breakfast." Susan set a basket of warm tortillas on a small table and glanced to the end of the bed. "Isobel, what happened last night? You look…rumpled."

Isobel touched her tender lips, remembering. "I'm all right, Susan."

"Did you and Noah…? Did he try to…?"

"No, it's nothing." She waved a hand in dismissal. "He wants me to go to Santa Fe. To Don Guillermo. Noah is…a problem. A problem for me. I'm sorry I agreed to the arrangement."

She tried to make the words ring true, but they sounded hollow and empty.

"Isobel," Susan spoke up, "if that cowboy is bothering you, we'll find a way to get you to Santa Fe. I know your don will protect you."

She herself knew nothing of the sort, Isobel admitted as she rolled a tortilla and took a bite. The more she thought about the man who had never written to her, never even sent a token of commitment to her mother, the less she trusted Guillermo Pascal.

And Noah Buchanan wanted neither a wife nor children to clutter his life. Besides, the vaquero was too common. Any connection between them was impossible.

Isobel forced a laugh as she stepped to the washstand. "Noah thinks he's a king," she told Susan. "He makes me wash dishes. He sends telegrams without my permission. He gives orders left and right."

Susan giggled. "He gives *you* orders?"

"Noah fancies himself my equal. But he has nothing."

"Nothing except a good job and a quick draw. Out West that can make a man a king. Look at Dick Brewer. He works for the Tunstall operation, but he bought land and a house, and he manages his own cattle."

"You were interested in Dick Brewer last night."

Susan's pale cheeks flushed. "I went outside for fresh air, and Dick came out, too. We talked."

"Talked?"

"Oh, Isobel, he's wonderful!" Susan hugged herself. "He's handsome and kind and strong. I've never met anyone so perfect. I love him, Isobel."

"Love, Susan? So soon? In Spain we say, *Lo que el agua trae, el agua lleva.* It means what comes easily can also go easily. Your parents should secure a well-to-do husband—one who can give you a fine home. I stayed in Dick Brewer's cabin. It's too small for a family. His land is nothing but rocks. Keep your thoughts from love and you'll be happier."

Susan shrugged. "My Mexican friends in Texas used to say, *Más vale atole con risas que chocolate con lagrimas.*"

"Better to have gruel with laughter than chocolate with tears," Isobel translated the familiar adage. Susan was teasing her now, and she didn't like it. It was bad enough that she'd hardly had any sleep, and that all night her mind had been possessed with thoughts of Noah Buchanan, but now she could hardly focus on her plans.

"I'd rather marry a cowboy like Dick Brewer," Susan said as she helped her friend dress. "I'd rather live in Dick's old cabin and bear him seven little roly-poly Brewers than go up to Santa Fe and marry someone like your rich Don Guillermo. You don't even know him. He would protect you as his wife, but he might not care a fig about you. He can give you a big house and jewels, but can he give you his heart?"

"What do you know about a good marriage, Susan?" Isobel challenged her. "The great families of Spain have made such unions for centuries. No one sits about moaning for love. We marry well because it is our tradition. I am obligated to marry Don Guillermo."

Susan embraced her friend. "Don't be angry, Isobel. We come from different worlds. To me, Dick Brewer seems like he stepped out of a dream."

"Dreams vanish, *pffft!*" Isobel clicked her fingers. "Like that!"

Susan walked to the window. "I always wanted to fall in love. I know it happened fast, but I do love Dick."

Fumbling with the unruly buttons of her wrinkled bodice, Isobel realized Susan looked different today. Filled with uneasiness at her memories of Noah's kisses, she hoped she didn't appear smitten, too.

"Let's go down to the mercantile," Susan chirped. "We need to sew you a gown that fits. You want to look pretty for Noah Buchanan, don't you?"

"Such nonsense you speak!" Isobel chided her friend.

Aware she was blushing, she snatched her white cotton shawl and wrapped it tightly around her shoulders as she and Susan set off. The day was sunny, and the frozen road had begun to thaw. Scraggly dogs and snuffling pigs wandered through the mud. Wisps of piñon smoke floated from beehive ovens beside the adobe houses that lined the road. The smell of baking bread hung in the morning air, mingling with the scent of bacon and strong coffee.

"Are you going to the fandango Saturday night?" Susan asked. "Folks are saying it'll help ease the tension in town. We could all use some fun."

Isobel shook her head. "I've already spent too much time in the company of rough American men."

"Last night, Dick asked me for the first three dances."

"And the wedding? When is that happy event?"

"Wedding!" Susan elbowed her friend. "Stop teasing, Isobel. I want to teach school for at least a year. After that, who knows?"

As she walked, Isobel pictured Noah as he'd been the night before, his arms around her, his kisses burning like fire on her lips.

"Susan," she said. "Did you hear Noah Buchanan say anything to Dick about me?"

"Not this morning, no. But last night Dick told me a few things about Noah."

"Yes?"

"He said that in the past few days it seemed like something was bothering Noah. Eating at him. Dick said Noah wouldn't talk about it, but…"

"But what?" Isobel's fingers tightened on her shawl. "What, Susan?"

"Well… Dick made me promise not to tell."

Isobel stopped in the middle of the street, her sodden hem swaying against boots caked with mud. "Susan, you must tell me. Noah Buchanan is bound to me by that silly, reckless vow we made. He's going to stay with me until I've found my father's killer and recovered my land titles. You must tell me everything you know about him."

Susan heaved a sigh. "If you must know… Noah writes."

"Writes? Writes what?"

"Stories. He hopes to publish them in a New York maga-zine. But Dick says that, with you to look after, Noah fig-ures he's going to have his hands too full to write. He sort of wishes he hadn't agreed to protect you so you'd testify."

Isobel stared down at the mud on her fine leather boots. Noah Buchanan was a *writer?* She tried to visualize his big shoulders bent over a sheaf of papers, a pen gripped in his powerful brown fingers—fingers more suited to wres-tling a steer than forming letters.

Noah had mentioned the woman in Texas who had read the Bible to him and taught him to spell and count. But what tales would a vaquero have to tell? Noah had no life beyond dusty trails and herds of longhorn cattle.

How dare he resent her for keeping him from his cow stories! Well, she must put all thoughts of the man out of her head and resume searching for her father's murderer, Isobel decided. She must forget the heat of his touch and the pleasure of his lips. The best she could do for herself—and for Noah Buchanan—was to finish her business in Lincoln Town and leave.

Chapter Six

"I must go to the courthouse," Isobel announced. Turning toward the building across from the *torreón,* she heard Susan give a cry of exasperation.

"The courthouse? But Isobel, what about shopping?"

"A new dress can wait. I must find out about my father."

Whitewashed caliche walls shaded by the deep courthouse porch reminded Isobel of her home in Catalonia. She tried to focus her thoughts. She must learn where the public records were kept. Later, she would ask about church records. Striding into the large room, her head full of plans and her vision blinded by sunlight, she almost bumped into Noah Buchanan.

"Isobel." He caught her arm.

"Noah." Their eyes met and held for a heartbeat. She tried to make herself smile, but her mouth had gone dry.

He took off his hat, his hair lifting and then settling against his head. "Morning, Isobel."

"Good morning."

In that brief moment it occurred to her that she had never seen as handsome a man in all her life. He was nothing at all like the *guapo* Spanish dons who had courted her. Noah wore his broad shoulders as another man might wear a relaxed and easy-fitting coat.

Clean-shaven and smelling like fresh rainwater, Noah had on a sky-blue shirt that matched his eyes. His battered black leather jacket hung unbuttoned to the gun belt and holster at his waist. Denim trousers skimmed his thighs. His fingers touched the brim of his hat as gently as they had cupped Isobel's cheek.

"Excuse me," she breathed out. "I need to find records… my father."

"Here, Isobel. I copied out the records for you." He set a sheaf of handwritten documents in her open palm. His voice was low as he related what he had learned. "Your father died on January eighteenth, 1874."

"No, it was seventy-three," she protested.

He pointed out the written evidence. "He was buried on the nineteenth. The report is sketchy, but you'll be interested in it."

Isobel stared at the documents—proof at last of what she had traveled so far to learn. But Noah drew her attention.

"Squire Wilson," he said, indicating a middle-aged man peering at them through a pair of foggy spectacles. "I'd like you to meet my wife, Belle, and her friend Miss Gates. Ladies, Squire Green Wilson is Lincoln's justice of the peace. The town holds district court here once a year. The rest of the time, it's a meeting room and dance hall."

The heavyset man stood. "Forgive me for not being more sociable, Mrs. Buchanan, Miss Gates. I was awake most of the night taking affidavits, issuing warrants, impaneling a jury and whatnot."

"Squire Wilson found the report you needed," Noah told Isobel in a tone she found patronizing. "Wasn't that nice, honey?"

She shot him a look as the justice absently leafed through a stack of papers on his desk. "Glad I could help out. I keep these records, and nobody ever takes a second look at 'em. 'Course, now with all the trouble, you can bet the bigwigs up in Santa Fe will come snooping around."

"Thanks, Squire." Noah caught Isobel's waist and turned her toward the door. "Let's go, sweetheart."

"Certainly, honey," she replied, echoing his manner.

Noah paid her no heed as they stepped out into the brilliant sunshine and began walking in the direction of the store. "Last night," he told the women, "the jury decided Tunstall was killed by Jimmie Dolan's posse. Several of the leaders, including Evans and Snake Jackson, were named, but no one has been arrested yet."

Isobel's heart began to pound harder. "And the rest of us? Did they mention me?"

"Nobody said a word about our being there." He was silent a moment before continuing. "Cavalry troops from Fort Stanton came to town late yesterday to keep the peace. Sheriff Brady ordered the Tunstall store to provide hay for their horses. Alexander McSween accused Brady of larceny for appropriating the hay from Tunstall's estate. So, Squire Wilson issued warrants for Brady and his men. The constable arrested the sheriff this morning and the squire released him on bond of two hundred dollars."

"Everyone is arresting everyone else," Isobel remarked.

"Tempers are hot and getting hotter by the minute. McSween is using his legal know-how to bring Sheriff Brady and Jimmie Dolan to justice for Tunstall's murder."

"Did Dr. Ealy assist in the postmortem on that poor man's body?" Susan asked.

"Both doctors performed the postmortem."

"And?" Isobel's curiosity grew as she strode alongside the strapping cowboy.

"Dr. Ealy recorded the truth," Noah said. "Tunstall's body was not only shot but abused. The report confirms what you said about Evans shooting the Englishman in the head after he was already dead."

A sense of relief washed over Isobel. "I must testify immediately," she declared. "Let's go back, and I'll tell the squire everything I saw. Alexander McSween has the upper hand, and my testimony will see Dolan, Snake and the others thrown straight into jail."

"Whoa, now." Noah slowed his stride. "You march into the courthouse with that story, and you're dead if Snake has half a chance to get at you."

"Mr. Buchanan," Susan cut in. "You just tell Isobel what happened to her father. Then we'll put her into some decent clothes and send her off to Santa Fe."

Noah paused, his eyes narrowing as they pinned Isobel. "Santa Fe?" he asked. "Is that what you want?"

"I want to know about my father," she told him softly.

"It's all in the report. He was shot once—in the chest. One of his guards was still alive when Dick Brewer found them on the trail."

"Dick Brewer!" Susan squeaked. "Dick found Isobel's father?"

Noah nodded. "He was riding to Lincoln for supplies. The guard told him a gang of twenty men had attacked their party. The man who killed your father wasn't the leader, but he was the biggest talker. After they'd shot all the travelers, the men stole everything. The guard died before Dick got him to Lincoln, poor fellow, and there wasn't enough evidence to indict anyone."

Absorbing everything, Isobel stared at the ink scribbled across the crumpled pages. Banditos had killed her father. Twenty men? But who?

"The Horrells?" she asked him. "Do you think they did it?"

"We'll ask Dick. He'll know more than anyone else."

"Let's go find him," Susan said eagerly.

Isobel shook her head. "Before we speak to Dick, I must bear witness to what I know about the murder of John Tunstall."

"Don't be a fool, Isobel." Susan's voice rose. "You should stay out of this. You'll be killed, just like your father was, and what good will that do anyone?"

Without responding, Isobel studied a store across the street. The two-story building was surrounded by soldiers sent from Fort Stanton to keep order.

"You are wise," she told her friend. "Let's purchase fabric for my new dress. Our first stop will be the store of Mr. Jimmie Dolan."

A haze of piñon smoke filtered over Lincoln as Noah escorted his wife, Belle, and the town's new schoolteacher onto the porch of Dolan Mercantile. Four white posts supported the porch roof, which was also a balcony. Unlike the flat-roofed adobe *jacales* lining Lincoln's single street, Jimmie Dolan's store had a sloping, shingled roof with three chimneys. Eight windows on the lower floor and eight above assured that Dolan and his employees were aware of any shopper's approach long before the front door opened.

"We need a code," Noah said to Isobel under his breath. "You can't testify unless we're sure the killers are the men we think they are."

"When I see the man who murdered Mr. Tunstall," Isobel said, "I'll say the word *yellow*. *Blue* will be the man who shot second."

"Isobel." He caught her hand. "You be careful. Don't lose your head in there."

"Of course not. Belle Buchanan never loses her head." She initiated a chat with Susan as the group stepped into the store. Noah lifted up a silent prayer for God to protect them all…and to put a lock on Isobel's tongue.

"Buchanan," a gruff voice called out from a group of men standing around an iron potbellied stove. "Don't you know better'n to come in here?"

Noah took off his hat as the men touched the six-shooters on their hips. "Don't get testy now, fellows," he told them. "My bride here is looking to make a new dress."

"A dress?" Snake Jackson stepped to the front of the group. "Get your saddle-sore backside outa here, Buchanan. Jimmie Dolan don't want no Chisum men—"

"There!" Isobel moved forward and placed a hand on Snake's arm. "Do you see that yellow fabric? Near the ladder? Will you get it for me, sir?"

For an instant Snake's focus slid across the room and scanned the rows of brightly colored fabric bolts. Then he jerked his arm away and spat a thick, arcing stream of brown-red tobacco juice into the brass spittoon near the door.

"Get yer wife outa here, Buchanan," he snarled, "before I blast the three of you to kingdom come!"

"That'll look good on the squire's books," Noah retorted, stuffing his hat back on his head. "Belle, honey, which bolt did you want Mr. Jackson to take down for you?"

"The yellow. That bright yellow silk near the ladder."

"Ah, Mr. Buchanan. I'm afraid this is not an opportune day for shopping." A short, slender man entered from a side door. He wore a black broadcloth tailcoat and trousers, a red vest and a stiff white shirt with a black bow tie. His hair was a thick mass of unruly curls.

Noah nodded a greeting. "Hello there, Jimmie. I'd like you to know my new wife, Belle. And this is Lincoln's new schoolteacher, Miss Gates. Ladies, meet Jimmie Dolan."

"Such a lovely store you have, Mr. Dolan." Isobel dropped the barest of curtsies. "I've already found a yellow silk that will suit me just fine."

"Didn't you hear the man?" Evans growled. "We don't want a Chisum man in our territory."

"You know, dear, I also favor that blue," Isobel told Noah, her voice breathless. She turned to Evans. "Sir, would you be so good as to fetch me that blue calico?"

"Don't you hear good, lady?" Snake started toward her, his eyes narrowing. "Jimmie Dolan ain't gonna trade with no Chisum—"

"It's all right, Snake, Evans." Dolan's speech carried an Irish lilt that might have sounded pleasant on another man. "Mrs. Buchanan, I'm afraid we've had a little trouble in Lincoln. Perhaps you'd better do your shopping another day."

Noah glanced at Susan, whose fragile face had faded from pale to white. The schoolteacher looked ready to faint. But Isobel gave Jimmie Dolan a coy smile.

"My dear Mr. Dolan," she said in a soft, buttery accent. "I am in the uncomfortable situation of having almost nothing to wear. May I see that adorable blue calico? Please?"

The Irishman glanced at the row of armed men lurking behind him. The one who was wearing a brass badge on his chest took a stump of cigar from his mouth.

"I believe Mr. Dolan just said he's not open for business," the lawman informed them.

"Sheriff Brady, what are you doing here?" Noah drawled.

"If there's trouble in Lincoln, shouldn't you be down at the courthouse? It wouldn't look too good if folks knew the sheriff was hiding out at Jimmie Dolan's store."

"Hiding out?" Brady snarled.

"Sheriff. Buchanan." Dolan put up his small, ring-bedecked hand. "Men, why don't you take your seats by the fire? I'll see that Mrs. Buchanan gets her fabric."

"Why, thank you, Mr. Dolan." Isobel awarded him a radiant smile. "How kind of you."

Noah had no intention of leaving her side for a moment. Dolan made his way around the counter and hooked the bolt of blue calico down into his arms. "It's fifty cents a yard, ma'am." He tossed the fabric on the counter. "That yellow silk is five dollars a yard."

Noah sensed Snake Jackson eyeing Isobel from his position against a wooden post.

"Five dollars. My goodness!" She fingered the yellow silk and then the coarse cotton printed with tiny white sprigs on a blue field. "And the width?"

"Twenty-two inches for the calico. Eighteen for the silk."

"I'll need at least twenty yards to make a dress, won't I, Mr. Dolan?"

Noah watched her turn the dull fabric this way and that. Then, unexpectedly, she turned to face Snake Jackson. "Is there something wrong, sir?" she asked. "You have been staring at me."

Without taking his eyes from her, he straightened. "You always wear that shawl, ma'am?"

Her cheeks paled. "May I ask why you would want to know that, sir?"

"I'm looking for a woman I seen in a shawl just like that one. A woman about your size—"

"Snake," Evans called out, rising from his chair. "Get over here, and leave them people alone."

"You have a mighty odd accent, ma'am," Snake went on as Evans approached. "Like Mexican talk, maybe?"

She tried to smile. "I've never been to Mexico, sir."

"Get your snake-eyed mug back here." Evans stomped up to the counter, a half-empty bottle of whiskey dangling from one hand. "'Scuse ol' Snake, here, ma'am. He thinks he's seein' ghosties ever'where."

"I am seein' ghosties. Mexican ghosties with little lace veils."

"Let's get out of here, honey," Noah said, reaching his arm around her shoulders. "We'll take ten yards of the blue stuff, Dolan. Mark it down, and I'll send you the money when Chisum pays me."

A slow smile spread over the Irishman's face. "You'll have a long wait for John Chisum to be paying you, Mr. Buchanan. I'm afraid he's in jail."

"So I hear. They tell me some stinkin' coyote of a man is behind it."

Dolan measured the yards of fabric, his face impassive. "The coyote is a smart animal, I'm told."

"Feeds on carrion," Noah shot back.

Isobel placed a placating hand over Noah's. "Have you buttons?" she asked Dolan, tucking the fabric under her arm.

"We don't carry buttons. Most people cut the buttons off their old clothes and sew them on their new ones."

"Hooks?"

"Those we have. I assume you'll be wanting thread?"

"Blue, of course."

"Do you have a sewing machine, Mrs. Buchanan?"

"Mrs. McSween has a Wheeler and Wilson machine—"

Susan blurted. "That is…she's in St. Louis and I'm sure she wouldn't mind if Mrs. Buchanan were to borrow it."

"McSween, eh?" Dolan squinted at her. "So you're working for Mac, are you, Miss Gates?"

"The lady's a schoolteacher," Noah spoke up. "She's here to teach kids how to read and write."

Snake sidled along the counter. With one dirty finger he prodded Noah's arm. "What I want to know is why you didn't do yer shoppin' at Tunstall's store, Buchanan."

"I reckon you'd know the answer to that, Jackson."

"And what's that supposed to mean, huh? You sayin' I done the Britisher in?"

Noah smiled. "I'm saying you'd know we couldn't shop at Tunstall's because it's shut down this morning. I didn't say you killed him. *You* did."

"Why, you—"

"All right, hold it there, now!" The voice of young Billy Bonney snuffed the argument as the Kid strode through the front door, followed closely by the town constable.

"We've come with a warrant," the constable announced.

At that, the store erupted. Guns drawn, men on both sides of the room rushed toward the fray. Susan screamed. Isobel grabbed her friend's hand and was making for the counter when Noah bundled both of them in his arms and drew them against his chest.

"Heads down!" he growled. Barreling between two Dolan men, he kicked wide the counter's swinging door. He huddled Isobel and Susan against the side of a three-foot-high black iron safe. "Stay here. Don't move till I come back for you, hear?"

As he drew his six-shooter, Noah gave the women a last glance. Cradling Susan's head in her lap, Isobel gazed at him, her eyes deep. For the first time in his life, Noah realized, someone else's life meant more than his own.

* * *

Wishing she had a gun, Isobel held the sobbing young woman. She scanned the rows of dry goods on the shelves behind her head. Black Leaf sheep dip. Tobacco paste. Pride of Denver soap. Glass lamp globes. Tins from the National Biscuit Company. Red Cross cough drops. Chase & Sanborn's packaged teas. She spied guitar strings, corsets, union suits, gloves and shoes. But no guns.

"Hold on!" a voice bellowed over the rest. "I got a warrant here, and you boys better calm down and listen to it."

Isobel peered over the countertop.

"This here warrant," the constable announced, "is signed by Squire Wilson for the arrest of James J. Dolan, Jesse Evans, Jim Jackson—"

"What fer?" someone shouted.

"For the murder of John Henry Tunstall."

Voices rose again, drowning out the constable. Isobel searched for Noah among the mob, but he was nowhere in sight. If only she had her pistol.

"As sheriff of Lincoln, I'm arresting you!" Sheriff Brady shouted. "All of you!"

"You can't do that, Sheriff!" the Kid protested. "We came in here to arrest these fellers. You can't turn around and arrest us."

"I sure can and do."

"On what charges?"

"Disturbing the peace."

The momentary burst of laughter was followed by a sudden scuffle. A gun went off. Susan shrieked. Isobel scrunched down, covering Susan's head in her lap. Not far from the safe where they hid, she spotted a derringer tucked at the back of a counter behind a cigar box. No doubt Jimmie Dolan had placed it there, but Isobel knew she could put it to good use herself. An ironing board leaned against a shelf, and she dragged it closer and propped it against the safe to form a makeshift barrier.

"Forgive me for leaving you, Susan," she whispered, "but I must have a weapon."

Crawling across the dusty floor, she reached for the gun. But when a hand clamped over her wrist, she let out a gasp.

"Isobel," Noah hissed. "What do you think you're doing?"

"A woman of honor can end a *lucha* between cowards like these filthy vaqueros!"

"You're crazier than a bedbug, lady. Let go of that thing." He pried her fingers from the pistol and tossed the weapon into an open drawer filled with packets of Putnam's fabric dyes. "Where's Susan? I've got to get the two of you out of this place before it blows."

"Here I am, Mr. Buchanan," Susan whimpered.

"It's okay, Miss Gates," he assured her. "Give me your hand, and we'll head out the back way."

Isobel crossed her arms and watched in distaste as Noah escorted the red-haired schoolteacher from the hiding place. Tears streaming, Susan buried her head against his shoulder.

"You'll be all right now, Miss Gates. Come on." Noah cast a warning frown at Isobel, then jerked on her arm and hurried the two women toward the back door.

The hubbub grew behind them as Dolan's men swarmed to help make the arrest. The closing door silenced the commotion inside the store.

"Let me go!" Isobel snarled, twisting against Noah's grip as he hurried her and Susan down the muddy road. "Where are you taking me?"

"Santa Fe. Let that don of yours try to keep his eye on you."

"He's not my don!" she snapped. "You're the man who

married me, Noah Buchanan, and I command you to treat me with respect!"

Noah stopped dead still on the road. "If I'm the man you married, Isobel, then you'd better do as I say. That means no pistols, no shooting, no taking matters into your own hands and getting somebody killed. If I'm your husband, I'm the boss. You hear?"

Isobel tossed her head. "What you want is a weak little nobody for a wife, yes?"

"That's right."

"Then you have married the wrong woman."

"You're right about that, too."

"Oh, no!" Susan cried out. "Here comes the Dolan mob with the constable and the others under arrest."

Noah stiffened. "The pair of you head over to Alexander McSween's house and sew Isobel's dress. I don't want to see hide nor hair of either of you around Lincoln Town today."

Simmering, Isobel stared at the towering cowboy who presumed to rule over her by his bartered title of husband. His blue eyes fairly crackled as he met her gaze.

"You got a problem with that plan, Isobel?" he asked.

"I can't take another minute!" Susan sobbed. Lifting her skirts, she ran down the road toward the McSween home. She had just passed the Wortley Hotel when a group of soldiers emerged and surrounded the approaching Dolan mob.

"My only problem on this day is you, sir," Isobel informed her counterfeit husband. "You forget that we made an agreement. You will protect me, and in return I will testify about the murder of John Tunstall. You have no right to treat me like a—"

"You left out part of our deal, darlin'," Noah cut in, pulling her against his chest as the throng of men drew near. "Your job is to be my sweet little wife until Chisum sells me some land."

Isobel tugged her shawl tight and hugged her packet of calico fabric as if it might insulate her from him. "A good wife knows how to protect herself."

"You and Susan were shielded behind that safe. You were perfectly secure."

"Susan. Ah, *sí*, poor Susan who weeps at the sound of gunfire. How happy she was to be taken under your wing like a helpless chick."

Noah's jaw dropped. "You're jealous. Jealous of Susan Gates."

"Jealous? Ha! She can have you, for all I care. I want a man who treats me like a lady."

"Then you ought to try acting ladylike instead of crawling around the floor to get at a gun."

"And allow myself to be shot by some dirty vaquero like the one who killed my father? Never." She lifted her chin. "I should never have agreed to marry you. I can take care of myself. I am good at shooting."

"You're good at a lot of things."

Her eyes darted up, and she read the twinkle in his. Her mouth twitched, and she shrugged her shoulders. "You know very little about me, *señor*."

"Seems to me I learned a few things about you last night, didn't I?"

At the mention of their kisses, she felt heat suffuse her cheeks. "You know nothing," she managed.

"I know that right now you're starting to look like a blushing bride. So, I'm going to head my pretty little wife over to Mac's house and set you to sewing up your new dress. All right?"

"Oh, yes, my strong, brave husband," she responded,

batting her eyes for effect. "I will stitch and bake—and weep for joy when I hear your footsteps on the porch."

"You do that, sweetheart."

Chuckling, Noah tucked Isobel close and strolled with her toward the adobe home. At the warmth of his arm around her shoulders, it occurred to Isobel that perhaps she wouldn't mind being a wife who would sew and bake and wait for her husband to come home at night. What a curious thought.

Chapter Seven

Isobel had never stitched a dress in her life. For that matter, she had never allowed plain cotton fabric to touch her skin—not until the day she wed Noah Buchanan and was compelled to wear one of Susan Gates's simple ginghams. But she had to remember she was no longer Isobel Matas, daughter and heiress of a wealthy Catalonian family. She was Belle Buchanan, wife of a poor cowboy.

All morning, Susan patiently taught her student how to sew. First Isobel learned to thread the black Wheeler & Wilson treadle sewing machine. Using a borrowed pattern that had been the model for nearly every dress stitched in Lincoln Town, Isobel learned to lay out the blue fabric and cut it to size. The bodice took some adjusting, for she insisted on hooks all the way up to her throat. Modesty was a definite requirement these days. She may have succumbed to Noah's charms once or twice, Isobel allowed, but she would not permit such intimacies to become commonplace.

As she snipped and pinned and tried her hand at finishing seams, Isobel thought about those stolen kisses. What could she have been thinking? She had made a simple agreement with Noah Buchanan. Each would use the other to get what they needed. How then had she slipped so willingly into his arms?

Oh, his kisses… Isobel shut her eyes as the memory seeped through her.

"Are you planning to gather that skirt or not?"

Susan's voice dissolved the memory of Noah's rough stubble against Isobel's cheek. With renewed determination to focus, she resumed sewing. Her feet tilted up and down to work the treadle, while her fingers guided the fabric. The soft cush-cush-cush of needle biting through cotton cloth lulled her. As the full skirt ruffled beneath her fingers and the long hours stretched on, she struggled to force images of Noah from her thoughts.

"How are you and Mr. Buchanan getting along?" Susan asked. Night was setting in and the lamps cast a golden glow over the swaths of fabric that had taken shape during the day. "We've avoided the subject all day, but I can't hold my tongue a moment longer. He seems like such a nice man."

"Nice, yes…" Isobel wet the tip of a thread with her tongue, knotted it and began to hem. "Nice…but common. Like the vaqueros on our hacienda. Strong and powerful but very ill-mannered."

"You still have your sights on Don Guillermo Pascal, then?"

Isobel smoothed the hem and leaned back in her chair. "Noah sent *Señor* Pascal a telegram last night. There has been no reply."

"Maybe he hasn't had time to answer."

"If a man wants to make a woman his wife, he will do anything for her. He will rescue her from peril. He will care for her at any cost."

"But for all you know, your don is on his way to Lincoln right now."

"He doesn't want me, Susan, and how can I blame him? I have nothing to offer."

"You're pretty."

Isobel laughed. "For a common man, a wife need only be pretty. But in my social class, wealth and land are necessary to forge a marriage."

"What will you do? You've come all this way to marry him."

"I always knew I must find my father's killer first. I must regain my lands and jewels. Then Guillermo will marry me."

"Meanwhile, you're married to Noah, and he's a very good man. You might consider just sticking with him."

"Oh, Susan, what a silly head you have! To think that I would ever consider Noah Buchanan in any serious way is loco. We have an arrangement. He's nothing but a vaquero and so plain. He has no land, no house, no cattle, nothing. His hands are large and rough. A workingman's hands. He's beneath me, Susan. How can I explain it?"

"You just did." Noah's voice echoed off the adobe walls of the little sewing room. Isobel and Susan lifted their heads at the unexpected intrusion.

"Noah," Isobel gasped.

"I came for you. It's almost dark."

She studied the hem of her new dress. Had he heard the horrible things she had said about him? Things she knew were weak excuses to hide the surge of emotion she felt every time she thought of him?

"Isobel learned a lot today, Mr. Buchanan," Susan reported, filling the awkward silence. "She threaded the Wheeler and Wilson. She's fine with a straight seam, too."

"But I sure do hate for the *marquesa* to have to wear such common duds."

Isobel stood, her face hot and her heart thudding. "The dress will suit my purpose. Shall we go?"

Noah shrugged. "Good night, Miss Gates. I hope you have a pleasant evening."

"Mr. Buchanan, do you suppose I might have a word with you? That is, if Isobel wouldn't mind waiting outside a minute."

"But of course," Isobel said.

She watched a pink stain creep up Susan's cheeks as the schoolteacher eyed Noah. Grabbing the blue dress, Isobel bundled it in her arms and stepped out of the sewing room. Why should she care if her friend had cast an eye on Noah? First, Susan was supposedly in love with Dick Brewer, and now she blushed and giggled over another man. Susan, it appeared, was an audacious flirt.

But what difference did it make to Isobel if Susan or any other young lady fancied Noah? She and he both intended the arrangement to end in an annulment. Let Susan Gates have the vaquero.

In a few moments, the sewing room door opened and Noah stepped out into the hall. Without a word, he escorted Isobel out of the McSween home.

"Nice night," he commented as they started down the road.

Isobel chose not to respond. Now that she saw things more clearly, she realized kissing Noah had simply been a result of the madness in this tangled town. But such foolishness was in the past. She knew what she had to do with her life. And she certainly understood Noah's place in it.

"Chilly, though," he said as he opened the front door of the Patrón home. "Mighty chilly."

When they had crossed through the empty front room to their bedroom door, Isobel opened her mouth to speak, but Noah addressed her first.

"Isobel, I heard what you told Miss Gates about me," he said. "I'm a plain, common vaquero. I'm beneath you."

"Noah, wait—"

"Hear me out. Last night I thought maybe we had found something good. I prayed about it all day—half the time asking God to blot you from my mind, half the time begging Him to let me keep you."

"You prayed to God…about me?" The very idea of approaching the Creator of heaven and earth with something so personal confused her.

"Yes," he continued, "and I didn't think I was going to get an answer anytime soon. But a few minutes ago, I heard what you said, and that made things clear enough. I'll give you plenty of elbow room from here on, Isobel."

"But I didn't mean it—what I said to Susan." She gestured emptily, aware that anything tender between them had been swept away by her careless words.

"I may be a common cowboy," he said, "but I've got my pride. Now, if you'll excuse me, I'll head back to Mac's place and bunk down in his barn."

Settling his hat on his head, he strode through the silent living room and left Isobel alone to wonder whether her husband would seek other, warmer arms that night.

In the morning Isobel ate the breakfast Beatriz Patrón brought to her room, then she slipped her new blue-cotton gown over her head. It was not a bad dress, she admitted, though it was hopelessly outdated. But evidently Lincoln Town had never heard of fashion.

What would Noah think of her dress? she wondered. And what did that matter anyway? She had offended him and cast him aside. Why should she give his opinion any credit?

But even as she thought it, she fell to her knees by the

bed and buried her face in the blanket. How many times during the night had she slid to the floor, folded her hands and attempted to address God as Noah had—as One who actually cared about her…about Isobel Matas and her insignificant desires.

God was majestic, a Lord who ruled over all the universe. What thought would He spare for a woman who longed to be held and loved and cherished? How could He truly care about a silly, headstrong girl up to her ears in trouble?

He didn't care, of course. God was busy tending to kings and priests, wars and famines, earthquakes and floods. But she needed guidance! Her father was dead, her mother thousands of miles away and her intended husband utterly silent. God would bother Himself with none of that, of course. She was alone.

Rising, Isobel stepped to the washbasin and brushed her hair. As stiff bristles slid through her golden waves, she wondered how to make the best use of this day. She could speak with Squire Wilson about the events surrounding her father's death. She might ask Sheriff Brady, too, though she could hardly trust what such a man might tell her.

Sweeping her hair into a knot, she had just begun to pin it when someone knocked on the door. Dropping the mass of hair, she swung around, fingertips at her throat.

"Yes?"

"Buchanan here."

Annoyed at the flutter that began in her chest at the sound of his deep voice, she strode to the door and pulled it open. Though images of Noah had drifted through her mind all night, she was unprepared for the sight of him. A clean chambray shirt showed beneath the ankle-length canvas duster coat he wore. His denim trousers ended in a pair of black boots. A pistol hung in the holster at his hip.

"We're going on a buggy ride," he informed her. "Bring your shawl. It's cold out."

Too disconcerted to protest, Isobel wrapped her white shawl around her head and shoulders.

"Straighten the bed," Noah ordered. "Good manners."

Isobel had never made a bed in her life, but she bent over to smooth the blankets. A buggy ride? Where had he gotten a buggy? What did he intend? And where had he been all night? With Susan?

She glanced at Noah. His square jaw gleamed from the morning's shave. His blue eyes glowed with the brilliant hue of the morning sky outside her window.

"Where are you taking me?" she asked.

"You'll see." He took her arm and set off through the house. He paused in the kitchen long enough to bundle a stack of freshly baked tortillas in a white napkin and hand them to Isobel.

"Thanks, Beatriz," he said to Juan's petite wife. "If we aren't back by sunset, send out a posse."

"Sunset!" Isobel exclaimed. "But I—"

"I'll be in Mac's rig, Beatriz," he said. Busy with her housework, the woman waved them on. Noah hustled Isobel across the porch and into the waiting buggy.

A pale yellow sun rose to light the Capitan Mountains as Noah drove the buggy toward the Rio Bonito's narrow valley. Purple shadows faded. Greens began to stand out. Sometime in the night, Noah had made up his mind to take Isobel out of town, where he could talk to her about things that needed to be said. And being so far from civilization, he would have time to calm her down before she did something fool headed. At least he could try.

Noah found he had a hard time keeping his eyes on the dirt track. Isobel looked mighty fine this morning. Her new blue dress with its ruffles and gathers showed off her figure in a way that made it hard for him to concentrate. Though she sat up straight on the buggy seat and held her chin high, she looked as sweet and mild as fresh milk.

But he knew better. Beneath that demure facade lay a woman with a tongue as sharp as barbed wire. He had felt its sting the night before when she had told Susan Gates her opinion of him. It didn't take much to set Noah Buchanan on the straight track. And Isobel had done just that. So much for the daydreams that had been rolling around in his head since the night he had kissed her. Daydreams weren't worth a barrel of shucks.

"Where are you taking me?" Isobel spoke up as the buggy passed the Dolan store, where the group of Fort Stanton soldiers lounged on the porch.

"Out of town."

"I guessed that much," she retorted.

Noah didn't let himself rise to the taunt. He wasn't about to start talking to her this close to town.

As the buggy rolled closer to the river, the barren terrain gave way to cedar shrubs mingled with piñons and junipers. Grama grass and bunchgrass, untouched by cattle or sheep so far from town, had grown thick the past summer. Now a dry gray-brown, it crackled beneath the buggy wheels.

The rig bumped and jolted along the rutted trail until Noah turned the horse into the woods. "I intend to speak with several men in Lincoln today," Isobel said. "I can't be away long."

"Eat a tortilla," Noah told her.

Letting out a sigh of exasperation, she crossed her arms. "Noah Buchanan, I—"

"If you aren't going to eat, hand me one. That Susan Gates is a bum cook. Good thing she's set her mind on teaching." He couldn't hold back a smile at the memory of the men hunkering down for breakfast at McSween's house. "Eggs looked like cow chips. And the bacon…well, a man could break a tooth on the stuff."

"Poor Susan," Isobel murmured.

"But she's a sweet gal anyhow. Whoa, now." He pulled the horse to a stop in a glade at the edge of a stream. "How's this?"

"For what?"

"For talking." He jumped down from the buggy and walked around to Isobel's side. When he extended a hand, she stood, lifted her skirt, and set her fingers on his palm. She was trembling, he noted as he helped her down, and he suddenly realized how unexpected—maybe even frightening—this excursion might appear to her.

"What will we talk about?" she asked.

He looked into her eyes, swallowed and hitched up his shoulders. "I'll put down a blanket, and we can sit a spell."

"Has something happened? Is it about Mr. Tunstall's murder?"

He rubbed a palm across the back of his neck. "I'll fetch that blanket."

She stood unmoving while he unloaded a wool blanket from the buggy and spread it on a patch of grass under a tree. Seating herself, she seemed to melt into a pouf of blue cotton.

"What I have to tell you isn't about Tunstall," he began as he sat down beside her.

"Then who?"

He took a deep breath. "I know who killed your father."

"Who did it? Tell me at once!" She clumped her skirt in knotted fists.

"Before you get bees in your britches, I want you to hear me out, Isobel. Do your best to think straight."

"I always think clearly."

He held his tongue about that comment as he continued. "Last night after I left you at Patrón's house, I went to McSween's place. Dick Brewer and I sat out on the porch jawing about this and that. I led him around to telling me about the day he came across that massacre on the trail."

"And?"

"And Dick let out a secret he'd never told. When he found the coach, the guard who was still alive gave him a good description of the man who shot your father. Dick knew right away who it was. The assassin would be long gone by the time the story came out, Dick knew, so the law would drag him back to Lincoln where no one wanted him. 'Course now he's back in town whether we like it or not."

"Who, Noah?"

"The Horrell Gang attacked your father's party—the same bunch that killed Juan Patrón's dad. But the guard told Dick that the man who pulled the trigger on your father had a heavy jaw, a flat nose and spiked-out red hair. His eyes were narrow slits."

"Snake Jackson," she whispered.

"You'd be hard put to find a man to match that description better than Rattlesnake Jim Jackson. This morning, Juan confirmed that Snake was riding with the Horrells back in seventy-three."

Isobel had shut her eyes, the expression on her face filled with pain. Noah could guess how it felt to learn the name of a man who had murdered someone you loved. He fought the urge to put his arm around the woman and hold her close.

But to Isobel, he thought, he wasn't worthy to give her comfort. He was just a no-account cowboy, and he had to keep his hands off.

"Now, Isobel," he said, crossing his arms to keep from

touching her. "Look at this situation straight-on. Snake Jackson murdered your father, but he just murdered John Tunstall, too. He's in a heap more hot water about that. He already has his eye out for a Mexican woman who saw him put a hole in Tunstall's chest. If he ever pins you as that woman, you don't stand a chance. And if he links you to the Horrell business, honey, your days are numbered."

Her eyes filling with tears, Isobel said nothing. Noah knew that she was remembering the moment Snake Jackson had shot the Englishman…and imagining the same man killing her father.

"Take me back to town, Noah," she said suddenly. "I must kill Jim Jackson."

"Kill him?" It was the last thing in the world Noah had expected her to say. He shook his head. "Lady, I just told you your life is in great danger, and you want to ride into Lincoln and try to hunt down a killer? A man who's in league with Dolan and Evans and the rest of those sidewinders?"

Her eyes flashed. "He murdered my father, Noah. What choice do I have?"

"Choice? Take your pick. You can head for Santa Fe and marry your fancy don—or sail back to Spain and settle down with your family."

She looked away. "I don't suppose you've had a telegram from Guillermo Pascal."

"Not yet, but the Pascals are busy folk. Ranching, politics, you name it. If I were you, I'd go home. I bet your mama would be tickled pink to have you back."

"I'm not wanted in Spain. No more than I'm wanted by Guillermo Pascal."

Noah let out his breath. Here was a fine to-do. She wouldn't go to Santa Fe because the don she'd come all this way to marry didn't seem to want her. She wouldn't go to Spain because her family didn't want her. So what did she plan to do—stay in Lincoln? Who wanted her here?

Not Noah Buchanan, that's for sure. He took off his hat, leaned back against the tree and closed his eyes. He had enjoyed that kiss the other night, but if she thought she could treat him like dirt and still expect him to protect her…

"What do you see?" she asked. "In Lincoln. What makes you stay?"

He studied the vast terrain. "New Mexico Territory has elbow room, fresh air, blue sky and plenty of sunshine. It's a tough land. Tough people, too. I like that."

"I see little about the people to admire."

"Most of them are hard as old boot leather. They've worked hard and lived hard. They're either good or they're bad. It's not hard to tell 'em apart. The way a man's heart is—the state of his soul—starts creeping out onto his face. The older he gets, the more he looks like the person he is inside."

"Perhaps you're right," Isobel said. "My father had golden hair, and his smile was gentle. Dr. Ealy's face is filled with peace. Susan Gates is lovely."

"She's easy on the eyes."

"You should marry her."

Noah sat up straight. "Marry Miss Gates?"

"She likes you. She would make you a good wife."

He gave a snort. "You've got two problems with that little notion. One is that Miss Gates has her cap set on Dick Brewer, and he's returning the compliment. Last night when we were alone, she asked me about him. I had only good things to say, of course. I don't imagine it'll be too long before we hear wedding bells."

"A wedding? But they barely know each other."

"They know enough—for sure more than you know your don."

"Don't speak of Guillermo Pascal," she said, knotting her hands in her lap. "It's not your concern."

"But the second hitch in your scheme to marry me off to Miss Gates *is* my concern. I'm already married—in case you forgot."

"I didn't forget," she said.

"Neither did I."

Their eyes met for a moment. Isobel swallowed and glanced away. "How do I look to you, Noah?" she asked. "Does my face show a hardness of heart?"

He took her hand from her lap, opened the fingers and studied them for a moment. "When I first saw you hiding behind that juniper, I thought you were a mite chilly looking. All those shiny green ruffles. Now I have you pegged as hardheaded, afraid of tying yourself down, scared to trust folk. That shows on your face, Isobel. It does."

She lowered her head.

"On the other hand," he continued, "being strong minded and gritty serves a woman well here in the West."

Taking a breath, she spoke in a gush. "Noah, last night you heard me say harsh and cruel things about you. They were lies. All of them. You're the best man I have met since the death of my father. You're gentle but also strong. And brave, intelligent, kind…"

"Whoa, I seem to have improved."

She smiled. "You are a good person. Noah, I'm sorry. What I said last night was wrong. I'm so sorry."

He studied her for a moment. "Isobel, if you didn't mean what you told Miss Gates, why'd you say it?"

Nervous, she lifted the hair from the back of her neck. Her long eyelashes fluttered as she struggled to voice her feelings. "I… I can't allow myself to think too well of you, Noah."

"Because I'm low class?"

"That has nothing to do with it. What is here for me? Nothing. I have no future. My paths to Santa Fe and Spain are blocked. My only hope now is to find Snake Jackson and get my land titles from him. I have nothing. I am nobody. How can I allow myself to look at anything but *revancha?*"

"Listen, Isobel, you can forget about revenge. I'm not letting you near Jim Jackson. The man wants to kill you, and he wouldn't think twice about it."

"What will you do with me?"

"After Tunstall's funeral tomorrow, I'll take you to Chisum's ranch. That's final. No arguing."

"And then? What then, Noah? What is to become of me? You can't hold me there forever. You don't want me any more than Don Guillermo or my family and—"

"I want you, Isobel. I don't understand why, but ever since I first laid eyes on you, I've cared about you. The future is in God's hands, but one thing's for sure. Everything's about to blow sky-high in Lincoln. I've got to get Chisum out of jail and keep Snake from getting his hands on you. All I can think about is right now. And right now, what I know I can't deny. The only truth I can see is that I want you."

Isobel let out her breath slowly. "If you want me, Noah, hold me. Kiss me now."

Chapter Eight

He could hardly believe she had said it. But she was a temptation, and at this moment, Noah could not resist. A woman who looked as Isobel looked, who spoke as she spoke, could not be ignored.

Thoughts of the uncertain future went clean out of his head as he bent to kiss her cheek.

"Isobel, darlin'," he murmured. "What are you doing to me?"

She stared up at him, her face filled with ten-derness.

With a sigh, he took her in his arms and kissed her sweet lips. And kissed them again. A cool breeze playing off the stream mingled with the warm sunlight shining on this patch of green grass. In the silent haven Noah felt as if he was a world away from the fear, bloodshed and anger pursuing them.

When her arms came around him, he knew they were in dangerous territory. Gritting his teeth, he drew back and forced his breathing to steady.

"I haven't had much schooling," he told her, "but I learned one thing a few years back. Put a hungry man and a willing woman together, and you've got trouble. I've read the Bible cover to cover a few times, and I figured out the smart thing to do is stick with God's plan for a man and a woman to get married before they do too much kissing."

Isobel relaxed in his arms, her cheek on his shoulder, her dark gold hair soft against his chest. "I have read many books, but never the Bible. The Scriptures are read to us in church. For me, such things as prayer, the Bible, the sacraments are of the old ways—respected but insignificant. Religion is a guide, not a law."

This surprised Noah. Most of the Mexicans and Spaniards he knew took their faith seriously. "Without those *old ways,* I'd have made a heap more mistakes than I did. Fact is, I don't put a foot out of bed every morning without praying first. I try to never make a decision unless I check it out with God first."

"You married me very quickly. Did you check with God?"

He shook his head. "Nope, and that's how come I'm as tangled up as a bull with its horns caught in a barbed wire fence. Only thing I can do now is pray that God will reach down His hand and untangle me."

She fell silent for a moment. "Noah." Her breath stirred his skin. "The day we met, you searched Dick Brewer's cabin for paper."

He tensed. "Yeah… I did."

"What do you write, Noah?"

His touched a strand of her hair, his fingers tracing the golden waves as he pondered her question. Finally he let out a breath. "Not much yet."

"The moment I first saw your hands—when you saved me from the bullet's path that day on the trail—I knew you were more than a vaquero. I knew you were an artist. Your hands are those of a poet."

He smiled at that. "I'm no poet, Isobel."

"Tell me what you write. Please, Noah."

"Just stories, mainly. They're all up here. In my head.

Stories about life on the trail. About things that can happen to a man when he's living off the land, when he and God and the cattle are his whole world. Yarns the men spin while they're sitting around the fire after a long day." He sighed. "It's probably a crazy notion."

"It would be crazier not to write down your stories."

"Maybe so, Isobel."

A white butterfly drifted over their heads. Noah watched, wondering how it had emerged from its cocoon so soon. Too soon. An early frost would likely end its life before summer. The white wings trembled, and the butterfly alighted on Isobel's shoulder. She didn't notice. Noah smiled.

He liked Isobel this way, he mused. She was soft and feminine in a way that made him want to do things he'd tried to put clean out of his mind. Things like protect, honor and provide for her. He wanted to keep her at hand so he could touch her hair and brush his lips across hers. He'd like to know her sweet arms were waiting for him at the end of the day.

"You must take me to town now, Noah," she cut into his daydream. "I must find Jim Jackson before dark. I cannot be denied *la venganza*."

It took him a moment to sift through the sunlit imaginings that had spangled his reality. *"La vengan—"*

"I must avenge my father's murder and retrieve the land-grant titles this Snake stole from the *familia* Matas. I know the name of the assassin, and I have no choice."

Noah stiffened and eased Isobel's shoulders away until she was at a safe distance. "I want you to hear me once and for all, girl. You're not a Matas any longer. You're a Buchanan. I swore an oath to keep you safe, and I always abide by my word. I'll go to Tunstall's funeral tomorrow, and the minute it's over, I'm taking you to South Spring

River Ranch. No arguing. And none of this revenge nonsense, understand?"

"I understand, Noah," she said.

She would not obey him, he thought to himself. Not at all.

That evening in Lincoln, Isobel eagerly listened to Juan Patrón's account of the day's developments. He was worried that Dolan's gang would attend the funeral the following morning. With Alexander McSween's party there—along with Tunstall's friends and employees—violence could be expected.

As predicted, McSween had demanded Squire Wilson charge Sheriff Brady and his bunch with the unlawful appropriation of property for using Tunstall's hay to feed Fort Stanton horses.

Brady was arrested and bound over to the grand jury for the coming term of court. Everyone in town, Juan explained, knew that the sheriff now sided squarely with Jimmie Dolan.

After dinner Noah insisted on patrolling Patrón's home and store. He circled the house through the night, checking windows and doors. Isobel could not sleep. She listened to his footsteps until dawn.

When breakfast ended, they joined the crowd gathered for the funeral. McSween had selected a burial plot east of Tunstall's store, just behind the land for the church that Dr. Ealy planned to build.

"John Henry Tunstall," Dr. Ealy said to begin the solemn service, "a mere twenty-four years of age, met an untimely death. The son of John Partridge Tunstall of London, England, our friend was brother to three sisters, whom he loved with an extreme devotion. Many are unaware that

John was blind in his right eye, but he overcame this difficulty with the determination of the gentleman he was."

Isobel studied the row of heavily armed men who made up the Dolan faction. Snake Jackson was not among them. They stood beyond a pile of newly turned earth beside the open grave. The casket, a simple pine box, sat unopened on the ground.

As the service began, Noah slipped one arm around Isobel. She glanced at Dick Brewer standing protectively beside Susan Gates. Like all the McSween men, they rested their fingertips lightly on their holsters.

The detachment of Company H, the Fifteenth Infantry, from Fort Stanton kept watch at a distance. Isobel surmised that Lieutenant Delany had instructed them to be a respectful but obvious presence. No doubt the soldiers were the only thing preventing a clash between the two angry groups.

"My text today is from the Gospel of St. John, Chapter eleven, verse twenty-five." Dr. Ealy cleared his throat as he opened the heavy black Bible. *"Jesus said unto Martha, 'I am the resurrection and the life; he who believeth in me, though he die, yet shall he live.'* We are to understand by these words that those who believe in Jesus Christ unto salvation will abide with Him in heaven after their earthly death."

Recalling Noah's declaration of absolute faith in God, Isobel reflected on the beauty and grandeur of the New Mexico Territory. At such a display, who could discount the power of the Creator?

"I'd like to ask now," Dr. Ealy said, "that we close this service with a hymn. Noah Buchanan, I'm told you're blessed with the best voice among us. As we stand here by the Rio Bonito, would you lead us in singing 'Shall We Gather at the River'?"

Isobel glanced at Noah in shock as he began to sing.

Yet another surprise from this man. His deep voice drifted over the stream and across the grassland toward the distant mountains.

"Shall we gather at the river, where bright angel feet have trod," Noah sang, "with its crystal tide forever, flowing by the throne of God?"

The entire company, even the Dolan men, joined in the chorus.

"Yes, we'll gather at the river,
The beautiful, the beautiful river;
Gather with the saints at the river
That flows by the throne of God."

Not knowing the words as the others did, Isobel shut her eyes and absorbed the vibrations in Noah's chest. Though it was a funeral, at this moment she felt more peace than she had known in the entirety of her life. She was folded in the arms of a man who had sworn to protect her. Sweet golden sunlight warmed her. The anger that had driven her to this land faded, leaving in its place the gentle lull of tranquillity.

"Soon we'll reach the shining river, soon our pilgrimage will cease," Noah sang.

"Soon our happy hearts will quiver
With the melody of peace.
Yes, we'll gather at the river,
The beautiful, the beautiful river;
Gather with the saints at the river
That flows by the throne of God."

Dick Brewer was weeping, his head bowed and his curly hair resting against Susan's. Alexander McSween mopped his eyes with a white handkerchief. When the song ended, the lawyer cleared his throat and announced that he had a message from Billy Bonney.

The Kid, Isobel recalled, was still in jail. A murmur of discomfort rippled through the crowd as McSween began to read. "Though I cannot be present for the burial of John Henry Tunstall, I want it known that he was as good a friend as I ever had. When Mr. Tunstall hired me, he made me a present of a fine horse, a good saddle and a new gun. He always treated me like a gentleman, though I was younger than him and not near as educated. I loved Mr. Tunstall better than any man I ever knew. Signed, William Bonney."

McSween folded the letter and placed it on the casket. As the pine box was lowered into the ground, Noah turned Isobel away from the scene.

"There's a meeting at McSween's house," Dick Brewer whispered. Noah had left Isobel's side for a moment to confer with his friend. "Folks are spitting mad that Sheriff Brady won't arrest anyone for John's murder. I think we ought to ask Brady outright what he means by it."

"I'm with you, Dick, but I can't stay for the meeting. I've got to get Isobel out of town. I told her about Snake Jackson murdering her father, and she's hot for blood. The woman's a spitfire, Dick, and—"

"Noah!" Dick grabbed his friend's shoulder. "Over by the tree. It's Snake. He's talking to Isobel."

Noah swung around, fingers sliding over the handle of his six-shooter. "Snake!" he shouted, half-sick with fear. "What do you think you're doing, talking to my wife?"

The heavy-jawed man straightened. "Buchanan, this Mexican ain't your wife."

"She sure is." Noah reached the tree just as Isobel

opened her mouth to speak. He grabbed her arm, stopping her words and pressing her toward Dick, who hauled her quickly out of earshot—and pistol range.

"You stay away from my woman, you hear?" Noah growled. "If I see you near her again, I'll bore a hole in you big enough to drive a wagon through."

"Forget it, hombre. The jig's up with your little Mexican *chiquita* now. This morning the stagecoach dropped a pile of fancy trunks at the hotel. The name on 'em was Miss Isobel Matas. Later on, that uppity Mexican so-and-so Juan Patrón came a-wanderin' into the hotel. He took one look at the trunks and then, all sneaky-like, he wrote a new name on 'em. Mrs. Belle Buchanan."

Snake gave Noah a triumphant smirk. "All through this sorry funeral, I been studyin' your so-called wife. She's the *señorita* who was in the woods the day Tunstall got laid out, ain't she? She was wearin' this Mexican veil."

He shook the fragile white mantilla in Noah's face. "And you know what your woman just told me? She thinks I'm the man who done in her Mexican papa a few years back. Well, guess what?"

Noah glanced behind him at Isobel. She was staring, white-faced, her eyes luminous with rage. "What have you got to tell me that I don't already know, Snake?"

"Just this. I'm the man who made her papa a free lunch for the coyotes. And I'm the man who's got what she came to Lincoln lookin' for—her package of fancy papers. And I'm the man who's gonna pull her picket pin the minute your back is turned. So get ready, Buchanan. The next funeral you sing your pretty songs at is gonna be hers."

"Why, you lowdown—"

"Now, just a minute here, gentlemen." The burly Lieutenant Delany stepped between the men. "Haven't the two of you got better things to do this morning? Especially here in the presence of the dearly departed."

Noah glanced at Tunstall's grave. It was nearly filled with dirt now, and the reality of it was a punch in the gut.

"Listen up, Lieutenant," he barked. "This man shot down John Tunstall in cold blood."

"Now, you don't know that, Buchanan," Delany countered. "You weren't even there."

"I was there, all right. And I've got a witness who'll swear the man who pulled the trigger on Tunstall was Jim Jackson."

"Aw, Buchanan, quit your jawin'." Snake laughed. "Tunstall's own men swore out a statement about who was at the killing, and your name weren't on it, nor the name of your witness. If Tunstall's men didn't say neither of you was there, how you gonna convince a judge of it? Huh?"

"Don't sell me short, Jackson," Noah retorted.

"Go on your way, Mr. Buchanan," the lieutenant spoke up. "You, too, Snake. Captain Purington charged me with the protection of life and property around here. Now, get along, the both of you."

Chuckling, Rattlesnake Jackson lumbered across the clearing. He gave Isobel a sideways glance and formed his hand into the shape of a gun. As he walked past her, he aimed at her heart and pulled the imaginary trigger. Tossing his head back in laughter, he sauntered along the side of Tunstall's store toward the Dolan Mercantile.

"If you know something about him, Buchanan," the lieutenant said, "watch your back. He used to run with the Horrells. Now he's in deep with Jesse Evans and the Dolan bunch. Steer clear of him, that's my advice."

"Thanks, Lieutenant." Noah tipped his hat and headed for the Tunstall porch, where Dick stood guarding the women.

As Noah neared, Isobel stepped out from behind Dick and ran to meet him. Noah caught her and pulled her close. "Why'd you tell him, Isobel? Why'd you tell Snake you knew he shot your father?"

"I was so frightened when he came suddenly from behind the tree. He put his hand around my neck!" Tears filled her eyes. "He called me unspeakable names. He told me that a Mexican had murdered his parents in Laredo, and now he would kill every Mexican he could lay his hands on. He said if I tell what I saw in the forest, he will strangle me. Oh, Noah, I was so afraid, and then my fear became anger, and I told him I knew he had murdered my father."

She bent and buried her face in her open hands. Sobbing, she allowed Noah to fold her into his arms. "I have no choice," she choked out. "I must kill that man before he kills me."

"You can't go after Jackson, honey," he murmured. "You're a woman. And a woman's place is somewhere safe and quiet."

"The pair of you better get out of Lincoln fast," Dick said, joining them. "Snake means what he says."

Susan touched Isobel's arm. "*Señor* Patrón told me your trunks came this morning. They're at the hotel."

"My trunks…" She looked at Noah.

"I'll borrow a buckboard from McSween. Dick, will you help me load up?"

"Count on it."

The women started down the covered wooden porch in front of Tunstall's store. Dick set off after Susan, but Noah stood back a moment.

Not far away, men stomped down the mound of soil that covered John Tunstall's grave. Odd, the peace he had felt as he had lifted his voice in song. He could easily imagine the joy he would feel standing with the saints at the river that flows by the throne of God.

But Noah wasn't ready for heaven yet. For the first time in his life he had touched the fringes of serenity. He had found a haven in the sweet kisses and warm embrace of Isobel Matas. He wasn't ready to let that promised land slip away. Not yet.

It took four days to drive the loaded buckboard to John Chisum's South Spring River Ranch. Concerned that Snake might ambush them, they bumped and jolted southeast along the edge of the Rio Bonito before making the slow climb over the foothills that bounded the Rio Ruidoso. They passed the Fritz ranch, and Isobel asked whether they might spend the night there. Noah shook his head.

"Emil Fritz died nearly four years ago, and the wrangle over his estate started the mess in Lincoln," he explained. "The Fritz family hired Alexander McSween to settle the will. Emil had once been Jimmie Dolan's business partner, so Dolan claimed the Fritz money was owed to his store. McSween refused to give up the inheritance. So Dolan accused him of stealing it."

"Everyone has accused everyone else," she said with a sigh. "One man arrests another…and then is arrested in turn. Both claim to be in the right."

"The main thing is that you and I have no part of either side," Noah said. "We'll settle at Chisum's ranch and bide our time until the trouble blows over."

"And what about Rattlesnake Jackson? Am I to let him escape justice?"

"You have no choice, Isobel." Noah set his hand on hers. "If Dolan's bunch wins this feud, Snake will have the law on his side. If McSween's group comes out on top, they'll lock Snake up without needing your testimony. Snake reminded me that the affidavits sworn after Tunstall's murder don't mention us."

Isobel fell silent. She was held hostage by a man who deserved the worst fate she could wish upon him. Ensnared, yes, but a cornered animal—one with spirit to live—didn't lie down and die. It fought. It snarled and clawed and bit. And perhaps...perhaps it won its freedom.

A silver pistol was nestled in the folds of her green silk gown, packed in a trunk on the buckboard. Isobel knew how to use that pistol. She had the skill and the desire. Now all she needed was the opportunity.

Focusing on the large brown hand that covered hers, she noted the fingers hardened with callus. This was a good hand. It held the promise of protection, nurture, passion.

Isobel knew Noah wanted her to be at peace. He hoped to mold her into the sort of woman to whom a simple blue-calico dress and white shawl might belong. He believed he could hide her away and erase the pain in her heart.

As darkness settled over the road, she studied his profile beneath the black felt Stetson. His face was outlined in the last ribbons of golden light. As the days had passed, Noah somehow had shed his common, dusty vaquero image. Isobel had almost forgotten the dark-bearded cowboy who had swept her onto his horse. In his place she saw a human being, a man who held hopes, dreams and desires in the palms of his rough hands.

It frightened her to think how much of herself she had given him, yet how little she knew him. Perhaps Noah was right to insist she step out of the fray and let someone else give Snake the fate he deserved. But this was not the way she had been brought up.

"Noah," she said as they rode on through the darkness. "You told me I have no choice but to abandon the revenge that calls me."

"No choice at all. You just give up the notion, like any woman with a thread of common sense would."

"What do you know about my people? About Catalonia?"

"Not much more than could fit in a thimble. I reckon it's part of Spain. That means everybody speaks Spanish—"

"We speak Catalan." She saw his brow furrow. "The Spanish government forbids us to speak our language, but we speak it anyway. We are fierce, artistic, political people. Catalonia leads the rest of Spain in the production of textiles. Barcelona has grown far beyond its fifteenth-century walls. We dream of autonomy from Spain."

"Autonomy? You folks want civil war—like the one we went through a few years back?"

"Why not? The rest of Spain is poor and ignorant. But we are a high-minded, cultured people. We have the Jocs Florals, our famous poetry contest. We have painting schools and choral societies. We love fraternity and liberty."

"Those sound like revolution words to me," he grumbled.

"In Catalonia, we do not sit and wait for our future. We have a heritage of progress. Change. We will fight for our freedom."

"So, you're one of these high-minded, revolutionary Catalonians. Is that what you're telling me?"

"What I'm telling you is this," she said in a voice so low the rattle of the buckboard wheels almost drowned it. "I am a Catalan. I have a noble spirit and blood of fire. My father has been murdered and our family heritage stolen. These are crimes I cannot allow to go unpunished."

"Now, Isobel—"

"I must prepare myself, Noah. I must find Jim Jackson. And then I must kill him."

Chapter Nine

Noah wasn't much in the mood to chat by the time the buckboard pulled into San Patricio. It was almost midnight according to the moon-silvered hands on his pocket watch. The little town lay in the valley where the Bonito and Ruidoso rivers joined to create the Rio Hondo was shut tight. Noah directed the buckboard into a wooded copse and set the brake.

Isobel sat shivering while he built a fire. They spoke little. She knew Noah regretted yoking himself to a Catalan firebrand. She was pondering the mule-headed vaquero she'd married. By the time they'd eaten the supper of tortillas and roasted meat Beatriz Patrón had packed, both were feeling positively hostile.

"Shall I sleep in the buckboard?" Isobel asked after washing the plates in a chilly stream while Noah banked the fire.

"Unless you'd rather pack a rifle and stand guard over your fancy dresses all night," Noah shot back.

Isobel tossed her head. "Better to appear foolhardy and defend one's possessions than to be so concerned for safety that one loses everything. To run is cowardly."

"Who're you calling a coward, woman?"

"Certainly I'm not the one who chose to flee danger."

"No, you're the one who was so scared she blabbered every secret we were trying to keep under wraps."

Isobel could hardly argue there. She had collapsed in front of Snake Jackson. But with the clarity of reflection, she realized she should have stood her ground with Noah and insisted they remain in Lincoln.

"A brave person may have a moment of weakness," she asserted, "but it is your stubbornness that prevents justice."

Without another word, she climbed onto the buckboard and settled in a pile of blankets in the midst of the trunks.

"Me stubborn?" Noah grumbled as he tended the horses. "She's so ornery she wouldn't move camp in a prairie fire. Spanish hothead."

Isobel pulled a blanket over her head.

"Thinks she's going to kill Jim Jackson," Noah muttered.

But as Isobel drifted to sleep, she heard him singing in a low, almost inaudible voice.

"On the margin of the river,
Washing up its silver spray,
We will walk and worship ever,
All the happy golden day.
Yes, we'll gather at the river,
The beautiful, the beautiful river;
Gather with the saints at the river
That flows by the throne of God...."

The sun was blazing high overhead when Noah drove down the trail to the home of John Simpson Chisum. Isobel descended from the buckboard, her face aglow with pleasure at the sight of the rambling adobe house built around a central patio.

"This is lovely!" she exclaimed.

"And well built." Noah slapped the side of the house with a gloved hand. "Long planks are buried inside the walls so no one can saw through it with a horsehair rope."

"The roof has a *pretil*," Isobel whispered.

"A parapet," Noah corrected. "That wall can protect a lot of armed men from attackers. The place is a fortress. And it's where I aim to keep you safe from Snake Jackson."

Isobel looked at him fully for the first time in many hours. "Is this where you stay, Noah?"

"My house is a few miles north. It's not near as fancy as Chisum's."

"Take me there. I want to see your home."

Noah's brow lifted. "You're not leaving Chisum's for a minute, hear? And while I'm on the subject, I've got a few things to tell you."

"Are these the thoughts that have made you scowl at the world today?"

Noah took off his hat, eyed it a moment, then spoke. "Until John gets out of jail, Isobel, we don't need to pretend we're married. Which is good because I don't want to let things get out of hand."

"You're unhappy because you kissed me?"

"Yes. Well…no." He met her gaze. "It's not good. Kissing. It *is* good, but it's wrong."

"Pardon me?"

He stuffed his hat back on his head. "We made this arrangement, and we plan to end it one day, right?"

"Yes," she answered. But it came into her mind as she spoke the word that she could not imagine the day when Noah Buchanan would ride out of her life as swiftly as he had ridden into it.

"So," he was saying, "I'm going to check on my place

while you stay here. You'll be safe. Nobody can get into John Chisum's house."

"Or out?" Anger flared. "You intend to imprison me."

"I intend to protect you. When John comes home, we'll act married again. After he sells me the land and we've found out what's become of Snake Jackson, we'll go our separate ways."

"And you'll be rid of me."

"You'll be rid of me, too, darlin'." He touched her chin with the tip of one finger. But he drew away quickly. "I'll take your trunks inside and then head upriver."

From the nearby corral, three men wandered over to the buckboard, and Noah greeted them by name. Isobel stood aside as Noah directed the removal of her trunks. Noah carried himself with a quiet authority that Isobel had never noticed. In his long coat, black hat and leather boots, he resembled a military officer. Tall and powerfully built, he stood well above the other men. But it was the confident air with which he gave orders that revealed his true position among them.

Isobel watched, trying to memorize him, yet trying to accept the truth that their marriage was a sham. The moments of tenderness meant nothing to Noah, and she must not forget that.

She walked toward the house, past the rosebushes, willows and cottonwoods. As she stepped into the front room, a voice called out.

"Mrs. Buchanan?" A small, plump woman extended a hand. "I'm Mrs. Frances Towry, Mr. Chisum's housekeeper. My husband and I moved here from Paris, Texas, a while back. He runs the harness and saddle shop. Our son works on the range. He's a good friend of your husband. 'Course, I don't know a soul who ain't fond of Noah. You got yourself a mighty fine man, Mrs. Buchanan."

"Thank you," Isobel said, mustering a smile.

"Welcome to South Spring River Ranch. And this here's our cook." She gestured to a chocolate-skinned man. "Pete, say howdy to Mrs. Buchanan."

As they greeted one another, Isobel began to see that John Chisum enjoyed the same lifestyle in which she had been reared. The house was large, cool and well-appointed with furniture and plush carpets. Mrs. Towry prattled on as she led Isobel to a fine bedroom.

"I'm gonna put you and your husband right here in Mr. Chisum's room. Now, don't look so shocked. See this beautiful bed?" A mattress, feather tick and bolster rested on an elaborately carved bedstead. "He won't touch this. Every night, he sets up his camp bed."

"But why?"

Mrs. Towry smoothed a hand over the embroidered shams. "Says it's too much trouble to fold up the bedding." A twinkle lit her gray eyes as she glanced at Isobel. "Mr. Chisum is known for pulling jokes. So…if he don't like his own bed, I'll settle you and your husband into it. See how that suits him."

Isobel didn't see how such a joke would endear her to John Chisum. Before she could protest, Noah entered the room, and Mrs. Towry scuttled out.

"Everything okay?" he asked, jamming his hands into the pockets of his denims, as though fearful he might touch her.

"It's good," she said, trying to smile.

"I'll be back in a couple of days. Don't go anywhere."

"Where would I go?"

"You've threatened to chase down Snake Jackson."

"If I leave, everyone will know I'm not Belle Buchanan. That would ruin your plan to buy land from Mr. Chisum."

"Isobel." He stepped closer. "I'll get my land one way

or another. That's not why I want you to stay away from Lincoln. Snake will kill you."

She shrugged. "If I'm dead, you won't have to bother with me."

"Listen, woman." He clamped her shoulders in his hands. "I swore to protect you, and I'm not backing down on that."

"You also swore to be my husband."

"I'm not your husband. Don't tempt me, Isobel."

"How do I tempt you? Tell me."

"Your eyes…your hair…your lips." He drew her against him.

"Noah," she murmured. "I, too, decided some days ago that I must look to my own future."

"That's right." His blue eyes searched her face.

"We are very different. And we want such different things from life."

"Isobel…"

"Kiss me once, Noah. Before you go."

"Isobel…" But his lips pressed hers in a kiss that broke the flimsy barriers of restraint. She slipped her arms around him as she had dreamed of doing. But in a moment, he broke away.

"I can't do this," he said, his voice strained. "No. It's not right."

"Then go, Noah Buchanan. Go to your safe little house. Run away from me. Run from every danger in your life."

"I'm no coward, girl. But steering clear of calamity is how I keep myself alive long enough for my dreams to come true."

"And going *mano a mano*—hand to hand—with calamity is how I make dreams come true."

He shook his head. "Isobel… Isobel."

"Goodbye, Noah." She turned away lest he see the tears

brimming in her eyes. This was the last time he would ever hold her, the last time their lips would touch. Their destinies called them in opposite directions, and each had to obey the beckoning whisper.

By the time the moon rose Noah had settled into the four-room adobe *jacal* he had built at the edge of the Pecos River. He checked on the old milk cow and dozen hens he kept penned in a roughshod barn. His neighbor downriver, Eugenio Baca, looked after the stock when he was gone.

By lantern light Noah meandered down to an old cottonwood tree and dug up his pail of money. It was all there—ten years' worth of scrimping and saving. More than enough to buy the acreage adjoining his home. As he reburied the pail and shifted the heavy slab of limestone back into place, he couldn't help but smile. He had the money. He had the wife. And pretty soon he'd have the land.

He slept well. The following morning, he swept and mopped, gathered eggs, milked his cow. Woman's work, but he was used to it. He couldn't imagine Isobel doing the common chores that made a house a home. She would expect servants to obey her every command. Good thing she was settled at Chisum's place.

The next day, Noah unpacked his pens and ink and started writing a story that had been tickling his thoughts ever since Tucson. Working hard, he stayed up half the night, his thoughts racing and the precious oil in his lamp burning. He could hear the men talking inside his head. He could smell the acrid tang of gunpowder and taste the dry dust in his mouth with each new sentence, each paragraph, each page.

He wrote all day Thursday. Almost forgot to milk the cow. Forgot to chop wood. Snow began to fall outside his window, but Noah didn't see it. He was out on the prairie, sun beating down on his shoulders, sweat trickling from his brow. He was shooting wild turkeys and riding a fiery black stallion and bunking down at night with an Indian blanket twixt him and the ground. Stars by the million twinkled overhead. The smell of blooming cactus filled his nostrils by day. The low of the cattle made music in his ears. Amazing how writing could transport you to another time and place.

Around three o'clock in the morning, Noah fell asleep at the kitchen table. His lamp flickered out. Snowflakes slipped in under the front door. Frost crept up the new glass windowpanes.

"Noah? Are you in there?"

He lifted his head. Running a hand across his chin, knocking ice crystals from his beard, he scowled at the shuddering door.

"Noah Buchanan! Open this door at once!"

No mistaking that voice. "Isobel," he croaked. "What in tarnation are you doing here?"

"I've come with my furniture, Noah."

What was that supposed to mean? he wondered as he tried to stand. Oh, no, must have forgotten to light a fire. He stepped to the door, suddenly aware he felt hungry enough to eat a saddle blanket.

"Isobel, what do you…" He was growling as he dragged the door open, but the sight of her stopped his words.

Oh, the woman was a beauty. Dressed in a royal-blue wool cloak with the hood pulled up, she stood like a queen on his porch. Her red gloves and red boots were the only spots of contrasting color, save her bright pink cheeks and lips. Her hazel eyes flashed as one eyebrow lifted.

"You have been drinking, Noah Buchanan," she announced.

Pushing past him with a sweep of her hand, she stepped into the icy room. At the sight of rumpled blankets, dirty dishes and the table piled with papers, she gave a cry.

"Shame, Noah!" She stripped off her gloves and headed for the woodstove. "I let you out of my sight and you become a *borrachón*. What have you been drinking? Whisky? Rum?"

Noah watched dumbfounded as she clanked open his stove door and began to build a fire. A lopsided effort that would smoke up the house before it caught flame.

"I had hoped we might never see each other again," she was saying. "I knew you planned to keep me from my appointed task."

"Killing Snake Jackson is not your appointed—"

"Unfortunately, my furniture arrived."

A prickly feeling wandering up his back, Noah looked out the front window. Two oxcarts loaded with crates waited by the porch.

"You brought the furniture here?"

"Storing it for me is the least you can do, Noah, since you have refused to help me go after Snake Jackson."

They stared at each other.

"Well, you look good anyhow, Isobel," Noah told her.

"You look terrible." Her glance fell on the table littered with reams of paper and inkwells. "You have been writing!"

"Finished my first story last night." Suddenly enthusiastic, he grabbed the sheaf of paper from the table. "'Sunset at Coyote Canyon.' That's the title. You wouldn't believe the ending. There's a no-good skunk of a fellow who sneaks up, and then…well…"

"And what happens?" Isobel settled on a chair, water from her cloak puddling around her feet as the room warmed.

"Well…" Noah fumbled. "Aw, never mind…"

"Is it ready to mail to New York? I'll take it to the post office when I return to Lincoln."

He studied the pages—scrawled handwriting, blotches of ink, scribbles where he'd added ideas that had come to him. "No, it's not near ready."

"I shall cook breakfast," Isobel announced. "You will read the story to me."

Without giving him opportunity to protest, she shed her cloak, rolled up her sleeves and set to work. "Read, Noah!" she commanded.

He cleared his throat, settled into a chair and began to speak aloud words that once had been only in his mind.

Isobel smiled as she tapped a spoonful of grease into the black iron frying pan.

"Up on the ridge a coyote began to howl," Noah read, "a sound that blended with the whine of the wind and the owls' soft hoot."

Isobel cracked six eggs, one by one, into the sizzling grease.

Chapter Ten

"Opal stood between Travis and Buck. In her arms she carried the newborn babe." Noah's voice lowered as he read the words. "She looked into the eyes of the stranger who had come to kill her husband. 'You'll have to shoot me first, Buck Shafer,' she said. 'I won't be parted from the man I love.'"

Isobel was absently stirring the third batch of scrambled eggs she had made that day. Eyes closed, she listened to the final pages of Noah's story.

They had eaten eggs for breakfast, lunch and now supper, and she had burned them the first two times. But she could do nothing but listen as his words transported her into the tale.

"Travis gazed into the face of his wife," Noah continued, "and at the sweet expression of his newborn son in her arms. 'We're all right,' Opal whispered as they stared at the man who lay dead on the floor. Then Travis and his family stepped outside into the flaming orange sunset of Coyote Canyon.'"

Noah placed the last page upside down on the rest of his manuscript. "In my mind, it came out better. The story flowed like water down a ravine. On paper it got jumpy."

His words drifted off, and he sat staring at the table as though he felt sick. "Just a bunch of scrambled words," he muttered, "like those eggs you're cooking."

From behind, Isobel slipped her arms around his neck. She pressed her damp cheek against his. "It is a good story, Noah."

"You're crying?" he whispered.

"If I read this story in Catalonia, I would know that canyon. I would see those people."

"What about Opal? You probably think I should have let her blast Buck Shafer to kingdom come, like you would have done."

Isobel came around Noah and knelt beside his chair. "Opal did what was right. She protected the baby."

"Isobel, why did you come here?"

"My…my furniture, of course."

He shook his head. "You're in quite a tangle. You want to be bold, shoot-'em-up Isobel Matas. But somewhere inside there's a Belle Buchanan who likes fixing up a house and cooking for her man. There's a woman who cries when a story comes out right. And there's a woman who can't stay away from the man she loves. The man she needs."

"You flatter yourself. I don't need anyone."

"You need me." He touched her cheek with a finger when she started to shake her head. "Yes, you do."

"No," she said, but her eyes again filled with tears. "Oh, Noah."

"There'll be other men for you, Isobel. Men who'll fit into your schemes better than I do."

She knew he was wrong. Not only was she a spinster, but in the days apart from him she had realized she wanted no one else.

"Isobel, you have to go back to Chisum's," he was saying. "I've got chores. And the cow—"

"The cow, the chores!" She pushed away from him and stepped to the stove. "Excuses. The truth for you is the same as for me. You love me."

"But I never let my heart take control. If I'm angry, I give myself time to cool down. If I care for a woman who's no good for me, I back away."

"I'm no good for you?"

"You're so good I can't stand to be this close and not touch. But, Isobel, what could come of it?"

"Then we shall bring in my furniture," she replied, striding to the door. "Stop gawking like a schoolboy and come along."

As Noah dragged the last velvet-upholstered chair across the dirt floor of his house. He had never seen so much furniture in his life. A huge wooden bed sat in pieces to reassemble. A settee and three chairs were lined up by the fireplace. Rolled carpets lay stacked in the bedroom. Dishes and fine linens cluttered the floor. An enormous, gold-framed mirror almost filled one wall.

Heading out the door to check on his cow just before midnight, Noah could hear Isobel singing Spanish ditties as she filled cupboards with her brightly painted plates and cups. How had he gotten into such a mess? A hot-blooded *señorita* determined to gun down Snake Jackson. A head full of stories that wouldn't hush until he wrote them down. A boss in jail, and a best friend sitting on a keg of dynamite in Lincoln. And now a house full of frilly velvet furniture.

As he returned to the house he heard a strange sound— *clickety-click-click, clickety-click, ding, clickety-click.*

What now? He shouldered into the front room. Isobel was bent over a small machine on his pine table. Her fingers darted around *clickety-clacking* on the machine as her eyes scanned his manuscript.

"What are you doing?" he asked.

"It's my Remington!" She swung around and laughed aloud. "It makes letters—like a printing press. I used my typewriter to keep records for our hacienda, but it came from America. See? E. Remington and Sons of Ilion, New York."

Frowning at the contraption, Noah studied the springs, ratchets and levers jumbled among a pair of spools and an inked ribbon. "What do you aim to do with it?"

"I aim to put your story into type before we post it to New York. Look, the first page is finished."

She held up a sheet of white paper with capital letters marching in a straight line across the top. SUNSET AT COYOTE CANYON BY NOAH BUCHANAN.

He whistled softly and sat down beside her as she began to touch the keys again. "Reads pretty good," he murmured as his story began to appear at the top of the unrolling paper. "Well, how do you like that."

"I like it," she said. Her slender wrists moved back and forth in a graceful dance. "When we send it to New York, they'll like it, too."

A smile playing at her lips, she *clickety-clacked* until a second page rolled out of the Remington. Noah leaned one elbow on the table and watched. He felt off balance. Hadn't he planned to stow Isobel safely at Chisum's house? Hadn't he decided there was no future in wooing her? She didn't want to be hooked up with a dusty cowboy for the rest of her life. He had never planned on a wife and family.

So why did her fancy Spanish furniture somehow feel just right in his adobe house? Why had it warmed his heart to walk in the front door and find her seated at his table?

He studied the gold ringlets that fell from the bun at the back of Isobel's head. She was wearing the blue dress again. The one she and Susan Gates had made. Little ruffles clustered around her neck. Little cuffs clasped her slender wrists.

"This part about the coyote I like very much," she said softly. "It makes me shiver."

The scent of her skin drifted over Noah while she spoke. Unable to resist, he trailed kisses up her neck. The *clickety-click* faltered. When his lips met her ear, the typing stopped altogether.

She faced him, her face a mix of tenderness and frustration. "Noah, you said you didn't…"

"But… I do."

"I'll type your story tonight and leave for Chisum's in the morning. You're tired. Go to bed."

He took her shoulders and turned her toward him. "I know what we said about the marriage, Isobel. And I know we meant every word. But there's no way I can be near you and not start thinking about what it's like to kiss you. You feel it, too, Isobel. I know you do."

"When you left, I sat alone in the big house of John Chisum and thought about my life, my future." She lifted her head and met his eyes. "Death runs close behind me. I feel its breath on my skin."

"Isobel, I'm going to take care of you."

"Listen to me, Noah. I have nothing to claim as my own. Nothing. My own death or the killing of a man—perhaps both—these are my only paths. My heart is desperate."

"You're making this worse than it is. Don't you know God has a good plan for you?"

"God? The God who permitted my father's murder? You put your faith in a tale no more true than this one." She pointed to his manuscript. "My future is in no one's hands but my own. Put yourself in my place, Noah. What would you do?"

He let out a breath. "I'd go after the man who stole my

land. I'd track down Snake Jackson. But you don't have to do that. You can go back to Spain."

"Once I was a noblewoman. Betrothed to a don, I was a lady of high breeding and exquisite taste. Now, my heart has been turned upside down. I care nothing for that life."

"It's this land—New Mexico. The mountains and streams."

"It's you, Noah." Before she could think clearly, she slipped her arms around him and kissed his lips.

"Mercy, Isobel," he murmured. Taking her in his arms, he held her close. "Isobel, no matter what we said, I'm not ever going to let you go. I hope you know that."

She shut her eyes and nestled against his shoulder. "Perhaps, Noah. Perhaps."

They set up the new bed in the front room. Isobel slept alone, her dreams tangled and frightening. Noah kept mostly to his room when he was in the house. For three days, no word of past or future was spoken between them. A gale of wind ushered in the first days of March. Snow quickly melted, dry leaves whisked away, shoots of green grass along the Pecos River pushed upward.

While Isobel continued unpacking and arranging her things, Noah went hunting. There was no scarcity of wild game along the river, and in no time flat he had bagged a brace of rabbits.

"Oh, Noah," she cried, her eyes bright with unshed tears as he laid them out. "They're bunnies!"

"They're food, darlin'."

He handed her a knife and taught her how to skin and dress the rabbits. With a kettle of simmering water, a handful of turnips and carrots from the root cellar and a dash of salt, he taught her to make stew.

As the aroma drifted through the *jacal,* Isobel lined the edges of Noah's cabinets with ribbons of white lace she had brought from Spain to wear in her hair.

"Curtains," she said aloud, musing on the glass windowpanes. "We must have curtains."

Noah straightened from the bowl of cornbread batter he was stirring. "What for? Nobody's around to look in."

"A home must have curtains. They let in the light just so...."

Noah rubbed his chin where he'd shaved that morning. "You know, when Mrs. Allison passed away a few years ago—"

"She's dead? Your Mrs. Allison?"

He nodded. "Some kind of a fever got her. Just like the one that got my mother." He fell silent for a moment. "Mr. Allison sent me a trunk from Texas. Things Mrs. Allison wanted me to have. I took one look inside and shut it quick."

"But why?"

"Aw, it was just the kind of stuff Mrs. Allison loved. I think I saw some fancy curtains in there, pictures of pink roses, silver spoons. It made me sad to look at them, being as they were Mrs. Allison's prized possessions."

Isobel watched the flicker of pain that crossed his face and realized the childless Englishwoman had been the only mother Noah had known. "Please show me the trunk, Noah."

Leaving the cornbread, he led her into a back room where he kept his stores. He raised the trunk's domed lid, and Isobel caught her breath.

"Lace curtains from Nottingham in England." She lifted the soft fabric and hugged it close. "Oh, they're exquisite."

A small grin tugged at Noah's mouth. "Exquisite, huh?"

The trunk was filled with treasures—a silver tea set, porcelain cups and saucers, bone china candlesticks. The heavy linen napkins and tablecloths were evidence of the woman's wealth, and her love for Noah.

Isobel lifted a heart-shaped pewter box and peeked inside. "Here's a letter. It's for you, Noah."

"Me?" He took the envelope on which his name had been written in a fine hand.

"Dear little boy," he read aloud. He cleared his throat as he glanced at Isobel. "Mrs. Allison always used to call me that—*dear little boy.*"

For a moment he couldn't read. When he began again, his voice was low. "I pray for you each day as you ride the cattle trails for Mr. John Simpson Chisum. Do be careful. These things I am sending will not fit well with your trail life, but they are all I have. Dear little boy, please remember our sunny afternoons reading books in the library. I have saved every letter you wrote me, one every…every week you have been gone. Dear little…"

Noah swallowed. He gazed at the letter, the muscles in his jaw working as he fought for control. "Dear little boy," he whispered, "I love you so much. Mrs. Allison. Jane."

He folded the letter and slipped it into his shirt pocket. Clearing his throat, he looked at Isobel. "I'd be pleased to hang those curtains for you now," he said.

Sunday morning as Noah sat reading his Bible at the pine table, he couldn't remember a time he'd felt so downright happy.

Not to say that Isobel wasn't more than a mite stubborn and sassy. But he didn't care a lick. In fact, he liked the way she took charge of the house. She unearthed the copy of *Beeton's Book of Household Management* that Mrs. Allison had given him the day he set out for New Mexico. Before he knew it, the young *marquesa* was elbow deep in cleaning and cooking.

Studying the array of bottles and jars she had turned upside down to dry on the fence posts, Noah smiled. As

she finished the dishes, she mentioned how nice it would
be if he would plow a patch of ground outside the kitchen.

Did the highfalutin *señorita* really mean to plant a garden? The idea of her staying on at his place sat well with
Noah. Especially if she could forget about the things that
had driven her to New Mexico.

They had spent only three days together, but the words
that ran ragtag around inside his head were sounding better all the time. Mr. and Mrs. Buchanan. The Buchanan
family. Well, well. Could you beat that?

Monday morning shaped up to be the prettiest day of
the year thus far. The sun appeared over the hills, the wind
died, buds began to unfold. Isobel had finished typing Noah's manuscript, bound it in cloth and sewed the packet
shut for mailing. She was laundering their clothes on the
ribbed washboard and tub on Noah's front porch. He had
saddled the horses in preparation for a ride out on the range
to show Isobel the land he intended to buy.

Her hair slicked back in a tight bun, Isobel had just bent
over the washtub when a raucous holler rippled down the
river valley. Chilled, she straightened. Noah came charg-
ing out of the barn, his six-shooter drawn.

"Isobel, get inside the house!" he shouted.

"I'll bring the rifle!" But she halted as Billy the Kid's
horse thundered up the bank, followed by those of Dick
Brewer and a slew of other McSween men.

"Hey, Buchanan!" Billy reined in his horse and swung
down. "Looks like you and the *señorita* are gettin' mighty
homey round here!"

He let out a hoot as the rest of the men joined him on the
porch. Noah had holstered his gun, but Isobel felt a sense
of growing dread. She should fetch the rifle by the door.

"Last I heard, you were in lockup, Kid," Noah said.

"Aw, they didn't have nothin' to hold me on. Got out the day after Tunstall's funeral."

"Things are bad, Noah," Dick spoke up. "McSween wrote his will and made Chisum executor without bond."

At this, Isobel realized that, even though Noah's boss was still in jail, McSween's action deeply involved him. No doubt whose side Chisum and Noah would take.

"McSween went into hiding on Tuesday," Dick continued. "We thought he might hunker down at Chisum's, but we went by this morning, and he's not there. Mrs. Mc-Sween left for Kansas."

"What about Dolan?"

"No one has arrested any of Tunstall's murderers. Snake Jackson and some other fellows are at Dolan's cow camp down the Pecos. We aim to round 'em up and see they get what's coming to 'em."

"You've formed a gang, Dick?"

"That's right. I'm the leader of the Regulators. Each man took an oath to stick together no matter what. We'll make arrests but we won't shoot on sight. Once we take Snake, Evans and the others into custody, they'll be tried when court sits in April."

"Squire Wilson made Dick a constable and the rest of us deputies!" Billy hooted.

"We want you to join us, Noah," Dick said. "We need you on our side."

Isobel's dreams—lace-curtained windows, a packet of pages bound for New York, a spring garden—began to fade. Noah kicked a heel against the edge of the step.

"I made Isobel a promise, Dick," he said finally. "I've got to stay here and protect her like I swore I would. If Snake gets his hands on her—"

"We'll both go with them, Noah," Isobel cut in, slinging his rifle over one shoulder.

"Isobel, what in thunder do you think you're doing?"

"Five years ago, Snake Jackson rode with the Horrell Gang," she told the men. "Five years ago, he killed my father and stole my land-grant titles. My desire to bring him to justice is as great as yours. I shall ride with you."

"Hold on now, Isobel," Noah began.

"We can't have a woman in the Regulators," Billy protested.

Isobel stepped to the edge of the porch. Inside her heart, she battled the urge to run to Noah's arms and release the past that haunted her. But she smothered the impulse. The last few days had been only a wonderful holiday from reality. With the arrival of the Regulators she understood at last that she would never be free…not until she freed herself.

Shouldering the rifle, she took aim at a bottle drying on a fence post. It exploded in a spray of glass.

She held out her hand. There was only a moment's hesitation before Billy the Kid set his own six-shooter in her palm.

"One, two, three," she counted as she calmly blasted more bottles.

No one moved. A faint breeze lifted white smoke from the end of the revolver. Billy let out a low whistle.

"The *señorita* can ride at my side any day," he said.

Noah was glaring at her. "Why?" he asked. "Why, Isobel?"

"How can I have a future when my past haunts me? I must go with them, Noah. I have no choice."

He shook his head and settled his hat lower on his brow. "Looks like you've got yourselves a couple more Regulators," he said, his voice resigned. "Now, Dick, if you'll excuse me for a minute, I reckon I'd better go take the cornbread out of the oven."

Chapter Eleven

The Lincoln County Regulators—eleven men and one woman strong—set out from Noah Buchanan's house on Monday, the fourth day of March, 1878. Each horse packed a heavy supply of arms and ammunition. Food was plentiful along the Pecos River, and spring was creeping across the New Mexico Territory. The Regulators planned to make camp each night in the hills, where they would be well hidden.

Two days passed without incident. That night, they camped a few miles up from the Rio Peñasco crossing.

"Noah," Isobel whispered from the folds of her blanket.

He lifted his head. "What is it? You hear some-thing?"

"No." She touched his arm. "Noah, I'm… I'm think-ing of dying."

"Dying?" He frowned. "What in thunder are you think-ing about that for?"

"If I'm killed, and if my lands are ever recovered from Snake Jackson, I want you to have them."

"Great ghosts, Isobel, you're not going to die. I prom-ise you that."

Ignoring his avowal, she propped herself on one elbow and gazed into the intense blue eyes. He looked haggard, his hair mussed from the day under a hat and lines deeply etched in his face.

"Noah," she whispered again. "You are a good man."

He reached out and stroked her hair with the tips of his fingers. "It'll be all right, Isobel. Go to sleep. I'm watching over you."

The next morning's travel was uneventful. But at mid-afternoon, the Regulators had just crossed the Peñasco when they rounded a hill and came upon five of Dolan's men.

"It's them!" Billy the Kid shouted.

Hearing the familiar voice, the Dolan five wheeled their horses, broke into two groups and took off overland at a gallop.

"After 'em, men!" Dick hollered. "They're Tunstall's killers."

Weapons drawn, the Regulators gave chase. Isobel caught no sign of Snake in the group, so she spurred her horse after the others. Noah's horse matched hers neck and neck. They rode over a ridge, skirted a patch of yuccas and thundered toward the river. Mud flying from their hooves, the horses pounded along the soft bank.

They'd ridden about five miles when one of the Dolan group's horses stumbled and fell in a tangle of thrashing legs. The rider cried out for help, but his two companions rode on.

"Leave him!" Dick shouted. "He wasn't in the posse that shot Tunstall. Stick with the others, men!"

Oddly pleased at being referred to as one of the men, Isobel lowered her head and guided her horse in a leap over the prone figure who had fallen. Grinning, she turned to Noah.

"Yeah, just watch where you're going, hothead!" he called, giving her a wink.

Soon their horses, too, began to flag from the long chase. As they ascended the brow of a low hill, they realized the other men were no longer in view.

"They've given out!" the Kid crowed. "I bet they're hiding in that patch of tule. Who's going in with me?"

Dick's riders followed Billy down a gully toward a large clump of thick-stemmed grass. As the Regulators closed in, an arm waving a dirty white handkerchief rose out of the tule.

"Hold your fire, men!" Dick shouted.

"Brewer, we give up! Don't shoot!"

"Come on out. We won't shoot. You're going back to Lincoln to stand trial."

As the pale faces of the three men appeared, Billy released the safety on his rifle. In the gully, the click sounded as loud as a gunshot.

"Put it down, Kid!" Noah grabbed the barrel.

"C'mon, fellers, we've got three of Tunstall's murderers," Billy argued. "Let's plug 'em and be done with 'em."

Dick assessed the skinny, bucktoothed boy. "To tell the truth, I'm sorry they gave up, too. If we'd shot it out, we could have finished 'em. But we took an oath, Kid. I promised to transport any prisoners I captured to Lincoln. Alive."

Billy spat. "I say shoot 'em between the eyes and save the court's time."

"No, Kid. I'm not gonna let you do it." Dick nodded to Noah and the others. "Take their weapons, men. Let's ride for Lincoln."

The party spent the night at Chisum's cow camp near the Pecos River. It bothered Noah that they had failed to capture two of the men. The Regulators' position was tenuous. A word from any of those two, and Dolan's men would ride after them.

As he watched Isobel sleeping, Noah wondered how he had made such a big mistake. If Dolan's bunch came to rescue their men, he honestly didn't know how he would fare at protecting his own hide, let alone Isobel's. She was good with a gun, but being hunted by heartless desperados was a lot different from shooting glass bottle targets.

The only thing he could think to do was pray. At Mrs. Allison's feet, Noah had formed a deep faith in God. He was far from perfect, but he tried to follow the Bible's principles. Isobel had no such regard for her Creator. In her quest to avenge her father's death, she was oblivious to the scripture Mrs. Allison had made him memorize: "Vengeance is mine, sayeth the Lord." Maybe Isobel had never heard it.

Was she a Christian? He studied the beautiful woman who had stolen his heart. The idea that a Dolan man might kill her sent a chill through Noah. Losing her would be torment. But then a lifetime wondering if her faith had been enough to see her into heaven? That would drive him loco.

He was still awake when the sun slid over the Pecos and roused the others. With their prisoners riding near the front of the line, the Regulators wound their way back up the Pecos toward South Spring River Ranch. At Chisum's place they learned that Dolan had organized a band of twenty men—and the posse's sole aim was to hunt down the Regulators.

"You think Dolan's posse might be planning to ambush us and rescue their men?" Dick asked as they rode toward Lincoln the following day.

"If we take the main road into Lincoln," Noah said, "we'll play right into their hands. I say we follow the trail through Blackwater Canyon."

"Good idea." After clapping his friend on the shoulder, Dick rode ahead to inform the others.

As the riders left the road, Isobel sensed a strange certainty that she had come home. The New Mexico Territory was not her beloved Catalonia, but here the sky was large and blue, the trees grew tall, rivers rushed through gorges, deer and jackrabbits nibbled grass damp with morning dew. Here rattlesnakes sunned on gray limestone slabs, and coyotes cried out to the moon.

Oh, she enjoyed her fine furnishings and silk gowns, but they could hardly compare to a land as raw and untamed as the spirit that flamed in her heart. With her hair braided and tucked under one of Noah's black Stetsons, her riding boots hooked in the stirrups and Noah's leather belt and holster at her waist, she felt she had found herself.

"I never got to thank you for typing my story," Noah said, leaning toward her. "I put it in my saddlebag so I can mail it when we reach Lincoln."

Isobel gazed into his warm blue eyes. "I enjoyed the typing. I liked your home very much, Noah."

He smiled. "We had a good time there."

As he reached to take her hand, gunshots rang through the canyon. Noah whipped his six-shooter from its holster. His left hand reached to shelter Isobel as he spurred his horse ahead of hers.

"Kid!" Dick shouted toward the front line. "Who fired?"

Noah and Isobel rounded a bend in the trail moments after Dick. On the ground lay three men spattered with blood.

"Who did this?" Dick barked. "Billy, you responsible here?"

The Kid shrugged and glanced at the other men riding with him in the front flanks.

"Speak up, Billy," Dick demanded. "We promised to bring back prisoners—and now we got three dead bodies."

Isobel slid from her horse. Once again, death. Barely breathing, she walked among the horses toward the corpses. As she took off her hat, her golden braid tumbled down her back.

"Isobel…" Noah took her arm, but she pulled free and knelt beside the latest victims of Lincoln County's violence.

"Here's what happened," Billy was explaining. "I reckon they was arguin'. One of 'em shot this feller, and then him and the other one took off. That's what happened, ain't it, boys?"

"Yeah," the others mumbled in assent.

Isobel stood and rubbed her bloodstained fingers together. "This man was shot in the back nine times."

"Like I said," Billy went on, "he was tryin' to git away. 'Course we shot him in the back."

No one spoke as they stared at the three dead men. Isobel felt sick inside. At least two of them had helped kill John Tunstall, but she didn't feel the expected sense of triumph at seeing his murderers slain.

"Fine way to regulate the law in Lincoln County," Noah spoke up, his voice tight. "Makes a fellow proud to be called a Regulator."

"What's the matter, Buchanan? You been lookin' at the world through lace curtains too long?" Billy jeered.

Noah stared at him a moment before turning away. "C'mon, boys, let's get these men buried."

The three Dolan men had been shot in Blackwater Canyon. Dick Brewer paid a group of Mexicans at a nearby cow camp to bury the bodies. His mood dark, the Regulators' leader said nothing as his posse traversed the canyon trail.

As night fell, Billy Bonney announced that he and the other men responsible for the three deaths would ride to San Patricio and hide in the hills until Dick had conferred with the law in Lincoln. When all was clear, the Regulators could regroup and make new plans.

Noah and Isobel elected to remain with the original party. He had no intention of leaving Dick to face a possible Dolan ambush. The winding canyon trail took another full day to navigate. As the three tied their horses to a post outside Alexander McSween's house, Isobel mentioned that exactly one week had passed since the Sunday Noah had read his Bible at the pine table in his home.

"So much has happened since that peaceful morning," she murmured. With a sigh, she stepped onto McSween's porch.

"Isobel!" Susan Gates flew through the door and embraced her friend. "Is it really you? Why, I took you for a man in that getup. Oh, Isobel, I thought I'd never see you again! And what has become of...of..." She scanned the faces. "Oh, Mr. Brewer... How nice to see you."

Susan clearly struggled to contain her joy at finding Dick alive and well. The handsome cattleman made no such pretense. He took two strides toward the woman, took her in his arms and kissed her full on the lips.

"Miss Gates, I'm back," he announced. "I'm here to say in front of all this company that I love you, and if you'll have me, I aim to marry you."

"Mercy!" Susan's eyes lit up as she clasped her hands at her breast. "Why, yes, Mr. Brewer. I'll have you. Indeed, I will."

"Thank you kindly, ma'am. And if you'll excuse me, I need to talk to a good lawyer."

"Reckon I'll do?" A tall man stepped from the shadows of the doorway.

"McSween?" Noah queried. "I didn't expect to find you here."

"Figured no one would shoot me in the back with Governor Axtell in town. Come on inside, Dick." He set a hand on the young man's shoulder and led him into the house.

"Felicitaciones," Isobel said to her friend.

"You couldn't have a finer husband, Miss Gates," Noah added as he brushed past her to follow the other men.

"My stars, what a shock!" Susan giggled as she gestured toward two wicker chairs on the porch. "Come sit down, Isobel, and tell me what brought that on. I've never seen Dick so bold."

"Dick Brewer is a brave man, Susan." Isobel settled on a weathered cushion. She summarized the events of the past days as Susan listened, the smile on her face fading as Isobel recounted what had befallen the Regulators.

"So what did happen to the three Dolan men out there in Blackwater Canyon?" Susan asked at the end of the tale. "Were they really trying to escape? Or did Billy just up and shoot them?"

"I don't know," Isobel acknowledged. "I think we may never have the full truth."

"You need to know what's happened here in Lincoln while you've been away," Susan said softly. "Governor Axtell came down from Santa Fe to investigate the troubles. He's Jimmie Dolan's good friend, so you can imagine how it all came out. Axtell refused to interview anybody on our side. Mr. McSween even risked his life to come back to town, but the governor wouldn't see him."

"Has Axtell done anything about the situation?"

"I'm afraid so. He voided Squire Wilson's appointment as justice of the peace."

Isobel reflected on the man whose careful record-keeping had helped her trace the events of her father's murder. "That's a great loss to the town," she said.

"The governor also declared that no one can enforce any legal process except Sheriff Brady and his deputies."

Isobel stood as Noah stepped onto the porch. Leaning one muscled shoulder against the doorjamb, he spoke. "Governor Axtell has outlawed the Regulators."

She gasped. "Then Dick had no authority to round up those men?"

"Not as of March eighth, the day they were shot in Blackwater Canyon. We're outlaws," he said. "Every last one of us."

"Oh, Isobel!" Susan cried out.

Noah took a step closer. "Isobel, you need to decide what you want to do. You can ride for Santa Fe tonight, or you can stay here under Alexander McSween's protection."

"And you?"

"Dick and I are heading for his farm on the Ruidoso River. We'll stay until court convenes April eighth."

"But that's three weeks away. I'll go with you."

"No, you won't, Isobel." His words left no room to protest. "I can't protect you there. Stay here or ride to Santa Fe. Your choice."

Isobel gazed into his blue eyes and knew she was not ready to leave them. Not yet.

"I'll stay in Lincoln," she told him. "I'll wait for you."

Isobel settled at Alexander McSween's house along with the Ealy family and Susan Gates. They had been her companions on the trail to Lincoln, and she was glad to rejoin them. But she knew the arrangement set them all squarely in the Tunstall-McSween camp.

Susan and Dick had spent not five minutes alone together before he and Noah set off. But that was enough to convince Susan that he wanted her for his wife—and the sooner the better.

Isobel tried to be interested in planning her friend's wedding. The two women studied the array of fabrics inside the closed Tunstall store. "The green, do you think?" Susan would ask. "Or would pink make a better wedding gown?"

But Isobel's thoughts were on a man whose face was imprinted on her soul. Dressing each morning, she recalled his admiration of her blue gown. Brushing her hair, she remembered him lifting a tress from her shoulder, turning it this way and that. Helping Mary Ealy prepare breakfast, she heard the clatter Noah had made as he'd searched for bowls, a frying pan, spoons.

Isobel had only to gaze out the window, and the scene brought Noah to her mind. Riding into town that first evening and sliding from her horse into his arms. Crossing frozen streets on the way to Juan Patrón's house. Lincoln had become a part of her life. Her life and Noah's, together.

"You love Mr. Buchanan," Susan declared almost a week after the men had ridden away. "Don't you, Isobel?"

She gave a weak smile. "The last time I told you how little Noah meant to me, he was standing just outside the door. Now…oh, how I wish he were here again."

Susan reached out and covered Isobel's hands with her own. "In the eyes of God, you and Noah are married. It's all right to love him. Do you want a husband? Do you want Noah?"

"I tell myself I want to capture Snake Jackson," Isobel said. "I want to regain my land titles. I want to marry Don Guillermo. But… Noah is the only man I've ever wanted in this way. I cannot imagine my life without him now."

"I've got news!" Dr. Ealy strode through the back door,

his coattails flying in the March breeze. "It's about Jesse Evans—one of the men who shot Mr. Tunstall."

"Have they caught him?" his wife asked.

"Evans and some of the others have been hiding out in the Sacramento Mountains. A few days ago they sneaked over to a spread near Tularosa to loot it. They were having a merry time of it, but then the owner showed up. He grabbed a rifle and started firing."

"Was anyone shot?" Isobel had realized at once that Snake Jackson often rode with the Evans bunch.

"Killed one and wounded Evans. Shot him in the wrist and the lungs."

"Lungs!" Mary Ealy exclaimed. "Oh, he can't last long."

Dr. Ealy snorted. "Guess again. Evans escaped to friendly turf in the Organ Mountains. Just this morning he decided to give himself up to the commanding officer at Fort Stanton. So there he lies—safe from the Regulators and receiving the finest medical attention in these parts. Save for my own skilled hands, of course."

"Is Evans a free man at the Fort?" Isobel asked.

"He's under arrest until court convenes in April. They'll try him under one of the old warrants he racked up—horse and cattle rustler, murderer, robber." Dr. Ealy shook his head. "And here's the humdinger of it all. Evans swore it was another man in the bunch who pulled the trigger on John Tunstall."

"Another man?" Isobel exploded. "But I saw Snake Jackson and Jesse Evans kill him!"

Clenching her teeth, Isobel turned away and stepped outside. Never mind about Evans. The real object of her mission was Jim Jackson.

If she could have no part in Noah's life…no station as a doña in the Pascal family…no rights to her father's land in Catalonia…then she had only one path.

   She must find Jackson.

   And only one man would know where he was hiding. Gazing up at the rolling green hills that rose above the river, Isobel made her decision. She would ride for Fort Stanton at once.

Chapter Twelve

Isobel knew Dr. Ealy and his wife would forbid her to leave McSween's house. Instead she took Susan aside and explained the situation. If she confronted Jesse Evans while he was under arrest at Fort Stanton, he would be forced to tell her where Snake Jackson was hiding.

"And what then?" Susan asked, panic in her voice.

"Then…only God knows."

Susan's protests did no good. Isobel's revenge would be complete only with the recovery of the land that belonged to her family. Vengeance was her only hope of peace.

Clad in borrowed denim trousers, chambray shirt and leather coat, Isobel set Noah's black Stetson over her gold braid and mounted her horse.

Reaching down, she took Susan's hand. "I shall return in a week. If not, you must write to my mother. Tell her I tried."

"Oh, Isobel!"

"And tell Noah…tell him that I loved him."

Fort Stanton was nine miles from Lincoln. Once under the authority of Kit Carson, it was now commanded by Captain Purington. The towering snow-covered peak of Sierra Blanca dominated the horizon on one side of the stone bastion. On the other rose the mountains of El Capitan.

Entering the fort with little notice from the guards, Isobel scanned the barracks, irrigation ditches and spaded garden plots. Homes dotted the enclosure, and she noted more women and children than she had expected.

Troops of the Ninth Cavalry Regiment—one of four black brigades organized after the Civil War—were stationed at the fort. Highly respected by area settlers, the soldiers protected them from Apache attacks.

Noah had told Isobel that five years earlier, Jimmie Dolan had been the fort's primary supplier of goods. Accused of defrauding the government, his services had been terminated. She assumed this meant the commanders would oppose Dolan in the Lincoln County conflict.

She was wrong. Noah had said the garrison's orders lay with the law in New Mexico. And the law upheld every move Jimmie Dolan made. Determined to speak to Jesse Evans, Isobel tied up her horse and entered a building that served as the fort's store, hotel and post office.

"Help ya?" The voice came from a row of mailboxes where a man was sorting through a stack of envelopes. "Name's Will Dowlin. I'm the trader and postmaster here."

"I want to speak with a medical prisoner."

"Jesse Evans? He's under guard at the hospital. Go to headquarters and ask for the officer in charge." The postmaster turned toward her. "Will you be needin' a room for the night…ma'am? Or, is it sir?"

"My name is Isobel Matas Buchanan. I seek Jim Jackson, the man who murdered my father. And no, thank you, I won't need a room."

As she prepared to step outside, Dowlin called to her. "Miz Buchanan, I wouldn't go tellin' folks you're lookin' for Snake Jackson. He's liable to start lookin' for you."

She tipped her head. "I certainly hope so, Mr. Dowlin."

* * *

Captain Purington was frustrated with the War Department, he told Isobel, and tired of being fettered in his efforts to control the troubles in Lincoln County. Fearing more problems, he at first refused her interview request. But after much pleading, he said if she was fool-headed enough to hunt down a man wanted for murder, so be it.

Late that night, Isobel was ushered into the Fort Stanton hospital. Dr. Appel, the physician who had been paid a hundred dollars to examine John Tunstall's body for the Dolan faction, pointed out Jesse Evans. The outlaw lay on a camp bed, his wrist and chest bandaged.

As she stepped to his side, she touched the place on her thigh where Noah's six-shooter had hung. The holster was empty, the gun confiscated by the guard.

"Hello, Mr. Evans," she said, her mouth dry.

The man stared at her, saying nothing.

She swallowed. "Mr. Evans, I'm looking for Rattlesnake Jim Jackson."

"Snake?" he wheezed. "What fer?"

"He murdered my father, Alberto Matas." The words came easier now. "It happened five years ago, when Snake rode with the Horrell Gang."

"Aw, not you again." Evans began to cough. He spat a globule of bright blood onto the white sheet.

Isobel saw that none of guards intended to move. "Here," she whispered, blotting his chin with a towel.

"Snake aims to kill ya, miss," he grunted as she tucked the towel around his neck. "Hates Mexicans."

"I'm from Spain."

"Don't matter. When he was a kid, some of your people done in his whole family. Besides, Snake seen you in the woods that evenin'."

"When you shot John Tunstall? Yes. I saw it all."

Evans coughed again. "If I tell you where Snake is and you go after him," he gasped out, "yer gonna git killed."

"If I were dead, I certainly couldn't be a government witness against you."

"Well, now…that sits purty good." He lowered his voice. "Snake's at the L. G. Murphy ranch, about ten miles northwest of the fort near White Oaks."

Isobel stood. "Thank you, Mr. Evans. I wish you a speedy recovery."

"Good luck, *señorita*. Yer gonna need it."

Isobel dismounted as dawn cast a pink light over the mountains. The Murphy ranch house sat atop a small grassy knoll in the distance. At this hour no one stirred.

Perspiration broke out on her temples as she drew her gun and crept through the scrub piñon and oak brush. What would Noah say if he knew what she was doing? No doubt he would berate her for taking matters into her own hands. One of his Bible verses would accompany the rebuke, of course. As if God even noticed a lone Spaniard stalking her father's killer.

It wasn't as though she really wanted to shoot Snake. If she could capture him and take him to the fort, Captain Purington would hold him with Evans until court convened in Lincoln. Then the law could hang them both.

Her breath sounded loud in the crisp morning air as she knelt beside a rail fence. No matter how distant and unfeeling God was, she needed divine help. Leaning her head against a post to whisper a quick prayer, she saw the faces of her father, her mother, her brother…and the gentle smile of Noah Buchanan. *Oh, Lord, keep him safe. Always.*

Cradling her pistol, she flipped open the chamber and counted the six bullets. As she clicked it back into place, a gloved hand clamped over her mouth.

"Don't scream. Don't move."

Fear knotting her throat, she struggled, twisting to see the man who held her. A dark hat, a bandanna, shadowed eyes. Gripping her hard, the man turned her to face him. Strong nose…unshaven chin…blue, blue eyes.

"Mule-headed woman," Noah breathed. "What're you doing out here?"

"How did you know I was gone?"

"Susan Gates sent for me."

"But…but I told her—"

"Enough's enough, Isobel. You're coming back to Lincoln with me."

She caught his arm. "Noah—look!"

The front door of the Murphy house swung open. Scratching his rumpled hair, Jim Jackson wandered onto the porch, a rifle in his arms. He wore only a red union suit, its buttons half undone. As he leaned the rifle against a porch post, Isobel wrestled free of Noah's grip.

"Jim Jackson!" she cried out. "Where are the titles to my land?"

"Get down, Isobel!" Noah hissed, drawing his gun as he tried to push her to the ground.

"I am the daughter of Don Alberto Matas—a man you murdered five years ago," Isobel shouted. "Where have you put my family's land titles and jewels? The ones you stole from my father's coach."

With a loud croak, Snake reached for his rifle, but Isobel cocked her pistol.

"Hold yer horses now, *señorita!*" he yelled.

"Shall I shoot you dead? Or will you talk?"

"Why should I tell you anything, *señorita?*"

"Tell me where you put the titles, or I'll blast off your head!"

"And I'll blast off yore sassy head!" Snatching up his

rifle, Snake crouched just as Isobel pulled the trigger. The bullet hit the front door. As she squeezed the trigger a second time, Noah grabbed her by the waist and hurled her to the ground. A bullet zinged past her head and buried itself in a tree trunk behind them.

"Someone's firing from upstairs!" Noah shouted.

"You made me miss my shot!"

"Head for that arroyo."

As Noah dragged her toward the protection of the nearby ditch, Isobel aimed at a face in an upper window and fired her third bullet. A return shot struck a fence post, causing a spray of sawdust and splinters to explode beside them. Isobel took aim at Snake as he scampered around the side of the house.

"Asesino!" she hollered, pulling the trigger. "Murderer! Thief!"

A slug plowed into the dirt beside her. Another hit a rock and ricocheted. As Noah was tugging her down into the ditch, she squeezed off her two remaining rounds.

"Oh, if I could only get my hands on that man—"

Her words hung in her throat as she caught sight of a crimson stain spreading across Noah's sleeve.

His blue eyes darted back and forth as he scanned the landscape. "C'mon—this way!"

"You're…you're wounded!"

"That's what happens when folks shoot at you, darlin'. Follow me."

Running in a crouch through the low shrubbery, they approached the road. The fire in Isobel's blood still pumped like lava through her veins. Yet the man she loved had been shot defending her.

"Get on now!" Noah lifted Isobel in his arms and slung her onto the horse. Swinging a leg over his own saddle, he shouted, "Go, Isobel! Ride like the wind!"

* * *

Pistol drawn, Noah rode just paces behind Isobel. If Snake and his cronies gave chase, it would be close. Noah's arm was on fire, and he knew that spelled trouble.

"Are you badly hurt, Noah?" she called over her shoulder.

"I'll live."

"Then we should circle behind the house. They won't expect it. *Por la venganza!"*

As she spurred her horse, Noah reined his. Busy thanking the Creator for a relatively safe exit, he hadn't quite caught her drift. Maybe it was the loss of blood, but his head didn't feel right. Hadn't he just rescued Isobel? Hadn't he just dragged her to safety as bullets flew around their heads? Hadn't he just gotten himself shot trying to get her away from Snake Jackson?

"Isobel!" he bellowed, goading his horse. "Isobel, get back here!"

A branch raked his hat from his head as he followed her horse's flying hooves through a thicket. Stifling a curse, he gritted his teeth.

"We'll take cover there," she cried, wheeling her horse around. "Behind the privy."

"Isobel!"

But she was off again. When her horse galloped across a stretch of open ground, shots rang out from the Murphy house. The horse shied, dancing sideways as Isobel fought for control.

Jaw clenched, Noah started across the clearing after Isobel. Bullets seemed to come from every direction. Feeling vulnerable without his hat, he hunkered down low.

"Isobel!" he called over the commotion.

"Noah—to the outhouse. My horse will follow yours. I can't leave now. I'm too close!"

"Close to getting yourself killed," he growled. "Get out of here, darlin', and I mean now."

Hostility bordering on hatred flashed from her eyes as she swung her horse away from the privy. He followed, this time steering clear of the road in case of an ambush. When they had ridden a couple of miles without hearing pursuit, Isobel reined her horse to a stop.

"Where are you taking me?" she demanded.

"Home."

"I have no home—and you just made certain of it."

"Snake Jackson won't give up those titles, Isobel, even with you shooting at him from behind a privy."

She shook her head and looked away. "How little you understand me, Noah Buchanan."

"You can say that again."

"At Fort Stanton, I will recruit soldiers. They'll be brave enough to fight by my side against Snake Jackson."

Noah snorted. "We're not stopping at Fort Stanton, Isobel. Or in Lincoln. I'm taking you to Chisum's ranch."

"You will have to keep your gun on me, vaquero, because I mean to return to the Murphy house. I know my mission."

"So do I, *señora*."

Cradling his wounded arm, Noah reached for his hat, then remembered he'd lost it. He ran a hand across his damp hair and let out a sigh. No hat. No breakfast. A hole in his arm. And one crazy spitfire. This arrangement was turning out to be some kind of fun.

As angry as she felt at being deterred from her goal, Isobel was worried about Noah's wound. She insisted on bathing his arm in the clear, icy water of the Rio Bonito.

"It's a clean wound," she informed him as they sat under

a tree near the stream. "The bullet passed through. God was with you."

"He's always with me. You, too."

"How can you say such a thing? He is God! If you saw the churches in Spain, you would understand His majesty."

"Honey, I see it just fine in the New Mexico sky. Majestic as He is, God told us, 'I will never leave you nor forsake you.' He loves us, Isobel."

"If God loved you, He would not have let a bullet go through your arm." As she bound his forearm with a strip of cotton torn from her petticoat, Isobel struggled against her own guilt. Noah had been injured protecting her. She didn't like it that such a man could be hurt. He had seemed so strong, so invincible. Like her father.

Noah brushed a strand of hair from her forehead. "Didn't your daddy ever let you do anything wrong, so you'd learn from your mistake and be a better person?"

Isobel thought back to the first time she had taken her horse over a fence. Though her father had warned her not to do it, he had stood by and watched as she disobeyed. When she'd fallen, he had been the first to her side.

"Why do you reject Him, Isobel?" Noah asked.

She tugged a necklace from inside her blouse. "I carry God with me, you see. You can never accuse me of rejecting Him."

Noah lifted the gold crucifix with his fingertips. "You carry Him, but you won't let Him carry you. You keep Him on this cross so He won't interfere with your plan to wreak vengeance on Snake Jackson. You think you can direct your own life, Isobel. But you're wrong."

"You know nothing about me or my plans. You treat me like a child—forcing me to run when I should stay and fight. You are a coward."

He turned his head, blue eyes piercing. "A coward?"

"That is what I said."

He gave a little grunt. "I must be slipping. I used to be a commonplace vaquero. Now I'm a coward."

"If you had stood by my side—"

"But you're right. We should have fought it out with Snake and his pals from behind the privy. Then, when Dick came to claim our rotting bodies, he could say, 'Yup, these two are dead as doornails, but they sure were brave.'"

"I have no intention of dying at Snake Jackson's hand," Isobel shot back.

"You have some kind of holy halo to keep bullets away?"

"Mock me if you will. I shall never run from my destiny, Noah. I am not afraid of death."

"Well, you and death can get together and have a little tea party one of these days. But until our arrangement is over, you're staying right here."

They set out again without speaking, and it was not long before they arrived at the gate to John Chisum's spread. Isobel caught her breath as they neared the house. Rose-bushes had leafed out and were beginning to bud. Once dry grass had brightened to a soft green. The stream ran high and swift through the valley.

Isobel softened as she recalled the sweet days she had spent with Noah on this land. Now he had brought her here again. If she went to his house, she would fall into that dreamworld again and surrender her quest. Or was a life with Noah her true quest?

She studied him as he unlatched the gate. It seemed forever since her hands had slipped over his broad shoulders. Since his arms had held her close.

"Noah," she said, "when will our arrangement be over?"

His eyes were soft as he regarded her. "When things calm down in Lincoln. When I'm sure you're safe from

Snake Jackson. When I convince Chisum to sell me some land."

"I see," she said, trying to imagine the day he would look into her eyes and bid her farewell.

"Howdy, Buchanan!" A slender, mustached man with deep brown eyes and thinning hair strode toward them. "Where's your hat, partner?"

"Looks like we may end our arrangement sooner than we thought," Noah spoke under his breath. "Here comes John Simpson Chisum."

Chapter Thirteen

John Chisum took Isobel's hand and kissed it. His thick brown mustache—each end waxed into a curly point—brushed over her bare skin.

"Hey there, you old coot," Noah said as he and Chisum embraced.

But the older man drew back with a frown. "What did you mean leaving your new bride at my place, Buchanan? I was mighty ashamed of you when Mrs. Towry told me about it. Especially when I realized that your wife had taken to sleeping in my new bed and hanging her shiny silk dresses in my wardrobe."

Noah turned to Isobel, who blushed a deep red. She lifted her chin. "But Mrs. Towry said—"

"Buchanan," Chisum cut in, "don't you know I've been cooped up in a Las Vegas jail for three months? Eating grub that ain't fit for man nor beast. Sleeping on a hard prison cot. Why, I've been living for the day I could get back here and stretch out on my pretty bed."

Mortified, Isobel spoke up quickly. "Oh, Mr. Chisum, please, I—"

"Now I reckon I'll just have to sleep on my old camp cot."

"Sir, I—I'm terribly sorry," Isobel stammered. "I had no idea. And certainly Noah never intended to offend you."

At this the cattle baron slapped his knee and burst into a gale of hearty guffaws. "Oh, I got you good there, didn't I, Mrs. Buchanan? I had you thinking your husband was in a heap of trouble, right? Camp cot—why, that's where I always sleep!"

Noah tucked Isobel under his arm and gave Chisum a punch on the arm. "You had us plumb tongue-tied, you old joker. I should have guessed what you were up to the minute you started in on her."

It took a moment for Chisum to control his laughter over the grand prank he had pulled. Isobel saw little humor in the situation.

"Don't you mind me, now," Chisum said. "Everyone knows I love a joke. Welcome to the family."

She mustered a smile. "Thank you, sir."

"Noah Buchanan," Chisum said as his sharp brown eyes studied Isobel. "I never would have figured you to settle down. But now that I've seen your enchanting bride, I understand. You folks come on into the house."

As Isobel and Noah followed, he turned and fixed them with another frown. "You know how I feel about gun fighting, Buchanan. A six-shooter will always get you into more trouble than it'll get you out of."

Without waiting for a response, he strode into the cool shadows of his front room. Isobel had already decided that John Chisum was the most eccentric man she had ever met. He swaggered when he walked. His speech was peppered with sarcasm and loud hoots of laughter. He loved practical jokes that were funny only to him.

But as Isobel entered the cattleman's opulent home for a second time, she was reminded that, as odd as he might be, Chisum was also a shrewd businessman.

"Two hundred miles along the Pecos River," he boasted as Isobel gazed out the front window. "Largest ranch in the territory. I dug those irrigation ditches between the roses and the orchard. Clear water. One hundred rosebushes. We'll have watermelons this summer. You and Noah come over for some *sandía*."

"I would like that," she replied.

Chisum fiddled with the waxed end of his mustache. "Tell me about yourself, Mrs. Buchanan. Your kinfolk. Your friends. What possessed you to up and marry my best trail boss?"

Isobel spotted Noah talking to Alexander McSween across the room. Evidently the lawyer had sought refuge at Chisum's ranch.

"My father owned land," Isobel replied, reminding herself to make Chisum believe that Noah was a happily married man. "Noah reminds me of him."

"You married for love?"

She glanced at Noah, whose blue eyes were on her. "I love my husband," she murmured.

"Reckon you'll like living in the territory?"

"I already do."

"Reckon you'll manage to settle ol' Buchanan down?"

"I already have."

"Then how'd he wind up with that bullet hole in his arm?" Chisum asked, leaning closer.

Isobel was ready. "He was protecting me, as a good husband should."

Chisum grinned beneath his mustache. "I like you, Miss Goldilocks. You're spunky. We'll get along fine."

He clapped his hands, and the room fell quiet. Isobel noted that others had entered the room, but she recognized none of them.

"Noah Buchanan, Belle," Chisum began, "I'd like to

introduce you to Alexander's wife, Sue McSween, just in from St. Louis."

A small woman with mounds of curled chestnut hair and almond eyes stood to greet them. Her small lips beneath a prominent nose turned up in a smile. An elegant violet brocade gown trimmed in white ruffles hinted at her husband's wealth.

"And here are Mr. Simpson, Mr. Howes and Dr. Leverson," Chisum continued. "Dr. Leverson has come down from Colorado to establish a colony here."

Isobel stared at the man and wondered at the ill-fated timing of his arrival in Lincoln County. When the guests resumed their chatter, Noah started for the front door.

"Buchanan, where are you off to in such a hurry?" Chisum asked, blocking his path.

"Thought I'd check on my place." Noah nodded in Isobel's direction. "I'll leave Belle with you, if you don't mind. She'll be safer here."

"I certainly do mind." Chisum glanced at Isobel. "Not that I wouldn't appreciate the company of such a lovely creature, but she's *your* wife. You'll need someone to tend that bullet hole of yours. Adios, partner."

Laughing heartily, Chisum hailed McSween across the room and swaggered off, leaving Noah gazing at Isobel.

"You make one move to escape, and I'll hog-tie you to this rail," Noah vowed as he and Isobel wrapped their reins around the hitching post outside his adobe home.

Isobel decided not to respond to such a vulgar comment. When she pushed open the front door and stepped into the familiar room, her annoyance wavered. The house smelled wonderful—crisp starch in the lace curtains, old leather coats hung on pegs, the charred remains of their last wood fire. From the kitchen wafted the aromas of ground coffee, cinnamon, lye soap. From the bedroom, the eucalyptus and lavender Isobel had packed among her clothes mingled with the bay rum cologne Noah sometimes wore.

She shut her eyes and stood for a moment, swept away by memories…laughter, as she and Noah hung curtains, giggles over too many onions in the rabbit stew, the soft *swish-swish* of the straw broom, the *clickety-clack* of the Remington.

"I mailed your story to New York," she said when she felt Noah moving behind her.

"Thank you, Isobel."

She turned to him. "It seems we go in opposite directions, Noah. You are for the quiet life. I am for *la venganza*."

He studied the oriental carpet beneath the velvet sofa. "I remember when you seemed happy with the quiet life, Isobel."

"I remember, too." Again, their eyes met.

"I've lived a rough life, Isobel," he said. "A man's life— rounding up cattle, warding off rustlers, going without decent food. My gun has sent three men on to their rewards—two cattle rustlers, a horse thief. Despite what you think, I'm no coward. But I've got to follow my dreams. It's time."

Noah gazed at her face, and she began to fear he could read her longing, her passion. Did he know how deeply she cared for him? Did he sense that she loved him?

"Then we'll keep apart," she said quickly. "Do as you wish. I'll do the same."

"Good. In a few days I'll talk to Chisum about the land I want to buy. As soon as we hear Snake is in jail, you can get on with your own business."

"Yes," she said in a low voice. "I understand."

But as she began removing her shawl, Isobel knew that every word she had spoken was a lie. She didn't want to stay away from Noah, though he had no use for her. He understood her quest, but he would never help her. When the time was right, he wanted to be rid of her.

Isobel slipped into Noah's life again as though it were something they had planned. He slept in the barn while she returned to the bedroom. Every morning when he walked into the house and smelled the eggs frying and the coffee bubbling, his heart lifted.

And there she always was—Isobel. Freshly scrubbed from her morning bath. Dressed in her blue cotton dress or one of the fancy Spanish outfits she'd refashioned. Her hair gleamed like sunshine, and her lips were always ready with a smile.

As they ate their breakfast at the white-clothed table, her plans spilled out in a gurgling stream. The house soon wore a new coat of caliche whitewash. The windowpanes sparkled. The floorboards squeaked of fresh wax. Noah repaired his fences and gave the barn a coat of red paint.

He sensed that Isobel was channeling her urge for revenge into labor as she spaded the deep, rich river soil beside the kitchen. In his storage bins she found seeds for corn, beans, peas and chilies. She cut the eyes from old cellar potatoes and planted them in rows beside the onion bulbs. Then he taught her how to dig irrigation channels from his ditch to her garden.

In the second week, Noah woke one morning with the idea of taking Isobel out to see the land he hoped to buy. He had no illusions that she would want to stay on with him. Many a sunset he had seen her standing on the back porch and looking in the direction of Lincoln Town. She kept her pistol beside the bed, and he knew if she could, she would ride out again in search of Snake Jackson and *la revancha*.

"Can you leave your laundering for a day?" he asked that morning as they cleared the breakfast dishes. "I thought we might go riding."

"To Chisum's?"

"No." He hung the iron frying pan on its hook. "Thought you might like to see the land I want to buy."

She scrubbed the entire kettle before nodding.

As the horses cantered through belly-high green grass, Isobel was sure she had never been so happy. Dressed in her riding skirt, shirtwaist and boots, she had placed one of Noah's old hats on her head.

She watched him riding just paces ahead, his shoulders broad above the straight line of his back. The wound in his arm had almost healed, and his hair had grown too long. She had considered asking if he would like for her to trim it, but they had not touched each other since returning to the house. The thought of lifting his hair in her fingers was… No, she could never cut his hair.

"I own a few head of cattle," Noah said, beckoning her. "They range with Chisum's herds. Now and again I round them up, see how many calves have dropped and send a few beeves to the railhead. I've saved a little money. Enough to buy a spread, anyway."

"A small one, like Dick Brewer's?"

"Smaller. Chisum staked his claim on this land, and he's fought off rustlers too long to let it go easy." He surveyed the rolling grasslands dotted with wildflowers and yuccas. The turquoise sky spread overhead like a clear lake. "Sometimes, I almost think I can look straight up into heaven and catch a glimpse of God."

"I have never seen my land," Isobel responded.

"Good country around Santa Fe. You'll like it."

Isobel nodded, though she knew she would never own that land unless she fought to reclaim it.

Noah led them beneath a tall tree and they dismounted. "This is a cottonwood," he said. "Remember what I told you last month?"

"You said the leaves in the wind would sound like a river."

"Listen."

She stood beside him in silence, head bowed, eyes shut. For a moment the only sound was the thudding of her own heart. Then she heard it. Whispering, rushing—the gurgle of cool, clear water.

"Yes," she whispered. "Yes, Noah."

She lifted her head and let the winds play across her eyelids. Dappled sunlight warmed her cheeks. Grass swished against her riding skirt. A warm mouth covered her lips.

"Noah!" Her eyes flew open, and she stepped backward.

"Isobel, wait," he said, catching her around the waist. "This has been too hard—you and me together like this. I've prayed day and night, and all I can see to do is ask you to stay here with me. I'll protect you, I swear it. I can't promise much, but I'll give you what I can. I'll give you a home."

"A home? Is that what you think I want from you?"

"It's better than what you've got now. It's better than nothing."

"Oh!" Pushing away from him, she walked around the cottonwood tree and leaned against the trunk. How could he be so blind? Didn't he see the longing in her eyes as she cooked for him? Didn't he feel it in his freshly polished boots, in the ruffles of white lace lining his kitchen shelves, in the neat rows of the garden? Didn't he know she wanted his heart?

Noah's love was her only hope of healing. Without it, her pain would drive her toward a violent destiny.

"Now, Isobel," Noah was saying, his head lowered like an angry bull's as he circled the tree. "I just offered to make good on this crazy marriage of ours. I offered you a home and all that goes with it. Can you tell me what gives you the all-fired uppityness to huff in my face and go marching off like I've insulted you?"

Her heartbeat pulsed in her throat as she watched his blue eyes roam her face. She sensed the power in him, and the need. His stance—shoulders set, legs spread, feet planted firmly—said nothing would get past him now. He wanted honesty. He wanted answers. And he wanted her.

She lifted her chin. "You think a destitute woman has no choices. She must surrender her dreams in exchange for security."

"So, I'm not good enough for you. Is that it?"

"I want more in my life than a house and food."

"Well, what is it you want?" he asked.

She stamped her foot and tossed her head. "I want passion!"

"Passion? Why didn't you say so?" He bent and kissed her. When he lifted his head, his eyes were deep pools. "I've been pussyfooting around you so long I'm about to go stark raving loco. Now, come here and kiss me."

Before she could stop them, her hands slipped around his neck and her fingers threaded through his hair. She stood on tiptoe, pressing her lips to his again and again.

Noah smiled down at her. "We can make it work, darlin'."

"I'm so weak in your arms. How can I say no when you do this to me, Noah?"

"This is why we're good together. This and everything else that's happened between us in that little house."

She kissed him again, and when she drew back, his blue eyes grazed over her. "Oh, Isobel," he breathed. "Oh, darlin'..."

She sighed, her eyelids heavy. "Noah, how can I ever leave you?"

"Don't leave me, Isobel. We'll head for Chisum's right now, and I'll get him to sell me the land."

She studied the nodding heads of silver grass in the distance. "Why not?"

He ran a finger down the side of her neck. "Not a reason in the world."

Arriving late that afternoon at South Spring River Ranch, Noah and Isobel walked hand in hand up the steps of the front portal. John Chisum opened the door before they could knock.

"Why, it's Goldilocks and Papa Bear!" he chortled. "Come on in! Plenty of guests here—two more won't hurt."

Clearly in no mood for Chisum's nonsense, Noah took his boss's shoulder and spoke in a low voice. "John, I want to talk to you."

"Sounds serious."

"It is."

Chisum held out a hand in the direction of the hall. "Kindly excuse us, Mrs. Buchanan," he said.

Isobel nodded, watching them go and wondering whether Noah's dream would come true at last. Dusting her skirt, she sat on the edge of a blue sofa.

"I don't suppose you've heard the news," Sue McSween said.

"News?" Isobel looked around her at the earnest faces of the woman, her husband and three other guests. A chill slid into her stomach.

"Rumor has it," Sue said, "that Sheriff Brady is threatening to place my husband in confinement."

"Jail," Alexander McSween clarified.

"The jail in Lincoln is no more than a hole underground." Sue glanced at her husband. "Some say the sheriff intends to run water into the jail and drown Mac."

"You cannot allow yourself to be taken," Isobel told the lawyer.

"I'm duty bound to be in Lincoln for the opening of court on April first—three days from now."

"But I was told the opening was April eight," Isobel declared.

"It's been garbled," Sue said. "We think District Attorney Rynerson, that great hairy ape, may have switched it deliberately so that in the confusion Mac could be arrested. Or ambushed and shot."

"No!" Isobel rose to her feet. "Not another good man. We won't allow it."

"We're all riding with Mac, Mrs. Buchanan," another of the guests put in. "Mrs. McSween, Mr. Chisum. All of us."

Isobel looked at McSween's protectors—every one of them soft-handed and pale. None wore a gun.

"Well, Miss Goldilocks," Chisum said as he stepped into the room. "Looks like you and your husband are landowners—soon as Buchanan produces the pot of gold he claims to have. Congratulations!"

Noah wore a broad smile. "I'm a mighty blessed man," he said. "A beautiful wife. Land. Good friends."

"I'm so happy," Isobel murmured as he drew her close.

Noah smiled. "Let's head for home, honey. I've got some digging to do."

"Noah," she said with a sigh. "First we must escort Alexander McSween to Lincoln Town. Sheriff Brady plans to kill him."

Chapter Fourteen

While Isobel recounted her conversation with the Mc-Sweens, Noah studied the determination in her face, the hope in the eyes of Sue McSween, the fear in the posture of Alexander McSween and the others.

"You go on home, boy," Chisum said. "Plow your land. Start a family. We'll watch over Mac. Some friends of yours are…uh…taking care of things in Lincoln Town. The Regulators."

"What about Dick Brewer? Is he with them?"

"No, I reckon Dick's still at his farm, mending fences and keeping a sharp eye on his own back."

Noah could never knowingly allow an innocent man to ride into an ambush. "I'll go with the rest of you," he announced. "You'll need protection."

Chisum shook his head. "Buchanan, you just spent a good quarter of an hour in my library explaining how you planned to lay down your six-shooter and start a family. How you're a loyal husband now. How you want to be a peaceful rancher. You're not changing your mind, are you? I'd hate to have to change mine."

Noah bristled. "I will lay down my gun, John. And I

do mean to ranch. But I'll never let the bunch of you ride into Brady's trap without my protection."

"All right, calm yourself." Chisum clapped Noah on the back. "You can ride with us—you and your wife. We'll make it a jolly jaunt, how's that?" Turning about, he leaned in the direction of his kitchen. "Mrs. Towry, we've got more company! Tell the cook to add two extra places to the dinner table!"

Early on April first, Noah and Isobel rode into Lincoln ahead of the others. They would make sure the Regulators were in place to guard the arrival of the McSween party.

"What do you think of Sue?" Isobel asked him.

For most of the journey, the two women had ridden together, surrounded by the men. Noah watched them talk and hoped they were forming a friendship.

He shrugged. "Never gave her much thought. Folks say she's got money smarts."

"Am I very much like Sue?"

"Sure you are. You're smart. You're determined."

"I'm also angry, opinionated, unforgiving."

"Whoa, now," he said. "I've seen those in you, but you have good qualities, too."

"Noah," she whispered. "I don't like Sue McSween."

"Aw, she's not so bad. Give her time."

"But you don't understand…." Her words trailed off. "In Sue, I saw a mirror of myself—a woman driven by a desire for land, power, wealth. I saw a bitter woman, Noah."

He reached over and took her hand. There were a lot of things he could have said—quick assurances, shallow denials—but he was beginning to appreciate what he saw in Isobel's face. A softness was growing, a melting of anger, a gentleness.

"I have been praying," she said as they rode past Juan

Patrón's house. "Praying as you do. I may…it's possible I may have been wrong about God…. I think He might be listening to me after all, and I need His help. I want to wipe away the reflection I saw. I want to change."

Before he could reply, Noah spotted Sheriff Brady. A rolled sheet of white paper under his arm, the sheriff stepped into the street. Four armed deputies accompanied him, two at each side.

"I wonder where they're headed," Noah said under his breath. "Courthouse, I'd bet."

"Maybe it's the mix-up in court dates," Isobel speculated as they rode past the *torreón*. "What time is it? No one's out."

Noah opened his pocket watch. "Nine o'clock."

An uneasiness seemed to hang over the street. The usual morning scents of piñon smoke and baking bread were absent. No children laughed or played outside. No women bustled toward the stores.

"Do you see any of our people?" Isobel asked. "Dick or Billy?"

"Squire Wilson hoeing his garden yonder. His son is out in front of the Wilson house. But—" Noah stopped short as a Winchester barrel appeared atop the adobe wall of John Tunstall's corral. Billy the Kid's face emerged behind it.

"Isobel, look out!" Noah shouted. A row of rifles bristled up from behind the wall, followed by the men holding them—all Regulators. A fusillade of gunfire shattered the quiet. A hail of bullets slammed into Sheriff Brady. For a moment he hung in midair, mouth open. Then he toppled to the street. One of his deputies staggered toward the courthouse, moaning for water. The other three fled.

Noah drew his six-shooter as he tried to steady his horse. "Get off the street, Isobel!" he roared.

In shock, she stared as Ike Stockton ran from his saloon

with a mug of water for the bleeding deputy. Billy the Kid jumped the adobe wall and dashed into the road where Brady's body lay. He bent to grab a fallen rifle.

"This is *my* gun!" he snapped at the dead man before tearing open the sheriff's coat and searching the pockets.

"Billy!" Noah yelled. A shot cracked from the window of a nearby house, and a bullet tore through the Kid's left thigh. Yelping, skipping for cover, he left a trail of blood across the dirt road.

"Noah—it's Squire Wilson!" Isobel cried, observing the man lying in his garden patch.

"Isobel, take cover!" Abandoning his horse, Noah sprinted across the road. The squire lay in a fetal curl, his hands wrapped around the backs of his thighs.

"I was hoeing onions," he moaned. "In this godforsaken town, can't a man even hoe his onions in peace?"

Noah rolled the man over, passing a hand across the wound where a bullet had ripped through both his legs.

"It's all right," Isobel whispered to the squire's son.

Noah frowned to realize she had followed him. Scooping up the fallen man, he started for the squire's house, where his hysterical wife stood in the doorway. She grabbed her son's arm and jerked him inside.

"Oh, is he gonna die?" she shrieked as Noah carried Wilson through the door. "My son, my son, are you all right?"

In moments, Noah deposited the squire on a bed and headed back outside again. "I told you to take cover!" he barked at Isobel. "I can't lose you, girl!"

Taking her arm, he rushed her through McSween's gate and onto the porch.

Susan Gates threw open the door. "Isobel, did they shoot you?"

"She's fine," Noah growled. "Now, get her inside and keep her safe. Tie her up if you have to."

Susan took Isobel's shoulders as Noah started out. But he stepped aside just as Billy Bonney staggered into the house. Face ashen, upper lip glued to his buck teeth, he gripped Noah's arm.

"Buchanan, I need Doc Ealy," he huffed. "I'm hit."

Noah had half a mind to let the Kid take what he deserved for pulling a dirty game on Brady and the deputies. But he slipped a supporting arm around the youth and helped him into a back room where Isobel huddled with Susan and the Ealy family.

"Billy took a bullet in the leg," he informed the women. "Where's Doc?"

"He went to help the squire," Isobel told him.

A skinny young man holding a rifle stood. "Dr. Ealy asked me to keep watch over the women."

Noah recognized him as Tunstall's store clerk. "Well, boy, I hope you're ready. The law is sure to come looking for Billy."

Everyone in the room gathered around as Noah laid the Kid on the bed. "Don't never get shot, ladies," he told the two little Ealy girls. "Hurts like fire."

"Kid, you did a fool thing gunning Brady down," Noah growled. "Ambushed him. What was that about?"

"It's not how it looked, I swear. All us Regulators snuck into town last night to keep an eye on things for Mac." Billy grimaced as Mrs. Ealy began cutting away the lower half of his trousers. "When we seen Brady headin' our way, we knew he was gonna arrest Mac and then flood the jail and drown him. Brady organized the posse that murdered Tunstall, you know, and he never arrested nobody for the killin'. As sheriff, he weren't never gonna get his dues, so we settled the matter ourselves."

"And then went through Brady's pockets," Noah said.

"I was lookin' for the warrant for McSween's arrest.

I knew Brady had it with him, but I didn't find it before them Dolan dogs shot me."

"The Regulators were at South Spring the other day," Noah said. "Did McSween and Chisum order you to ambush Brady?"

Before the Kid could answer, Dr. Ealy hurried into the room. "George Peppin just declared himself sheriff," the doctor puffed, jerking off his spectacles and cleaning them with the tail of his frock coat. "A Dolan man, of course. They're saying McSween's behind the ambush, even though he's not in town. Peppin sent a message to Captain Purington to bring troops from Fort Stanton. They've sworn to arrest McSween and the Regulators, and they're coming after Billy first."

"Why me?" Billy hunched up onto his elbows. "A whole passel of us shot at Brady."

"Oh my!" Dr. Ealy seemed to see the youth for the first time. He peered at the wounded leg. "I don't like harboring a criminal, but Christian duty binds me. Mary, fetch my bag."

While Noah looked on, Dr. Ealy drew a silk handkerchief through the raw hole in Billy Bonney's leg. Isobel and Susan mopped the trail of blood from the back door to the bed. Mary Ealy kept an eye on the window while the store clerk sawed a hole in the floor of an adjoining room.

"Here comes George Peppin!" Mary cried out. "He's got some deputies and a bunch of others. They've followed the blood in the street. Oh, what shall we do?"

With Peppin pounding on the door, Dr. Ealy hastily bandaged Billy's leg. The doctor and Noah helped the wounded man into the next room and lowered him into the hole in the floor. They handed him a pair of pistols before replacing the boards. The women placed a carpet and a rocking chair over the spot.

With Noah standing watch, Isobel settled into the chair, and Susan took a stool nearby. The two Ealy girls crawled onto their laps.

Taking the Bible from a table, Isobel began to softly read. *"The Lord is my shepherd, I shall not want. He maketh me to lie down in green pastures. He leadeth me beside the still waters. He restoreth my soul."*

Peppin stomped into the room, his boots thudding on the wood floor. "We seen the trail of blood leading to the door, Buchanan, and we aim to find out where Billy Bonney has got to."

"You're wasting your time, Peppin," Noah answered. "My wife is reading the Good Book to calm the children."

Peppin snorted as his deputies began overturning furniture, tossing pillows to the floor, ripping curtains in their search for the Kid. Isobel kissed the cheek of the girl on her lap, and continued.

"Yea, though I walk through the valley of the shadow of death, I will fear no evil, for Thou art with me."

She rocked on the loose floorboards while the intruders tore up the house. If Sue McSween was unhappy with Dolan's men before, Noah realized, she was going to be furious when she saw what they had done to her home.

It was all he could do to stand by while the men smashed china plates, tore velvet upholstery and uprooted ferns. Isobel stroked the little girl's golden hair and kept rocking. As the vandals stormed out of the house, Isobel's voice continued.

"Surely goodness and mercy shall follow me all the days of my life," she read. *"And I shall dwell in the house of the Lord forever."*

The McSweens' home was raided two more times that day in search of Billy the Kid. The final inspection was undertaken by Captain Purington and twenty-five caval-rymen from Fort Stanton. Billy stayed hidden with his six-shooters under the floor, beneath Sue McSween's carpet and the Bible-reading Mrs. Belle Buchanan.

Isobel tried to calm her fears as Noah left to intercept the McSween party as they got to Lincoln. Later, Noah reported that Isaac Ellis, a McSween sympathizer, had put the group up in his house on the outskirts of town. Pep-pin, Captain Purington and his soldiers wasted no time in arresting McSween on the warrant retrieved from Sheriff Brady's body.

"Mac refused to surrender," he told Isobel that evening as they sat on a bench on Juan Patrón's back porch. "He said Brady's death canceled Pippin's status as deputy and didn't make him sheriff."

"But you told me Mac turned himself in," she said.

"He surrendered to Captain Purington on the condition they take him to the garrison and hold him in protective custody until court convenes next week."

"Such lawless men, all of them."

"You should have heard the shouting match between Purington and Mac's buddy Dr. Leverson. He's English, but he's got friends in high places. Says he knows the secretary of the interior, Carl Schurz. And he's pals with Rutherford B. Hayes."

"The president of the United States?"

"Yup. Leverson accused Purington of ignoring the Con-stitution by searching the house without a warrant," Noah explained, chuckling. "Finally the captain cursed the Con-stitution and Leverson for a fool. So Leverson started urg-ing the soldiers not to obey a captain who would show such contempt for the Constitution. By that time, Purington was mad as a rattler on a hot skillet."

Isobel shook her head. "Everyone in Lincoln is so angry. I'm… I'm afraid, Noah."

He slipped his arm around her and kissed her forehead. "I'm here with you, darlin'. Nothing's going to happen to either of us."

"Who told the Regulators to assassinate the sheriff?"

Noah pondered for a long time. "I don't know. I'd like to think our men are better than that. But, Isobel… I'm just not sure."

"Will it calm down now that the soldiers are here?"

"Captain Purington's got a twelve-pound mountain howitzer and a Gatling gun at Fort Stanton. Fear of him bringing them to town ought to keep folks in line. District court will bring a lot of people to town—people who don't want to get shot at."

Isobel leaned into Noah's embrace. "I don't know where Snake Jackson and my land-grant titles are. I saw two more murders today. That makes six since I came to Lincoln County."

An image of Noah's adobe house filtered through her thoughts. She wondered how the cow and the hens were faring. Would the corn and beans have sprouted in her garden? How high was the river flowing? Had it rained?

Her sigh drew Noah's attention, and he cuddled her closer. "Isobel, I've got my land, and I've got you beside me. I'm not going to let those slip away. Not for anything."

"But what will happen next?"

"This evening when one of the boys sneaked into the McSween's house to fetch Billy out from under the floor, he told me Dick Brewer had called a meeting of the Regulators. Brady was a Dolan man, but he wasn't a bad fellow. The Regulators are going to be unwelcome in Lincoln Town."

"Do you think Dick wants to disband the group?"

"Probably. He's never been a man for violence." Noah brushed a strand of dark gold hair from Isobel's shoulder. "I'd like to hear what he has to say. I trust Dick's judgment. I'd lay down my life for that man."

"Let's go to the meeting," she whispered.

"It's a good safe distance from Lincoln," Noah assured her. "At a place called Blazer's Mill."

To reach Blazer's Mill, Noah, Isobel and the Regulators rode through friendly territory. Dick Brewer joined them at his farm. As they journeyed west, they picked up five new sympathizers.

Noah and Dick insisted Isobel ride close to them. Dick was furious about Brady's murder. The killing betrayed the true purpose of the Regulators, he said, which was to bring law and order to the county. He wanted to disband the group but the Regulators were still needed.

Members of the posse who had shot John Tunstall roamed loose—at least two hid near the little town of Tularosa, not far from Blazer's Mill. A huge number of Tunstall's cattle had been stolen and driven to San Nicolas Spring near the Organ Mountains. The spring, too, could be reached from Blazer's Mill. Worst of all, Dolan had put a bounty of two hundred dollars on any Regulator. If the group dispersed, bounty hunters could pick them off.

Isobel studied the two men, one slender and finely carved, the other massive, as if hewn from stone. Noah and Dick were notches above the other Regulators. They were clean men, their guns polished, their horses groomed. Both were intelligent and skilled, yet they avoided violence.

As she rode the grassy trail along the Rio Ruidoso, Isobel began to see a picture of the future. At first her thoughts seemed childish, but soon she began to pray her dreams could become real.

She and Noah would live as husband and wife in the adobe house beside the Pecos River. They would own land and run cattle. She saw their children scampering through the front yard or wading in an irrigation ditch…little girls in pigtails…little boys with scuffed knees. A lush garden grew beside the house, rich with peas, beans, corn, chilies. Laundry flapped on a line, the New Mexico sun bleaching the linens a pure, brilliant white. Chickens scratched in the dust. The aroma of *biscochitos* drifted from the kitchen window. Lace curtains billowed in the breeze.

Dick and Susan Brewer would visit, their buckboard full of children. Laughter would fill the house as the families ate together. Isobel and Susan would discuss children and recipes. Noah and Dick would linger on the porch after the little ones had gone to bed. They would speak in low voices about their land and livestock.

"Billy was a good kid till they killed Tunstall," Noah was saying. "Now he's angry, reckless, hotheaded. He never thinks about the future. All he wants is revenge."

Dick glanced behind at the youth—little the worse for the shot that had torn up his leg a few days earlier. "Billy and Tunstall were pals. Tunstall was the first man to accept the Kid and try to help him."

"I'll talk with him after lunch." Noah checked his pocket watch as the group rounded a pile of logs beside the mill, then entered a corral near Dr. Blazer's foursquare house. "Maybe I can make him see sense."

Isobel's usual fire-and-ice demeanor seemed to have suddenly melted, Noah noted as they dismounted. She wore a peaceful, faraway gaze. It worried him.

That morning, she had pinned her hair high on her head, all swooped up in curls and waves. Gold tendrils danced around her neck and forehead. Isobel had already earned

the Regulators' respect for her shooting and riding. Today
her beauty had won their devoted admiration.

Noah grunted. Those poor, female-starved cowboys
wouldn't know how to behave around a woman like Isobel. But they flirted and made eyes at her all the same.
Some in the bunch were said to be downright handsome.
Ladies thought the Kid was a charmer. He could dance
better than any man Noah knew, and when he felt like it,
he could be amiable—so long as a person didn't stare at
those buckteeth and droopy eyes.

Most of the Regulators had been in the woods the night
of Noah's wedding and knew it was a sham, but Isobel
made it plain she belonged with him. She slept near him
each night on the trail. She rode at his side. She followed
him with her eyes.

Now, at Blazer's Mill, she was introducing herself to
Mrs. Godfroy, the wife of a government agent who rented
the house from Dr. Blazer.

"I'm Mrs. Noah Buchanan," Isobel said.

The woman smiled. "Would you and your friends like
some dinner?"

Dr. Blazer, a dentist, had leased his house as headquarters for the Mescalero Indian Agency. Mrs. Godfroy was
known for serving a fine meal, and the men looked forward
to eating there before hunkering down to talk things over.

They were settling around the table for a meal of stew
and cornbread when Noah glanced out the window. A
small cloud of dust drifted up from the road the Regulators had just ridden. Now Noah spotted a lone mule and
rider—a small man, loaded down with pistols, cartridge
belts and rifles. He carried his right arm at an odd angle.

A wash of ice slid down Noah's spine. "Boys, looks
like we've got a visitor," he said. "Yonder comes Buckshot Roberts."

Chapter Fifteen

"Buckshot Roberts was in the posse that shot Tunstall!" Billy Bonney shouted, grabbing his rifle and angling toward the window. The other men pushed away from the table and went for their weapons.

"Roberts is a bounty hunter," the Kid said. "He'll be after that two hundred dollars Dolan put on our hides."

"Hold it, boys!" Dick called. "I've got a warrant for Buckshot's arrest. Let's get him to surrender."

"Surrender," Billy muttered. "I'd rather put a bullet through him."

"Frank, you know Buckshot Roberts pretty well." Noah addressed one of the two Coe brothers. "Why don't you talk to him?"

"No problem." Frank buckled on his six-shooter and left the room.

Noah handed Isobel a Winchester. "Buckshot Roberts is almost too crippled to lift a rifle," he said in a low voice. "But he's fought Indians and Texas Rangers, and he'll stand up to all fifteen of us if he's pushed. I want you to stay close to me."

She nodded, disconcerted to see these armed men in a

dither over a single bounty hunter riding a mangy mule. What could one man do against so many?

Frank Coe had begun talking to Buckshot from the porch. Watching from a window, Dick shook his head. "Frank just stepped out of my line of vision. Three of you boys go arrest that little varmint."

Mrs. Godfroy was in a tizzy. "Mr. Brewer, you can't shoot your guns around this place! Those men are standing by a door that leads to Dr. Blazer's storage room. He's got a Springfield and a thousand rounds of ammunition in there."

"Roberts, throw up your hands!" A voice outside the window cut off Mrs. Godfroy's warnings.

"Hold on," Buckshot Roberts shouted back.

A blast of gunfire followed. Mrs. Godfroy screamed. Everyone inside the house raced for the back door. Noah grabbed Isobel's hand and ran behind a water trough near the corral. They crouched there, breathing hard as they loaded their Winchesters.

Isobel peered around the trough and gasped. "Buckshot's wounded!"

Noah jerked her back to cover, his blue eyes flashing. "Careful, Isobel. The man is a deadeye shot."

"But he was hit—his stomach was covered with blood."

"Gut shot." Noah took off his hat and wiped his brow. "He won't last long."

Just then, Charley Bowdre and George Coe dashed around the water trough. "Loco little spitfire!" Bowdre spat. "He drew on me, so I shot him—but he won't quit! He blew off my cartridge belt and mangled George's finger."

Muttering curses, George Coe bound his hand with a bandanna. "Blasted off my trigger finger right at the joint, ornery little—"

"Buckshot hit Billy," Bowdre cut in. "I don't know where he is now."

Isobel peered around the trough at the crippled bounty hunter who had managed to shoot four men. In the doorway to the storage room, he lay stomach down on a blood-stained mattress. His rifle was aimed at the trough.

Perspiration trickled down Isobel's temples as she took cover again. "Dick's coming our way."

As he slid in next to Noah, Dick yanked off his hat. "How many shot here?" he asked.

"Two. George Coe and Bowdre," Noah answered. "They'll live."

"A shot skinned Billy's arm—says it matches the one he took in his leg the other day."

"How's Mrs. Godfroy?" Isobel asked.

"Screaming that Buckshot's in a room full of ammo. I'm going to that stack of logs near the sawmill to get a better look. If I don't talk him into surrendering, he'll die on that mattress."

Noah grabbed Dick's arm. "Let me talk to him."

"I'm leading the Regulators, Noah. I'll do it."

Without waiting, Dick ran in a crouch toward the pile of wood a hundred yards from Buckshot Roberts. Noah handed ammunition to Bowdre, whose gunbelt had been shot off.

"Dick's behind the logs," Isobel reported. "He's trying to get a better look at—"

"No!" Noah roared.

Too late. Dick lifted his head just above the line of logs. Buckshot took aim and fired. The bullet struck Dick between the eyes, and he toppled over.

"No!" Noah's cry echoed. "No!"

He started for his friend, but Bowdre and Coe dragged him back. Trembling, Isobel sank against the trough.

"He's gone, Noah," Coe barked. "Let's get out of here before Buckshot kills us all."

As he grabbed Isobel's arm with his bloody hand, a hail of slugs splintered the trough, causing water to stream out the holes. As soon as the shooting paused, the three men hustled her toward the corral.

The remaining Regulators were already on their horses. Several men blocked Noah to keep him from heading back to his friend. As the group sped away from the mill, Buckshot continued firing.

"Dick," Noah groaned. "We've left Dick."

"Brewer's dead, Buchanan," Billy Bonney said. "The Godfroys will bury him."

Noah lapsed into silence. But when Isobel gazed at the man she loved, she saw his tears.

For almost two days Noah said nothing. When the Regulators arrived at Dick Brewer's ranch, they gathered on the porch to talk. Isobel joined them, but she noted that Noah sat a short distance away, hat in hand as he studied the ground.

"We need a new leader," Billy declared. "With Dick dead, we got even more reason to blast them Dolan snakes to kingdom come."

"You want to be leader, Kid?"

"Sure!"

A disgruntled muttering followed, then Frank Macnab spoke up. "I'll put my name in the ring, boys. Everybody knows I'm a cattle detective. Makin' war on rustlers is my job, and the Dolan bunch is no better than a pack of thieves. I reckon I can get myself deputized easier than any of you."

"He's right," Charley Bowdre said. "Macnab is used to trackin' folks down. I'd stick by him as leader."

"Me, too," Frank Coe added.

"Aw, nuts," Billy said, flinging down his hat.

Noah stood. "I'm going to round up Dick's cattle and take them to Chisum's ranch for safekeeping," he said. "I'll cast my lot with Macnab."

"You stickin' with the Regulators, Buchanan?" Bowdre asked. "Nobody'd think you was yeller if you wanted to leave. With Dick gone—"

"With Dick gone, I've got a job to do," Noah spat. "It's called revenge."

Without a glance at Isobel, he stalked off the porch and headed for his horse.

Isobel heard Noah's boots on the porch of Dick Brewer's cabin. After the Regulators left, she baked a batch of biscuits and cooked a thick cream gravy. It wasn't much of a meal, but she knew Noah liked it.

Head down, he entered the front room and hung his lariat on a nail by the door. Without looking at Isobel, he sat on a stool and took off his boots.

"Noah," she tried, his unfamiliar reticence distressing her. "I… I made your supper."

He stepped to the table and sat in one of Dick's rickety chairs. Isobel split the biscuits with a fork and ladled gravy over them.

As he ate, she turned over memories of the first hours they had spent alone together. Here in Dick's cabin, Noah had taught her to wash dishes, their hands touching in the warm, soapy water.

But Dick's death had changed Noah into this unspeaking, angry bull of a man. A man who frightened her.

"Will you have more biscuits?" she asked.

He shoved his plate at her.

"How many days will it take to round up the cattle?" she asked as she filled it.

He chewed a bite so long she thought he wasn't going to answer. Then he lifted his head. "You were right all along. When someone you care about gets killed, you don't stand back and let things take their course. You don't wait for the law. Not in Lincoln County."

"Noah, what are you saying?"

"I'm saying that Dick Brewer got killed—as fine a man as any to walk God's green earth. Buckshot Roberts deserves to die for killing Dick. Jimmie Dolan, Snake Jackson, Jesse Evans—the whole passel of them—deserve to die. And I aim to bring them to justice."

"You mean you'll try to kill all those men yourself?"

"I mean I will kill them." He pushed his plate back and stood. "I understand you, Isobel Matas. Finally, I understand."

He went into the bedroom. Isobel sat at the empty table staring at the chipped plates and blinking away tears. Her vision of a little adobe home on the Pecos faded. The kitchen garden would never bear fruit. There would be no laughing children, no laundry flapping, no *biscochitos* baking. Susan and Dick would never visit. The dream was ashes.

Dick Brewer had not owned many cattle. Even so, the drive from his place to Chisum's South Spring River Ranch exhausted Noah and Isobel. At night, they took turns sleeping and guarding the herd. During the day, they worked to keep the cattle out of the river and move them east.

Caring for Dick's cattle was the least Noah could do for his friend. After meeting Susan Gates, Dick had told Noah about his desire to raise a ranching family on the vast New Mexico range. He had confided that he hoped every one of his children would have Susan's red hair and gray eyes.

Choking down the knot in his throat that rose every

time he thought of Dick, Noah studied Isobel from a distance. Her riding skirt was dusty from days in the saddle. Her white shirtwaist hung loose. The long gold curls that turned men's heads were shoved beneath one of Dick's old hats.

Isobel had buckled on one of Dick's holsters, and her pistol now hung at her thigh. A leather cartridge belt studded with bullets girdled her hips. Noah would have figured her for a tough trail hand if not for the soft glow in her eyes each time she looked at him. Where was her fire?

As they camped each night, she cast sweet smiles Noah's way. Her hands gently spread his blanket on the thick grass. She never tried to make him talk as they sat beside the campfire. Instead she cooked, dusted his Stetson and read aloud from his Bible.

Her tenderness was almost enough to weaken him to the point of shedding tears. But when he lay alone in the dark, he saw Dick rising from behind that stack of logs…a bullet slamming into his forehead…his body jerking backward…crumpling.

No! Dick's death demanded justice, and Noah was the man to deliver it.

Noah and Isobel drove the cattle onto Chisum's spread and left the herd with the hired hands. They found Chisum's square ranch house empty of guests. But Mrs. Towry, the housekeeper, knew all about the shoot-out at Blazer's Mill.

"Buckshot Roberts died the day after you left," she said as they sat on the sofa in Chisum's front room.

"Gut shot," Noah mumbled.

"Major Godfroy and Dr. Blazer sent to Fort Stanton for a doctor. I don't know why they wanted to save that rotten bounty hunter. Dr. Appel drove down from the fort, but it was too late. They buried Buckshot Roberts right beside Dick Brewer."

Noah clenched his teeth to suppress a curse and stared out the window.

Mrs. Towry continued. "Mr. McSween is at Fort Stanton. District court was to start in Lincoln this morning. Everyone thinks Judge Bristol will be staying at the fort for protection. Soldiers will stand guard every day at court. The town should be safe now."

Isobel glanced at Noah. "I'm going to Lincoln," she said. "I want to be there for the trials."

Noah frowned but made no move to dissuade her. "Fine. We'll go."

Mrs. Towry took in a breath. "But Mrs. Buchanan has been on the trail for days with those reckless Regulators. Herding cattle like a common cowboy. It's plain indecent the way you've treated your bride. Why don't you take her home? The fellow who looks after your place told me a coyote got into your chicken coop. Your milk cow got scared and broke loose. Court will go on for weeks, and if I was you, I'd check on my place."

"Well, you're not me, Mrs. Towry," Noah said, standing and slinging his saddlebag over one shoulder. "I have business in Lincoln."

"It is one thing," Isobel said, throwing open the guest-room door, "to mourn your friend. It is quite another to be rude."

"What did you say?" Noah emerged from behind an ornate bamboo screen, his shirt in his hands and his face dripping wet.

"You were impolite to Mrs. Towry." Isobel tried to keep her eyes on his face. "She was trying to help."

"And I was trying to make my point." He stepped back

behind the screen. Amid splashing water, she could hear him muttering. "That house is in the past…crazy idea anyway…writing stories and all that nonsense…"

Isobel marched around the screen. Noah was bent over the washstand, scrubbing his hair with soap. Sputtering, he came up for air. As he blindly reached for the towel, his hand inadvertently touched Isobel's shoulder.

She sucked down a gasp. Taking the linen towel from its brass hook, she handed it to him. For a good minute he rubbed his hair and face.

Then he lifted his head to stare at Isobel. Bright blue eyes shone in a face so haggard and tormented her heart ached.

"Noah," she whispered. "What happened to you?"

"The best man I ever knew got a bullet between the eyes. And now he's buried next to his killer. If you don't think that turns my stomach—"

"Sit down, Noah Buchanan," Isobel cut in, pointing a finger at the chair near the window. "Sit. Now."

"I'm busy."

"Sit!"

Casting her a black look, he obeyed. She drew a fresh linen towel over his shoulders and around his neck, tying it in back.

"What are you—"

"It's time for a haircut," she said. "My husband may act like a barbarian, but he won't look like one."

She rummaged through a drawer until she found a pair of scissors. "When I was a girl," she said, snipping at his sideburns, "I was afraid."

"Afraid of what? You lived on your fancy hacienda with your rich clothes and your rich parents. What was there to be scared of?"

"Many things." She smiled as she drew the comb through his hair and cut the ends. "I was afraid of my horse."

"Your *horse?*"

"Yes, I was terrified of him. One day my father took me aside and brushed away my tears. He said, 'Isobel, *mija,* you must change your fear into anger. Anger will make you strong. And with that strength, you will control your horse.'"

She snipped the back of Noah's hair. "From that time, I hid my fear behind the curtain of anger. No one, nothing, could frighten me. I have pursued revenge with that anger—never letting anyone see my fear."

"Are you afraid of Snake Jackson, Isobel?"

"I'm afraid of losing the ones I love."

He reached up and took the hand that held the comb. "You lost your father. I lost Dick. You hide your fear. I hide my pain. What's so bad about that kind of anger, Isobel?"

She searched his bright blue eyes. "Once a man taught me that there was more to life than fear and pain and anger," she said. "That man showed me how to laugh at bubbles in dishwater. How to weep over a beautiful story. He taught me that God loves me...that because the Lord is my shepherd, I need fear no evil. That His Spirit comforts me—even in the valley of the shadow of death. Because of you, Noah, I am learning how to really live."

He stood suddenly, knocking back the chair as he moved away from her to the window. Isobel watched as he leaned an arm against the sill, his fist clenched.

Stepping to his side, she laid her hand on his back and ran her palm down the taut muscles. He let out a breath and turned to her, his eyes red.

"That man died, Isobel," he whispered in a hoarse voice. "The moment that bullet hit Dick Brewer's forehead, the old Noah Buchanan died. Buckshot Roberts's bullet blew away that part of me. I feel anger now, nothing else."

"Come, Noah," she said, taking his hands and drawing him near. "Let me remind you of other things."

Isobel shut her eyes as their lips touched. He kissed her cheek, her neck, and she felt protected in his arms. "Noah, we could be so good together."

She slipped her arms around him, but when her fingers threaded through his hair, he stiffened and pushed her away.

"No, Isobel," he growled, his eyes icy, distracted. "I can't. I've got things to tend to."

Pushing away from her, he strode across the room. She heard the door slam as she stood alone, needing her husband.

Chapter Sixteen

On the long ride to Lincoln, Isobel pondered her future. Though she knew Dick Brewer's murder had changed the silent man who rode at her side, she had no doubt that deep in his heart Noah would remain the same. The intense pain he felt over the loss of his friend proved that his gentle nature had not been erased.

"I've been considering," he said as they neared Lincoln. He hadn't spoken more than a few words for three days, and his declaration surprised Isobel.

"What have you considered?" she asked.

"I think it's time we ended our arrangement."

She tried to squelch the dismay that rose inside her. "Why is that?"

"We've pretty much wound things up. I helped you find the name of your father's killer. I protected you from Snake Jackson and the others. You can't testify against Evans and Snake, because the Regulators didn't name you as an eyewitness in their first report. So you're off the hook on that. District court will put an end to Lincoln's troubles. Dolan might go free because of his connections in Santa Fe, but his men will wind up behind bars."

"And I helped you get the land you wanted from John Chisum. So our contract is fulfilled."

"Reckon so."

Isobel nodded, but inside she felt frantic to sort out the real meaning behind Noah's words. Did he want to be rid of her? Did all that had passed between them mean nothing? Or did he love her and fear for her safety as he carried out his plan to avenge Dick Brewer's death?

"What will you do now?" she asked. "Continue as Chisum's trail boss?"

He scowled at the sun-dappled road. "You know what I'll be doing."

"Buckshot Roberts is dead. What more do you want, Noah?"

"I want to bring Jimmie Dolan down."

"Will you ambush him on the street like the Kid did Sheriff Brady? Will you become a bounty hunter like Buckshot Roberts?"

"I'll do whatever it takes, Isobel. Dick wouldn't let Tunstall's death rest. I'm not going to let Dick's death rest. And the man behind both murders is Jimmie Dolan."

"What's to become of me while you wreak your revenge?"

"Look, I didn't take on your entire future the night I married you, Isobel. We struck a temporary bargain. Do whatever you want."

"Then I shall ride with you in pursuit of Jimmie Dolan."

"No, you won't!" He whirled on her, his blue eyes flashing. "I've already lost Dick, and I'm not going to lose…" He bit off his words. "Stay at McSween's house through the trials. Susan Gates will be in a fix over losing Dick. She'll need comforting."

"And what about you, Noah?"

"I don't need your comforts, Isobel. You saw that three days ago."

"Three days ago, I saw a man whose best friend had been murdered. One day you'll wish me near."

"No, I won't. If I need a woman, I'll find one with no strings attached. I don't want to be tangled, Isobel."

"And I tangle you."

"Yes, you do."

"So, you will throw away your stories, take down the lace curtains, let the kitchen garden go to weeds. Those days with me meant nothing. You'll forget our laughter, my burned eggs, the typewriter—"

"Don't. Just don't talk about that, Isobel. I don't want to hear it."

"You said you wanted to make our marriage real. You took me to Chisum's house to buy land for us."

"That was before Dick got killed." He reined his horse and studied her, his eyes dark. "I'm sorry I steered you wrong, Isobel. Sorry I made you think there could be a future for us...like I was good for you."

"You are good for me."

"No. You don't know what kind of people I come from. I told you about Mrs. Allison and her library. But my daddy was a gambler. He left after I was born. My mother sold herself to keep food in our bellies. Then she died of a fever and left all us kids orphans. I'm no better than Snake Jackson. His folks left him an orphan, too. It was only the luck of the draw that got me on as a stable hand with the Allisons."

"Luck? Don't you mean God? Didn't He put you with Mrs. Allison? Are you not the man who reads the Bible and prays each day? The man God shaped to write 'Sunset at Coyote Canyon'? Who was that man, if not you?"

"But I've got my daddy's roving blood, Isobel. I'm a

wanderer. Chisum didn't want to sell me land because he thought I couldn't sit still long enough to care for it. I may have fooled you into thinking I was a good man, but the truth is, I've got an outlaw's heart."

Isobel blinked at the tears blurring her vision of Lincoln's dusk-shrouded road. So this was how Noah would end their union.

"It is your choice," she told him. "I am now both Isobel Matas and Belle Buchanan. You are a good man and a rootless drifter. Neither of us can continue to be both. We must choose. Choose well, Noah."

Lest he see the tears that spilled down her cheeks, Isobel dug her heels into her horse's sides and rode for the home of Alexander McSween.

When Isobel arrived, she found Susan Gates very ill. Dick Brewer's death had come as a terrible shock, and nothing Dr. Ealy had tried helped.

While Isobel wept with her friend, she cried her heart out to God. How could Noah let her go so easily? How could he turn his back on what they had begun to build? *La venganza* was not worth such sacrifice.

Days passed, and Isobel saw nothing of Snake Jackson or the wounded Jesse Evans and their bunch. Though the town swarmed with people, she often escaped to sit beside her father's grave. Don Alberto Matas really had died, she accepted finally. She would never see his golden hair or hear his laughter again.

Hoping to catch a glimpse of Noah, she stopped at the courthouse several times. He was nowhere to be seen in the crowded room.

Isobel breathed a sigh of relief when district court concluded on April 18, and that evening Dr. Ealy brought a summary of the news. Most of the trials, he said, had turned in favor of the McSween faction. For the killing of John Tunstall, indictments had been brought against Jesse Evans, Jim Jackson and several others as principals, along with Jimmie Dolan as accessory. But of the principals, only Jesse Evans could be found. He was put under a five-thousand-dollar bond. Dolan was arrested and placed under a two-thousand-dollar bond. The judge continued his case.

For the killing of Sheriff Brady and his deputy, four indictments had been handed down—all to Regulators. For the killing of Buckshot Roberts, only Charley Bowdre had been indicted. Since neither Bowdre nor any other Regulators were to be found, no arrests could be made. The sheriff held the warrants.

Alexander McSween was cleared of criminal charges, and Fort Stanton released him. The grand jury indicted Jimmie Dolan for encouraging cattle stealing.

Sitting in a rocker beside Susan's bed later that evening, Isobel recognized that Noah's prediction of peace in Lincoln had come to pass at last. But when someone began hammering on the back door, she tensed, remembering the day she had helped hide Billy the Kid under that very floor.

Dr. Ealy opened the door. "Noah Buchanan—good to see you again!"

Noah stepped into the room and swept off his black Stetson. "I need to talk to Isobel," he said. His focus flicked to her. "Would you step outside for a minute?"

Isobel glanced at Susan. The ache in her friend's face mirrored what she saw in Noah's. Taking her white shawl from the peg by the door, she stepped onto the back porch and looked up at the sliver of moon hanging just over the roofline.

"I'm riding for Santa Fe tomorrow morning," Noah said. "If you want, I'll take you to the Pascals'."

Isobel ached to feel Noah's arms around her. But she saw that his intentions toward her had not changed.

"Why Santa Fe?" she asked him.

"This afternoon, Dolan left Lincoln headed that way. Rumor has it he's planning to talk to Governor Axtell and Tom Catron, the U.S. district attorney for the territory. Catron holds a lot of property mortgages and loans around these parts. Axtell and Catron are both in the Santa Fe Ring, and if Dolan gets their help, he can turn things to his favor pretty quick."

"And you mean to stop him?"

"Legally, if I can. If not…" He shrugged.

"Why must you be the one to pursue Dolan?" she asked. "Billy is always hot for blood. Let him do it."

"The Regulators are in hiding, and nobody's after me. Besides, I know how to talk to men like Catron."

Isobel pondered the painful consequences of riding with Noah again, bearing his rejection day and night. And what of Guillermo Pascal? Her betrothed had never responded to the telegram sent so long ago. Surely he would not want Isobel to appear on his doorstep like some windblown beggar.

But when she looked into Noah's blue eyes she heard herself whisper, "Yes. I will go with you to Santa Fe."

The sun had not risen when Isobel rode through Lincoln Town at the side of Noah Buchanan.

"Don't let him get away from you," Susan had whispered as she had hugged her friend goodbye. "He's a fine man."

But what good had it done Susan to fall in love, Isobel wondered. Dick Brewer had been killed as easily as Noah might be. Now Susan had to live with loss for the rest of her life.

Loss and rejection seemed to hound the women of Lincoln County. It would not be long before Isobel had to face the rebuff of Guillermo Pascal and his family. She could no longer deny her land grants had been lost forever. She would return to Catalonia with nothing but heartache to show for all her months in New Mexico.

Yet—against all better judgment—Isobel loved Noah Buchanan. She knew she could live without him. She also knew she didn't want to. God had given her one week in which to win the heart of her husband. Would He help her mend the rifts between them?

Noah chose a difficult passage over the mountains to Santa Fe. He hoped Jimmie Dolan might have opted for a longer but safer route up the Pecos River. If Noah had his way, he would beat the Irishman to the capital and speak with Catron first.

Climbing the mountainous trail with Isobel only a few feet behind gave Noah time to think. He wasn't sure what had driven him to the McSween house to propose such a venture. The moment he had stepped through the front door and had seen Isobel sitting on the rocker by Susan's bed, he knew he ought to back right out the door and run.

Great stars, she had looked beautiful that night! Waves of golden hair had hung shimmering over her shoulders. She must have sewn a new dress, a pink confection with ruffles at the wrists and around the neck.

On seeing him, she had risen from the rocker with her hazel eyes shining. When he had taken her out in the moonlight, it had been all he could do to keep from gathering her up in his arms and kissing her the way he wanted to.

He turned around now to check on her. She wore fancy Spanish riding clothes—a black outfit that covered her neck and swung down to her boots. She had swept her hair up into a tight knot high on the back of her head.

But Isobel was no *marquesa* on this ride. Around her waist hung a belt studded with a row of bullets. Dick Brewer's old hat dipped low on her brow, and she looked ready for battle.

Letting out a breath, Noah focused on the winding trail. He had to force away memories of their days in the little adobe house by the river. He had to forget the letter that had come to him in Lincoln saying his story had been passed to a magazine editor in New York.

There was no room for dreams in the real world, and he'd better not forget it. For too many years he had believed people were better than they were. He had prayed for a peaceful future. He had expected to become a writer.

Nonsense, all of it. It had taken the death of his best friend to show him. People were liars, cheaters, murderers. A man in the West could bet his bottom dollar a bullet would put him in the grave.

It was no good getting attached, Noah reasoned—especially not to a pretty Spaniard who made a fellow lose sight of the facts. He clenched his jaw and made up his mind he could last one week on the trail alone with Isobel and not get tangled. He had to.

With the help of the Good Lord, he would keep his mind on the job at hand—bringing Dolan down. He had to resist taking Isobel into his arms…and into his heart.

On the first day of May, 1878, Noah and Isobel caught a glimpse of the Pascal hacienda. As they approached the house in the rolling foothills of the Sangre de Cristo Mountains, Noah struggled to swallow the lump of grit in his throat. The Pascal spread was a grand affair—much grander than his ramshackle home and milk cow. This house had a roof of red tiles and a deep, shady porch. From its perch on a pole near a flowering lilac bush, a green parrot eyed the two riders.

Sleek black horses pranced for their trainers in a nearby corral. Fat cattle, belly-deep in green grass, dotted the foothills. Caballeros in leather chaps and wide-brimmed hats rode among the herds.

As Isobel and Noah dismounted, a man in a blue uniform greeted them.

"I've brought Isobel Matas," Noah explained. "The Pascals are expecting her. I sent a wire from Lincoln almost two months back."

The man's dark eyes swept up and down, taking in Isobel's dusty riding clothes, pistol and battered felt hat. With a taut smile, he extended a hand. "Won't you come inside?"

Isobel waited on the sofa in a grand salon while Noah paced, his hat swinging in his hand. Through large glass windows he studied the hills. Then he focused on the interior of the elegant home.

"Looks like your dream's about to come true." He halted, his deep voice echoing off the wooden vigas on the ceiling.

"The Pascals have a fine home," Isobel noted.

"I expect you'll be happy. I'll send your furniture and trunks—if you still want them."

She fiddled with the string that bound her holster to her thigh. "How long will you stay in Santa Fe?"

"Don't worry about me. I'll be busy bringing Dolan down…and getting our marriage annulled." He started pacing again. "Just do your best to get this fellow to keep his end of the bargain he made with your father."

"Are you so eager to be rid of me?"

His eyes darted to her face. There was a moment of silence as each gazed at the other.

"This was the plan, wasn't it?" Noah said. "I was to take you safely to your fancy don."

Isobel stood. "But, Noah, that was before—"

"Buenas tardes. Good afternoon." The chocolate-rich voice drew their attention to the doorway. Tall, with slick black hair, a thin mustache and crackling brown eyes, Don Guillermo Pascal removed his hat and gave the slightest of bows.

"Señorita Matas," he said. "What a lovely surprise."

Noah took a long look at the man who soon would be Isobel's husband. And a dandy he was. He wore a brown suede suit with black leather trim and rows of buttons. At his hip hung a pistol with a carved ivory handle. Every inch of his holster and gun belt had been tooled. And on his feet gleamed the shiniest pair of pointed-toe boots Noah had ever seen.

He glanced down at his own leather boots, crusted with dried mud and worn down at the heels. His denims had been washed hundreds of times and were threadbare to prove it. The cuffs of his chambray shirt had frayed so badly there was no point mending them. A layer of dust had coated his hat, and his duster smelled of saddle leather and old horseflesh.

Don Guillermo glided toward Isobel and took her hand. Lifting it to his lips, he placed a kiss on her fingertips.

She smiled.

When the Spaniard lifted his head and saw that flash of white teeth and those full lips, Noah knew right off Isobel had won her man. His eyes sparkling, Don Guillermo bent for a second kiss.

"Cariña, you must be exhausted from your journey," he said. "I'll order a servant to prepare your room. You must bathe and refresh yourself before dinner."

Isobel tipped her head.

"You may go, *señor*," he told Noah. "Señorita Matas will have no further need of your services."

With that he stepped through the door, boot heels ringing sharp *rat-a-tats* on the tile floor.

Noah fixed his eyes on Isobel. Her high cheekbones held a flush that told him she'd been pleased by the attentions of the elegant *señor*. He tried to squelch the image of the man ever touching Isobel again. His prickly mustache poking into her lip as he kissed her. His long, thin fingers toying with her hair.

"Noah—"

"Isobel—"

Their words overlapped. She cleared her throat. He stuffed his Stetson on his head and crossed his arms over his chest.

"You will leave me here?" she said. It was more a plea than a question.

He walked to the door. "Take care, Isobel."

As he crossed the long hall, Noah passed a woman who must have been Guillermo's mother, hurrying to meet their guest. A black lace mantilla billowed behind her.

"¡Ah, Señorita Matas—que bonita!" the woman cried. *"¡Bienvenidos, cariña!"*

Noah hightailed it to his horse and rode away, thinking how glad he was to have Isobel off his hands. Yes, sir. No looking out for somebody else's skin. No wild-goose chases after Snake Jackson.

He had to admit they'd had a good time together, all in all. The cowboy and the *señorita*. Memories filtered through his mind—the first moment he saw her in that new blue dress, the night she slipped off her horse into his arms, the way she typed page after page of his story, the hours she spent working that kitchen garden, the way she fit so perfectly against him as he held her....

But she was where she'd always wanted to be—with her rich Spaniard instead of some old dusty…what had she called him?…vaquero.

Isobel didn't need to be out riding the trail, hiding from bad hombres like Snake Jackson and sleeping under the stars. She deserved a fine hacienda, fat cattle, fiestas. She deserved a man like Guillermo Pascal.

Noah reined his horse and looked over his shoulder at the hacienda. He would never forget the woman he loved.

Chapter Seventeen

Doña María Pascal gave her eldest son the privilege of showing their visitor around the house and grounds. Isobel searched in vain for any sign of Noah as she walked down a flagstone path lined with blossoming red roses.

When Don Guillermo extended a hand to assist her over a bridge, she had no choice but to take it. Tucking her arm through his, he drew her close.

"So you came all the way from Catalonia?" he asked.

Isobel nodded. "A telegram was sent from Lincoln. I've been in New Mexico more than two months."

"But *cariña,* you should have come directly to Santa Fe. If I had known—"

"Known what?" she retorted, losing patience. "You knew my father had been murdered and the land-grant titles stolen. My mother sent a letter saying I was traveling to New Mexico—so you knew that, also. What did you not know, *señor?*"

"We speak honestly, I see." He took a breath. "Very well, *señorita.* I did not know you were so beautiful."

The honest avowal caught her off guard. "How can my appearance possibly matter in this situation?"

"It matters very much. To me." Stroking his narrow

black mustache, he eyed her. "At my father's death, I became the head of our family, and I lack nothing. Your land appealed to me when your father offered it as part of the betrothal agreement. But I've acquired much property since. If I regain your titles—and I have no doubt that I can—I will absorb the land into my own. The jewels, of course, are of value, as well. Land, jewels…these I have in plenty. But women are scarce in this rough land."

"Especially beautiful women?"

He smiled. "You are a beautiful woman with a quick mind. Our fathers were wise to have arranged our marriage."

"You intend to follow through with it, Don Guillermo?"

"Only time will tell, Señorita Matas."

In the following days, Isobel spent much of each day nosing through local newspapers. Don Guillermo had little patience for her preoccupation with reading and marking the latest events in Lincoln County. If she didn't participate in the activities of the estate, he informed her, he would have the newspapers removed from the house.

Isobel did her best to behave as a future doña in the *familia* Pascal. After all, she had once made a marriage of convenience—why not again? But the answer was obvious. She had grown to love Noah Buchanan with a passion she knew could never be matched. Even so, she wrote a letter to Dr. Ealy, asking where he had registered the hasty marriage and how she might end it with equal quickness.

Guillermo Pascal was not unpleasant, she admitted to herself. His appearance was tolerable. His manners were impeccable. But what attraction could she possibly feel for this self-absorbed, shallow man?

And so, reading the *Cimarron News Press*, she wept over the memorial Alexander McSween had written for

Dick Brewer. His glowing praise reminded her of the deep loss Noah and Susan had suffered.

Editorials in the *Santa Fe New Mexican,* the *Trinidad Enterprise and Chronicle* and the *Mesilla Independent* volleyed the situation in Lincoln County back and forth— some writers favoring Dolan, others praising the bravery of McSween and the Regulators.

Jimmie Dolan began to defend himself in the newspapers. Isobel felt his whining letters only revealed his many weaknesses.

A short notice buried in the *New Mexican* brought her hope for Noah's case against Dolan. James J. Dolan & Co. was temporarily shuttering its mercantile in Lincoln due to unstable conditions. Was it possible the outcome in the district court had driven the tyrant from the county?

More good news came when Alexander McSween wrote that he had been authorized by John Tunstall's father in England to offer a reward of five thousand dollars for the apprehension and conviction of his son's murderers. Isobel knew this would improve the reputation of the Regulators, even though they themselves had been outlawed. Bounty hunters would set their sights on Snake Jackson and the rest of Dolan's bunch.

When Guillermo left the hacienda to look after his properties in Santa Fe, Doña María began joining Isobel on the patio. At first they simply enjoyed the sunshine and fresh air wafting down from the Sangre de Cristos. But soon the elder woman began leafing through newspapers, too.

"This cannot be good for the Regulators," Doña María commented one afternoon as she was browsing the *Cimarron News and Press*. "They're killing again in Lincoln County."

"Who died?" Isobel craned to read the news over the doña's shoulder.

"Somebody shot a man at the Fritz ranch on the Rio Bonito—Frank Macnab."

"Macnab was the leader of the Regulators! Who shot him?"

"The Seven Rivers Gang—from the Rio Pecos."

Isobel tried to breathe. More men had joined the Dolan forces. And they'd murdered Frank Macnab, leaving the Regulators leaderless again.

"Oh, more trouble here," Doña María said, trailing a finger down the text as she read. "George Coe shot one of the Dolan bunch. It says the Fort Stanton soldiers have returned to Lincoln to keep order, and the Seven Rivers men surrendered to them."

"Is Captain Purington holding them at the fort?"

"Colonel Dudley runs the garrison now." The doña turned to Isobel. "You were in Lincoln. Do you favor Dolan or McSween?"

"McSween is good and honest," Isobel answered. "He carries no gun and tries to make peace. Jimmie Dolan used his mercantile to cheat the United States government so badly his business was banished from Fort Stanton. Now he plays games of deceit on the landowners. His men are murderers and thieves."

The old woman leaned forward, brown eyes sparkling. "It's like a bullfight, yes? One strong and brave struggling against another, also strong and brave. Who will win?"

"I don't know, Doña María."

"Together we watch this bullfight, Señorita Matas."

Isobel nodded, feeling the first spark of companionship since her arrival. "We watch together."

The doña laughed and clapped her hands. "¡*Olé!*"

* * *

Isobel enjoyed sitting with the matriarch on the portal. But she soon saw that her dreams of helping run the Pascal hacienda were impossible.

No one in the family would hear of her riding out to see the cattle. She was kept inside, fed, pampered and clothed by the finest dressmakers in Santa Fe. She spent the days with the doña—stitching and playing cards.

But no matter how hard she tried to play the dutiful betrothed, she could not erase Noah Buchanan from her heart. Was he still in Santa Fe? Surely not after all this time. What had become of his quest for justice against Jimmie Dolan?

Almost a month had passed since Noah had ridden away from the Pascal hacienda. The newspapers never mentioned his name. Susan Gates wrote to Isobel twice, but she said nothing about the cowboy.

Dr. Ealy sent a letter saying he had registered the Matas-Buchanan marriage with Squire Wilson. When Governor Axtell had voided Wilson's appointment as justice of the peace, it had complicated matters. Wilson was still recovering from his wounds, but he had assured Dr. Ealy that he would find a way to look back through the records and see what could be done to quickly annul the union.

Feeding sunflower seeds to the green parrot one morning at the end of May, Isobel heard someone join her on the portal. She supposed it was Doña María, for they always sat together at this time of day to read and chat.

Over the weeks, Isobel had weighed her options and decided to return to Spain. After Dr. Ealy confirmed the dissolution of her marriage to Noah, she would rejoin her family as a confirmed *soltera*, a spinster. She had chosen that day to tell the doña about her plan, so she was surprised when Don Guillermo touched her arm.

"Señorita," he said.

She gasped. "Oh, *señor*, you startled me."

"Forgive me, but I must speak with you about our betrothal." He folded his hands behind his back. "I have contacted territorial officials in Santa Fe regarding your family's stolen land titles. It should be little trouble to restore them."

"But my family was told the thief had started transferal proceedings. How have you settled it so easily?"

"I have connections, *cariña*." He gave her a small smile. "I have found it agreeable that we should wed. The ceremony will take place at the end of three weeks."

"Three weeks!"

"Have no concern, Isobel. I have arranged everything. The food, the entertainment, your gown, the church. The first banns were published in this morning's newspaper. You and my mother, I am certain, will peruse the announcement at your leisure."

"But what about my family? My mother?"

"I have written to confirm the details," he continued. "My mother is amenable to the union, as are my brothers."

"And what about me?" Isobel said. "Did you ask for my consent, Don Guillermo?"

"You gave your consent five years ago when you agreed to the betrothal. You confirmed it the day you walked through my door."

Isobel looked away. "Five years was a long time ago. I admit, I have come to care for your mother and your family. Once, becoming your bride was the summit of my aspirations. But, since coming here, I have had time to consider my future. I intend to return to Spain."

"Spain? Certainly not! I won't allow it. Our families

signed a betrothal agreement. I have begun proceedings
of land transfer from your name to mine. The wedding is
arranged, *señorita,* and you will marry me."

"That's not much of a proposal, Pascal."

The deep voice from behind a boxwood hedge startled
Isobel.

"Noah?" She caught her breath as the cowboy rounded
the hedge.

"Don't draw your gun, *señor.*" Noah leveled his own
six-shooter at the Spaniard.

"What is the meaning of this?" Don Guillermo demanded.

"I've come for Isobel."

"Señorita Matas is my betrothed. She will go nowhere."

"I hate to break it to you, but Isobel is my wife. Mrs.
Buchanan, to you. I married her the day we met—February eighteenth, 1878, three months ago."

Guillermo turned on Isobel. "Perhaps you can explain
what this man is—"

"I've come for you, Isobel," Noah cut in. "We've got
urgent business in Lincoln County."

Isobel could hardly speak in the presence of this man
she had believed she would never see again. "What happened?" she managed.

"Seems like snakes are always after you, sweet-heart."

Speaking to Isobel, Noah holstered his gun, but his blue
eyes never left Guillermo's face. "Tom Catron—one of the
territory's biggest snakes himself—let slip a little fact the
other day while we were chatting. Seems his district attorney's office has been working on behalf of the Pascal
family to secure a packet of stolen land-grant titles from
a fellow named Jim Jackson."

"Snake?" Isobel's eyes darted to Don Guillermo.

"A couple of years back," Noah explained, "Snake Jackson went to Jimmie Dolan and told him he had the Matas family's Spanish land-grant titles. Dolan took the matter to his pal Catron in Santa Fe. Catron approached the Pascals to see if things could be done under the table in a way that could benefit everyone. Don Guillermo could buy off Catron, Dolan and Snake, get the land he wanted and never have to get hitched to a spinster. I'm told he's been known to enjoy the company of many women."

"But I came to New Mexico and upset your plans," Isobel said to Guillermo. "Then you decided you liked me well enough, after all."

Noah grunted. "Pascal realized he could marry you, get the titles legally and cut the other men out of the deal. With his connections inside the ring, he knew he wouldn't have much trouble."

"The ring?" Doña María's voice was shrill across the garden. "What ring is that?"

"It's nothing, *mamá*." Don Guillermo held out a hand to keep his mother back. "A little business between Señor Buchanan and myself."

"Business?" Embroidery bag in one hand and newspapers in the other, the doña elbowed past her son to face Noah. "Speak frankly, *señor*. I've heard many rumors about this ring. What do you know?"

"Your son is a member of the Santa Fe Ring, doña," Noah said. "He's in with Governor Axtell, Tom Catron and the other scalawags trying to own New Mexico. Guillermo has doubled the Pascal family land holdings since your husband's death, ma'am. These days, nobody gets land in the territory so easily without connections."

Isobel glared at Guillermo as she recalled his words to her minutes before, *I have connections, cariña.*

The doña's eyes narrowed at Noah. "You accuse my son of illegal dealings, vaquero."

"He's a liar, *mamá*," Guillermo interjected. "The fool even claims to have married Señorita Matas!"

Doña María turned to Isobel. "Who is this man?"

Isobel knew she could deny everything Noah had said. She could marry Don Guillermo and have her hacienda, horses, gardens, fiestas. Her children would be of pure Spanish blood, a proud dynasty.

Then she looked into the cowboy's blue eyes.

"Noah Buchanan speaks the truth," she admitted softly. "He is my husband. For my protection, we wed in haste. I came here planning to marry your son, but now I understand who he really is. I shall return to Spain."

"But the wedding? And my grandchildren? And what about our newspapers, *mija?*"

"You have been good to me, Doña María," Isobel said, kissing her gently on each cheek. "I thank you."

Her heart lighter than it had been in many weeks, Isobel lifted her skirts and started for the stables. It seemed that God had heard her prayers and chosen to smile upon her after all.

"I made appointments with Governor Axtell and District Attorney Catron," Noah was saying as he and Isobel sat on a blanket beside a flickering campfire. "Then I took a room at a hotel and began to write."

"Another story?"

"An argument against James J. Dolan." Noah paused for a moment, recalling how with each stroke of his pen he had tried to force his longing for Isobel deep inside his heart—with the hope it would stay hidden forever.

"I kept after Catron every day," he continued, "until he agreed to look into Dolan's finances. The more he dug, the more he saw the extent of Dolan's business troubles."

Isobel shook her head. "One man betrayed so many."

"Turns out Catron was endorsing Dolan's notes to the tune of more than twenty thousand dollars. Now Dolan is deeply in debt to the district attorney. A few months back, he mortgaged all his property to Catron as security for the notes, and he got a new note for twenty-five thousand dollars. This month he took out a second mortgage."

"So Dolan's mercantile is bankrupt?" Isobel said. "The man is ruined?"

"Catron was trying to keep him afloat so he wouldn't be saddled with the debts. But Dolan shut down his store, and he's been barred from making deliveries of flour and beef to the Mescalero agency. I reckon if he leaves Lincoln County, broke and defeated, I'll feel like Dick's death has been avenged."

"I'm happy for you, Noah."

He shrugged, realizing nothing could fill the place Dick Brewer had held in his life.

"I read that Macnab was killed," she spoke up.

"Yeah, sad to say. I'm hoping Dolan's bunch will disband and things will settle down in Lincoln. It's what I was trying to accomplish all the time I was in Santa Fe."

"It seems you were successful."

"I nearly let you marry Pascal." Noah flipped a twig into the fire. "When I read the wedding announcement in the paper this morning, I couldn't sit still. I'd already found out enough about Pascal to hook him into the ring. I deduced he was the silent partner Catron said was planning to take your land grants. 'Course, I didn't know for sure till I bluffed him this morning."

"That was a bluff?"

Noah shrugged. "A good guess."

"Noah, why didn't you leave me with the Pascals?"

He stared at the fire awhile before answering. "I couldn't let you marry Pascal, Isobel. You deserve better."

"What sort of man do I deserve, Noah?"

"Maybe you'll find a decent fellow when you get back to Spain."

"In Spain I will be a *soltera,* a spinster. When people learn I broke the Pascal betrothal, my name will be dishonored. Don Guillermo will spread the story of my rash marriage to a common vaquero. Even with an annulment, I will be too old to marry."

Noah couldn't imagine any man in his right mind turning Isobel down. Not one thing about her failed to move him. Her hair lying dark gold on her shoulders. Her smooth neck. Long arms. Long legs.

But there was more to Isobel than beauty. He'd almost forgotten how easily they could talk. She made him laugh and think and create and dream. He loved everything about the woman.

But how did she feel about him? He had given her no promises, no tender words of commitment, no hope for a future with him. Then he had abandoned her to the Pascals.

She might not want to spend her life with a man who still felt his friend's death like a knife in his gut. If Dolan somehow rode out his troubles, Noah couldn't let the matter go. Nothing would change that.

"Now that your *venganza* against Jimmie Dolan is accomplished, how will it be between you and me, Noah?" Isobel asked in a soft voice. "Will it be as before—at home by the Rio Pecos? Or will you drive me away again?"

"Isobel…" It was more a sigh than a word. "Great stars, you make things hard on a man."

"And you make things hard on a woman."

Their eyes met and held. "What do you want?" he asked. "Do you want to try to get your titles from Snake before Pascal gets his hands on them? Do you want to own your own spread up here in the north? Do you want to go back to Spain and live a quiet life, away from all the guns and killing?"

When she didn't answer, he spoke the final option. "Or do you want to be hooked up with a dusty cowboy who can't even promise you a tomorrow?"

Isobel gazed at the fire. "I may never live happily ever after. But I want to live happily today."

"Come here, Isobel." He took her hand and drew her into his arms. "You know, I made a fine show of myself in Santa Fe. Bought some fancy duds, ate good food, slept on clean sheets. Every day I worked to whittle Jimmie Dolan's empire into pieces."

"Were you happy?"

"I was miserable. Walked around looking like a throw-out from a footsore remuda." He shook his head. "I thought revenge would feel good."

"But you taught me how foolish it was to try to steal vengeance from the hand of God. I gave up my quest just as you began your own."

"We've taught each other an awful lot." He slid one hand up her arm. He hadn't touched a woman since leaving her with Pascal. All his desires seemed dead—killed along with Dick Brewer.

Sure, women had made eyes at him in Santa Fe. But he loved Isobel. Only Isobel.

Now, holding her, he felt a rush of need stronger than he'd ever known. Something inside his soul longed to connect with hers. A spiritual ache had resurfaced the moment he had seen her that morning, standing in the garden in Santa Fe.

"Noah," she murmured as she snuggled against him. "I couldn't let Guillermo Pascal come near me. It was impossible for me to think of any man but you."

"The minute I saw your name on that wedding announcement, I grabbed my saddlebag. Didn't give it a second thought. Just got on my horse and headed out to fetch you. I had to have you with me again."

"I don't know how I once thought of you as a common man. Each day I was alone, I ached for you."

"I love you," he whispered, kissing her lips, slipping his fingers into her hair. This was the union, the bonding, the oneness he needed.

"I love you, too," she whispered against his ear.

"I'll stay with you, Isobel. Rain or shine, darlin', you're mine."

Chapter Eighteen

On the journey from Santa Fe to Lincoln, Noah's desire to write came back in a flood. He spent two nights guarding Isobel and roughing out a story on paper he had tucked into his saddlebag. A young orphan boy, a hungry wolf, marauding Apaches, twists and turns. When he read it to Isobel, she declared it even better than his Coyote Canyon tale.

Their final day's ride took them to the little town of White Oaks. While Noah tended the horses, Isobel stopped at the mercantile, where she hoped to learn news of Lincoln from the shopkeeper. She was looking at a length of yellow calico when Noah stepped into the store.

"Isobel, come with me. Now." Taking her arm, he ushered her quickly to the back door.

"Noah? What's wrong?"

"I spotted Dolan at the feed store," he explained as they mounted their horses. "He's back in Lincoln County. And he's brought the Kinney Gang with him. Follow me—and stay close."

When they were safely into a thicket of aspen trees, Noah pulled his horse to a halt. Isobel drew up beside him.

"Who's Kinney?" she asked.

"Cattle thief, murderer, robber. Roams the Rio Grande Valley—mostly around El Paso. John Kinney is ten times meaner than Jesse Evans or Snake Jackson. Looks like Dolan hired the Kinney Gang to do his dirty work."

Her heart faltering, Isobel lifted up a silent prayer for guidance. Did Dolan's return mean that Noah's efforts to ruin him had failed? Would the man she loved set her aside again in his pursuit of vengeance?

"Let's go back to Santa Fe, Noah," she begged. "We should stay out of the trouble this time."

He took off his hat and wiped his sleeve across his brow. "I have to get to Lincoln and warn McSween. With Peppin as sheriff, Dolan back in town and the Kinney bunch roaming the county, things could get bad for the Regulators."

He slapped his hat against his thigh. "Blast this whole ugly mess!"

Isobel's shoulders drooped as her dreams sifted away. Noah was staring up through the trees at a patch of sky, as if waiting for God to speak. Finally he put on his hat and turned to her. "I'll take you to Chisum's ranch. It's the safest place I know."

"But you won't have time to warn McSween. Noah, I'll go with you."

"No. I'm not going to lose you, Isobel. Not again."

"Don't tear us apart. Please, Noah." She caught his hand. "The safest place for me is at your side."

He shook his head. "All right, I'll take you to Lincoln. But, darlin', I'm afraid things are shot to pieces again."

"We're together, aren't we?" she said, forcing a smile. "How bad can it be?"

Warned by Noah and Isobel, the Regulators rode out of town, shattering Lincoln's newfound serenity with the thunder of horses' hooves. Minutes later, the Kinney Gang rode in.

Isobel and Noah hurried to John Tunstall's store, where Susan Gates and the Ealy family had taken rooms. Isobel talked briefly with her friend while Noah watched through a curtained window as John Kinney rode up and down the street, as if to say, "Look, folks, I'm here and I'm in charge."

Noah was fingering his pistol in frustration when Isobel leaned against his shoulder to kiss his cheek. "Susan is better," she whispered. "She started teaching school. That seems to have taken her mind off her loss."

"I'm glad to hear it." Noah mustered a smile.

Isobel knew his thoughts. Maybe Susan had recovered from the death of her fiancé, but he would never get over the loss of his closest friend.

"Dr. Ealy says I should stay here," she told him. She peeked out the window at Kinney. With a shudder, she took Noah's hand. "I want to be with you."

"Some of the Regulators rode for San Patricio. The others planned to hide at Chisum's. I say we head to Chisum's. If we ride fast, we may be able to catch them."

Once they had agreed on a plan, it took only moments for Isobel to bid her friends farewell. Then she and Noah slipped out to the hitching post where their horses were tethered.

"Kinney and his men are roaming all around here, Isobel," Noah warned. "Stay close to me. We'll ride for the woods and keep under cover until we're clear."

She nodded, her heart hammering at the prospect of impending danger. Noah led their horses down a slope toward the Rio Bonito. Isobel was trailing not five paces behind when she heard a cry.

"It's Buchanan!" someone shouted from the street. "He's a Chisum man! Get him!"

Noah whipped out his six-shooter. "Isobel, ride around me!"

She spurred her mount forward while Noah covered them with his gun. Horses crashed through the underbrush behind Isobel as her gelding charged into the river. Holding the reins with one hand, she pulled her pistol from its holster. Branches raked her arms. A bullet smashed into a tree trunk just ahead. Splinters flew.

"Isobel, ride!" Noah shouted behind her as he fired at their pursuers.

She lowered her head to the horse's neck. On the hill above the stream, the Huff house and the *torreón* flew past. "I'm headed for the hills, Noah! Follow me."

Her horse galloped out of the streambed and began climbing the foothills. She glanced behind to see Noah riding only a few yards ahead of the outlaws. At their head rode a hulk of a man…a man with a lantern jaw and slitted eyes.

Snake Jackson.

Muffling a scream, Isobel watched the outlaw gang break into two groups.

"Rattlesnake, you and your men stay with those two!" Kinney shouted. "We'll ride for San Patricio and round up the rest of 'em!"

"Keep going, keep going!" Noah flew past Isobel and gave her horse's flank a slap. "Snake's after you."

Anger surged as Isobel buried her head against the horse's neck and rode for her life. With each heartbeat, she saw her father's face, his golden hair, his gentle hazel eyes. She saw John Tunstall in his dapper tweeds. She saw blue-eyed Dick Brewer, curly hair tossing in the breeze.

And she saw Snake Jackson. She heard his mocking cries, hoots of derision, jeering laughter.

A bullet splatted into the dirt beside her. She swung around. Noah was returning Snake's fire, his arm stretched behind him and his six-shooter blazing. Chisum's ranch was a three-day ride, Isobel realized. How could she and Noah possibly hold off Snake Jackson and his men? Darkness was hours away. Their horses couldn't keep up this pace much longer. In a moment Noah would be forced to reload.

She scanned the hills for cover. Nothing but scrub piñon and cedar. The horses crashed through evergreen branches, scenting the air with the sweet smell of tree sap. But Isobel's nostrils were filled with fear. She was about to die by Snake Jackson's hand—just like her father. In her besotted love for Noah Buchanan, she had forgotten her true purpose. Now she would pay for her failure with her life.

Gritting her teeth, she turned and fired three wild shots at Snake. The outlaw lifted his head and whooped. "Missed me, *señorita!* But I'm gonna git you!"

"Isobel," Noah hollered, flying past her again. "Stay in front. Let me do the shooting!"

She lowered her head and surged past him. Why had she let herself grow lazy and sloppy? She and Noah had dallied on the road from Santa Fe. Then she had waylaid them to comfort Susan Gates. Now they would both suffer for her weaknesses.

Her horse pounded around a bend, hooves kicking up dirt and old pine needles. The animal had begun to slow. Noah rode against her again, blue fire in his eyes.

"Find cover!" he called. "Your horse is going down."

She skirted the base of a hill and spotted a stone outcrop halfway up. Pointing so Noah could see without giving them away, she guided both horses through the trees.

Wheezing, foam dripping from its mouth, her horse slowed to a trot. Fear acrid on her tongue, Isobel slid to the ground and began to run. She clambered over a boulder and slid across a rock ledge.

At that moment a burning pain tore through her shoulder, shattering flesh and muscle. She tumbled behind the rock.

"Isobel!" Noah's urgent whisper came from a few paces away.

She clutched at the searing pain in her right shoulder. A warm liquid seeped onto her fingers.

"Snake winged you." Noah was peering between two boulders as he spoke. "They're coming this way. I need your help, darlin'. Please try."

She attempted to sit up, but her stomach turned and bile rose in her throat. "Noah," she groaned.

"Can you load this, Isobel?" He tossed a six-shooter into her lap. "If I can turn Snake and his men back, I'll have time to work on your shoulder. But if we can't hold them off—"

A bullet sent rock fragments flying past them. Isobel clenched her teeth and flipped open the pistol's chamber. With effort, she pried the cartridges from Noah's gun belt. Then she slid the bullets into their slots and clicked the gun shut.

Noah grabbed it and tossed a second empty six-shooter onto her lap. The hot metal burned through the thin fabric of her skirt. As she began to reload, bullets slammed into the stone around their heads. Cries rang out through the hills. Horses galloped past. Isobel continued loading Noah's two six-shooters, his rifle and her own small pistol. Pain fogged her mind. Blood soaked her sleeve and trickled onto her fingers.

Now and then Noah peered at her, his eyes dark blue

with concern. "Isobel, darlin', hold on for me," she heard him whisper. "Don't give up on me now."

Then the firing stopped. Smoke cleared. The tang of gunpowder lifted. Warm arms came around her. Noah laid her out across the ground, her head resting on a pile of soft pine needles. Streaks of orange, blue and purple painted the sky. Noah's face appeared.

"Rest now, sweetheart," he murmured. "Snake's gone, and I'm going to patch you up."

She heard her sleeve tear and shut her eyes. Noah's voice drifted in and out. "Dear Lord, help me. The bullet's still in here. Isobel, darlin', I've got to take this thing out. Hold on to me, now."

A searing pain in her shoulder cut through the fog and brought her sharply awake. A scream rose in her throat. Then it faded away with the pain, the knife, the bullet. Blackness swam over her and took her away.

Isobel opened her eyes to find Noah seated on top of the rock outcrop. He had lifted his face to the heavens, but his eyes were shut. His lips moved silently. Brilliant morning sky framed his profile, the straight nose and square jawline, the sweep of dark hair.

Shifting, Isobel tried to ease the throbbing pain in her shoulder. Noah heard the movement and scrambled from his perch.

"Isobel?" He crouched beside her. "Isobel, darlin', are you awake?"

She tried to speak, but her throat felt parched as desert sands. Noah smoothed the hair from her forehead.

"I got the bullet out," he whispered. He dug around in his shirt pocket, then held up a flattened piece of lead. "Take a look at that, would you?"

She tried to grin, but the pain in her shoulder pounded

unbearably. Noah adjusted the wool blanket that pillowed her head.

"You've lost a lot of blood," he said. "I need to get you back to Lincoln."

"No!" she croaked. Snake and Kinney would find them there. She wanted to go someplace safe where they could be together and forget Lincoln's trouble.

"Doc Ealy is the only one around these parts who can patch you up right. I've seen gangrene, Isobel, and I'm not going to let that happen to—"

"No!" She grabbed his arm with her good hand. "Not Lincoln."

"We can't stay here. Snake'll be back. And soon. I've got to get you out of here."

"Chisum's," she mouthed. "Please, Noah."

"That's a three-day ride for a fit horse and a healthy rider. I don't imagine you can even sit up straight, and you've been in and out of consciousness all night."

But the thought of being so close to Noah's little adobe house drove Isobel to struggle up from the pallet. Blood siphoned from her face, but she threw the blanket back.

"All right," Noah said, grabbing her shoulders before she fainted. "I knew you were mule-headed, Isobel, and I can see you mean business. Come on, you'll ride with me."

He tethered her gelding behind his horse and then settled Isobel in his arms. They kept away from the river's edge for fear of ambush and stopped often to drink, rest or tend Isobel's shoulder. In the midst of her daze she could hear Noah growling about Jimmie Dolan and Snake Jackson. In between she heard the soft refrains of hymns.

Once Noah prayed out loud, a fervent plea. He spoke in that tone Isobel had heard so often—as if God were a father with whom a man could talk about his deepest needs.

Somewhere in the feverish mists, she remembered the

wedding ceremony in the Lincoln County forest and her fears that God would punish her for such a hasty, selfish union. Perhaps this was God's chastisement—her wounded shoulder, her terrible fears, her hopeless love for Noah Buchanan.

But even as she pondered a rebuking, angry God, she heard Noah's voice. "God is love," he sang.

"His mercy brightens
All the path in which we rove;
Bliss He wakes and woe He lightens:
God is wisdom, God is love."

Several times each day Noah bathed Isobel's shoulder and changed the dressing. The slightest jolt sent a searing pain that nearly made her scream. Noah fashioned a sling to hold her arm close against her body. She couldn't eat. Only water from the Rio Hondo kept her going.

Their journey took many more than three days, but they could go no faster. Accepting that, Isobel nestled against Noah, her mind wandering from memories of her father to hanging lace curtains, typing pages of a story, galloping along mountain trails, baking *biscochitos*.

Through these memories wove a deep baritone.

"E'en the hour that darkest seemeth
Will His changeless goodness prove;
From the gloom His brightness streameth:
God is wisdom, God is love."

June was nearly gone when Noah's horse trotted the last few yards down the road to Chisum's house. The scent of blooming roses perfumed the air, and Noah's spirits rose in spite of his fears for Isobel.

About the only words she had said were how much she wanted Noah to stay with her, never leave her, always be near. As hard as it was to acknowledge, he now knew without a doubt that he loved Isobel Matas Buchanan.

In the frozen instant he'd watched her tumble behind that pile of rocks, his heart had nearly stopped. When he'd made it to her side and had seen her life's blood oozing out of that shoulder wound, a red rage had filled him. The fear of losing her had convinced Noah that he loved her.

If Dick Brewer meant a lot to him as a pal and confidant, Isobel meant far more. They could laugh, talk, even cry together. He had told her his dreams of writing, his ambitions and hopes for his land and future. And she shared hers with him. The thought of losing her was more than he could bear.

But the trouble with Snake Jackson would continue unless somebody stopped him. With Jimmie Dolan and now John Kinney fueling his fires, Snake wasn't about to back off. All three needed a dose of strong medicine. Lead poisoning would do the trick, and Noah knew just the man to deliver it.

"Darlin', after I settle you here I'm going back to Lincoln," he whispered into Isobel's ear as they neared the hitching post in front of the Chisum house. "Don't get your feathers ruffled about it. When I'm sure you're in good hands, I'm going after Snake and Dolan."

"Noah, they almost killed me!" Her hazel eyes filled with terror. "Please don't go."

"I'm going *because* they almost killed you." He took her hand. "The way I see it, Isobel, the only way to stop killin' is to kill. You were right about that. My big speeches about being strong enough to stay out of the trouble were like spittin' in the wind."

"Noah, I can't lose you. Not again."

But he was already handing her down to the waiting arms of Mrs. Towry and the men who had rushed to meet the riders. She recognized the faces of several Regulators before she was carried into a cool room, tucked into bed with a damp cloth on her forehead and abandoned.

"Noah!" she croaked. "Noah, please!"

But her voice echoed off the bare walls.

Chapter Nineteen

Noah sat at Isobel's bedside for three days. She was exhausted from the ride, but her pain had eased. Better still, the shoulder wound was healing well.

Mrs. Towry tended Isobel like a mother hen. Tongue clucking, she bustled back and forth, fetching ointments from John Chisum's medicine box, chicken soup, fresh bandages and cool, sweet lemonade. Finally Isobel was able to sit up on her own and then walk about the room while leaning on Noah's arm.

One morning after breakfast he settled on a chair by her bed. "Today's the Fourth of July," he said, his blue eyes twinkling. "Know what that means?"

"A celebration of the day the United States declared its independence from England." She smiled at Noah's patriotism despite the fact that New Mexico was still a territory.

"When I lived in Texas," he said, "Mrs. Allison used to fix a picnic for everybody. Feel up to a picnic today, darlin'? Me and some of the other Regulators thought we'd ride over to the Pecos."

"What about Sheriff Peppin's posse?" she asked. "Aren't they staying in Roswell?"

Isobel had heard that the hastily assembled posse included notorious outlaws known as the Seven Rivers Gang—led by deputies Marion Turner and Buck Powell.

"Aw, they're just a bunch of rascals," Noah said.

"But they're fifteen men, and we have only twelve. Some of ours will have to stay behind to keep an eye on Mr. Chisum's place."

"Regulators have been riding between the Pecos and the ranch without any trouble from that posse. I just thought it would be fun to get you out of the house. You can ride in the buckboard. Take in some fresh air. Think you're up to it?"

A day in the outdoors appealed to Isobel. If she rode in the buckboard, she could wear a dress. Just the idea of putting on a fresh gown, brushing her hair into artful waves, setting her feet in a pair of slippers instead of heavy leather boots—

"I'd love it!" she exclaimed.

He bent over the bed and kissed her cheek. "I'll give you half an hour. Mrs. Towry's fixing a basket. She might come along with—"

"Buchanan!" Billy Bonney kicked open the door and charged into the room. "Buchanan, hit the rooftop! It's Buck Powell and the Seven Rivers Gang."

"What do they want?"

"Who knows? Me and the Coe boys was ridin' back from Ash Upson's store this mornin'." Billy brandished his six-shooter as he spoke. "Twelve of 'em jumped us! It was a runnin' gun battle all the way back to the house. Now they're takin' potshots at the boys on the roof. You gotta get up there and help afore somebody gets killed!"

Noah glanced at Isobel, but before she could say anything to try to hold him back, he dropped his hat on his head and drew his gun.

"Stay away from the windows, Isobel," he called back

as he and Billy ran from the bedroom. "And don't go looking for trouble!"

She watched the door slam shut as their boots pounded
down the hall. "I found trouble when I married you," she
murmured, settling back against her pillow. "And you
found it when you married me."

The shooting went on all day and most of the night.
The picnic was abandoned, though Mrs. Towry got a big
holiday meal onto the table anyway. The Regulators took
turns coming down from the parapet roof to eat before
heading back upstairs.

It was clear to Isobel that the Regulators were confident in their position. With Chisum's fortifications and a
large supply of ammunition, they were having no trouble
holding off Buck Powell and his posse. Isobel and Mrs.
Towry spent the night in the central courtyard of the house.
If not for the occasional burst of gunfire, it would have
seemed idyllic.

Roses in full bloom scented the air. Beds dragged onto
the patio offered down comforters, pillows, bolsters, shams
and embroidered sheets. But the two women sat up most
of the night, speculating on how the battle was proceed-
ing and worrying about the men.

At dawn the following day, Isobel woke with a gentle
hand on her shoulder. "Buck Powell and the others have
gone," Noah said. "We think they've headed to Lincoln
for reinforcements."

"Has anyone been hurt, Noah?" she asked.

"We've had the upper hand the whole time." He gave
her the hint of a smile, then his face grew solemn. "I've
been talking with the other Regulators, Isobel. We figure
we can't end this trouble without all-out war on Jimmie
Dolan."

"War?" Isobel whispered.

"Justice, darlin'. Dolan is responsible for too many deaths. Any way you look at it, Isobel, he's got to be put away."

In silence she gazed at the embroidered coverlet, lit pink with the sunrise. She ran one finger over a red rose entwined with green leaves.

"And then there's you," Noah added before she had a chance to speak. "Snake Jackson won't rest until he kills you, Isobel. He's got nothing to lose by pulling your picket pin. And he's got plenty to gain—the land titles, money from Pascal and Catron, elimination of an eyewitness, and one less 'Mexican'—"

"I'm Spanish."

"Isobel!" Noah clenched her hand tightly. "Hear what I'm saying. Your life is in danger."

"I know that," she said, rubbing her shoulder.

"The Regulators will ride to Lincoln this morning. A couple of the boys are headed to San Patricio to round up the rest of the bunch. Everyone plans to meet at McSween's house and decide how to finish this business. Isobel... I'm going with them."

She snatched her hand from his. "What's happened to you, Noah? What has become of the man with gentle hands who lifted me from the path of a bullet? Where is the writer who would rather leave a fight than shoot an enemy?"

"That man is gone."

"Oh, Noah..."

"I've been around a few years, darlin', but I didn't learn what was what until I met you. The fact is, Isobel Buchanan, I love you. I'm not going to let Jimmie Dolan or Snake Jackson or anyone else hurt you. Never again. And the only way to fight fire is with fire. Gunfire."

"Noah, please don't do this!"

"What's happened to my little spitfire? When we met, you were bent on vengeance. If I had helped you instead of trying to stop you, Snake Jackson might be dead right now—instead of wounding you with a bullet. You were right. It's time for revenge."

He stood suddenly, knocking back the wooden chair. "I'm going now." He settled his hat on his head. "Heal up, Isobel, you hear?"

He started across the patio, and she called his name. But he didn't turn.

"I love you, too, Noah," she whispered.

Moments later, Isobel heard the drumroll of horses' hooves as the Regulators rode away. She eased herself to the floor and stood. In the week since the shooting, her arm had grown stronger, and she was able to move it more comfortably now. She made her way into her bedroom and gazed out the window.

A light cloud of brown dust trailed the men, and an overwhelming sense of loss enveloped her. What she had known and loved of life was about to end.

Mrs. Towry crossed the garden near the window, a basketful of roses on her arm. She waved at her guest. "Shootin's over, honey. It's safe to move around."

Isobel tried to smile. "May I join you in the garden?"

"You still look mighty pale." The older woman shook her head. "Such high talkin' them boys was doin' this morning. I wish Mr. Chisum was here to preach some sense into 'em. They think they're gonna be heroes—shootin' up Lincoln and killin' all their enemies. What next?"

"Noah went with the others, didn't he?"

Mrs. Towry nodded. "Good thing, too. He's the most levelheaded of the bunch. He should be leader of the Regulators. Doc Scurlock ain't a bad feller, but your husband's got horse sense. He reminds me of Mr. Chisum—smart, peaceable, strong. I sure wish Mr. Chisum would hurry back from St. Louis.... Well, honey, come on out to the garden."

A week had passed since the Regulators' departure when Mrs. Towry rushed onto the porch where Isobel was stitching.

"Mrs. Buchanan! Look what come in the mail from Lincoln. I bet your husband sent it."

Isobel grabbed the letter and tore open the envelope. "Dear Mr. Buchanan," she read aloud.

"It is my great pleasure to inform you that your story, 'Sunset at Coyote Canyon,' has been accepted for publication in our magazine, Wild West. It will run in five installments, beginning in December. Congratulations. Enclosed please find a check for the sum of fifty dollars. Wild West would like to see more of your fine writing, Mr. Buchanan.
Sincerely, Josiah Woodstone, Editor."

Mrs. Towry frowned as she studied the envelope. "This ain't from Mr. Buchanan, is it?"

"Noah's story," Isobel said. "It's going to be published."

"Mr. Buchanan writ a story?" Mrs. Towry muffled a laugh. "Ain't what I expected of a cowboy like him, but here's fifty dollars to prove it's true. That ought to go a good way toward payin' off the land he bought from Mr. Chisum."

Isobel gazed at the letter. Noah's story would be published. His dream would come true. But where was he now, this man with a gift so few possessed? No doubt he was in Lincoln warring with someone who would still his voice with a bullet through his heart.

It was her fault, she thought, tucking the letter into her pocket. If she hadn't been so headstrong, so determined to seek out Snake Jackson, Noah wouldn't be caught in Lincoln's troubles.

When they'd met, he'd been on his way to buy land and write stories. He was the man Mrs. Towry had described—peaceable, gentle. Thanks to his untimely marriage to a selfish Spanish woman, he had tossed away that cloak and assumed the one she had brought—revenge. Now, because of Isobel, he was chasing down Jimmie Dolan with an outlaw's bloodlust.

She had ruined Noah. While he had taught her to find the beauty in life, she had taught him to seek vengeance. From Noah she had learned to cook meals that would satisfy, to plant a garden, to value marriage and home. She had discovered that what she wanted most was love. Noah's love. She ached for him. Nothing else in the world mattered.

Leaving Mrs. Towry to her flower arranging, Isobel hurried to her room, found her saddlebag and groped around inside. Yes—her pistol. She contemplated the weapon for a moment before tossing it onto the bed.

Quickly she changed into riding clothes and leather boots. She transferred Noah's letter from the New York publisher into a pocket. Stopping by the kitchen, she took some bread and cheese, along with a knife and a box of matches. After stuffing these items into the saddlebag, she slung it over her good shoulder and slipped out the door.

Fussing over the roses, Mrs. Towry hummed on the porch. Isobel left the house through a back door. In the corral, she selected a horse that had not yet been unsaddled from a morning's ride. Pain shot through her shoulder as she mounted.

"Now," she breathed as she goaded the horse's flanks. "Take me to Lincoln. I have to save my husband."

Though Isobel knew the trail, travel was more difficult than she had anticipated. Riding alone, she had to be alert for outlaws who roamed Lincoln County's roadways. Perhaps it had been foolish to leave her pistol behind, but Isobel never again wanted to touch a weapon. As she rode she recited the words she ached to say to Noah.

I was wrong! Wrong! Revenge is not the way. Leave it to God, my love. Come home with me to the little adobe house by the river.

Would she ever get the chance to say those words? Isobel prayed as she had heard Noah pray—the deep and soul-drenching pleas of her heart. "Please, dear God, let Noah live. Let me atone for my errors. Allow me to lead Noah away from violence and into a life of love."

Each night she lay bundled in blankets and listened to the rush of the river. As she gazed at the stars through piñon branches, Isobel recounted her life and its many blessings. Noah Buchanan was the greatest blessing of all. Before it was too late, she had to convince him to leave Lincoln.

Though her shoulder had regained strength and flexibility, she knew how easily the pain could resurface. For the rest of her life, she would bear a scar—a round patch of smooth, tender skin, a reminder of the man who had killed her father and had tried to kill her.

Her fourth night on the trail, Isobel camped at the spot where the Rio Hondo met the Rio Bonito. Lincoln lay only a few miles away, and her sleep was restless.

Early the next morning she rose as dawn was breaking over the mountains. In the pale purple light she took the kitchen knife from her saddlebag and cut off a slice of cheese and a hunk of bread. After eating, she set Dick Brewer's old hat on her head and mounted her horse.

Isobel had not been riding long when she noticed a horse and rider coming toward her on the trail. Her pulse began to pound in her neck and temples. Could it be Noah? The man removed his hat and tipped his head.

"Mornin', *señorita*," he said.

Isobel's breath hung in her throat. "Jim Jackson."

"Most folks call me Snake."

She glanced around for a path of escape, but he was already drawing his six-shooter.

"Me and some of the boys just happened to be passin' Casey's Mill yesterday," Snake said, casually taking aim at her heart. "One of the hands mentioned seein' Mrs. Buchanan ridin' all alone. That's when I realized I hadn't finished a job I started the other day. Seems yer like a cat, huh? Nine lives."

"Mr. Jackson, you can see I'm unarmed," Isobel said. "I'm going to Lincoln to find my husband. I have no business with you."

"No business with me? What about this here packet of papers I been carryin' around for five years? Ain't that yer business, *señorita?*" He slapped his saddlebag and gave her a wink. "Took it off yer papa, y'know. The day I shot him dead."

Isobel clenched her jaw. Snake had ridden close enough now that she could see his eyes set deep beneath his heavy brow.

"Now, don't deny it," he teased. "You been chasin' me ever since you come to Lincoln County, *señorita*. First you seen me do Tunstall in. Then you figured out I blew yer papa to kingdom come. You followed me to Murphy's ranch and tried to shoot me. Then back to Lincoln where you and your Mexican-lovin' husband tried again to gun me down."

"You chased us from Lincoln," Isobel corrected.

"Aw, well, it don't really matter now. Point is, it's time for one of us to finish the game. I reckon it better be me."

"I renounce my claim, Snake. Take my family's land. Take our jewels. Just let me go to Lincoln."

"What's this? Has the little she-devil lost her fire?"

"Yes, I have. I'm through fighting. I'm going to pass you in peace and go on my way."

Flicking the reins, Isobel rode toward Snake. Their horses brushed on the narrow trail. She kept her focus straight ahead and tried to push back the terrible images of blood and death. Don Alberto Matas. John Henry Tunstall. Dick Brewer. Sheriff Brady.

"Oh, *señorita*." Snake grabbed her arm, nearly jerking the wounded shoulder from its socket. As he pulled her backward in the saddle, he released the safety on his six-shooter. "I'm afraid we got unfinished business."

"Let me go, Snake!" she ordered.

"You really thought I was gonna let you ride by me?"

"I hoped you would be man enough to holster your gun." She stared into the slitted eyes. "I have no quarrel with you, so set me free."

Smiling, he raised the gun to her head and jabbed it into her temple. "Yer dumber than I thought, *señorita*. See, I got a lot of killin' to do to make up fer the bunch of Mexicans that murdered my parents."

"I had nothing to do with that," she gasped as cold steel pressed against her head. Pain wrenched through her shoulder where he pinned her against him. "I want only peace. Let me go. Please!"

"Somebody's gotta pay. Might as well be you."

With his last word Snake pulled the trigger. An instant before the blast, Isobel tilted her head and sank into the saddle. The bullet blew off Dick Brewer's hat and slammed into a tree. Both horses bolted, but Snake still gripped Isobel's arm. The horses struggled, turning in circles. With her free hand, Isobel fumbled for the knife in her saddlebag.

Snake muttered a curse. He righted his gun and took aim a second time. Isobel whipped the knife across his arm, and the six-shooter tumbled onto the grass in a spray of blood.

"Curse you!" Snake yelled.

He lunged at Isobel and both riders tumbled to the ground. The air whooshed from her lungs. She rolled, trying to escape, but Snake tangled her legs with his as he pulled his own knife from his belt.

"Now," he growled. "Now we'll see."

Just as he lunged for her throat, she stabbed his back. Her knife sank into flesh and struck bone. Snake bellowed and bolted upright with the pain. Then his knife flashed downward and buried in her arm, not an inch from the bullet wound.

"Stop!" she shrieked, twisting in agony.

"I'll kill you first."

He yanked the knife from her arm and went for her throat a second time. She squirmed and thrust. Her blade buried deep in his stomach. He shuddered.

Barely able to breathe beneath his weight, she tried to jerk her weapon away but lost her grip on it. If only she could escape…now…while he was wounded. She tried to push out from under him.

Snake reared. His eyes flashed with hatred. She grasped at the swinging steel in his hand. The blade nicked her cheek, and she screamed.

Blood seeped from the corner of his mouth and still he grappled with her. He caught a handful of her hair and twisted her head backward, grinding her scalp into the dirt. She could see nothing but trees. Her throat exposed to his blade, she waited for the final slash.

"*Señorita*," he mumbled. As he slumped forward, she felt his knuckles brush her neck.

"Dear God, help me!" Isobel labored to catch her breath. She lay beneath Snake and listened as the last gurgle of life left his chest. Gasping, she shoved his body to one side and struggled to her knees. At the scene of horror, she cried out.

Snake Jackson lay on the ground, her knife buried in his stomach. His blood puddled on the road. "I've killed him," she whispered. "I've killed him after all."

She buried her face in her bloodied hands. Bile rose in her throat. She staggered up and hung over a tree branch, retching with fear and revulsion. Tears streamed down her cheeks and dripped pink bloodstains in the grass. For a moment she could do nothing but lean against the tree and cry.

How had it come to this? Once she had longed to end the life of Jim Jackson. But now…now that she had killed him…

"God," she murmured. "Dear God, forgive me!"

Weak and in terrible pain, she lurched down to the river, filled her hands with water and splashed her face. Cradling her injured shoulder, she slumped into the grass, stretched out her legs and shut her eyes.

She had no idea how long she lay still. With every breath she saw Snake's face. She had taken his life. She had killed. Covering her eyes with her good arm, she wept more bitter tears. Once, she had imagined satisfaction, even joy, after her revenge was complete. But death was ugly, senseless.

She had to find Noah and turn him from the same path. It was her only hope of atonement.

In time, she struggled to her feet. The two horses grazed side by side near the trail. She studied Snake Jackson's body for a moment, then she touched each eyelid to press it closed before she walked to the horses.

She knew what she must do. She had battled for her birthright with her own life and had won it at the cost of another's. Slipping her hand inside Snake's saddlebag, she found a slender packet. Her father's neat handwriting graced the yellowed envelope. "Spanish Land-Grant Titles," the words read in both English and Spanish. "The Possession of Isobel Matas."

Bowing her head, Isobel held the packet close. Land. With it, she could draw the hand of any eligible man in New Mexico or Spain. She could have Don Guillermo or any other husband she chose. She would be a landowner at last.

But there was only one man she wanted. It was time to find him.

Chapter Twenty

When Isobel rode into Lincoln that night, Sheriff George Peppin met her on the road, his rifle drawn from its scabbard. The middle-aged man, known to many in town as "Dad" Peppin, frowned.

"Mrs. Buchanan? Is that you?"

"Yes, it is." She tucked a wisp of her hair behind her ear, as if that might tidy her appearance. "Do you know where my husband is? It's an urgent matter."

"He's holed up in McSween's house with the other Regulators. Don't you know what's goin' on here, ma'am?"

"I've come for my husband. That's all I know."

"Well, you can't just ride into town and—"

"Who's this?" Jimmie Dolan rode out of the shadows, a dark hat perched on his thick, glossy curls.

"It's Noah Buchanan's wife," Peppin said.

"What happened to you, woman? You're covered in blood."

"Never mind my appearance, sir," Isobel told the Irishman. "I've come for my husband."

"Your husband is camped out with fourteen other outlaws on the roof of Alexander McSween's house," Dolan spat. "They've knocked holes in the parapet and made the place a firing range."

"I'll go and fetch him, then."

"And my men will shoot him to the ground the minute he sets foot out of that house. This is war, Mrs. Buchanan. Twenty of McSween's men are inside José Montaño's store. Nearly as many are over at Isaac Ellis's store."

"I'll speak to Juan Patrón. He'll help me."

"That Mexican grabbed up his family and rode to Las Vegas like a banshee was after him. Five McSween men are camped at his house."

"If McSween has taken the town," Isobel said, "how do you propose to keep me from my husband?"

"Because my men hold the *torreón*," Dolan shot back. "And now I've got you." He gave Peppin a nod. "Take this woman to the Cisneros house, Sheriff. We'll hold her there. Maybe we can use her to bargain with."

"Hold me?" Isobel exploded. "James Dolan, I will not be made a prisoner—"

"Take her away, Peppin."

The sheriff nudged Isobel with the end of his rifle. She refused to move.

"Mr. Dolan," she said, "I own the finest land in New Mexico. I took my title papers from Snake Jackson this morning. If you'll set my husband free, I'll give them to you."

"Land, eh?" Dolan squinted at her. "You took those titles from Jackson? Rattlesnake Jim Jackson? Did you kill him?"

Isobel looked away. "You'll find his body on the road to Roswell where the Bonito and Hondo rivers join."

"You're a banshee yourself. Hand over that packet, ma'am," Dolan commanded, drawing his own gun.

"I don't have them with me," she retorted. "You don't

think I'm so foolish as to carry valuables into this murderous town, do you? I buried them. But if you'll set my husband free—"

"Ah, just take her away, Peppin. I'll get the titles later. Can't have a banshee roamin' the town, can we?"

"Mr. Dolan, this woman is wounded," the sheriff said. "I'd better take her over to Tunstall's store and let Doc Ealy have a look at her."

"Any woman who could kill Snake Jackson and steal those land titles he's been so proud of all these years can't be underestimated. Especially if she's tryin' to break out one of the Regulators. Give her husband and the rest of McSween's bunch a look at my ace-in-the-hole. Then take her to the Cisneros house. And lock her up tight."

"Yes, sir."

The Irishman rode away into the darkness. Peppin gave Isobel an apologetic shrug and prodded her forward.

"Will you send Dr. Ealy to me, Sheriff?" Isobel asked as they neared a three-room adobe house opposite McSween's. "Jackson wounded me in the shoulder. Please, I need help. Dr. Ealy won't cause trouble. He's a missionary—a man of God."

"I'll do what I can for you, Mrs. Buchanan."

Peppin paraded Isobel past Alexander McSween's house, but it was so dark she couldn't be sure Noah saw her. The Cisneros family had fled Lincoln, the sheriff told her, as had most of the town's peaceable citizens. Dolan had taken the Cisneros house, though it was too small to hold many fighters. Peppin led Isobel to the front bedroom, locked her in and stationed an armed man at the door.

From a curtained window, she could see a row of silhouettes lining the roof of the McSween house across the street. She tried to identify Noah among them, but there was not enough moonlight to see clearly. For some time, she waited in hopes that Dr. Ealy would come—not so much to tend her wounds as to reassure her that Noah was all right.

When no one came, she bathed her wounds in a washbasin and lay back on the bed. Though she had not planned to sleep, the sun was well up when she was awakened by the sound of her bedroom door swinging open.

"Breakfast, Mrs. Buchanan?" Her young guard walked in with a loaf of bread under one arm and a pot of hot coffee in his hand. His other hand rested lightly on the handle of his pistol. "Sorry to bust in on you. If you don't mind my sayin' so, ma'am, you don't look too perky this mornin'."

Isobel attempted to smooth her wrinkled shirtwaist while the guard set the bread and coffee on the dresser.

"Say, did you really kill Rattlesnake Jim Jackson?" he asked, giving her a sideways glance. "That's the rumor."

"Yes, and I'd rather not discuss it," Isobel informed him. "When will I be set free?"

"Soon as things settle down. Dolan sent a letter to Fort Stanton askin' for soldiers."

Isobel studied the young man whose limp, blond hair hung almost to his shoulders. "Thank you for this information," she said.

He smiled. "I reckon John Kinney and the rest will hightail it up from San Patricio when they hear what McSween's done. Dolan thinks his posse will be here by this afternoon."

"And then?"

"A shootin' match, I'd guess." He backed toward the door, keeping his eyes on his prisoner. "I'll be outside if you need me. Just holler."

"What is your name, sir?"

"Ike Teeters. I'm from Seven Rivers."

"You're in the Seven Rivers Gang?"

He chuckled, showing a row of uneven teeth. "Not hardly. My eyes don't see too good from a distance, ma'am. Truth be told, my shootin's downright pitiful. But I can do guardin' work. I'm fine at that."

"Why don't you wear spectacles, Ike?"

"I ain't got the money. Chisum pushed my family off our land, and it's all we can do to get by."

"John Chisum?"

"Who else? Us Seven Rivers folks is small cattlemen— law-abidin', hardworkin' fellers—and we can't do nothin' against a powerful man like him. We joined Dolan to fight Chisum."

As he was shutting the door, Ike poked his head back in. "I'll see if I can get you a doctor, Mrs. Buchanan."

As he spoke, John Kinney's posse rode into Lincoln and began shooting at the McSween house, their bullets shattering windows and gouging holes in the adobe walls. When the Regulators returned fire, Isobel spotted Noah on the roof. His black Stetson moved back and forth behind the parapet.

The gunfight raged until sunset. As darkness brought an end to the shooting, Ike managed to slip Dr. Taylor Ealy across the street to the Cisneros house. The missionary doctor hurried to Isobel's bedroom with his bag of medications and bandages.

"Dr. Ealy," Isobel couldn't contain herself as he brushed aside her hair to take a look at her shoulder. "Can you get a message to Noah? Please help me save my husband's life!"

"Your *husband*? I see things have taken an interesting turn since that hasty wedding in the forest. Good thing I got nowhere trying to annul your marriage."

"Noah and I are still married?"

"In the eyes of God and the territory of New Mexico you are." The doctor patted her hand. "Now, you must try to rest. With more than sixty gunmen on his side, McSween has the advantage. Dolan's posse numbers just forty."

"Is it all-out war, then?"

"Only God knows," he said as he placed a clean bandage on her wound. "I'll try to speak to Sheriff Peppin about you. If you're being held for the death of Jim Jackson, you deserve the chance to post bail. If Dolan is holding you hostage, it's illegal."

As he prepared to leave, gunfire again erupted on the street. Ike Teeters burst into the bedroom. "Doc, you better get back to Tunstall's store. They're shootin' it out again, and I'm only supposed to protect Mrs. Buchanan."

Dr. Ealy hurried for the door.

"Take my message to Noah!" Isobel called out. But the door slammed behind him. As she crawled into bed, she breathed a prayer for her husband's safety. She recalled his vivid blue eyes, his bronze skin, his dark hair, his gentle hands. *Dear God,* she lifted up her prayer. *I'm responsible for one man's death. Please keep it from becoming two.*

Dawn on the fifth day of Isobel's imprisonment brought the customary pop of gunfire as the sniping began again. She changed into a dress Ike had found in the house, a simple gown of pale yellow cotton. As bullets slammed into the wall outside, she washed and combed her hair. Then she knocked on her bedroom door.

"Ike," she called out. "I must speak with you."

He unlocked the door and stepped into the room. "Yer lookin' spunky this mornin', Mrs. Buchanan. I've just about got yer breakfast ready."

The loaf of bread and pot of coffee was more food than many people in town would have by now. Supplies were running low, and children would be hungry.

"I can't eat, Ike." She held her aching shoulder. "I must see my husband. Will you escort me across the street?"

"Aw, I can't do that, ma'am. It's against Dolan's orders."

"Please, Ike! After I talk to Noah, you can bring me back here. Hold a gun on me if you like."

The young man scratched his scraggly locks. "It'd be risky. Things is hot out there this mornin'."

"Just let me go—"

"What on earth is that?" At the sound of shouting and horses' hooves, Ike bolted to the window. Isobel rushed to his side.

"What's goin' on, ma'am? I can't see nothin'."

"It's soldiers from Fort Stanton," she cried.

"Wahoo! That means we got the army on our side, Mrs. Buchanan!" Ike did a little dance around the room. "Count 'em for me, would ya?"

"There's Colonel Dudley," she said. "Four officers. Eight...nine...ten...eleven black cavalrymen. More than twenty white infantrymen. And they've brought cannons!"

"It's the howitzer!" Ike whooped as he squinted to see. "Dudley's brung the howitzer! She's a twelve-pounder. And there's a rapid-fire Gatling gun comin' along behind. Dolan's won the war now. Mac might as well give up."

Isobel sank onto a chair and buried her face in her hands. It was too late. Too late. The soldiers had come to obliterate Alexander McSween's forces. Among the dead would be Noah Buchanan.

Chapter Twenty-One

Before Colonel Dudley and the soldiers could take positions, Isobel saw several Dolan men run to Alexander McSween's house and begin pouring coal oil around the wooden window frames.

"What do they mean to do?" she asked Ike, clutching his arm.

"I reckon they're gonna try to burn out the McSween bunch."

"Burn them!" Isobel rose to her feet, but Ike pushed her out of bullet range.

"Don't worry yerself none, ma'am," he drawled. "That house is made of adobe brick. It ain't gonna burn worth a lick."

"But the window frames. And the roof. Oh, Ike, you must take me across the street at once. I have to save my husband."

"Settle down, now. Tell you what. I'll step outside and see if I can find someone who can tell me what the soldiers is plannin'."

The moment Ike left the room, Isobel pushed at the window casing in an effort to dislodge it. But the stout wood frame was embedded in adobe, and it refused to give. She ran to the door and tried the knob, but Ike had locked it. Frantic, she raced to the window again.

"Noah!" she shouted. Taking up a chair, she began smashing it against the window. "Let me out, Jimmie Dolan!"

"Hey, there!" Ike barged into the room. Isobel flew at him, fists pummeling as she tried to push past him. He grabbed her arms and shoved her back from the door. She stumbled and fell to the floor, sobbing.

"What's all this, ma'am?" Ike said after he'd locked the door behind them. He bent over her and laid a hand on her back. "You know I can't let you out, Mrs. Buchanan. I got my orders."

She shrugged away from his hand. "My husband is in that house! I must see him."

"You wouldn't get near McSween's place even if I did set you free."

Her heart breaking, Isobel struggled up from the floor, ran to the window and looked out.

Ike spoke softly as he joined her. "When McSween's men saw Colonel Dudley was back in town, they hightailed it out of here. He ain't got nobody left but the men in his own house. I hear they've stacked adobe bricks inside to make a barricade."

Isobel leaned her forehead against the window frame. Noah was inside Alexander McSween's house. Noah and a few others. How could they hope to hold out against an army?

"Where is the colonel?" she asked. "I must speak to him. If he fires those guns at McSween's house, he'll kill everyone inside."

"He's setting up camp down the street. Dudley may be a hard-drinkin' man, but he's got some smarts, too. He sent messages tellin' McSween and Dolan that he's in town to protect the women and children. He said if anyone fires on his soldiers, he's gonna blow 'em to kingdom come."

Isobel moaned. "That means Dolan's men can fire on the McSween house without fear of hitting a soldier. But with troops everywhere, no one inside the house can shoot back. It's not fair."

"'Course it ain't. That's war for ya." Ike patted her arm. "Now let me bring in yer breakfast, Mrs. Buchanan. There ain't nothin' you can do. Anyhow, you won't be the first widow in Lincoln County. Believe me."

Sauntering away, he unlocked the door, slipped through and relocked it from the outside. She could hear him whistling as he banged around the stove, preparing her breakfast.

Isobel was given no opportunity for escape. Shortly after noon, Dolan's posse filled the house. The men outside the locked door were laughing about their sure victory as they loaded their rifles.

Unable to keep still despite the throbbing pain in her shoulder, Isobel drew a chair to the window. Some of Dolan's men approached the McSween house and began to pry loose bullet-torn shutters, and smash windowpanes with their rifle butts.

She had no doubt that Alexander McSween must die. How many would die with him? Noah Buchanan… Billy Bonney… Sue McSween? She had barely thought of the woman when out of the house marched Mrs. McSween herself.

Head up, she strode down the street toward the *torreón*. If anyone could stand up to an army colonel, it was Sue McSween with her sharp tongue and quick mind.

But the moment she was safely away from the house, Dolan's men began pouring coal oil over the windows. A flame sprang up at the back of the house near the kitchen.

A pillar of smoke rose as the fire crawled from one room to the next.

Isobel sat helpless at her window. Her throat ached from choking back tears. Several times she was certain she saw Noah's silhouette, but he took cover before she could call out to him. Smoke poured from the windows as hazy figures moved around inside.

Murmuring prayers, Isobel saw images of Noah flicker through her thoughts. The evening he had lifted her onto his horse and carried her into the shadows of the pines. She could recall the smell of him…leather and dust. She remembered his clean-shaven face, the handsomest she had ever seen. She thought of the tender way he had held her, kissed her, loved her. His clear voice rang through the valley with hymns. His strong hands wrestled cattle…and wrote stories.

Oh, Noah! If only she could change the past.

"Naw, she's Buchanan's wife!" Ike's protest carried into her room. "Leave her be, fellers."

"C'mon, Ike. Let's have a look at her. Ain't she the one sent Snake Jackson hoppin' over coals?"

"Yeah, Ike! Let's take a gander at Buchanan's woman."

"Boys, if I did that, ol' Dolan would skin me alive."

Someone guffawed. "He means to string her up for murder, don't ya know?"

"Murder?" another hooted. "Hoo-wee!"

Isobel swallowed at the thick knot in her throat. Murder? But of course. What chance would she have to prove her innocence? Dr. Ealy had treated her wounds, and the surgeon had felt no compunction over lying about the condition of John Tunstall's corpse. He could certainly make it look as though she had not acted in self-defense but had stabbed Snake Jackson to death.

Feeling ill, she studied Mac's house—enveloped in raging flames. Now Sue McSween marched back down the street to her burning home and went inside, seemingly oblivious to the conflagration.

Moments later, Sue left again and crossed to John Tunstall's store, where Susan Gates and the Ealy family had hidden. At once, the Dolan posse began to set fire to that building. Mary Ealy ran out of the store carrying the two children and set them on the road. Her husband followed with a stack of Bibles in his arms. Susan raced outside with textbooks in hand and slates under one arm.

"Susan!" Isobel cried, pounding on the window. "Susan, please look at me!"

But now soldiers drove a wagon to the front of Tunstall's mercantile. The troops quickly loaded the Ealys' few possessions into the wagon. The Ealys and Susan climbed on board, Susan clutching one of the little girls in her arms, and the wagon rolled away.

"Susan!" Isobel yelled her friend's name one last time, but the petite red-haired schoolteacher evidently had seen too much. White-faced, she stared blankly ahead, her large gray eyes fixed on nothing.

The wagon made a final trip from the Tunstall store as darkness fell over the valley. It carried Sue McSween's organ, more of Dr. Ealy's books and a large sack of flour. By this time flames had raged through the entire McSween house. The blaze lit the mountains on both sides of town. Shooting increased until all Isobel could hear was the crack of gunfire and the roar of flames.

She hung against the window frame, not caring whether she died by a random shot. No one could still be alive inside the burning house. Noah was surely dead. She ached with hopelessness. But just then, she saw several figures suddenly run from the back of the house. Gunfire intensified. A silhouetted man crumpled to the ground.

For a moment the shooting halted.

"McSween said he'd surrender," someone shouted outside her door. "Bob Beckwith is goin' in after him."

From the window Isobel tried to make out what was happening. She heard a voice cry out from the yard of the burning house. Alexander McSween?

"I shall never surrender!" he roared.

At his words bullets flew. Bodies tumbled to the ground. Rifles blazed away. Dolan's men poured out of the Cisneros house, leaving Isobel completely alone.

She saw more men—Regulators who had tried to save their friends in McSween's house—jump from the window of the Tunstall store. Dogs barked. Flames leapt higher.

Sounds of victory erupted from the McSween courtyard as Jimmie Dolan's men began to prance about and fire their guns in jubilation. Isobel sank onto her chair, watching the devilish dance around the fire.

"McSween's dead!" someone crowed as he ran past her window, a jug of whisky in his hand. "McSween's dead! McSween's dead!"

"How many killed?" another man cried from the porch of the Tunstall store.

"Got 'em all. All the Regulators are dead!"

"Six dead in the courtyard!" someone else called out. "Naw, five. All shot dead. McSween's one of 'em!"

"Wahoo! We got 'em all. Every last one of them blasted outlaws!"

Isobel covered her face with her hands and began to cry. Noah…beloved Noah. Dear God, let him rest in peace.

Chapter Twenty-Two

Isobel slumped in her chair, her arms folded on the windowsill and her head resting on them. The acrid tang of smoke filled her nostrils. Shots continued to ring out, as they had most of the night. Someone had broken into Tunstall's store, and men were still carrying away the looted goods. Isobel could hear them laughing as they drank whisky and boasted about their victory.

Sniffing, she shut her eyes. She had not slept, and now the first purple light of dawn was beginning to streak the sky. How could she sleep? How could she ever go on? But, of course, it wouldn't be long before Jimmie Dolan remembered her. She would face her own death soon. It hardly seemed to matter.

Memories of Spain and the rich pastures of Catalonia drifted through her thoughts. Horses cantering over green hills. White cliffs. A crashing blue sea. Grapes. Grazing sheep.

And then she saw New Mexico. Blue sky arching heavenward. Fragrant piñon trees. Gurgling streams. Yuccas covered with thick white blossoms. Spiny cacti garlanded in pink blooms.

She imagined she was bending to pick one of those cactus flowers. Leaning forward, her hair fell over her shoulders. She straightened and placed the blossom in a pair of strong, sun-weathered hands.

"Noah," she whispered. "Noah."

"Isobel…" The voice came from somewhere outside herself. She tried to turn her head to see his face, but the wound in her shoulder hurt too much.

"Isobel…" She heard her name again. Or was it the wind whispering through the junipers? "Isobel…"

A warm hand stroked down her neck. She jumped. The chair tumbled backward on the floor as she struggled to her feet. And there he was…the tall hero of her dreams. Noah Buchanan.

"Didn't mean to scare you, darlin'," he said, "but we don't have much time. Got to get out of this place while Ike's keeping watch."

Isobel blinked. "Noah? Are you alive?"

"Me, Billy Bonney and a couple of others made it out of McSween's house in the dark just before the shooting got really hot. I'm not sure who made it and who didn't because I took off in this direction to find you. I didn't even know you were in Lincoln till I heard you shouting for Susan this afternoon."

He stopped and rubbed his hand over his forehead. "Mac got killed, you know. Dolan's men shot him. I saw it all."

"Noah…" It was the only word Isobel could force out of her mouth.

"C'mon, darlin'. Ike won't be able to steer those drunkards away from the house much longer. Let's head out."

Isobel moaned as Noah lifted her into his arms and carried her from the room that had been her prison for five days. She tilted her head to see Ike Teeters standing in the doorway.

"Good luck, Mrs. Buchanan," he said, giving her a friendly wave. "You're fine company, ya know? Easy to talk to. Say, send me a letter when that first little one gets borned. Juanita can read it to me. She knows her ABCs real good."

For the first time in many days she was able to muster the trace of a smile. "Thank you, Ike. I hope Jimmie Dolan won't harm you. He'll come looking for me to hang me."

"Hang you? Naw, I just made that up. Didn't want them drunks to get their hands on ya, is all. Dolan might've forgot he even had you. I shore ain't gonna remind him." He gave her a snaggletoothed grin. "Well, so long. Guess it's time for me to go join the boys."

As Ike stepped out the front door of the Cisneros house, Noah carried Isobel out the back. His horse was waiting, and Noah settled his wife against his chest before spurring the horse away from the scene of murder, bloodshed and mayhem.

They rode through the hills, skirting the road as the morning light filtered through the trees. When they had reached a clearing safely away from danger, Noah reined the horse.

"Ike told me Snake tore into you," he said gently.

Isobel gazed into eyes the color of the New Mexico sky. "I killed him, Noah. I was wrong to do it, even though I was fighting for my life. It's not my place to take a life. I know now, revenge is not the way."

"And I won't need to make Snake pay for what he did to you." For a long time he gazed at the gray smoke marring the sky over Lincoln Town. "The minute I figured out it was you yelling at Susan Gates through the window of that house across the street, all the bluster went out of me. I just wanted to get to you—protect you. The push to avenge Dick's death seemed downright worthless compared with the chance to build a life with you."

"Oh, Noah, I was sure you had been shot or burned alive," she murmured against his neck. "I thought I had lost you forever."

"I couldn't let that happen, darlin'. I love you too much."

A smile tilted her lips. "And I love you, Noah Buchanan."

"Good," he said, giving her a hug. "Love's about all we've got, because I don't intend to take you anywhere near Lincoln County again. I'm going to write John Chisum and cancel the purchase of the land. We'll go north somewhere and start over. I can run cattle for someone up there. We'll build us a little place—it may not be much—but it'll be ours and it'll be clean and safe. Isobel, I'd like to give you children. I'd like to provide for you and protect you—"

"And write stories for me?" With the hint of a giggle, she drew out the New York letter she had transferred to the pocket of her yellow dress. "'Sunset at Coyote Canyon' is to be published, Noah. And the magazine wants more of your stories. I'll type the second one you wrote, shall I? I'll use my Remington. Maybe we'll live on the land I won back from Snake Jackson. It's beautiful, rich pasture just north of Santa Fe. Green country with mountains covered in whispering aspens."

But Noah heard nothing. He bent and kissed Isobel's lips. His arms tightened around her, seeking solace for all those empty days…enfolding the woman with whom he would share a lifetime in this land of enchantment.

Epilogue

For my readers who are as interested in the historical portrayal of the Lincoln County War as in the love story of Noah and Isobel Buchanan, I offer this final note.

BILLY BONNEY (alias Billy the Kid)—Escaped from the burning McSween house with several other Regulators just minutes before Alexander McSween was shot. Lived for three more years, during which he engaged in more killings and daring getaways. He was shot to death on the night of July 13, 1881, by Sheriff Pat Garrett, a former friend. Billy was twenty-one years old.

JIMMIE DOLAN—Financially ruined, he brought himself back to power and wealth through an advantageous marriage and several shrewd business moves. Took over the Tunstall Mercantile in Lincoln and the Tunstall ranch on the Rio Feliz. Later served as county treasurer and territorial senator. Died a natural death on February 26, 1898, at age fifty.

SUSAN GATES—Moved to Zuni, New Mexico, with Dr. Taylor Ealy and his family. Taught school to the Indians there. Married Jose Perea, a young Presbyterian minister. Later moved with her husband to Jemez and then to Corrales, New Mexico, where she became the mother of a son.

TAYLOR AND MARY EALY—Served as missionaries in Zuni, New Mexico, from 1878 to 1881. Returned to Pennsylvania, where Dr. Ealy began a medical practice and a profitable baby powder company. More about the Ealy family can be read in *Missionaries, Outlaws, and Indians,* edited and annotated by Norman J. Bender.

JOHN CHISUM—Returned to Lincoln County after the Seven-Day War. Built a new home, the "Long House," at South Spring River Ranch. Developed a malignant tumor on his neck. Went to Kansas City and Arkansas for treatment but died in Eureka Springs on December 20, 1884. Buried in Paris, Texas. Read more about John Chisum in *My Girlhood Among Outlaws,* by Lily Klasner.

JUAN PATRÓN—Moved his family to Puerto de Luna, New Mexico, after the Lincoln County War. There he was murdered by hired assassin Mitch Maney on April 9, 1884. Patrón was twenty-nine years old. Maney's case never went to trial.

SUSAN McSWEEN—Started her own ranching venture in Three Rivers, an area distant from Lincoln. Remarried in 1884. Obtained a divorce in 1891. Became wealthy through skilled management of her vast land and eight thousand head of cattle. Considered "a woman of genius." Died in 1931 at age eighty-six.

The following books, among others, provide a well-rounded view of the history of the Lincoln County War:

Violence in Lincoln County, 1869-1881, William A. Keleher

Pat Garrett: The Story of a Western Lawman, Leon C. Metz

Maurice G. Fulton's History of the Lincoln County War, Robert N. Mullin, ed.

John Henry Tunstall, Frederick W. Nolan

Billy the Kid: A Handbook, Jon Tuska

Billy the Kid: A Short and Violent Life, Robert M. Utley

High Noon in Lincoln: Violence on the Western Frontier, Robert M. Utley

Merchants, Guns & Money: The Story of Lincoln County and Its Wars, John P. Wilson

* * * * *

Acknowledgments

In writing *The Outlaw's Bride,* I traced the historical events of the Lincoln County War in New Mexico. Except for the fictional participation of Isobel Matas, Noah Buchanan and Rattlesnake Jim Jackson, the characters and the sequence of events are as accurate as I was able to uncover in my research. Although any errors are my own responsibility, I owe my thanks for research assistance and inspiration to Tim Palmer, Terry Koenig, Lynn Koenig, Lowell Nosker, Bob Hart and the Lincoln County Heritage Trust, Jeremy and Cleis Jordan of Casa de Patrón, Father John Elmer, Sylvia Johnson, Nita Harrell and Sue Breisch Johnson.

Deep appreciation goes to my editor, Joan Golan, and my agent, Karen Solem, for their constant support and encouragement.

Renee Ryan grew up in a Florida beach town where she learned to surf, sort of. With a degree from FSU, she explored career opportunities at a Florida theme park and a modeling agency and even taught high school economics. She currently lives with her husband in Nebraska, and many have mistaken their overweight cat for a small bear. You may contact Renee at reneeryan.com, on Facebook or on Twitter, @ReneeRyanBooks.

Books by Renee Ryan

Love Inspired Historical

Lone Star Cowboy League: The Founding Years

Stand-In Rancher Daddy

Charity House

The Marshal Takes a Bride
Hannah's Beau
Loving Bella
The Lawman Claims His Bride
Charity House Courtship
The Outlaw's Redemption
Finally a Bride
His Most Suitable Bride
The Marriage Agreement

Visit the Author Profile page at Harlequin.com for more titles.

DANGEROUS ALLIES

Renee Ryan

I am sending you out like sheep among wolves.
Therefore be as shrewd as snakes
and as innocent as doves.
—*Matthew* 10:16

To my dear friend and BBS cofounder, Staci Bell.
Thank you for your support through the years.
You might buy all my books, but I'm your biggest fan!

Chapter One

20 November 1939
Schnebel Theater, Hamburg, Germany
2200 Hours

They came to watch her die.

Every night, they came. To gawk. To gasp. To shake their heads in awe. And Katarina Kerensky made sure they never left disappointed.

Tonight, she performed one of her favorites, Shakespeare's *Romeo and Juliet*. In typical Nazi arrogance, Germanizing the arts hadn't stopped at simply eliminating "dangerous" persons from cultural life. The Chamber of Culture had continued its purification function by also ruling that Shakespeare—in German translation, of course—was to be viewed as a German classic, and thus acceptable for performance throughout the Fatherland.

Leave it to the Nazis to claim the English playwright as their own.

In spite of her personal reasons for hating the Third Reich, Katia loved the challenge of taking a role already performed by the best and making Juliet her own.

For a few hours on stage her world made sense.

Now, poised in her moment of mock death, her hair spilled past her shoulders and down along the sides of the raised platform on which she lay. She held perfectly still as her Romeo drank the pretend poison and collapsed beside her.

She could smell the brandy and sweat on Hans as the foul scents mingled with the mold growing on the costume he hadn't washed in weeks, but Katia thought nothing of it. She was a professional and approached the role of Juliet as she would any role, on or off the stage. With daring conviction.

Hitting his cue, George, the bald actor playing Friar Laurence, made his entrance. As the scene continued to unfold around her Katia remained frozen, her thoughts turned to the actors who should also be sharing the stage. She was one of the lucky ones. Instead of playing a star-crossed lover doomed for eternity, she could have been among many of her peers thrown out of the theater due to whispers—often untrue—of their Jewish heritage or socially deviant behavior.

For now, at least, she was safe. As she was the daughter of a Russian prince, Vladimir Kerensky, fame had been her companion long before she'd stepped onto a stage.

Would notoriety be enough to keep her safe?

The Nazi Germany racial policy grew increasingly violent and aggressive with each new law. If anyone checked Katia's heritage too closely they might discover her well-kept secret.

To the Germans, she was merely a real-life princess playing at make-believe. A natural, as her mentor Madame Levine had always said. Good skin. Innate talent. Beautiful face and hair. All added to the final package. But the brains? Katia kept those hidden behind the facade of ambition and a seemingly ruthless pursuit of fame.

If the Germans only knew how she really used her talents. And why.

Opening her eyes to tiny slits, she tilted her face just enough to cast a covert glance over the audience. Her latest British contact was out there waiting. Watching. Bringing with him another chance for her to fight the monster regime and protect her mother with means she'd been unable to use to defend her father.

She drew in a short breath and focused on becoming Juliet once more. The scent of stage dust and greasepaint was nearly overpowering. Dizzying. The spotlight blinding, even with her eyelids half-closed. Nevertheless, Katia remained motionless until her cue.

"The lady stirs…."

As though in a trance, Katia rose slowly to a sitting position. She fluttered her eyelashes and let her arms drag behind her. Arching her back, she held her arms limp, making the motion appear effortless.

Presentation, Madame Levine had taught, was the difference between a rank amateur and a true artist.

Pitching her voice to a hoarse whisper, she said, "O, comfortable friar! Where is my lord?" The muscles in her arms protested, but she continued to hold them slack.

Katia wrapped her temporary role of the doomed Juliet around her like a protective cloak then tossed a confused, sleepy look over the audience. "I do remember well where I should be." She sent the audience a long, miserable sigh, then wiped the back of her wrist across her brow. "And there I am."

Pushing a shaky smile along her lips, she let it cling to the edges of her mouth for only a moment before hiding it behind a pout. "Where is my Romeo?"

Friar Laurence tugged at her as he began his impassioned speech to make her leave the tomb with him.

Ignoring his pleas, Katia peered around. She blinked once. Twice. Then turned her head away from the audience.

Friar Laurence came to the end of his speech. "I dare no longer stay."

Katia focused her attention on the actor lying next to her, narrowing her performance down to this final moment. Nothing existed before. Nothing after. Just this handful of lines. A few moments when escape was possible.

Feigning horror at the sight of her dead husband, she allowed a lone tear to trail down her left cheek. In a tragic whisper she recited her next lines, pretended to search desperately for a drop of poison in the vial she rescued from Romeo's clenched fist, then listened to the lines spoken offstage.

She pulled her brows into deep concentration. "Yea, noise? Then I'll be brief." She made a grand show of searching Romeo's belt. On a gasp, she widened her eyes. "O happy dagger!"

Snatching the fake blade, she raised it high above her. Arching, she tossed back her head, snapped it forward again, then locked her gaze on to the thin blade. "This is thy sheath…"

With a dramatic flourish, she stabbed herself just above her stomach. "There…rust, and let me die."

Swaying, she sucked in her breath, buckled over in pain, and collapsed on top of Romeo.

As the rest of the cast trooped in for the final scene, Katia remained unmoving, only half listening to the words of the rest of the play.

Knowing her performance had been one of her best, she tried to ride the wave of success. But the joy remained elusive this evening, as it had each night since the Nazis had discovered Madame Levine's fraudulent papers.

And just as the Lord had done back in Russia during

the revolution, God had abandoned Germany. Now most of the people Katia loved were dead, imprisoned or worse.

Her mind raced back to the last time she'd seen her mentor, now shipped off to Neuengamme, for her lie as much as for her Jewish heritage. There had been no warning, no time to help.

Would Katia's mother be next? The quick burst of fear came fast and hard at the thought.

Why didn't Elena Kerensky see that no one was safe in Nazi Germany, not even Russian royalty? Why didn't she understand that the very people who had killed Katia's beloved father—for no reason other than his distant relation to the Romanovs—were no different than the Nazis? Hitler could easily broaden his definition of a Jew to include anyone with only one Jewish grandparent, rather than the current definition of two.

At that thought, fear played in Katia's head, taunting her and convicting her. She would not allow her mother to die for so small a reason.

Katia was no longer a helpless eight-year-old witnessing the death of her loving father and loss of her beloved homeland. She was no longer an innocent who believed prayer was the answer, that God cared enough to stop the violence. As an adult she put her trust only in herself, not in a hard-hearted God who allowed courageous men like Vladimir Kerensky to die at the hands of their enemies.

At least now, as a British informant, she had the means to protect one of her parents.

A sense of control surged. The power of it danced a chill up her spine, giving her a foundation of order beneath the chaos.

The actor playing the Prince of Verona said his final line, dragging Katia back to her immediate job for the evening. "For never was a story of more woe than this of Juliet and her Romeo."

The applause broke out like a rumbling stroke of thunder. With a convicted heart, Katia rose to take her bows.

She was ready to begin her next mission, ready to fight the Nazis, ready to stop the tyranny before it swallowed up her mother and others like her.

Avoiding the crush of people milling around backstage, Lieutenant Jack Anderson leaned a shoulder against the wall behind him and watched Katarina Kerensky in action. She accepted the congratulations from her fellow cast members and adoring fans with understated grace.

In stark contrast, the overbright laughter and din of heavily accented voices sounded like a gaggle of geese, rather than a celebration of a remarkable woman's acting triumph.

Out of instinct and years of training, Jack surveyed his surroundings. He eyed the tangle of ropes and pulleys on his right, the large circuit box on his left. Extra props were set in every available spot. Dusty costumes lay strewn over a large paint-chipped box. There seemed to be no order, no organization. A full hour in this world and he knew the chaos would drive him mad.

The putrid odor of sawdust, human sweat and unwashed costumes took away the mystique of the fantasy world he'd watched come alive less than an hour before. From his seat in the twelfth row, the actors had glittered under the lights. Here they looked haggard, wilted.

Except for one.

The woman he'd come to meet was a surprise. And he was only half-sorry for it. Even as the thought rolled around in his mind he realized he should have had some instinct, some internal warning, that this mission wasn't going to be as tidy as the new chief of MI6 had claimed. Not with a woman like Katarina Kerensky involved.

Clearly, the British had a hidden agenda. But were they using this mission to ferret out individual loyalties, or was there a darker motive? Had the spymasters grown to distrust Jack and set a trap for him? Or was Kerensky their target? Given Jack's direct relationship with Churchill, the latter was far more likely.

Jack now admitted, if only to himself, that he hadn't prepared enough for his first glimpse of the famous actress. His sudden inability to catch an easy breath was like having a destroyer deposited on his chest. Later, when he was alone, he would sort through his messy emotions and decide what to do with them. For now, he had to disconnect. Focus.

Analyze the potential dangers.

She turned in his direction, tilted her head slightly and fixed him with a bold stare. Their gazes locked and held. A jolt of discomfort shot to the soles of his feet. He fought to keep his breathing slow and steady. But this woman made him *feel*.

The emotion wasn't real. It couldn't possibly be real. And yet…

The sudden flash of vulnerability in her eyes before she buried the emotion behind a bored expression gave her an air of innocence that Jack didn't dare consider too closely. It was simply a well-honed weapon in her female arsenal. He had to remember she was an actress *and* a spy. Nothing but lies would come from her mouth.

With a mental shake, he pushed aside his initial reaction to the woman and focused only on measuring her as a potential ally. Or enemy.

He quickly took in the hair, the face, the perfect fit of her costume. Her skin was smooth and flawless. Her features delicate. Her eyes were large and slightly slanted, the color of the sea in a bitter storm. Her hair was a deep auburn, almost chocolate except when the light hit it and revealed an array of gold, red and orange.

Absently, Jack shoved at his own hair, surprised to find he was sweating. Blinking, he shook himself from the trance she'd put him in.

She was good. He'd give her that. But with those fabulous eyes no longer locked with his, the unsteady rolling in his gut slowed. She may have knocked his brains around—which was probably intentional—but Jack was back in control of his wits.

Before tonight he had always believed the Bible's David a fool to let a woman turn him into a murderer and adulterer. But Jack hadn't fully understood the power of a beautiful woman.

Or the danger. Until now.

Chapter Two

In spite of the dim lighting backstage, Katia easily picked out her contact by the single bloodred rose he wore on his lapel. He stood on the fringe of the post-production party, his face hidden by the shadows. She couldn't decide if the lack of light made him appear mysterious. Or sinister.

He lifted two fingers in silent salute then settled his broad shoulder against the wall behind him once more.

Katia didn't particularly like the way he watched her with those long, speculative looks. The quiet intensity in him made her heart beat in hard jerks. How much did he know about her? Did he know her secret?

A sense of unease skittered up her spine, but she boldly kept her eyes on his. She drew a careful breath. The man made her nervous. The tingling weakness in her limbs distressed her further, until she realized he was deliberately trying to intimidate her.

Another man who underestimated her.

Annoyance replaced her anxiety. Katia hiked her chin up a notch. Many before him had seen her as a liability. And, like them, this one would ultimately come to view her as his greatest asset.

Or he would fail.

As he continued to study her with those smart, patient eyes, she felt a quick churn of hope in her stomach. But that made no sense. She refused to allow his assessment to go unmatched. With equal intensity she ran her gaze across him.

On the surface he looked like a young, wealthy German out for an entertaining evening at the theater. Dressed in an expensive tuxedo, black tie and crisp white shirt, he could pass as a financier. Maybe a bored aristocrat. Even one of Hitler's secret agents or a henchman for Heinrich Himmler.

Her breath came short and fast at that last thought. Did the Nazis know she was a mole for the British? Had they sent this man to trap her?

If it wasn't for the red rose, she'd give in to her fears. The operative's behavior certainly wasn't helping matters. His stance was anything but friendly. The intense control he held over his body spoke of hard physical training. Probably military. An officer, no doubt. A man used to giving orders, and having them obeyed.

She wanted to distrust him immediately.

She found herself intrigued instead.

He turned his head into the light, a gesture that allowed her to see his face for the first time without dark shadows hindering her inspection.

His sharp eyes and tall, lean body reminded her of a big cat. Unwavering, patient. And very, very dangerous.

Code name, Cougar.

It fit him to perfection. With his dark blond hair, piercing blue eyes and strong, obstinate jaw he could hail from any number of northern European countries. Austria, Norway, Great Britain.

Germany.

She turned from that disturbing thought and focused her

full attention on her understudy, pretending grave interest in the other woman's enthusiastic compliments.

Unable to stop herself, she slid another glance at her contact from beneath lowered lashes. The watchful look in his eyes suddenly vanished and, just as quickly, a pleasant smile rode across his lips.

The effortless charm put her on instant alert.

He shoved away from the wall and began pacing toward her. Slowly, deliberately.

The hunter stalking his prey.

A little stab of panic penetrated her attempts at calm. No. She would not show weakness.

He stopped in front of her, an inch closer than was polite, then offered a formal nod. Her understudy melted away, muttering something about needing a plate of food.

The scent of musk, expensive tobacco and dominant male was far too unsettling, the handsome face far too attractive.

In a purely self-defensive move, Katia gave her head an arrogant little toss. Lifting a single eyebrow, she concentrated on the planned greeting she was supposed to use with him tonight. "Did you enjoy the play?"

He nodded and stuck to the script, as well. "It was enlightening."

The words rolled off his tongue in perfect German, with just a hint of Austria clinging to the edges.

Relief had her fear smoothly vanishing. He was her British contact, after all.

She kept to the words MI6 had given them for this first meeting. "I'm glad."

"Perhaps we could discuss the finer points of your performance in a more private place?"

She swallowed but held his stare. He was following the

script, so why did she get the sense he was toying with her? "Yes, I would like that."

His smile deepened in response, revealing a row of straight, white teeth. Her heart gave one powerful kick against her ribs. The charm was there, urging her into complacency, and yet his eyes were so stark and empty.

For a moment she glimpsed something that looked like despair behind his flawless performance, giving her the impression that this man needed someone to reach him, perhaps even to save him.

For a second she felt herself softening toward him, but only for a second. This was no romantic interlude. This was a serious game of war. Loss of control, even for a moment, meant death. And then who would protect her mother?

Katia quickly adjusted her thoughts by focusing on her mother and all they had to lose if Katia became reckless.

She started to take a step back but her contact captured her hand, turned it over and studied her palm.

Her pulse raced at his light touch.

Not wanting to draw attention to them, she tried to ease her hand free, but he released her first.

"Perhaps we should go to…" He allowed his words to trail off, as planned, giving her the choice of the location for their real meeting.

Happy to take the lead, she cocked her head toward a room off to her right. "My dressing room is just over there."

Her territory.

His smile turned into a roguish grin. "Perfect."

The boyish tilt of his lips made her want to believe everything he said from this point on, even when she knew— knew for a *fact*—he made his life telling lies and using intrigue to accomplish his mission.

She opened her mouth to speak, reconsidered and then snapped it shut. Let him take command for a while, as expected.

"You were remarkable," he drawled, his words no longer following their scripted first meeting. His expression dared her to remark on his audacity.

She couldn't. She was too busy trying to shove aside the pleasure that swelled inside her at his impulsive remark. If there was anything she didn't trust it was a spontaneous, sincere compliment. It hit at a vulnerable spot deep within, the place no one had touched since her father's murder. The place that had once believed in a loving God.

She lifted a shoulder, pretending his deliberate shift in the conversation didn't bother her in the least. "Dying onstage has its own unique drama. Poetic and sizzling." She smiled, opened her heart just a little. "Wonderful, really."

His eyebrows drew together in an expression of genuine fascination. "Is that why you do it, then? For the drama?"

They both knew he wasn't talking about the stage.

Oh, he was a smooth one, intentionally forcing her further off track with an intriguing question. She would not be defeated by such a transparent maneuver. "Among other reasons."

She slanted him a warning glare. His questions were getting too personal. Too insightful. Too…dangerous.

Just how much did this man know about her?

Their association was supposed to be simple. But the curling in her stomach told her this mission had become entirely too complicated already. She had to remember they would work together only three days, then never see each other again.

She wouldn't even learn his real name. As far as she was concerned, he was Friedrich Reiter, a wealthy shipbuilder who frequented the theater.

Pushing the spark of remorse aside, Katia touched his arm, but then quickly dropped her hand at the shocking sense of comfort she felt on contact. "Why don't we—"

Her words were drowned out by voices coming from the backstage door leading into the alley.

Happy greetings rang out, one after another. Katia turned toward the sound of a familiar feminine voice, barely catching sight of her elegant mother before being greeted with a kiss on her cheek.

Taking a step back, Katia scooped a breath into her lungs and tried to focus her chaotic thoughts.

What was her mother doing here, tonight of all nights? Elena Kerensky rarely attended the theater and she never appeared backstage. Mingling with the masses was simply *not* done. It was one of her mother's cardinal rules.

So what had sparked this unprecedented visit?

Katia took another long breath and swept a furtive glance over her mother. Elena Kerensky was still a striking woman at forty-seven, one who knew how to dress for any occasion. Tonight, she'd chosen a form-fitting gown of ice-blue that matched the color of her eyes. She'd pulled her pale blond hair into a refined chignon, showing off the expensive jewels around her neck. The ensemble made her look every bit the brave Russian princess in exile.

"My darling Katarina." Elena spoke in her trademark breathy whisper. "You were lovely this evening. Perfectly charming. I am a very proud mother."

For a moment Katia's practiced facade deserted her. She, unlike her mother, had very few rules in life and only one unbreakable commandment: never, under any circumstance, involve her mother in a mission.

She had to send Elena on her way before propriety required Katia to introduce the MI6 operative. Even though he had backed off a few steps, most likely to give her room to deal with this unexpected interruption, he remained close.

To further complicate matters, her mother wasn't alone. She'd brought her favorite escort of late, Hermann Schmidt, a cold-hearted naval officer in his early fifties.

Despite the air clogging in her throat, Katia needed to concentrate. What was Elena thinking? Not only did Schmidt hold the high-ranking position of captain in the *Kriegsmarine,* he had an unholy obsession for the Fatherland and a stark hatred of Jews.

Perhaps her mother didn't recognize the risks. Or perhaps she was simply hiding in plain sight.

"Katia, my dear, you remember Hermann?" Elena swept her hand in a graceful arc between them. "It was his idea to come backstage and congratulate you personally."

Which could mean…anything.

Far more worried about her mother's safety than the British operative standing to her right, frightening possibilities raced through Katia's mind, each more terrible than the last. Her heartbeat slowed to a painful thump… thump…thump.

How could her own mother willingly choose to align her loyalties with a Nazi like Hermann Schmidt? It was true, the Nazis hated the Communists as much as Elena Kerensky did, but that did not make them—or this man— her ally. Especially when Elena carried such a dangerous secret hidden in her lineage.

Katia would have to speak to her mother in private. But not now. Now, she had to don the comfortable role of silly, spoiled daughter. "Good evening, Herr… *Korvetten-kapitän.* It is always a pleasure to see you."

Schmidt's eyes narrowed into hard, uncompromising slits. "It is *Kapitän zur See,* Fräulein Kerensky. Just as it was the last time you made the same mistake. And the time before that."

"Oh, dear, of course."

Arrogant beast.

Tossing her head back, Katia gave a little self-conscious giggle. "My apologies. I never seem to be able to distinguish the ranks of the *Kriegsmarine.*"

She continued chattering nonsensical words that indicated her ignorance of all things military, ever mindful of the British operative moving back to her side once again. Beneath her lashes, she slid a covert glance his way, quickly catching the doubt in his bearing.

And why wouldn't he be suspicious of her now?

Katia's mission was to help him gain access to the blueprints of a Nazi secret weapon, a revolutionary mine that had sunk countless merchant ships over the last three months. Yet here she was, fraternizing with a U-boat captain.

Then again…

Perhaps she could use the Nazi's unexpected appearance to her advantage. How was the British spy to know that Hermann Schmidt was not one of her most useful contacts?

The key was to keep Hermann thinking she was an imbecile, all the while convincing the British operative she was a brilliant actress in a necessary performance to protect her mother.

Tricky. But achievable.

Elena, however, provided the one complication Katia could not defuse with any of her well-practiced roles. "Darling, please do us the honor of introducing your…*friend.*"

Chapter Three

The moment all three gazes turned toward Jack his gut twisted into a hard knot. For a fraction of a second all the intense emotions—the guilt, the anger, the need for vengeance—threatened to break free and sweep away his control. But if he relaxed his guard for a moment, no matter the cause, someone would end up dead tonight.

Hardening his resolve, Jack searched Kerensky's face for signs of a hidden agenda. There was obvious distress in her eyes, a clear indication this interruption was not planned. But the woman was a world-renowned actress, one who knew how to drag sympathy out of a man.

He would be a fool to trust her.

As though sensing his reservation, she flashed him a smile and he lost his train of thought. Clenching his jaw, he forced his heartbeat to settle. Yet, no matter how hard he concentrated, he couldn't look away from those remarkable eyes staring into his.

Kerensky blinked once, twice, finally breaking the spell between them. "Herr Reiter," she began, addressing him by his assumed alias. "This is my mother, Elena Kerensky, and her escort, Hermann Schmidt."

Acknowledging the woman first, Jack took Elena's hand

and touched his lips to her knuckles. "It is an honor to meet you. I now see where Katarina gets her beauty."

"Thank you, Herr Reiter. You are very kind." She turned to her companion and motioned him forward. "Come, Hermann, say hello to Katarina's friend."

As expected of all loyal Germans, Jack stepped back and gave the required Third Reich salute. "*Heil* Hitler, *Kapitän zur See.*"

The Nazi returned the gesture with quiet relish. "*Heil* Hitler."

On the surface, Hermann Schmidt looked like a typical naval officer, but there was something in his arrogant stance that turned Jack's blood to ice—an unyielding ruthlessness that he'd seen in too many high-ranking Nazis.

It was the same look that now stared back at him from the mirror every morning.

Was Jack becoming one of them?

Was he losing the last shreds of his humanity?

With each new mission, he played roulette with his soul. He could no longer expect God to hear his prayers or his pleas. Not after the horrors he'd committed in the name of war.

There could be no turning back, no chance of forgiveness. He had to start thinking like the man he was: a man with no future, no hope and a single goal—to hunt and destroy the enemy that had stolen his life from him.

Patience, Jack told himself. In spite of the urgency of his current mission, in spite of the tight deadline, time was his ally. He'd worked too hard building his cover to let an unexpected player in the game throw him off balance now.

Cutting through his thoughts, Elena Kerensky cleared her throat. "Herr Reiter, I don't believe we've met before. Have you known my Katia long?"

Jack noted the concern in the woman's eyes and decided

to use it to ferret out how far Kerensky was willing to go to help the British.

"I've known *Katarina*—" he rolled her name off his tongue in a slow caress "—long enough to come to the conclusion that she is a remarkable woman whom I wish to know better."

Hitting her cue perfectly, Kerensky slid her arm through his and smiled up at him with unmistakable affection. "What a lovely thing to say, darling."

With surprisingly little effort, he returned her smile as though they'd already become lovers.

Her gaze filled with female vulnerability, and she snuggled closer to him.

He ran a fingertip along her cheek.

There was a time when the God-fearing man Jack had once been would have been appalled by their blatant sexual undertones. But that was before Jack had walked with the enemy, before he'd become an embittered U.S. sailor infiltrating the SS.

Much like this famous actress, he played whatever role was necessary to accomplish his mission.

And yet...

As he stared into Kerensky's beautiful green eyes, Jack couldn't stop himself from wishing they'd met at another time, and under different circumstances. He wondered if her performance was a remarkable display of acting ability, or something else. Something inherently truthful? Or something coldly sinister?

In that instant, the words of his father came to him. *Always remember, Jack, a woman has more power to destroy a man than any other weapon.*

Jack's pulse soared through his veins. Was Kerensky playing both sides? Had the Germans found out about his deception? Were they using this accomplished actress to bring him down at last?

Subterfuge. Hidden agendas. Jack no longer knew where the intrigue ended and reality began. Even in his own mind he could no longer discern how much of Jack Anderson lived inside him, and how much had become Friedrich Reiter, the deadly SS henchman. Every new mission blurred the line between the two, threatening Jack's soul bit by bit.

A smart military man always knew when to hold his ground, and when to retreat. For now, his work was done.

Tapping into the ruthless man the Nazis had created, the one who coldly witnessed brutalities without flinching, Jack extracted himself from Kerensky's grip. Ignoring the sense of loss that took hold of him, he turned to her mother then nodded at Hermann Schmidt. "It was a pleasure meeting you both."

Keeping his eyes on Kerensky's face, he took her hand in his and raised it to his lips. "I look forward to our next meeting, my darling."

She made a soft sound of distress, but they both knew she wouldn't voice an argument in front of her mother and the Nazi officer. It was a small victory, to be sure, but a victory that put Jack firmly in control of the mission.

He couldn't have planned a more perfect finale to their first meeting.

Katia stared in muted astonishment as the British spy turned on his heel and headed toward the exit with ground-eating strides.

What now?

A wave of nausea hit, and for the first time all evening her smile threatened to waver. She stood perfectly still until the moment passed.

The man had gunmetal nerve, she'd give him that. Not only had he antagonized a high-ranking Nazi and her own mother with his boldness, he'd left Katia to deal with the messy consequences. Yet, even with frustration burning at the back of her throat, something about the British operative left her wanting...what?

What was it about the man that urged her to let down her guard, if only for a fraction of a second? For a moment tonight, with their arms twined together and their gazes bound in intimate familiarity, she'd forgotten all about playing a role. She'd merely been a woman enthralled with an intriguing man.

From the first moment their gazes had locked and held, she'd sensed her British contact was someone who knew what it meant to be an outsider. Just like her.

Was he a man she could trust?

A lethal thought.

Blind faith, she reminded herself, was nothing more than weakness, a trap that ultimately led to a one-way invitation to the concentration camps.

Another sick spasm clutched in her stomach, but she held her expression free of emotion. If the operative said he looked forward to their next meeting, then she had to believe there would indeed *be* a next meeting.

All was not lost.

For the moment, she simply needed to concentrate on placating a stunned parent and her suspicious escort.

Sliding a quick glance toward her mother, Katia cut off a sigh of frustration. Elena stood tall, her full attention focused on the British spy as he left through the back door.

"I don't trust that man," she muttered, regarding the exit with suspicious eyes. "Tell me again how you know Herr Reiter?"

Rule number one in espionage was to keep as close to

the truth as possible. "He is a dear friend, one I see whenever he comes to Hamburg on business."

Hermann Schmidt made a noise deep in his throat that sounded like a growl. "What, precisely, *is* his business?"

The uncharacteristic display of interest in her affairs chilled Katia down to the bone. This grim-faced Nazi was not a person with whom her mother should be spending her time. He was a formidable enemy, one who could ruin Elena if he uncovered her secret.

On full alert, Katia played her role cautiously. The key was to keep it simple. Consistent.

"I'm sure he told me once." She tapped a finger against her chin. "I seem to remember him saying he owned a company that supplies the Third Reich with materials for the war."

Schmidt's features turned hard and inflexible, matching the severity of his tightly buttoned uniform and crisp white shirt underneath. "What sort of materials, exactly?"

Katia blinked at his impatience, the cold heat of the dangerous emotion flashing in his eyes. Fortunately, to Hermann Schmidt, beautiful equaled stupid.

The knowledge gave Katia a surge of courage, and a strong conviction to play this role to her utmost ability. Fluttering her lashes, she placed her hand on his arm and gave him an empty smile. Now, if only she wouldn't throw up and ruin her act. "Is it really so important?"

"Yes." He leaned over her, his eyes communicating an unmistakable ruthlessness. "It is *very* important you try to remember exactly what sort of business Herr Reiter owns."

"You don't have to take that tone with me." Katia dropped her hand and pretended to pout, all the while gauging Schmidt's mood from below her lashes. Why would a mere naval officer care what a man like Friedrich Reiter did for a living?

Before Schmidt responded, Elena pushed in front of him and softened her expression. "Try concentrating, dear."

"Yes, all right, Mother. I shall try."

She let out a sigh, careful not to overplay her role. This was no game. One misstep and her mother's life could be in danger.

In truth, the British had told Katia very little about her contact. Standard operating procedure. For all she knew, Friedrich Reiter was exactly who he pretended to be—a wealthy Austrian shipbuilder.

Having stalled long enough, she drew her eyebrows into a frown. "Yes, I remember now. He is in construction. Or…shipbuilding, perhaps? One of the two."

Schmidt's lips flattened into a hard line. "Which is it? Construction or shipbuilding?"

She flung her hair over her shoulder, fully into her role in spite of the German's open hostility. "Who can remember such tedious details?"

"You seem to have no problem remembering countless pages of dialogue."

She gave him a pitying look and put the royal princess in her voice. "Herr Reiter is a patron of the arts and he adores me. Nothing else matters beyond that."

Although he quirked an eyebrow at her, Hermann Schmidt visibly relaxed. "Of course, how could I have forgotten where your priorities lie?"

The sarcastic twist of his lips gave Katia pause. Like so many of his kind, this man was far too sharp to fool for long.

It was time to change the subject.

"Let's not talk about Herr Reiter anymore." She turned her focus back to her mother. "I had no idea you were coming to the theater this evening. You said nothing of it this afternoon at tea."

A slow smile spread across Elena's face. She looked at her escort with a question in her eyes. "Should I tell her?"

He nodded slowly, but there was a possessiveness in his gaze that had Katia swallowing hard.

Elena took both of Katia's hands in hers and sighed. "Hermann and I have marvelous news to share with you."

Katia looked from one to the other. At the happy expression they exchanged, a sick feeling of dread tangled in her stomach.

Oh, no. Please, please, no. "What…what news?"

"We are engaged to be married."

"Why, that's…" Katia's breath caught in her throat. Even if the Lord had long since abandoned Katia, God could not be so cruel. "I… I'm speechless."

"I've been waiting for your mother for many years." Masculine pride danced in Schmidt's eyes as he spoke. And something more. Something dark and ugly. And very, very determined. "Now I have her at last."

Elena moved to the Nazi's side and positioned herself shoulder to shoulder with him. "As you know, Hermann and I were childhood friends, before I met your father."

"I remember." Katia had to sink her teeth into her bottom lip to keep from shouting at her mother to wake from the nightmare that held her in its clutches.

How could Elena, a devout Christian with a secret Jewish grandfather, agree to marry a man whose only god was Germany and whose professed savior was Adolf Hitler?

"Congratulations." She nearly choked on the words. "I am very happy for you both."

"Oh, darling." Elena pulled her into a tight embrace. "I am so glad you're pleased."

"I only want you to be happy," she whispered into her mother's hair before stepping back.

"Hermann has three days before he ships out again."

Elena's breath caught in her throat and tears shimmered in her eyes. "It is my fondest wish that all three of us spend time together during his visit."

Three days? How was Katia to complete her mission for the British with her mother demanding all her time? An unprecedented flush of desperation made her words rush out of her mouth. "But I am in the middle of a play. I have to be here every night and I—"

"Don't worry, darling." Elena patted her hand. "We'll simply spend the days together then have a late supper after your performances." Her tone was full of determination, a tone Katia knew well. In this, Elena would not relent.

Katia's composure threatened to crack, then she remembered her British contact's open declaration for her affections.

The man's game had been an act, but a brilliant, impromptu one that could be used to her advantage now.

Her best chance was to continue the ruse. "I'm sorry, mother. I have already promised Herr Reiter I would spend the rest of the week with him."

Elena dismissed the argument with a quick slash of her hand. "Cancel your plans. You must take this opportunity to get to know Hermann."

Knowing better than to argue at this point, Katia nodded. "Let me see what I can do."

Unused to having her wishes denied, Elena took the vague promise as complete agreement. "Good. Now that that's settled, we would like you to join us for a celebratory supper this evening."

Supper? Tonight?

Katia couldn't bear the idea of breaking bread with Hermann Schmidt. In truth, she feared it with all her heart. But she feared her mother being alone with the man far more. "I would like nothing better. Just give me a moment to change out of my costume."

Without looking back, Katia fled to her dressing room. Weary from the drama of the evening, she sat staring straight ahead and rubbed her left hand as if it ached. A shocking wave of panic gripped her heart, making her breath sit heavy in her chest.

Overwhelmed, she buried her face inside her palms and fought back the tears burning behind her eyelids.

She was so…incredibly…tired.

How she wanted to accept MI6's invitation to escape this godforsaken country and live in England for the duration of the war. But Katia couldn't leave Germany without her mother. And Elena Kerensky would never leave. Not with her recent engagement to her childhood friend, a man who happened to be a ruthless Nazi naval officer.

How would Katia protect her mother now?

Chapter Four

After bidding Elena and her escort good night, Katia shut the door with a soft click. Pressing her eyes closed a moment, she released a sigh of frustration.

The night had gone worse than expected.

Already, she could see that *Kapitän zur See* Schmidt was going to be a problem. It had been foolish of her to hope otherwise.

The female in her wanted to kick something in frustration. The royal princess in her had been trained too well to give in to the childish display of emotion. The spy in her needed to quit stalling and formulate a plan.

Glancing at the mail laying on the entryway floor, she decided to ignore responsibility a little while longer. Food first, plan second. She hadn't been able to touch her meal at the restaurant, not with Schmidt firing off pointed questions between scowls.

Clearly, the Nazi neither liked nor trusted her.

Good. At least she knew where she stood with the man. That would make her planning less complicated. She would use her fiercest weapons of cunning, lies and schemes.

Oh, but she was in a despicable business. Thankfully, she'd created many roles for use in her arsenal. By taking on other personas she kept the real Katia separate from the spy.

Rounding the corner, she caught sight of a man lounging in a chair in her east living room. Her chest rose and fell in a sudden spasm, the only outward sign of her inner distress. Otherwise, she stared at the British operative with nothing more than mild curiosity on her face.

He'd tugged his tie loose and had left the ends hanging on each side of his neck. He'd also opened the top three buttons of his shirt, revealing a smooth expanse of corded throat muscles.

Even in his relaxed position, there was a hard edge to him that somehow complemented her feminine decor. This man was one hundred percent rugged male, the quintessential alpha. Although he sat in a chair covered with pink and yellow fabric, he radiated masculinity.

Which did nothing to improve her mood.

How many surprises must she endure in one evening?

"You have exactly sixty seconds to tell me what you're doing in my home, Herr Reiter." The calm, detached voice was one of her most useful tools.

For an instant she thought she saw a deep male appreciation in his eyes, but he blinked and the moment was gone.

She lifted her chin a fraction higher. "Well?"

He didn't respond. Nor did he rise to greet her, as would have been the polite thing to do. Perhaps by remaining seated he was reminding her whom he considered in charge of the mission.

Unfortunately for him, he had the particulars wrong.

"You now have twenty seconds to start talking before I throw you out of my home."

Leaning farther back in the chair, he hooked an ankle across his knee then glanced at the clock on the mantel. "Actually, we're now down to fifteen."

Her earlier desire to kick something turned into an overwhelming urge to kick *someone*. By sheer force of will she reminded herself that this stranger was to be her partner for the next few days. Their success would bring the British closer to defeating Hitler. A heady prospect.

Katia might be able to carry out her end of the mission alone, but she needed Friedrich Reiter to deliver the plans to MI6. That did not mean, however, she had to make this conversation easy for him. "Tell me, Herr Reiter, how did you know where to find me?"

"It's my business to know certain, shall we say…" He made a vague gesture with his hand. "Things about you."

There was something in the way he met her gaze that brought matters to a very basic level between them. Another time she might have enjoyed the challenge of discovering the real man beneath the layer of polish and subterfuge. For now, she could only wonder what motivated him to risk his life for Great Britain. Personal gain, as most of the spies she'd met before him? Or was he answering a higher call?

Either way, the clock was ticking. She couldn't afford the luxury of delving into his inner psyche right now.

"What sort of…*things?*" she asked from behind a well-positioned smile.

He slowly unfolded his large frame and rose. As he strode toward her, she shrank back a step, as much startled by her reaction to him as by the intensity in his gaze. He stopped a mere foot away from her, his heat chasing away the sudden cold that had slipped under her coat.

For one small moment, time seemed to stop and wait for him to speak.

"For instance. Your mother never joins you backstage after a performance." His gaze stayed locked with hers. *"Never."*

Her fingers flexed by her side. Already, the man knew too much. "This evening was a rare but happy occasion."

"Special enough for her to choose a high-ranking *Kriegsmarine* officer as her escort?"

Katia stiffened. She should have known he would go straight for the heart of the matter. "Hermann Schmidt is a friend of my mother's. He is nothing to me." She nearly spat the last of her words. But not quite.

Eyes still locked with hers, Reiter moved yet another step closer then brushed aside a strand of hair that had fallen over her eye.

Katia held perfectly still.

"Did you know that your left eyebrow twitches when you're upset?" He tucked the hair behind her ear.

It took everything she had not to jerk beneath the impact of his soft touch. He was using familiar tricks against her, but she knew this role well. She'd worn it like a protective shield when she'd accepted the company of some of the vilest men in Germany in order to gather valuable information for the British.

The fact that Friedrich Reiter's blatant attempt to throw her off balance was working shifted the power in his favor. "Hermann Schmidt will not be a threat to our mission. I give you my word."

She was not surprised when he closed his hand around her arm. She was surprised, however, that his grip was gentle. In contrast, a rough warning filled his gaze before he released her.

He'd made his point.

"I trust no one's word, Katarina." No longer playing the role of seducer, his cold-eyed regard slid over her. "And I take nothing on faith. I believe only in my well honed ability to see through a lie."

With the steel in his voice and the military glare in his eyes, she almost buckled. *Almost.*

This man was formidable.

In spite of the pounding of her heart and the bead of sweat that slid between her shoulder blades, she had to stay focused. It helped to remember that without her, there was no mission.

"Well tonight, Herr Reiter, you are misreading the signs."

The air grew tight and heavy between them. His gaze turned harsher, deadlier, the layers of polish peeling away to reveal a cold, merciless man.

But was the transformation real or just another act? Either way, she recognized the strategy of a back-alley brawler when she saw it. If this spy expected to intimidate her with his act, he was in for a disappointment.

Jerking her chin, she swept out of his reach and began roaming through the room. Step by step, she discarded her gloves, her coat and finally her hat.

On her second pass, she strolled within inches of him, proving to them both she was back in control of her nerves.

Obviously unaware of her internal struggle, he dropped into the wingback chair closest to him and flicked on a nearby lamp. Relaxing, he watched her in a very masculine way that sent her pulse skipping fast and hard through her veins. He played this game well.

"You seem to be making yourself comfortable," she said.

He gave her a crooked grin. The gesture transformed his features, making him look almost upright. Trustworthy. Decent?

Games inside games. Secrets inside secrets. How she hated the intrigue of espionage.

A jolt of weariness struck her then, making her feel hollow with an unfortunate mixture of exhaustion and doubt. She was not overly fond of the sensation.

"You might as well sit," he said, indicating the chair facing him. "This could take a while."

Knowing he was right, that the sooner they discussed their mission the better, she cleared her expression and sank into the offered seat.

Before she could settle in, his demeanor turned all business. "Tell me how you know Schmidt?"

Katia gripped the arms of the chair until her knuckles turned white from the tension. She was growing more than a little irritated by the spy's lack of faith in her. *She* was the one with far too much to lose, while he would be free of this tyrannical country in a matter of days. "Hermann Schmidt is a friend of my mother's. End of story."

"How close are they?" he asked. *Asked.* Not demanded. Oh, no, nothing so crude. Had he demanded an answer from her, she would have known how to respond. But now, she was…confused. This cunning spy had his own repertoire of schemes and tricks.

With another sigh, she folded her hands in her lap and settled into their polite clash of wills. She decided to answer with the truth. "They are to be married shortly."

"When did they become engaged?" Although his expression never changed, his voice dropped to a low, hypnotizing timbre.

Nearly seduced by the soothing tone, dangerously so, Katia barely managed to keep from gritting her teeth. She wasn't used to handling a man this clever with his words, or this cunning with his voice. "I don't see the point—"

"When?"

She could feel the anger in him now. This interrogation had moved to a more hostile place.

Very well.

Katia knew exactly what to do with male anger. "I don't know, precisely." She spread just the hint of a pout across her lips. "They only told me the happy news this evening."

Happy news? Rage flowed through her at the ridiculous notion. The Russian Revolution had already stolen her father. And now the evil Nazi regime had its claws in her mother.

Memories of her dead father swept across her mind, coming stronger than usual tonight. No matter how illogical, she couldn't stop torturing herself over her failure in Russia.

She'd been too small, too insignificant to challenge the revolutionists. She had prayed, though. Without ceasing. For one full year.

God had remained silent.

By the age of nine, Katia had stopped praying altogether. She hadn't spoken to her Heavenly Father since.

With the hollowness returning to her stomach, Katia curled her hand into a tight fist. Never again would she count on an absent God who remained silent at her most desperate hours. Katarina Kerensky would do whatever it took to ensure her mother was spared the same fate as her father.

"You're upset by your mother's choice of husbands."

The unexpected softness in Reiter's voice had Katia shaking her head to keep her mind focused. She could handle his suspicion and distrust. She could even handle his subtle attempts at seduction—those were all part of the game they played—but this…this…*understanding?* It unnerved her.

"My thoughts on the matter are of no consequence." She spoke in a detached, unemotional tone. "The choice is hers to make."

"Nevertheless, you would have chosen differently for her."

There was that hideous compassion again. Open, honest and very real. Another game? A trap? "We are through with this topic. My mother has nothing to do with our current mission."

He opened his mouth to speak then shut it again and nodded. "Perhaps you're right. However, Hermann Schmidt—"

"Is my problem."

The spy's expression changed with the speed of a torpedo bearing down on its target. No longer relaxed, eyes hard, he sat coiled like a snake ready to strike. "Let's talk straight, shall we?"

"And here I thought we were."

Ignoring the interruption, he rose and moved to tower over her. "I've been given the task of stopping a Nazi naval secret weapon. Now pay close attention, Katarina. Imagine my shock when I meet my German contact at the assigned time, and a high-ranking officer in the *Kriegsmarine* shows up, as well."

"Mere coincidence, nothing more."

A dangerous glint flashed in his eyes. Katia tried not to squirm under his scrutiny. She wanted to stand, to move away from his ugly suspicion, but he blocked the path by crouching down in front of her.

"Coincidence?" He contained his energy well, but she knew he could strike at any moment. "There is no such thing."

She would not show fear. She would not draw away. She would go on the offensive instead. "Aren't you overreacting just a bit?"

"I call it being cautious." He leaned forward, stealing

nearly all of the space between them. "Will your mother's fiancé interfere with our mission?"

She knew he was crowding her on purpose, trying to intimidate her with his superior size.

The game was all about power now. *This* was a game she knew how to play, and how to win. "Choose whatever you wish to believe. I admit I am unhappy about my mother's impending marriage, but you must trust that I will handle Hermann Schmidt directly."

With a snort of disgust, he pushed away from her and returned to the chair he'd occupied a few moments earlier.

She started to explain, to clarify the situation for them both, but he cut her off with a hand in the air. "Is he one of your informants?"

It was an understandable question, one he had every right to ask. One she would answer truthfully.

"No." She held the pause for effect, gaining control from his surprised expression. "Hermann is simply my mother's fiancé, a man who hates the Communists as much as she does."

Reiter slowly sat back and steepled his fingers. "I see."

Unfortunately, Katia was afraid this man saw far too much. Would he prove more of a problem than Hermann Schmidt? Katia could barely contain a wave of terror at the thought.

But no matter how afraid she was, she would not give in to any outward sign of vulnerability.

Not until she was alone.

Blinking away her emotions, she lifted her chin. "Finish with your questions, Herr Reiter. You're fortunate. I find I am in an obliging mood, after all."

A single eyebrow lifted. "How do you plan to 'handle' your mother and her fiancé?"

In an attempt to gather her thoughts, she looked at the

open window on her left. A light breeze joined in a ghostly waltz with the sheer curtains. The scent of coming snow shivered in the air, promising a thin coat of white by morning.

"I'll know more when I meet them tomorrow morning." Some unnamed emotion rose up. She shoved it back with a hard swallow. "They are picking me up at 0900."

"That's going to be a problem."

"Not if—"

"I go the rest of the way alone." The lethal expression in Reiter's eyes was enough to make even the bravest woman quiver in fear. She held his stare anyway, knowing that he was waiting to see what impact his declaration would have. She waited to see how long he would wait for her.

Games inside games.

The deceit and smoky undercurrents were growing with every tick of the clock.

Another minute passed.

And then another.

At last, Reiter broke the silence. "Tell me where the blueprints are hidden and I'll be out of your life forever."

"That won't be possible. You need me with you."

"You won't be available. You have a future stepfather to entertain." His voice was very soft. Very dangerous.

"You don't understand," she insisted. "You *need* me."

His eyes narrowed. "Why you?"

She didn't move, didn't breathe, afraid if she did she would break down and blurt out too much information. Keeping her secret to herself kept her and her mother alive. "Since I'm the one with the intelligence, you have no other choice than to rely on me."

His eyebrows slammed together. "In other words, if I don't allow you to come along, you won't tell me where the plans are hidden."

"That about sums it up."

"Are you trying to blackmail me, Kerensky?"

"Yes." But he didn't need to know why.

"An honest answer at last," he said, an odd hint of approval in his gaze.

His reaction threw her off balance. *Again.* What was she supposed to do with him now?

"Go ahead." He gestured for her to continue speaking. "You might as well tell me the rest, the part you're intentionally hiding from me."

She pretended to misunderstand him. "I don't know what you mean."

He simply looked at her.

She held perfectly still, dreading the obvious question to come. *Was she a Jew?*

But he surprised her once again.

"Tell me, Katarina," he drawled. "Why don't the British trust you?"

Chapter Five

Three. Four.

Five.

Jack counted each emotion that flashed in Kerensky's eyes. Up to this point, she'd proven herself inventive, bold and cunning, all necessary qualities for a spy. But in the soft moonlight, with so many emotions running across her face, she looked fragile, and surprisingly vulnerable.

In spite of Jack's distrust, a cold chill of fear for her took hold. If she *were* working for the British, which all the signs indicated, then she was playing a dangerous game with her life.

Why take the risk?

Jack had personally witnessed the hideous forms of torture the SS used to get answers. He'd watched in steely silence as the toughest men were utterly destroyed under the perfect blend of physical pressure and mental interrogation. The experience had cost him his soul. A reality he'd long since accepted, or at least lived with as atonement for his sins.

But now, as weariness kicked in, he didn't know if he could watch this woman suffer the Nazis' ruthless brand of interrogation. Unless, of course, she was working against him. Even then…he wasn't so sure.

The woman confused him. She made him want to return to simpler times, when the love of a sovereign God was concrete in his mind. When Jack had dealt with situations beyond his control by tapping into the knowledge that the Lord was bigger than any circumstance man could create.

But that was a long time ago, a lifetime ago.

Jack knew better than to take anything for granted, especially the actions of a trained professional.

Still on his guard, he gave Kerensky a look a few degrees short of friendly and continued waiting her out.

One beat, two beats, three.

At last, she broke. "The British don't," she began as she sucked in a harsh breath, "they don't trust me?"

Her reaction pleased him. The bitter resentment in her tone meant he'd actually shocked her. He had the upper hand now. Though he doubted she would accept the shift in power for long.

In his years as a spy, he'd never met a woman who could hold her own against him. Before Kerensky. Her determination was as forceful as his. For that alone, his gut told him to take a chance and trust her to do her share in the mission.

He restrained himself.

Until he discovered if she was an ally or a shrewd double agent he would not relax his guard.

"Look, Kerensky." He pushed to his feet. "Let's rid ourselves of this ridiculous power struggle and get on with the business at hand."

In response to his frankness, her composure slipped just a bit, but not enough to give Jack a sense of her real motives.

She was good. Very, very good.

With practiced grace, she stood and then paced through the small, stylishly furnished room. "If what you say is true and the British don't trust me, then it must be because they know about my...my mistake."

Her voice hitched. Part of her act? Probably. "What sort of mistake?" he asked.

Before responding, she roamed through a set of double doors with a liquid elegance that spoke of her stage training. Jack followed her, taking special note of how she gained immediate confidence once she had the physical barrier of an antique wooden table between them.

"It's not what you think," she said.

He willed himself to remain calm. In his line of work, losing his temper got a man killed faster than bullets. "It never is."

"You don't have to be snide. The information I gave MI6 was correct." She dropped her gaze to the table, drew a path of circles with her fingernail. "At least, it was at the time I sent it."

"Of course."

She slapped her palms on the table and leaned forward. "Your attitude is not helping matters."

"Nor is your penchant for withholding valuable pieces of information."

Head held high, she marched around the table and stopped long enough to let out a soft sniff of disapproval before she continued past him.

Keeping the woman in his sight, Jack trailed after her as she went back into the adjoining room and turned to face him. Folding his arms across his chest, he leaned against the doorjamb.

Neither said a word, each silently assessing the other. Jack considered the tactical scenarios and possible outcomes. The only wrong questions were the ones he didn't ask. "My patience is wearing thin. What mistake did you make, Katarina?"

Regardless of the flicker of uncertainty in her eyes, she held his gaze. Brave woman.

"Karl Doenitz moved his headquarters this morning."

Jack dragged a hand through his hair and resisted the urge to let loose the string of obscenities that came to mind. "How very inconvenient for us all. Except, of course, for the Nazis."

"Now you're being paranoid."

"I was trained to be paranoid." He drilled her with a hard glare. "And I'm very good at my job."

She sighed. "I realize this sounds bad, but Karl Doenitz is still in Wilhelmshaven. He's moved from Marinestation to Sengwarden."

Jack caught the quick, guilty glance from under her lowered lashes. "Which means you don't know where the plans are any longer."

"I—"

"This trip to Hamburg has been a waste," he said, more to himself than her. "For nothing more than countless hours of...*games*."

"Oh, I promise you, this is no game. I know where the plans are. It's just—" She broke off and looked away from him.

"It's...just?" he prompted with what he considered heroic patience.

Apparently, he could control the work, the decisions, even the risks. He could not, however, control this... *woman*.

"The plans are locked in a newly built cabinet. My key will only open the old one."

"That's it?" Jack had to resist the urge to laugh in relief. "That was your mistake?"

He'd dealt with worse. Much worse. Missions were always more complicated than they first appeared on paper. Real life had intricacies that tended to create a powder keg of unexpected problems.

"Are you just going to stand there staring at me?" she demanded. "Didn't you hear what I said?"

"I heard. You gave the British outdated information."

"I gave them *wrong* information. I never get it wrong. Never."

"Until now."

She inclined her head slightly, her expression giving nothing away. "Until now."

"So we make a new plan."

He didn't add that this was just the sort of tangle that had first led him into the heart of Germany two years before—the type of unexpected twist that ruled his every move. Disorder was so much a part of who he'd become, he'd long since accepted the realities of living without certainty. He didn't especially like the ambiguity of never knowing the outcome of a mission or when the next twist would come, but he bore the pressure with steely grit.

He had no other choice.

"Make a new plan," she repeated. "It's that simple for you?"

"Nothing is ever simple."

In fact, the possibilities were endless, but Jack was exceptionally skilled at finding the perfect solution inside the less perfect ones. "Tell me exactly where the plans are and I'll come up with an idea. Or better yet, get me some paper and something to write with. I think better with a pen in my hand."

She sank into a chair with an uncharacteristic lack of grace. "There is one more complication you should know about."

Jack felt like he was free-falling without a parachute. His tight control over dangerous emotions was slipping, and that made him furious. Nothing shook him, and no one caught him by surprise. Even when the real Friedrich Reiter had come to kill him, Jack had kept his wits about him enough to prevail in the deadly clash. There'd been no time for prayer, no begging the Lord for assistance, just reflex.

And now…here…with this woman…he was in another situation where his control was being tested.

Enough. The feminine manipulation ended now. "Let's have it," he said, pure reflex guiding his words. "*All* of it."

"As you wish." Narrowing those glorious eyes of hers, she jumped up and planted a hand on her hip. "The admiral keeps the key to the cabinet on a ring he carries with him at all times, except when he sleeps. Whereby, he sets the key chain on the nightstand by his bed."

The roll in Jack's gut came fast and slick, surprising him. He didn't take the time to analyze the emotion behind the sensation. "And you know this how?"

Taking three steps toward him, Kerensky pursed her lips and patted his cheek. "That's my business, darling."

He grabbed her wrist. "Not if it's going to endanger my life."

"Which it won't." She dropped a withering glare to his hand, waited until he released her. "Now, back to what I was saying. Since I alone know where the key is located, all I have to do is sneak into the room while Doenitz is asleep and—"

"No." Whoever went in that building had to respond instantly if discovered. Jack was the trained killer. She was simply a mole who gathered information. He was the obvious person for the job. "*I* will break into the admiral's private quarters."

Her smile turned ruthless, deadly. The change in her

put him instantly at ease. They were finally playing on his level.

He smiled back at her, his grin just as ruthless, just as deadly as hers.

She appeared unfazed.

"Here's the situation, Herr Reiter, and do try to pay close attention. There are only two ways into Admiral Doenitz's quarters. Through the front door or through a small window into his bedroom."

The thrill of finding a solution had Jack rubbing his hands together. "Now we're getting somewhere."

"The window leading into the admiral's room is small." She dropped her gaze down to his shoes and back up again. "Far too small for you."

"Then I'll go through the front door."

She was shaking her head before he finished speaking. "To get through the front door you would have to pass through six separate stations, with two guards each. They rotate from post to post on twenty-minute intervals, none of which are synchronized. Translation, that's a minimum of six men you would have to bypass at any given time."

"It's what I do."

She flicked a speck of dust off her shoulder. "Needlessly risky. Especially when I can get through the window and back out again in less time than a single rotation."

Jack's mind filed through ideas, discarded most, kept a few, recalculated.

"I'll ultimately have to get past those guards the night I go in for the plans," he said.

More thoughts shifted. New ideas crystallized, further calculations were made.

"I'll just take the key and the plans all at once." He blessed her with a look of censure, testing her with his words as much as with his attitude. "Translation: we go to Wilhelmshaven tonight and finish the job in one stroke."

She jabbed her finger at his chest. "You're thinking too much like a man. Go in, blow things up, deal with the risks tomorrow."

"Not even close." If anything, Jack overworked his solutions before acting on them. It was the one shred of humanity he had left.

"Two nights from now Karl Doenitz will be in Hamburg, at a party given for him by my mother." She raised her hand to keep him from interrupting. "And before you say it, that also means the key will be with him in Hamburg, as well."

"Keep talking while you get the paper I asked for."

She remained exactly where she was. *Naturally.*

"Here's how it's going to work," she said. "I get an impression of the key tonight, make a copy tomorrow, then go back the evening of the party and photograph the plans."

"Why not just steal the plans tonight and be done with it?"

"And alert the Nazis that the British have discovered their secret weapon? No." She shook her head. "We need to photograph the plans when no one is around and replace them exactly as we found them."

Her plan had a simplicity to it that just might work.

"And while I'm inside Doenitz's private quarters," she continued, "you get to do what men do best."

"And that is?"

"Protect my back."

If Jack didn't let his ego take over, he could see that her idea had possibilities. Perhaps, under all the layers of subterfuge, they thought alike. Maybe too much alike.

The woman was proving smart enough and brave enough that if he let down a little of his guard he might begin to admire her. Too risky. Emotional attachments, of any kind, were a spy's greatest threat. Especially when he had no real reason to trust his partner.

"Your plan has merit," he said. "But I only have two more days to get the plans and return to England. With the timeline you presented, there's no room for mistakes."

She nodded. "Then we make no mistakes."

"We? Haven't you forgotten something?"

Her brows drew together. "No, I'm pretty sure I've thought through all the details."

"Your mother is throwing the party for the admiral. Your attendance at such an illustrious occasion will be expected. How are you going to pull off the last of our two trips to Wilhelmshaven while at a cocktail party in Hamburg?"

Her expression closed. "I'll handle my mother. She won't even miss me."

"And her fiancé? Somehow, I doubt he'll be so…inattentive."

"I'll deal with him, as well."

He gave her a doubtful glare.

"You're going to have to trust me."

Trust. It always came back to trust. But Jack had lost that particular quality, along with his faith in God, the same night the real Reiter had come for his blood.

"And if you're caught tonight?" he asked in a deceptively calm voice.

"I won't be."

"*If* you are."

She lifted her chin, looking every bit a woman with royal blood running through her veins. "Failure is never an option."

Jack's sentiments exactly.

If he took out the personal elements running thick

between them and ignored the fact that Kerensky was a woman—a woman he couldn't completely trust—not only could her plan work, but it had a very high probability of success.

Her voice broke through his thoughts. "It's getting late. The drive to Wilhelmshaven will take almost two hours each way."

He glanced at his watch, looked at her evening gown and jewels then down at his own tuxedo. "We both need to change."

"Yes. We'll take my car, which is still at the theater." Which they both knew was only three blocks from her home.

"Right, then. We'll meet outside the theater at—" he began before he checked his watch again "—0130 hours. I trust that suits you?"

Head high, she moved to the front door and jerked it open without looking back at him. "Of course."

He reached around her and swung the door shut with a bang.

She spun about to glare at him. "What are you doing?"
Reminding us both who's in control.

With nothing showing on his face, he angled his forearm against the wall above her head and waited until her eyes lifted to his. "I leave the way I came."

She took a hard breath but held his gaze. For an instant, he was struck again by her determination and courage.

The back of his throat began to burn.

"Then I drive," she said without blinking.

"By all means." He pushed away and headed toward the open window, but then he surprised them both by returning to her and cupping her cheek. "I'm warning you now, Katarina. At the first sign of trouble, we abort. No questions asked."

"Whatever you say, Herr Reiter." The mutinous light in her eyes ruined any pretense of compliance on her part.

Jack sensed he was in serious trouble with this woman. He had to get matters back in his control. "One more thing," he said.

She angled her head at him.

"Make sure you dress warmly." He shifted to the window, dipped and then swung his leg over the ledge. "It's going to be a long, chilly night."

Chapter Six

The drive to Wilhelmshaven began in silence, and continued that way for most of the journey. Sitting in the passenger's seat, Jack surveyed the passing landscape. There was no horizon, no clear distinction between land and sky, just an inky blend of dark and darker. An occasional shadow slid out of the night, only to retreat as they sped by. Wind shrieked through the invisible slits of the car's windows.

Concentrating on the road, Kerensky drove cautiously, with both hands on the wheel. She hadn't looked at Jack since they'd left the city limits of Hamburg. Which was just as well. Between the poor quality of the road and the poorer quality of the car's headlights, driving required her undivided attention.

He took the opportunity to study her out of the corner of his eye. She was dressed head to toe in black wool. Black pants, black sweater, black gloves—the perfect ensemble for blending with the night. She'd slicked her thick, fiery hair off her face and twisted it into an intricate braid that hung halfway down her back.

He could almost feel the vibration of her carefully contained energy. Like a sleek, untamed animal poised for a fight.

She baffled him, tugged at him. She had a face meant for the movies and was so lovely his chest ached every time he looked at her. But he also knew how much depth lay below that exquisite surface.

Never once had he caught a hint of the corruption or selfishness that drove most spies. His instincts told him that she had her own personal agenda for working with the British. Those same instincts also told him that her motivation was connected to a dark secret she kept well hidden from the world.

He understood all about dark secrets and hidden motives, as well as the moral confusion that came from lying and stealing every day. For too many years, Jack had relinquished his Christian integrity—*no,* his very soul—to carry out other men's agendas. German. American. What did it matter if he was Jack Anderson, Friedrich Reiter, or someone else entirely? One face, two names, no identity. Those were the legacies the bureaucrats had created for him.

Now this woman, with her strength and determination, made him think beyond the mindless killing machine he'd become. She made him toy with the idea of a future beyond the war. He suddenly wanted something…more. More than hate. More than vengeance. Something that went beyond his own humanity.

Worst of all, the woman made him hope for a better world, where belief in God meant something beyond a faded memory.

This was the wrong business to feel emotions, *any* emotion, especially ones that made him soft toward a woman.

"You're too beautiful," he blurted out.

She whipped her head around so their gazes met in the dim light.

She gave a deep sigh of frustration before returning her attention to the road. "It's called *heredity*."

Heredity. Right. The word tugged at a thought hovering in the back of his mind. Jack forced himself to remember he was having this conversation for her benefit. "Your beauty could be used against you." He'd seen it often enough.

"Or to my advantage. Lucky for you, there's more to me than a pretty face." She sounded weary, as though she'd given this speech countless times before.

Jack wasn't impressed. He was responsible for keeping them both alive. He had to be able to predict her behavior and gauge what she would do if she ended up in a crisis. "This mission depends on your quick reflexes and ability to think on your feet. For at least five minutes you'll be alone inside the *Kriegsmarine* headquarters."

"I'll only need three."

He did his best not to react to her bravado. "Wrong attitude. You can't be impatient. Impatient equals careless. And careless equals one dead female spy."

A nerve flexed in her jaw. "Have I given you the impression that I'm stupid?"

"One mistake is all it takes."

"It won't be mine."

She returned to clenching her teeth.

He returned to holding on to his temper.

"Fancy words, Kerensky. Will you be able to back them up?"

He didn't know her well enough to judge for himself. And for five long minutes he would be unable to control the situation, unable to protect her if Admiral Doenitz awakened. Jack knew she was hiding something from him. And he thought he knew exactly what it was. *Heredity.*

If he was right, the woman could not be caught. Ever.

He knew what they would do to her, where they would send her.

No emotion. He reminded himself of his personal motto that kept him alive. *Nothing personal.*

Who was he kidding? "How much Jewish blood runs in your veins?"

Her sharp intake of air was barely audible, but he'd heard it all the same. Already knowing the answer, he found himself holding his breath, waiting for her response to his bold question with a mixture of dread and hope. When she held to her silence, he wondered if he might have been wrong in his assessment.

Jack Anderson was never wrong. "How much?"

Her hands tensed on the wheel, the only sign of her agitation. Making a soft sound of irritation, she adjusted herself with a swoosh of wool against leather. "We do not speak of these things in Germany. We do not even whisper them in the dark confines of a car."

He had no easy response. She was right, of course. Even if she was only part Jewish she could not reveal such a secret to him.

No emotion, he reminded himself again. *Nothing personal.*

"Consider the subject closed," he said.

She locked her gaze with his for a full heartbeat, two. Three. Then she began a very slow, very thorough once-over of him. Since the road ahead of them was long and straight, he sat perfectly still under her perusal. He owed her that much at least.

Eventually, she turned her head back to the road. "We're nearly there. Soon, this will all be a distant memory for us both."

Jack took a hard breath. He wished he could ignore the risks of going through the front door with nothing more than a loaded gun. This would be a good time for prayer, if he was still a praying man. "Are you sure I won't fit through the window?"

She snatched her eyes off the road, looked at his chest and then shook her head. "You won't."

Her voice sounded strong, confident, but she looked bleak. And her hands shook slightly.

Was she having second thoughts? Had he thrown her off balance by accusing her of being a Jew?

He knew touching her was a bad idea. *Don't do it,* he told himself. *She is not a harmless female. Not this one.*

He ignored his own warning and reached out, lightly fingering a lock of hair that had come loose from her braid.

She took a shuddering breath.

He dropped his hand. "I don't like the idea of sending you in there alone."

Her shoulders stiffened and all signs of her distress disappeared. "We've been through this already. I'm going into that room, end of discussion."

"What discussion?" he muttered.

She flipped him a smug look. "Exactly."

"Careful, Kerensky." Jack jammed a hand through his hair. "You're treading on razor-thin ice with me."

She bared her teeth. "Good thing I'm light on my feet."

"You're a difficult woman."

"So I've been told." She cleared her expression and pointed ahead of her. "Look up there, on your right. The harbor."

In the next instant, before he could stop her, she swung the car down a dark alley and cut the engine.

The night swallowed them, pitching the interior of the car into blinding darkness. A hot, nagging itch settled in his gut.

Unable to make out anything other than a heavy nothingness, Jack squinted into the eerie gloom. Still…*nothing*.

A sudden blast of anger left his nerves raw.

It was too dark. Too remote.

Too isolated.

He'd allowed Kerensky to park the car facing toward the back of the alley. If an ambush awaited them, there would be no getting out alive.

Very, *very* stupid.

He touched the panel in his sweater where he'd sewn a cyanide pill into the stitching. Trained to choose death over revealing secrets, Jack Anderson knew his duty. He'd seen men with stronger convictions break. He'd seen innocent men break, too. Jack would not join their ranks. Too many lives were at stake. The Nazis could never be allowed to get to the information he had stored in his head.

Suicide was the only solution. His own damnation was well worth the lives he would save with his permanent silence.

Tonight, however, there was a woman's life at stake. He would make sure the choice between disclosure and death never happened. Jack would do what he must to ensure the cyanide pill made it through another mission unused.

"Turn the car facing out," he said, his voice flat and hard.

"What?"

"Either do what I say, or I do it myself."

"I…" She shifted in her seat, then sighed. "Of course. I wasn't thinking." Her voice held a slight shake, as though she'd stunned herself with her thoughtless behavior.

Another act? Or was she still upset over their conversation about her "heredity"? Upset enough to make a mistake in the admiral's room, as well?

Before he could question her, she started the engine and

put the car in gear. Jack stayed planted in his seat as she made quick work of the direction change.

Once she threw the brake, a thin bar of light from a nearby streetlight slid across the front of the car's hood.

Better.

"Do you want to go over the hand signals one last time?" he asked, relief making his voice softer.

"No." She cut the engine again, tapped her temple two times. "Got it all in here."

Jack plucked the keys out of her hand before she could pocket them.

"What are you doing?" she growled.

Hardheaded, inflexible, full of pride. Did everything have to be a battle with her?

"You can't carry these with you." He jingled the keys in front of her nose. "Too much noise. And if you're caught or hurt or any number of possibilities, I'll need to be able to drive the car out of here."

She opened her mouth to argue. Again.

He merely looked at her.

Her snort was quick and full of wounded pride. "It must be quite a burden, being perfect all the time."

"You have no idea."

"Humble, too."

He ignored her goading. "Details are the most important aspect of any mission. Forget just one and a man *or*—" he gave her a meaningful look "—a woman will end up dead before there's a chance to rethink the situation."

"So you're the detail man." A statement, not a question.

Jack allowed himself a smile. "For better or worse, Kerensky, tonight we're a team. You might as well accept it."

And so should you, he told himself, as he tucked the keys underneath the driver's seat. "Let's go."

Nodding, she picked up the black knit cap sitting on

the seat next to her and began tucking her braid into it. Her eyes took on the excited gleam of a child's at Christmas. "Curtain up."

Such eagerness to get the job done, such conviction. I remember feeling that once, a lifetime ago, Jack thought.

Where did my convictions go? When did they go? The answer was simple enough. The day the Nazis sent the real Friedrich Reiter to kill him.

Lord, he started to pray, then cut himself off. This was a time for action, not a time for useless prayer that would bring no immediate help to the mission.

Jack gave Kerensky a sharp nod. "Let's go."

As one, they climbed out of the car and snapped shut their respective doors without making a sound.

A few steps and the cloak of the alley's gloom lifted. Icy damp air hit Jack's face as it sliced off the sea. Sand and wet leaves waltzed around his ankles and clung.

Kerensky repositioned her hat. Jack took a moment to check his weapon, a 9 mm Luger P08—the most effective German handgun available. He examined the magazine, a simple eight-round in-line box, and then clicked the safety mechanism in place.

Kerensky's eyes lingered on his gun's tip. "Do you really think that's necessary?"

"You don't?"

She took a steadying breath. "I—"

"This isn't make-believe, Katarina. And I won't give false assurances. Get that straight right now. Bad guys with guns are out there." He hitched his shoulder toward the harbor.

Dragging her eyes away from his weapon, she looked at him dead-on. "And you always go in prepared. Is that it?"

"Exactly."

She didn't argue the point further. "I understand."

He placed a hand on her shoulder. "No heroics. We abort at the first sign of trouble."

"Right."

Without another word, she turned on her heel and set out at a clipped pace. Jack let her walk exactly three steps before he reached out and stopped her again. "Remember, Admiral Doenitz will be in that room tonight. Sleeping. We do this quietly."

The intense green eyes that met his were level and clear. "I'm a cat. He won't know I'm there."

As she headed out again, Jack went into automatic mode. He memorized their route. Keeping the harbor always on his left, buildings on his right.

Stop. Gauge. Check bearings. Move on.

Again and again, he kept to the pattern as Kerensky wove them toward their destination. She led him along six streets, each thirty-eight strides long. On the seventh road they moved onto an open sidewalk lining a small park, passing four squat, identical stone buildings.

Kerensky stopped moving at the corner of the eighth street. She looked to her left, then to her right. Darting across an alley, she flattened against the closest wall.

Motioning with two fingers, she indicated the building on her left. The two-story structure was made of colorless granite and stood guard over the drab waters that led into the North Sea.

Closing the distance, Jack mouthed a warning. *No mistakes.*

Grimacing, she clamped a hand on his arm and folded him deeper into the shadows with her. She then gestured to the impossibly small window above their heads. Silently measuring the dimensions, Jack admitted to himself that she'd been correct. He'd never fit through the tiny opening.

Unfortunately, she would.

No second chances. No margin for error.
No turning back.
The mission was under way.

Chapter Seven

Although the stingy moon gave a mere suggestion of cold, pale light, Katia could still make out the expression on Friedrich Reiter's face. Grim. Resolute. She didn't need much imagination to know he considered her completely unsuitable for the task that lay before them. She could practically hear his mind working, gauging, assessing.

She couldn't fault him for his skepticism. With his unexpected question about her Jewish blood, he'd nearly thrown her off balance enough to make her as inept as his silent accusation claimed.

How could he have guessed her secret? And in so little time? Had she given herself away? The thought scared her beyond reason and she experienced an irrational urge to cry. With one simple question, Reiter had turned Katarina Kerensky into an amateur.

And now Friedrich Reiter had all the advantage. Which was too deadly to contemplate.

Remembering her mother, and all they had to lose if Katia allowed anyone or anything to distract her, she pulled out her most effective weapon—a sultry smile.

Reiter's expression remained implacable.

The man was a rock, the personification of cold, chilly

calm. Katia could probably learn from his technique. In fact, next to him, she felt like a bit player in a second-rate theater company.

As he continued to stare at her with unyielding eyes, her stomach flipped inside itself. She rubbed a hand over her belly, afraid the knots were there to stay.

At least for the rest of the evening.

Tapping his watch, Reiter pulled her attention back to the mission. He held up five fingers, silently reminding her that he would give her no more than the allotted time to get the job done once she was inside Doenitz's room.

She inclined her head in a brief nod.

A corner of his lips lifted in a sarcastic twist as he made a stirrup with his hands and crouched low. When she hesitated, he elbowed her to get moving.

Sighing, she kicked off her shoes, planted one foot in his cupped palms and placed her hands on his wide shoulders. For a second longer she merely stared into his eyes. In that beat of silence, something unnamable passed between them. Something that sent a shiver of foreboding up the back of her neck.

This man was not like the rest. He was pure danger, yet he was also a man she needed on her side.

Acutely aware of the hard muscles bunching under her fingertips, Katia was instantly reminded of her vulnerability, that she carried a dark secret underneath all the layers of acting and subterfuge. For a brief moment, she had the dangerous sensation of wanting to lean her head on those broad shoulders and let Friedrich Reiter carry her burdens for a while.

A normal reaction, she told herself, considering the stress she was under and the unwanted reminder of all she had to lose. Still, she had to stifle any further weakness—especially of the feminine kind—if she wanted to concentrate on the job she had to do.

Tonight there could be no mistakes.

At Reiter's impatient grunt, she shoved off the ground and pivoted in his hands. With a quick push, he lifted her toward the windowsill above her head.

Fully exposed now, the wind slipped icy fingers of cold and wet below the neck of her sweater. The breath rushed out of her lungs, but she steadied herself by flattening her palms against the wall in front of her.

Breathe, Katia. Focus on one task at a time.

Unable to see much in the dim light of the moon, she used her sense of touch to guide her. Careful to keep her movements slow and silent, she clung to the ledge with one hand, tested the latch of the window with the other. The rough metal gave way under her gentle push.

Luck was finally on her side. She knew Reiter would scoff at the sentiment. He didn't seem like a man who would rely on anything other than cold, hard logic.

She could use some of his sharp focus right now. It was times like these she just wanted…out.

But then what? Leave her mother in Germany, in the clutches of a man like Hermann Schmidt?

Unthinkable.

Convinced once more, Katia pushed the window forward another few inches, gripped the ledge with both hands and pulled herself up.

Precise and whisper quiet, each movement made with careful purpose, she inched past the windowsill. One last push from Reiter and she was through the window. She twisted midfall and landed on the floor with a soundless thud.

The window slid shut behind her.

No turning back now.

Blinking, she did a quick visual scan of the room, but was unable to see past her nose. She debated whether to take a step forward or wait in frozen immobility until her eyes adjusted to the darkness. Choosing the latter, she put her other senses to work.

Her ears picked up soft snoring coming from the other side of the room, slightly to her left. The scent of salt and sea and musk filled her nose. The smell wasn't unpleasant, exactly, just...strong.

As the inky gloom turned to a muted gray, Katia slowly reached to her left. Her hand connected with a large dresser. She blinked several more times, finally able to distinguish the dark shapes of the furniture from the shadows cast throughout the room.

She flicked a glance to her right, counted two additional, smaller dressers. A washbasin was perched on a table off to her left. The expected bedside table sat next to a small bed that contained a lump buried under a blanket.

Doenitz.

The sight of the sleeping admiral had her shifting a couple inches to her left. Caught between impatience and fear, her natural reflex was to rush her steps in order to get away from the man as quickly as possible. But she forced herself to think of Doenitz as a nameless, faceless blob, rather than a decorated admiral with enough power to kill her on the spot if he awoke.

She wondered if she would feel this strong aversion to him if she didn't know who—and what—he was. Now was not the time to ponder such a question.

One minute down.

And counting.

The floor beneath her stocking feet sparkled in the dim moonlight. Someone had obviously taken the trouble to polish it on a regular basis.

Admiral Karl Doenitz was as fastidious as the rumors claimed.

It was a good reminder for her to touch nothing or, at the very least, to put everything back in its precise place if she did.

Edging closer to the bed, she saw that the key ring was exactly where she'd been told it would be.

Her source was as reliable as ever.

Unfortunately, the intelligence hadn't been complete. She'd expected to find just one key, not four—*four!*

One minute, thirty.

Regardless of the ticking clock in her head, Katia took ten full seconds to simply stare at the key ring. *What now?* She didn't have enough wax to make an impression of all four keys. Nor the luxury of confirming her choice with the actual cabinet containing the plans.

That left her only one option.

Guess.

Doenitz chose that moment to grumble and shift in his sleep.

Katia dropped to her knees and melted into the shadows. As the cold heat of fear slammed through her, the air clogged in her throat, making it difficult to take a breath.

Turn your fear into action, she told herself. *Fear into action.*

Ah, but the fear wasn't going to settle so easily.

At least Reiter was just outside the window. The thought made her feel more confident. Safer.

She could do this.

Swallowing, she concentrated on slowing her heartbeat and waited patiently for Doenitz to relax back into his snoring.

After several very long, very tense seconds, the admiral's breathing found its rhythm again. On her hands and knees, Katia scooted forward and around to the right side of the bed. Reaching above her head, she clamped her fingers over the cold metal key ring.

Taking a quick inventory, she discovered that three of the keys were long, thin, with identical rounded tops. Just like…house keys?

The fourth was shorter, and fatter than the rest, just like—dare she hope—a cabinet key.

Yes. She nearly offered up a prayer of thanks. If she thought God was listening, she might have.

Instead, she dug in her pocket, pulled out the small box containing the special wax. Flipping open the lid with her thumb, she lifted the entire ring of keys and made the impression.

Three minutes down.

Careful to avoid making any sound, she set the keys back on the table and fanned them out in the same order as she'd found them.

Box in hand, she let out the breath she'd been holding. Backing slowly toward the window, she turned around at the last second and realized the window was too high for her to reach without assistance. She lifted her hands above her head, but found no ledge to use.

A chair sat just to her left, but was perched at an angle that wouldn't do. One small pull, a quick readjustment and the angle of the chair was right at last. Seconds later she was up and through the window, tumbling straight into Reiter's arms.

His warmth enveloped her.

Before that moment, she hadn't realized how cold she'd been inside Doenitz's room. Insanity overrode logic and she snuggled into Reiter, pressing her cheek against his broad shoulder. She took a shaky breath.

For a ghastly second, she wanted only to stay in the

shelter of his arms. Her fingers flexed against his chest, then relaxed.

His hard breathing was unmistakable, and she wondered if he was battling emotions anything close to the ones she was fighting.

She turned her head to look at him directly. His eyes, unblinking and very, very close, lit with a question. She lifted the box she still clutched in her hand, and then grinned like a fool.

He smiled down at her, his expression softening just enough to have her wonder if he had a bit of human blood running through his veins after all.

Before she had a chance to ponder the thought, he dumped her to the ground and tugged her around the corner. She barely had time to catch her balance and pocket the wax impression before he shoved her from behind. "Go, go, go."

She took off running in the direction in which they'd traveled earlier. One foot in front of the other. Legs pumping fast. Feet pounding faster. Cold wind slapped her face.

Run. Run. Run.

She heard Reiter closing in behind her, protecting her. The sensation gave her the courage to pick up the pace.

Three blocks later, he pulled her to a stop and yanked her into the shadows with him.

Handing her shoes back, he blessed her with a look of satisfaction. His smile gleamed in the moonlight.

He wasn't even breathing hard.

"Well done," he said. "You made it with a full minute to spare."

Still panting, she closed her eyes against an overwhelming desire to bask in his praise. "Nerves of steel."

A lie if ever she'd told one. A bead of sweat trickled

along her hairline, a sure sign of the stress she was trying to hold at bay.

She forced her breathing to slow, clamping down hard
on the string of hysterical laughs trying to bubble out of
her. Madame Levine would be pleased with her control.

At the thought of her former mentor, Katia's joy dis-
integrated. Would her mother be sent to a camp, as well?
Would Schmidt figure out their secret, as Reiter had done
so quickly in the car tonight? What if the U-boat captain
already knew? What if he had his own plans for them,
plans that included a trip to the camps?

There was so much at stake, so much to lose. So much—

"We're not safe yet," Reiter reminded her.

Fear scrambled to the surface. "I... I know."

If they were caught now, all their planning would have
been for nothing.

What if Katia was caught tonight? Would the Gestapo
come for her mother—not because of her secret heritage,
but because Katia had tried to fight them?

Elena would suffer unfairly for her daughter's actions.
Was she risking too much by helping the British? But what
else could Katia do? God had long since taken His hand off
Germany while too many sat back and did nothing. As a
result, Hitler's power had reached unstoppable proportions.

A surge of fear shimmied along the base of her spine.

She would not panic. She would not panic. She would
not—

"Stay focused, Katarina." Reiter took her chin in his
hand and gave her a long, measuring look. "Concentrate
on one thing at a time."

"Yes." She swallowed. "Of course."

"Let's get back to the car," he said.

"You have to let me go first."

"Right." He dropped his hand, his expression as unreadable as always. "Stick close."

"Like glue."

He took two steps then stopped and turned back to her. "No. I have a better idea."

With a casual shrug, he wrapped his arm around her shoulder and gently tugged her next to him. The gesture sealed them into a single unit. Subtle. Powerful.

Unnerving.

Katia struggled to think over the wild drumming of her pulse. She hadn't felt this safe since her father died. She distrusted the sensation completely. "What are you up to?"

His slow smile oozed charm and sophistication, creating an intimacy between them that quite simply scared her to death. It was then she realized what he had planned.

"From this moment on, we're a couple."

Under the circumstances, the tactic made perfect sense.

"We need to make this look good…" He lowered his voice to a caress. *"Darling."*

"I'm the trained actress," she reminded him. "Watch and learn from the professional."

She then gave him the kind of smile that usually scrambled men's brains.

He lifted his eyebrows in response. "Perhaps a bit obvious, Katarina. But you have the right idea."

"You want obvious?" She batted her eyelashes at him, and then trailed a fingertip along his jaw.

They stared at one another awhile longer, each breathing heavier than the situation warranted, but then they both laughed. The spontaneous gesture added the right touch of lightheartedness to the scene.

To an outside observer, they looked like two lovers sharing a long night of, well, whatever their imaginations wanted to dream up.

Playing it for all it was worth, Reiter continued looking at her in the way a man looked at the woman he loved.

The swift ache of loneliness came fast and hard. Reality came faster.

This was a ruse, she reminded herself.

They were spies. On a mission. Nothing more.

Get it straight, Katia.

"Lead the way, Herr Reiter," she said in a perfectly steady voice.

"By all means."

They walked arm in arm for three full blocks, the perfect picture of romantic bliss, but as they rounded the last corner, Reiter slowed his steps. And then…

The unmistakable grind of a hammer sliding into place rang in her ears.

"*Halt!* Or I'll shoot."

Chapter Eight

Jack froze.

Right here, right now, what he did next would determine all of their fates. His initial instinct was to turn and fight. But he made himself slow down, think offensively, and consider other options first.

Anticipation shimmered along his skin, tightening his muscles, making him more aware, more alert. And ready to strike. A quick hit to the three vital points—throat, nose, temple—was all it would take.

It would be so easy to succumb to impulse. Friedrich Reiter would have no qualms over killing a guard.

Jack Anderson wouldn't either, if it meant protecting the woman beside him. But Jack also knew better than to make such a rash mistake.

The Germans were meticulous record keepers. Once the guard was found, a report would be made. The grounds would be searched. And before long, Kerensky's little un-invited jaunt into Doenitz's room would be discovered.

The mission would be over before it had really begun.

The rhythmic sounds of Kerensky's breathing reminded him of her presence. This was why he preferred to work alone. What if she was captured and interrogated tonight, what if she got hurt in an escape attempt, what if…

No. *Think in terms of absolutes,* he told himself, *not ifs.*

He would do this right. With cold, hard pragmatism.

No emotion. Nothing personal.

And, lo, I am with you always…

Jack nearly flinched at the unexpected thought. Where had it come from? An old Scripture memorized from youth, or a reminder straight from God?

Jack couldn't be certain. So he focused on the only reliable sources he had at his disposal. His brain. And his skills.

Without moving, he took note of the line of fog snaking along the waters of the distant harbor. The vapor would eventually shroud the entire town in its milky-white mist. Perfect cover for escape.

"Get your hands in the air." The order was spat in clipped, rapid-fire German. "Now."

In one part of his mind, Jack counted off seconds. The rest of him searched for a solution that would keep all three of them alive. Measuring, gauging, he dropped a quick glance on to Kerensky. She met his gaze with hard steel in her eyes.

Good. She wouldn't buckle.

"Do it, or I'll shoot," came the order. The voice was angry and a little desperate now. Jack knew from personal experience that desperate was the same as reckless.

Just what they needed—a desperate, reckless Nazi with a loaded rifle pointed at their backs.

After giving Kerensky's shoulder a brief squeeze, Jack lifted his hands in the air above his head. She took a hard breath and did the same. By his calculation, less than fifteen seconds had passed since the guard's initial command to halt.

"Turn around," came the next order. "Slowly."

Jack slid another glance at Kerensky. Her eyes were narrowed into determined, pale green slits surrounded by spiky dark lashes.

"We do this together," he whispered.

She nodded. "Together."

As a unit, they pivoted to face the enemy. For a split second, time came to a standstill and the world waited for one of them to make the next move.

Jack took a quick accounting of the guard. Dressed in a *Kriegsmarine* uniform, the rank of midshipman was evident by the single bar on his shoulder strap. The sailor was shorter than Jack, slighter and much, much younger. Nothing more than a boy, really.

A boy who carried a 98 Mauser infantry rifle, with its five-shot clip, and simple, strong action that could pierce a man's—or woman's—heart at this close range with little to no mess.

Not the best of situations.

But not disastrous, either. As long as Jack kept his head thinking and his emotions shut down.

"State your name and your business." The voice was still strong, firm even, but the sailor's eyes reflected hesitancy, as though he sensed Jack's superior rank in spite of the civilian clothing.

Easing into the role of authority, Jack brought his hands to his waist. Palms facing forward, he took a deliberate step forward and addressed the sailor by his official rank of sub-lieutenant. *"Fähnrich zur See—"*

The rifle jerked. "Get your hands back where I can see them."

Jack knew exactly what he had to do now. A plan began formulating in his head. Placate first. Stall. But, at all costs, avoid bloodshed.

He took another step forward, careful to keep from spooking the guard any further.

However, Kerensky—the careless, rash woman—chose that moment to join the conversation. "Oh, honestly, this is ridiculous," she said, lowering her hands slowly, but without an ounce of hesitation. "*Fähnrich,* there must be some mistake. Although, I'm sure it's nothing we can't work out."

The sailor's eyes narrowed. "Do I know you?"

Jack recognized the curling in his gut as a mixture of anger and fear. He'd almost had things under control. Why hadn't the woman kept her mouth shut?

"Let me handle this," he hissed at her, his eyes burning with silent caution that only an idiot would ignore.

Kerensky, of course, chose to disregard the clear warning. Why he'd expected any differently was a mystery to him. With a flick of her wrist, she yanked off her cap. Her braid tumbled down, down, down, landing in a soft thump against her back.

Holding back a string of oaths, Jack took another step forward, shifting to his right, until he stood between her and the guard.

The sailor's face went dead-white as he craned his neck to look around Jack. "You... You're Katarina Kerensky."

So much for anonymity.

She pushed Jack aside and gave the sailor one of her brilliant smiles. "Why, yes. Yes, I am."

Wonder of wonders, the boy's shock turned into immediate adoration, and the rifle's nose tipped toward the ground. Well, well. Kerensky was using her fame to dazzle the kid. Rash, yes. Careless, most definitely. But maybe, just maybe, workable.

"I grow weary of this silly game," she said.

Jack agreed completely.

The gun tipped lower still. Another minute and the rifle would be Jack's.

"Yes, I, that is, I thought you were a threat."

"A threat? Oh, you can't be serious." She let out a tinkling laugh and tugged her braid over her left shoulder. Twisting the tip around her finger, she managed to look feminine, frivolous and very nonthreatening.

From the glint in the sailor's eyes, it was clear the boy felt genuine embarrassment over the incident. Jack wouldn't have believed it if he hadn't seen it for himself. Even through the haze of his frustration, he knew the wisdom of letting the woman play out the charade to the bitter end.

"Fähnrich—"

"My name is Franz Heintzman, Fräulein Kerensky."

"Well, Franz…" She looked up and smiled into his eyes, all grace and charm in the gesture. A fairy-tale princess come to life. "You don't mind if I call you by your first name, do you?"

"I'd be honored."

"You see, Franz," she continued. "My, uh, friend and I were taking a stroll along the quay for some fresh air after…well…" She flipped her braid back over her shoulder and left the rest unsaid.

The sailor blinked. "But why here in Wilhelmshaven?"

Kerensky leaned forward, crooked her finger at him until he drew closer to her. "We wanted privacy this evening. I—" she straightened, reached out and clasped Jack's hand for a brief moment "—or rather *we,* don't want others to know of our liaison just yet."

Jack actually heard the kid swallow. It was all over now. Battle lost. Surrender inevitable. He almost felt sorry for the boy. Almost.

The power of the woman was amazing, mind-boggling.

Jack didn't know whether to tap her on the back in admiration or wring her pretty little neck for taking such a risk.

"Yes, yes, I think I understand," Franz said. Then he looked at Jack again, the earlier suspicion in his eyes replaced with unmistakable envy.

Kerensky had been wrong about one thing. Her beauty wasn't a weapon. It was mass destruction.

As though sensing his silent awe, she gave Jack a quick smile then pivoted back to the sailor. "Franz, dear, perhaps we could keep this incident our little secret?" She circled her hand in a gesture that included all three of them. "Maybe pretend you never saw us here tonight?"

Clearly wavering between doing his duty and making friends with a famous actress, the sailor looked from her to Jack and back to her again. "I'm not sure I can do that."

Kerensky turned him facing toward the harbor and hooked her arm in his. "Let's talk plainly, shall we?" Lowering her voice, she created an intimacy between them that had the boy blinking rapidly. "I really don't want anyone to know about my visit here, for obvious reasons. What would make this easier for you?"

"Well, I don't suppose—" He stopped and looked everywhere but at her.

"Yes?" She patted his hand, blessing him with a look that had his Adam's apple bobbing in his throat.

"I have a two-day leave next week. And, I would really like to see your latest play."

"Done." She went on to explain where he could pick up his ticket, adding a promise to meet him backstage—in her dressing room—after the performance.

At the excited beam in the boy's eyes, Jack had seen enough. It was long past time to end this farce.

Kerensky was no longer star of this show. Jack was.

Drawing alongside her, he gave a brief smile to the

midshipman. Then, in a perfectly reasonable tone, he said, "Darling, it's getting late. We should be on our way."

Instead of arguing with him, wonder of wonders, her eyes filled with relief. "Yes, yes, of course."

Not one to miss an opportunity, Jack took immediate advantage of the woman's startling cooperation. With his mind on escape, he eased Kerensky closer to him, while offering a quick farewell to the boy.

Jack waited just long enough for Kerensky to say her own farewell before wrapping his arm around her shoulder and steering her in the direction of the car.

Although the guard had fallen under Kerensky's spell quickly enough, Jack knew their luck wouldn't last. German military training was too strong, too thorough. It wouldn't be long before the boy came to his senses and took them to his commanding officer for questioning.

Jack picked up the pace.

Chapter Nine

Three minutes and two blocks later, Katia let out a deep sigh of relief. Surprised at the need to rest in Reiter's protection a little longer, she had to resist the urge to retreat farther into the safety of his casual embrace.

For one, they weren't alone. She sensed rather than saw the sailor's presence still behind them, watching. Waiting. Perhaps even wondering if he'd made the right decision in letting them go so easily.

She wanted to look over her shoulder, but Katarina Kerensky *never* looked back.

Instead, her eyes shot to Friedrich Reiter's face. His expression was impassive, his steps slow and lazy. She wasn't fooled for a second. She could feel the tension slicing through him. His entire body may have looked relaxed, but there was no doubt in her mind that he was wound tight, ready to attack if the need arose.

The thought was as comforting as it was disturbing.

She knew he could have taken out the sailor in a matter of seconds, but something had held him back from killing the young man.

Had it been a deep sense of morality? Or had he simply been maintaining the integrity of the mission, ensuring no signs of their presence were left behind? A dead or injured guard would have been an unmistakable calling card.

One they would not have been able to take back.

Swallowing hard, she felt unusually restless and uneasy. Perhaps it was because she knew so little about the man walking beside her. And yet, she trusted him completely.

Odd. Katarina Kerensky trusted no one except herself. A Scripture came to mind, one her father had taught her during the dark days of revolution. *But they that wait upon the Lord shall renew their strength; they shall mount up with wings as eagles; they shall run, and not be weary...*

Because the verse had brought her father great comfort, Katia had memorized it, as well. Along with his other favorite verse, *My grace is sufficient.* Even in his last moments, Vladimir Kerensky had never lost faith in God.

Could Katia ever trust the Lord again, like she had as a child thanks to her father's righteous example? After years of relying on her own strength, she doubted it would be as easy as making a decision on a cold night in Wilhelmshaven.

Still...

Hope and bitterness warred within her. She didn't know whether to laugh or cry, to surrender to the Lord or continue in her own strength like always. Up to this point, she'd done well on her own.

But now?

Now things were...different.

And she feared the man walking beside her had everything to do with the change.

She needed time to think, to sort through her confusion, but they weren't safe yet.

"We better make this look real," she whispered. "I'm sure our new friend is still watching."

"Excellent idea." Reiter stopped, turned her until she

faced him directly. The intensity in his gaze made the air hitch deep in her lungs. She couldn't bear the way his eyes searched her face, but she was too mesmerized to look away.

"Our man's less than fifty yards behind you, on your left," he said, leaning down to touch his forehead to hers. "We have to get this right the first time."

"You don't need to worry about me. Let's not forget who just saved whom."

He pulled back and rewarded her with a quiet smile. She decided his quiet smiles were the most dangerous. "Gloating, are you?" he asked.

"Absolutely." She leaned into him, blinked like a cowering fool, because, well, why deny the truth? She wanted him to kiss her. And wasn't that incredibly shocking?

His grin never faltered. In fact, to the untrained eye, he looked completely smitten with her. If Friedrich Reiter needed a career after the war, the man could make a fortune on the stage.

Dropping his head until their noses were an inch apart, he waited a beat. "I'd expect nothing less from you."

He was making her nervous, and that made her angry. Not to mention incredibly afraid of losing control. She tried not to bristle, but temper mixed with confusion and fear twisted into a hard knot in her stomach, and had her wishing for a little more privacy. So she could kick him in the shin. "Why do your compliments always sound like insults?"

His expression softened. "Just part of my charm."

"Of course."

Watching him closely, she didn't move, didn't breathe. An eternity passed before his lips touched hers. They pressed, retreated, pressed again. A moment passed, then another. By the third, her knees gave out and she stumbled into him.

"Well done, that should convince him," he said as he helped her find her balance, then set her at arm's length.

His voice sounded too steady. Too sure. How could the man remain that unmoved when her own legs were literally giving way under the weight of her reaction to their short, meaningless, pretend kiss?

She had to cling to his shoulders to keep from tripping into him again.

He gave her an odd look, almost sad. "Let's not overdo it, Kerensky."

With a few quick maneuvers, he tucked her under his arm again, and led her toward the car.

"Our man just left," he informed her.

"I know."

Needing distance, she took a step away from him, but he tightened his grip on her shoulder and pulled her back against him. "He could come back," he explained at her questioning stare.

"Right." But how was she supposed to calm her scrambling pulse when he wouldn't let her have room to breathe?

Enough was enough. She was through being the only one off balance. "I saw your look of shock when I started talking," she said. There. That should get an interesting reaction out of him.

For the first time that night, his steps faltered. "Shock doesn't begin to describe it."

"Oh?" She smiled sweetly at him, fully aware that she was baiting the human equivalent of a wild animal. What was the old saying about pulling a tiger by his tail? Did the same apply to cougars?

"Try frustration, anger, sheer terror for your safety. That sailor had his full attention on *me,* which is exactly where

I wanted it. What I did not want," he said as his voice filled with reproach, "was him noticing you."

She was starting to get seriously insulted. "As if I can't take care of myself," she muttered.

"By revealing your true identity? That's how you take care of yourself?" He blew out a frustrated breath. "It's a wonder you're still alive."

"But I am. And so are you. Thanks to me, I might add."

"What happens if your name shows up in a report, Katarina? Did you think about that when you were playing the famous actress out for a little tryst with her…friend?"

"Revealing my identity made it more believable. You'd see that if you'd look past your colossal ego. Let's say my name does end up in a report, so what? All it will say is that Katarina Kerensky and her unnamed friend decided to come to this obscure little village to avoid stares. My idea was just short of brilliant."

"If you do say so yourself."

"Weren't you the one who said you wanted us to appear as lovers, in case someone saw us?" She gifted him with a smug grin. "But, no, wait, you were too busy thinking like a soldier back there, instead of a regular man."

His eyes, a deep, troubled blue that had judged her just minutes before, now looked…weary. "All right, you have me there."

She stared at him, her eyes going wide in spite of her attempt at playing nonchalant. "You admit it?"

They rounded the corner to the alley and he made a grand show of opening the car door for her. "Haven't you ever met a man who can admit when he's wrong?"

"Actually, I haven't," she said as she lowered herself to the seat.

He scooted her over with his hip and then settled in next to her. "Then let me be your first."

Having a man, especially such a large man as Friedrich Reiter, sitting this close to her made the inside of the dark car seem too crowded, too confining.

Blinking at him, she shifted farther across the seat, but when he dug the keys out of their hiding place, she froze. "Shouldn't I drive again?"

"No. You need to get some sleep. But before you settle in, let me have the box." He opened his palm to her.

Too exhausted to argue with him, she slipped the wax impression into his hand without a word.

After pocketing the tiny box in his jacket, he turned his attention to starting the car and steering out of the alley.

Once they were heading toward Hamburg, Katia busied herself with watching the passing scenery. Dark clouds drifted in odd patterns across the sky, converging in front of the moon and plunging the landscape into an eerie darkness. Apprehension slithered up her spine, making her shudder from the weight of the sensation.

A still, small voice whispered a warning in her mind.

Something didn't feel right about tonight, something she couldn't quite name. Not just the incident with the guard, but something else entirely, something to do with the mission.

Had she missed another important detail?

Trying to remain calm, she ignored the odd shivers dancing along her skin. But the sense of foreboding wouldn't go away.

Worrying was useless. So, she forced her mind to run through every detail of her time in Doenitz's room. The initial entry, dropping to the floor, making the impression of the key, her swift exit, the...

Oh, no!

No, no, no, no, no.

How could she have been so careless? In her haste to

get out of the room, she had moved the chair to a slightly different angle below the window.

She'd exited quickly, quietly and, what she had thought at the time, efficiently. Only now did she realize that she'd left the chair out of its original position.

After all her planning and all her posturing, she'd made a second mistake in so many days. They would have to abandon the mission now.

She needed calm. She needed strength, the same strength her father had tapped in to in his final days in Russia. *They that wait upon the Lord shall renew their strength; they shall mount up...*

No, wait. She was allowing the stress of the evening to do her thinking for her. She'd only left the chair marginally out of place. No one would notice the shift in its position unless specifically looking.

Friedrich Reiter had done this to her. With his dead-on suspicions about her Jewish blood and *pretend* kisses, he'd made her doubt herself and her abilities. He'd made her think she wasn't in control of her own destiny, when she'd been just fine on her own for years.

She'd never failed to complete a mission successfully.

She would prevail in this one, too.

Admiral Doenitz would never discover her tiny mistake. She was almost sure of it.

Chapter Ten

21 November 1939, Wilhelmshaven
Kriegsmarine headquarters, 0630 hours

Before his anger turned into an uncontrollable fit of rage, Admiral Karl Doenitz needed to cool his temper. It was, after all, his duty to remain calm in front of his men. Walking would help, but at the moment he couldn't find a decent patch of floor to pace across.

Feeling caged, he wove through the maze of humanity in his private quarters and went back into his office. Even here, members of his handpicked staff inspected every inch of the room.

They'd been searching for over an hour, but had found nothing missing, nothing out of the ordinary. Except, of course, the chair.

Breathing slowly, deliberately, he worked his hands at his sides, flexing, relaxing. Flexing, relaxing.

Someone would pay for this.

Blowing out a hard breath, he stalked back into his bedroom and stared at the chair still sitting at its slightly awkward angle under the small window opposite his bed.

Air wheezed out of his lungs, clogging his throat until he had to gulp for a breath.

Someone had actually infiltrated his private living quarters of the BdU, in spite of the increase in guards. In spite of the added precautions with the recent move.

The question was why? And why hadn't anything been taken?

Doenitz detested espionage and the intrigue that came with it. Just two months into the fight against England and this war already had more than its share of both. Nevertheless, he would adapt.

BdU Admiral Karl Doenitz *always* adapted.

With clipped steps he returned to his office and picked his way to the window behind his desk. Looking beyond the fishing vessels riding at anchor, he focused on the mouth of the harbor. A sharp wind gusted off the North Sea, frothing the dark waters with ragged whitecaps.

Shifting his focus to the U-boat pens peppered along the entrance, a swell of pride overwhelmed the other emotions raging inside him. Military duty was his calling. But the sea was his home.

Karl Doenitz was the *Kriegsmarine*. His U-boats were the first line of offense in the Führer's bid to seize power throughout Europe.

This break-in was an irritant that must be dealt with swiftly. He had to discover precisely what the intruder had been after. Only then would he turn his full attention back to the war with Great Britain.

Did one have to do with the other?

Nothing else made sense.

The British actually believed they could cope with the German U-boat threat. They were wrong, of course, and must continue in their misguided thinking. The strength of the U-boats and their advanced weaponry must remain secret.

Doenitz strode to the cabinet that held maps, plans, strategies and codes—all the weapons that would propel the Fatherland into the greatest power the world had ever seen. Stooping to study the lock, he ran his finger along the outer rim. The cold, smooth metal warmed under his touch.

As he continued to consider the lock, he caught a flicker of movement to his right. Rising, he turned to face Captain Emil Kurtz, his chief of staff. Even at this early hour the man glistened in the service suit required of all administrative officers. Doenitz took note of the immaculate blue uniform tailored to perfection and nodded in approval.

With perfect military precision, Kurtz saluted. "*Heil* Hitler."

Doenitz returned the gesture. "*Heil* Hitler."

"The search is complete, Herr Admiral. We've found nothing missing."

Doenitz's anger reared at the news. He coated steel over the emotion. "Any signs of tampering?"

Cool, composed, Kurtz's eyes cut from the cabinet back to Doenitz. "None, except the misplaced chair."

Doenitz nodded, his mouth firming into a determined line. The intruder had been careful, but not careful enough. The chair proved that much. One mistake always led to another.

He and his staff were simply missing the obvious.

As though reading his mind, Kurtz asked, "Do you want us to continue searching?"

"Make another sweep. In the meantime, I want to review the individual reports of each man on watch last night."

"Yes, Herr Admiral. I will get them to you right away."

"I also want to speak with every guard, personally."

Kurtz nodded. "I will arrange it at once." Eyes flat with concentration, he added, "We will find the intruder."

Certainty swelled. "I have no doubt."

Oh, yes. They would discover the identity of the guilty party. If not this morning, soon. Patience was the key.

Instincts honed in the heat of battle warned Doenitz that this was only the beginning.

The intruder would be back.

And Admiral Karl Doenitz would be waiting.

At exactly 0638 hours, Jack carefully checked for suspicious activity and, finding none, he bound up the front steps leading into the *Vier Jahreszeiten* hotel.

The historic building was a palace of old-world elegance. Never let it be said that Friedrich Reiter didn't know how to travel in style.

Ignoring the luxury of the gold filigree and yards of brocade-covered furniture, Jack strode to the front desk and obtained his room key. After a friendly, albeit brief, conversation with the sleepy-eyed clerk, he headed toward the staircase and to his suite on the third floor.

Jack had no doubt the clerk would make a note of his comings and goings. The report would further validate the charade of a man sneaking out for a clandestine meeting with his lover. He'd begun the act at the theater last night. Katarina Kerensky had added another layer to the ruse in Wilhelmshaven. Like it or not, Jack had to continue playing out his part.

With that loose end neatly tied up, Jack set his mind on blissful solitude, food and a hot shower, not necessarily in that order.

He took the steps two at a time, mentally reviewing the events of the last few hours.

For several obvious reasons, he would prefer not to continue his association with the famous actress. For one, now that Jack had the wax impression, he wasn't sure he needed her on the mission anymore. Not to mention the fact that he didn't trust aggressive females with fancy eyes and brave attitudes.

Who was he trying to convince?

Katarina made him remember the Godly man he'd once been. She made him want to search his mind for Scriptures he'd buried there as a child. Verses such as *The Lord is my strength,* and *We know that all things work together for good to them that love God.*

For two years, Jack had thought little of God or His word. Tonight, the Lord had been in his head every step of the way. Long-forgotten Scriptures had come to mind, seemingly out of nowhere.

Was the Lord trying to tell him something?

Jack was too short on sleep to know for sure. He needed to focus on the mission right now.

He would think about God later.

Unlocking the door to his hotel room, he glanced at his watch—0640 hours.

He'd been in Germany less than twelve hours, but that didn't mean his presence had gone unnoticed.

He began a systematic search of the suite, checking his subtle detection devices for signs of tampering. Starting on his right, he circled the perimeter in a counterclockwise direction. The single strands of hair, each placed over knobs of closed doors, were still intact, as were the invisible slices of tape over random drawers.

Patrolling past the sitting room, he moved into the bedroom, explored the adjourning bath, and then went out onto the balcony.

He'd found no signs of unwanted entry or tampering.

Relaxing his shoulders, he turned and looked out over

the city. Fog, wet and gray, slithered over the buildings in a glossy haze. There was an eerie post-dawn quiet as the morning cold swept in off the water and slapped him in the face.

Restless now, Jack was unable to enjoy the beauty of Hamburg. He strode back into the sitting room, shutting the balcony door behind him. Sinking into a large, overstuffed chair, he let the tension from the evening's events drain out of him.

It was only a matter of time before the SS contacted him. Friedrich Reiter was too important to Heinrich Himmler's personal agenda for his return to Hamburg to go unnoticed for long. Jack would be ready.

At the thought of facing Himmler again, he felt a familiar rush of emotion surge through his blood. Guilt, he wondered? Or conviction. He wasn't sure anymore. He'd long since lost his moral compass.

He closed his eyes against the thoughts colliding into one another in his mind. Kerensky had slipped past his well-honed defenses, tapping into the man he'd once been. And now he couldn't stop thinking about all he'd lost that long ago night when he'd first met the real Friedrich Reiter.

Jack let out a harsh breath.

He would never forget the exact moment he'd stared into the eyes of his assassin, a Nazi secret agent who had come to kill him and assume his identity. The physical similarity between Jack and Friedrich Reiter had been uncanny. No, terrifying.

When Reiter had pulled the knife, Jack had had little choice but to defend himself. The fight had been long and brutal. The ending nasty.

Murder, self-defense, whatever word was used to describe what had happened in that back alley, a man was dead because of Jack Anderson.

Absently, he shoved at his hair, as though the gesture would rid him of the dark memories sliding through his brain and tangling into a knot of regret. Would the guilt ever go away? Would he ever look at his hands and not see the blood?

What was a man capable of when he stopped feeling guilt? Jack feared he was close to finding out. He'd become that embedded in his life as a spy.

He hadn't started out cold and unfeeling. When he'd decided to become Friedrich Reiter he had believed he'd been called to a higher good. He'd vowed to risk his life for innocent blood, as many other warriors had done in the Old Testament. He'd accepted the killing—not murder, killing—as part of the job. No different than a police officer.

MI6 had been more than willing to aid his quest. With special training, forged documents and the addition of a slight Austrian accent to his otherwise perfect German, Jack had literally turned into the man who had come to kill him.

The transformation had been so complete Heinrich Himmler himself believed Jack *was* Friedrich Reiter. Short of checking dental records, there was no possible way of telling Jack's real identity.

The line between Friedrich Reiter and Jack Anderson had begun to disappear. Until tonight. While looking into Kerensky's eyes, Jack had remembered the man he'd once been. And now, Scriptures learned long ago were coming to mind.

Trust in the Lord with all thine heart; and lean not unto thine own understanding. In all thy ways acknowledge Him, and He shall direct thy paths.

The Scripture was a powerful reminder of where Jack should put his faith.

Yet how could he acknowledge God in the travesty that had become his life?

Deception was a rotten business. He'd learned quickly that he could trust no one. As a result, he'd become a hard man. Cynical. Faithless. All necessary to stay alive. The moment he became complacent, he became vulnerable.

Take tonight, for instance. He knew he should have never kissed Kerensky. Regardless of the need to present the impression of intimacy, the reflex to pull her into his arms had been too fast, too strong and entirely too powerful to deny.

What had been glorious one moment now haunted him. *Nothing personal. No emotion.* Who was he kidding?

He bolted out of the chair and started pacing through the room. Hovering on the brink of emotions too dangerous to explore, he turned his attention to less frustrating matters of reports and organization.

Taking action, he set a record on the phonograph. German walls had ears, Hamburg walls more than most. As soon as the poignant strains of a Wagner opera filled the air, Jack went in search of the radio components he'd camouflaged inside the actual construction of his suitcase.

As he crossed into the bedroom, he checked his watch again—0655 hours.

On a small table near the window, he spread out a power lead, adaptor, aerial wire, connection cables, dial and Morse key. Working quickly, efficiently, he connected cables and made a mental list of the information he would transmit to the British.

He draped the aerial wire over the dresser, connected the Morse key and dial tuning it to the prearranged frequency.

Using his personal five-digit series of codes, he made

initial contact with the Brits, waited for the go-ahead to continue.

As was true of all agents, Jack's Morse style was as unique as his fingerprints. If the Germans happened to discover he wasn't the real Friedrich Reiter they could very well try to force him to continue transmitting wrong information.

Their efforts would be to no avail, of course. Jack would simply pause an extra beat after every word that started with *T* or *O,* thereby alerting the British he'd been compromised.

A minute passed. And then another. Finally, Jack received the go-ahead from London.

With cool precision, he tapped out his message in the prescribed code that would be translated before landing on his superior's desk then sent on to Churchill himself for review.

ARRIVED OKAY STOP
MET BUTTERFLY STOP
PHASE ONE COMPLETE STOP
BEGINNING PHASE TWO OVER

Per standard operating procedures, there would be no response until 1430 Hamburg time. Jack took apart the radio and returned the components to their original hiding places.

He peeled off his sweater, loosened the top button of his shirt, and then pulled out the small cardboard box from his pants pocket. Flipping open the top, he studied the impression Kerensky had made of the cabinet key. Clear, precise. She'd done an excellent job.

But what if the plans weren't in the cabinet anymore? After the mistake she'd made over the change in location of Doenitz's headquarters, Jack couldn't trust the woman's intelligence.

He needed a backup plan. His best possibility would be to make contact with someone on the inside of Doenitz's staff, preferably someone who worked in the main building of the *Kriegsmarine* headquarters, a naval officer, someone who…

Schmidt. Of course. The U-boat captain engaged to Kerensky's mother.

A plan began formulating. When Jack had left Katarina this morning, she'd reminded him that she was to spend the rest of day with her mother and Schmidt. Jack had promised to find her later in the evening, after he'd had the key to Doenitz's cabinet made. However, now he would make sure they met much sooner.

With just the right amount of maneuvering, *Kapitän zur See* Schmidt could very well give Jack invaluable intelligence, without ever knowing he'd done so.

The tactic was a long shot, at best. Certainly dangerous, and would probably come to nothing.

But this was war. Jack had to take the risk.

Chapter Eleven

Katia used a heavy hand on her makeup. Not out of vanity, but to cover the consequences of her sleepless night. Friedrich Reiter might have thought she'd dozed during their ride back to Hamburg, but in truth Katia had spent most of the time wondering whether or not to confess her mistake in Admiral Doenitz's room.

Ultimately, she'd chosen to remain silent on the matter. At this point, what was done could not be undone. Yet, even as she tried to convince herself she'd made the right decision, a stab of guilt snaked through her stomach and she rose from her chair with a feminine growl on her lips.

She should have trusted Reiter with the truth. She knew that now. Nothing could be gained from withholding such an important piece of information. She must tell him the next time they met.

Satisfied with her new decision, she snatched her brush off the dressing table and moved to the closest window on her left. With an uncharacteristic lack of grace, she began yanking at the knots in her hair.

Tugging, tugging, tugging, she stared at the scene in front of her with unblinking eyes.

Sunrise over the rooftops of Hamburg made a magnificent picture, one she usually stopped to appreciate. But as Katia continued brushing her hair, she barely noticed the ribbon of golden light threading between the orange-and-red-tinted spires.

And then, after a painfully hard yank, a wave of despair crested inside her.

She was in too deep.

She wanted out.

But she couldn't leave. Not with her mother in such obvious danger.

Overwhelmed with too many emotions to sort through all at once, she admitted the truth to herself at last. Katarina Kerensky, a jaded woman who'd long ago lost hope, desperately wanted to believe good would overcome evil in the end.

Even after witnessing her father's senseless murder, even after accepting that the Nazis were in charge, Katia wanted—no, she *needed*—to believe that God hadn't abandoned the German people altogether.

God?

Where had that thought come from? She didn't believe the Lord cared anymore. Or did she?

My grace is sufficient.

Was it? Could she trust in the Lord again? Was there enough of Vladimir's daughter still in her to take that leap?

She wasn't sure. How could she put faith in a God who allowed a man like Hitler to rise to power?

She was just overly tired this morning. That had to explain her desire to rely on anyone other than herself, especially an invisible God.

Her mind wasn't working properly. She was confused over her mistake in the admiral's private quarters, stunned by her strange reactions to her new partner. Surely that explained her leaning to set aside her disillusionment and put her trust in a silent God.

The loud knock on the door made her jump. Happy for the interruption, she took a deep breath and checked the time. Her mother and fiancé were a full twenty minutes early for their scheduled outing with Katia.

Moving back to her dressing table, Katia studied her reflection in the mirror. She looked too haggard, too world-weary for the part she must play this morning.

Breathing deeply, she took a long, slow blink. The gesture wiped away the creases of worry on her brow. Another blink settled a vacant look into her eyes. A quick sigh, one last shudder, and finally she became the royal princess with little on her mind beyond the superficial. "Much better."

She thought she was back in control. Until the minute she opened the front door and the cold wind slapped ice-edged fingers against her face. Forcing a silly smile on her face, Katia braced against the frigid attack and took in the sight of her visitors.

Dressed in a cashmere coat made in her signature color of soft blue, Elena Kerensky stood arm in arm with her fiancé. Both held themselves proud and precise. But where Elena's arrogance came from her royal breeding, Schmidt's haughtiness had a sheen that was equal parts brutality and condescension. On closer inspection, his tailor-made *Kriegsmarine* overcoat looked like the work of Wilhelm Holters, the premier tailor of the Third Reich.

Nothing but the best for this Nazi.

Katia hid her cynicism behind a little sigh of pleasure. "Mother. Hermann. What a lovely surprise. You're early."

"I'm afraid I was the eager one," Elena said. "I so want you to get to know Hermann better."

She lifted an adoring look at her companion and squeezed his arm. Schmidt smiled down at Elena with similar admiration. But Katia thought she recognized a look of cunning flash in his eyes.

Did he sense Elena's secret? Did he have a dark plan already in place?

Before Katia could pursue the frightening thought, Schmidt turned his bold scrutiny on to her. "May we come in? Or are we to stand on your doorstep all morning?"

The man was, beyond question, the most arrogant Nazi Katia knew. And considering the company she kept, that was saying a lot.

Tread carefully with this one, Katia.

Hidden beneath several layers of foolish woman, she cocked her head at an agreeable angle. "Oh, dear, forgive me. Do come in."

She moved to her left, blessing them both with a happy smile as they passed by.

Once inside, Schmidt turned on his heel and handed Katia the bouquet of roses he'd been holding behind his back.

"For you," he said. "I understand they are your favorite."

He held her stare with a challenging look in his gaze.

Katia remained expressionless, fiercely so, but her mind raced in frantic chaos.

She hated white roses. No, she *detested* them. They reminded her of happier days when her father would bring a bouquet to both her and her mother for no particular reason.

Elena knew of Katia's aversion. Why would she allow Schmidt to make this cruel gesture?

A test, perhaps? But who was running the show, Schmidt or her mother? And was Katia supposed to react with outrage or complacency?

To avoid revealing her confusion, she quickly took the bouquet and buried her nose in the blooms. The scent made her stomach churn in anguish and a sense of loss besieged her. How she missed her beloved father. His faith had been strong, even in the moment of his death.

In comparison, Katia's faith was weak, practically non-existent. But she was growing weary of relying only on herself and her quick thinking. *They that wait upon the Lord shall renew their strength.*

She swallowed her trepidation. "Thank you, Hermann. They're very beautiful."

"Go put the flowers in water, darling." Elena patted Katia's hand, the gesture reminiscent of when she had been a child with a hurt that needed soothing. "Then we'll leave for our outing."

At the odd note of apology in her mother's eyes, tears pricked at the back of Katia's eyes. What was Elena trying to tell her?

Unsure of the meaning behind the undercurrents traveling between them, Katia made herself breathe evenly. "I'll only be a moment."

Elena nodded, an obscure smile playing at the edge of her lips. "Good girl."

Ice clutched around Katia's heart. This secretive woman was not the mother she knew. Was Elena trying to tell her something? Something only the two of them would understand?

In an attempt to keep her hands from shaking, Katia concentrated on the task her mother had set before her. She filled a vase with water from the kitchen sink, all the while keeping her attention on her guests in the adjoining room. Thankfully, her home had an open floor plan.

As though staged by a seasoned director, Elena remained in plain view while Schmidt idly moved from one room to another. From beneath her lowered lashes, Katia traced his every step.

As he made his way systematically from one end of her house to the other, he ran his index finger along a table, a chair, another table. He craned his neck to look into a room off to his left, another on his right.

Clearly, he wasn't attempting to be subtle with his search. All the while Katia's mother simply watched him as though nothing was out of the ordinary with his bold inspection.

Were the two working together? Could Katia not even trust her own mother? A woman with far more to lose than most?

My grace is sufficient.

Even now, Lord? Are You in this room with me now? Or am I alone, like always?

"So," Katia said, forcing her fingers to arrange the flowers one at a time. "Where do you two want to eat this morning?"

"I think we should go to our favorite little café near the *Rathausmarkt,*" Elena said, turning to face Katia directly. "The Engel café. You know the one."

Katia caught the silent warning in her mother's eyes.

Sudden fear snapped to life, leaching into her muscles and nearly causing her knees to buckle. *Breathe,* she told herself. *In. Out. In. Out.*

But no matter how hard she tried to remain calm, the floor seemed to shift beneath her and she couldn't stop thinking about the danger her mother was in with her Nazi fiancé.

Swallowing, Katia moved back into the main living area and set the roses on a table near the door. "Yes. *Yes.* I adore the Engel café. I think that will do nicely."

Elena nodded at her in…approval?

Unaware of the silent communication between mother and daughter, Schmidt completed his final pass through the living room and stopped at Elena's side. His eyes held the same glint of fanaticism Katia saw in the most treacherous Nazis of her acquaintance. She had no doubt the kind of man Schmidt hid under the *Kriegsmarine* uniform.

The knowledge gave her an odd rush of confidence.

She knew exactly how to deal with monsters like this man.

If she was careful—and Katia was always careful—a relationship with Hermann Schmidt could prove valuable.

Besides, the more she kept an eye on the terrible man, the more she could keep a protective watch over her mother. One thing was certain, something wasn't right with Elena Kerensky.

Katia had to find out what.

"Now that I've put the flowers in water, why don't we leave for the restaurant?" she suggested.

Elena nodded at her again, her motherly approval as clear as glass this time. "Excellent idea, darling."

Gathering her handbag and coat, Katia forced her mind to work quickly. This was not the first time she'd been in a dangerous situation like this. In fact, she'd acted this role a hundred times, with a hundred different Nazis like Hermann Schmidt. The part fit her as well as the gloves she slid onto her hands.

But with her mother's involvement, the stakes had risen. Katia had to make this her most masterful performance to date.

Chapter Twelve

A band of low-flying clouds swallowed the last patch of sunlight, turning the Hamburg sky a stark shade of gray. Jack gauged the weather with the eyes of a trained sailor. Satisfied the rain would hold, he edged closer to the Engel café and studied the three diners through the large, plate-eglass window on his right.

The Nazi propaganda machine couldn't have staged a more perfect scenario. The handsome naval officer, dressed in all his military glory, dining leisurely with his two beautiful companions as though the war was already won.

But as convincing as the scene appeared on the surface, Jack knew first impressions were deceiving.

He shifted closer and instantly registered the odd still-ness in *Kapitän zur See* Schmidt. Obvious mistrust glared in his eyes, eyes that never left Katarina's face as she chatted happily away. For her part, the woman had slipped into the role of silly daughter once again.

Jack's stomach churned with anger. Katarina Kerensky played a deadly game with a *very* dangerous man.

At least she had chosen a table directly in front of the window overlooking the town square. Her position put her in the line of vision of anyone who passed by the restaurant, including Jack.

It hadn't taken much to discover that Katarina and her mother frequented this café. Had Kerensky been expecting Jack to come looking for her? Was she worried about being in such an intimate situation with her mother and Hermann Schmidt? Perhaps her boast that she could "handle" the two had been nothing more than false bravado.

A protective instinct surged again, making Jack want to race into the café and snatch Katarina away. Away from men like Hermann Schmidt. Away from Germany. Away from anything that would put her in danger.

Jack shook his head.

What was wrong with him? Katarina Kerensky was no amateur. She knew the risks.

Jack feared for her anyway.

As if to mock his foul mood, the clouds split open and a ray of sunshine speared a path from him to the café. The added light gave Jack a better view of his surroundings. Leaning against a monument built to commemorate the Great War veterans, he checked the perimeter around the café before he moved into position.

Activity in the town square was down at this hour. A row of plants lined the walkway next to the restaurant, while a scatter of empty chairs peppered the deserted area under a faded green canopy.

Overhead, the spire of the St. Nikolai Church punched above the rest of the buildings, as if to proclaim its steadfast presence despite the surrounding evil. The church's intricate design outshone the ordinary Hamburg rooftops. There was a time in which Jack would have seen that as a sign of God's very real presence in his life, reminding him that he wasn't alone.

Draw nigh to God, and He will draw nigh to you.

Was it that easy? Could he simply turn to God and know he would be welcomed home?

Before, Jack would have answered his own question with a resounding yes. Not anymore. The day he'd become a spy had been the end of simple answers to hard questions.

Setting his mind back on business, Jack aimed his gaze on the interior of the café and studied Schmidt more precisely. Even from this distance, he could see that the German's eyes belonged to a warrior. When the Nazi wasn't glaring at Kerensky his gaze darted around the interior of the café, assessing each table.

Was he looking for something specific?

Or someone?

No doubt, the man had checked out Jack's background by now. He'd be stupid not to investigate Friedrich Reiter after the tension in their first meeting backstage at the theater. But again, Jack wasn't going to rely on supposition or visual perceptions. Now that he was here Jack needed to find out whether *Kapitän zur See* Schmidt was going to be a threat to his current mission.

No time like the present.

So do not fear, for I am with you... I am your God.

The fresh reminder of God's promise settled his mind.

Pushing away from the monument, Jack sauntered toward the café. He didn't bother with stealth as he entered through the front door. Friedrich Reiter feared nothing and no one. Intentionally drawing all eyes to him, he wove through the crowded restaurant at a leisurely pace.

Disregarding Schmidt's glare and Elena Kerensky's worried lift of an eyebrow, Jack took Katarina's hand and brushed a kiss across her knuckles. "What a happy coincidence finding you here."

She lifted her gaze to his. For a split second, their stares connected with a force that nearly flattened him.

"Herr Reiter," she said. "This is a surprise." Her voice was filled with obvious pleasure.

Even knowing this was an act for her companions' benefit, Jack found himself swallowing. Hard. "A pleasant surprise, I hope."

"The very best." She practically purred.

Loyalties tangled and warred inside him. He was beginning to feel the stirrings of deep emotion for this woman. The kind of stupid feelings that got a man killed if he went in unprepared.

I am with you... I am your God. Jack smiled. A little.

Katarina blinked, slowly. "You remember my mother and her..." She motioned to Schmidt. "Friend."

With a grand show of reluctance, Jack shifted his attention to the couple across the table. "Of course."

"Please, won't you join us, Herr Reiter." Elena Kerensky motioned him to the empty chair at their table.

"Thank you." He settled into the offered seat and studied Katarina's mother with open interest. She stared at him with equal boldness. Her eyes were filled with a hundred questions, but she held her tongue.

"I hope I'm not interrupting something important," he said solely to her.

"Not at all. We were just preparing to order." Her tone was affable enough, but there was obvious distrust in the stiff angle she held her shoulders.

She was reserving judgment. Smart woman.

Hermann Schmidt, however, had come to his conclusions already. He glared at Jack with disdain.

The naval officer must have discovered information about Friedrich Reiter that didn't sit well with him. Jack looked forward to finding out just what the other man had uncovered. It would be an opportunity to gain necessary information about his alter ego's growing reputation.

Relishing the upcoming confrontation, Jack smiled the smile of a predator.

Schmidt returned the favor.

Katarina looked from one to the other then cleared her throat. "Hermann was just telling me about his recent commission." She smiled at him. "Admiral Doniky himself gave the orders."

"Doenitz," Schmidt corrected with a large dose of annoyance.

She gave him a vacant look. "Who?"

"We just went through this, Katarina. Not Doniky, *Doenitz*. Admiral Karl Doenitz."

She sighed heavily. "Oh. Yes, that's correct. Doe-nitz. I don't know why I can't get that right." She turned her attention to Jack. "Isn't it amazing that Hermann knows a *real* admiral?"

She looked and sounded enthralled with the idea, but only in a superficial way. There was nothing of the spy in the woman now.

Impressed with her acting abilities, Jack smiled at her with an indulgent grin, the kind a man gives the woman he adores.

"And best yet. Hermann has promised to introduce me to the admiral tomorrow evening at mother's party."

Jack pulled her hand in his and laced their fingers together. "How lovely for you, darling."

He kissed her knuckles then swiveled in his chair so he could place a smile on Elena. "It must be quite an honor to have such an illustrious man attend your party."

Elena lifted an elegant shoulder. "The admiral will not be the first high-ranking official in my home."

Below her lashes she slid a warning glare in his direction, a look meant only for him. If Jack wasn't mistaken, she'd just told him not to press the issue any further at this time.

Jack went instantly on guard. Why would she make such a threat? Was Elena Kerensky the one he needed to worry about and not Schmidt? He gripped Katarina's hand a little tighter.

Elena looked down at their joined hands. "You will come to the party, Herr Reiter? As Katia's escort, of course." Her smile was sleek and polished and impossible to read.

Jack inclined his head. "I would like nothing more."

Katarina let out a sweet laugh. "Oh, lovely."

Schmidt brought his glass to his mouth, the gesture drawing Jack's attention. The officer took a long swallow and then set it carefully back onto the white tablecloth—a little too carefully. "Elena, darling, would you and Katarina be so kind as to find our waiter and tell him that we are ready to order?"

Elena opened her mouth to speak.

Shaking his head, Schmidt raised his hand to stop her. "I would like a moment alone with our new friend."

She looked prepared to argue but then stood abruptly. "Yes, of course, Hermann. Whatever you wish." She held out her hand to her daughter. "Come along, darling."

"Why do I have to go, as well?" With the perfect blend of surprise and hurt pride, Katarina furrowed her brow. She played her role well today.

"We need to allow the men a moment to speak privately," Elena explained.

Wide-eyed, Katarina looked from Jack to Schmidt to Jack again. He could only guess what the actress was really thinking behind the empty look she swept across him.

"But I want to stay with—"

"Come, Katia." With a firm hold on her arm, Elena all

but dragged Katarina out of her chair. "We shall be back shortly," she said to Schmidt.

"*Very* shortly," Katarina added over her shoulder as she stumbled after her mother.

Schmidt waited until the women moved out of earshot before speaking. "You are not the first man to succeed with Elena's daughter."

"I am fully aware that she is quite popular with men."

Schmidt's eyes turned mean. "Nor are you the second, third or fourth. She goes through them quickly."

Jack resisted the urge to hit the man square in the face. "Better and better. I won't have to teach her anything."

Seeing that his scheme wasn't working, Schmidt switched tactics. "Let us dispense of these verbal niceties, Herr Reiter, and get straight to the point."

Jack drummed his fingers on the table in a show of vast impatience. "And here I was having such fun."

"I know you are a rogue SS operative." Schmidt paused to sneer. "One of Heinrich Himmler's handpicked lackeys."

Allowing the cold, bitter shell of Friedrich Reiter to envelop him, Jack narrowed his eyes and put the entitlement of an SS *Sturmbannführer* in his manner. No one was allowed to question a major in the SS with such blatant insolence. *No one.* "You are well-informed. For a sailor."

The insult hit its mark, but Schmidt quickly hid his reaction behind a casual shrug. "I have my sources."

"Who are these sources?" Even his voice took on Friedrich Reiter's ruthless timbre.

"That is not important. What I want to know is how long the SS has been following me?"

Following him? "Why would we be interested in you?" Jack looked at his wristwatch and feigned boredom, but every cell of his being stood on high alert. "You are nothing more than a U-boat captain."

Schmidt pressed his lips into a firm line and refused to respond. But the damage had been done. Clearly, the man had a military secret the navy didn't want the SS to know about. He'd made a stupid mistake. The arrogant Nazi had no idea who he was dealing with.

But before Jack could begin his own subtle interrogation, the women returned to the table.

Soothed by Katarina's presence, Jack had to remind himself not to stare too hard at her. Something about the way she smiled at him, with that secret look in her eyes, mesmerized him. He couldn't take his eyes off her.

This was an act on both their parts, but one that made him want to rid himself of Friedrich Reiter once and for all. Katarina Kerensky made him want to forget his drive for revenge and recapture the man he'd once been. A simple naval engineer who loved his God and his country. In that order.

In fact, he wanted—

It didn't matter what he wanted. Jack Anderson's life was no longer his own. He was a man with blood on his hands. There could be no forgiveness for him now. No matter how close he drew to God, God would not draw close to him. Why would He?

Jesus came to save sinners, all sinners, a small, distant voice said in his mind. Was it just a memory from Sunday school? Or truth?

As though sensing his internal struggle, Katarina reached out and squeezed his hand. For one dangerous moment, Jack allowed a thread of hope to rope through his bitterness. He pulled her hand to his heart and held it there.

She flattened her palm against his chest and smiled at him, *really* smiled. "I took the liberty of ordering for you, darling." Her voice shook with emotion. "You will stay?"

He pulled her hand to his lips. "I am at your disposal."

His voice sounded raw in his ears. Something powerful was happening inside him and it scared him.

Katarina's smile widened. "Lovely."

They continued staring at one another and Jack found himself allowing his own smile to spread.

The gesture felt foreign.

Schmidt cleared his throat, drawing Jack's attention once again. "Now that that's settled. Why doesn't Herr Reiter tell us something about his life growing up in Vienna?"

Well played.

If Schmidt had done his research, and Jack had no doubt that he had, they both knew Friedrich Reiter spent very little time in Vienna. But by his condescending expression, he seemed to be buying the ruse that Jack was here to pursue Katarina for purely romantic reasons.

To be sure, it was always best to warn off a dog before the fight got ugly. Releasing Katarina's hand, Jack slid deeper into his role of SS henchman. For a brief moment, he allowed Schmidt to get a good look at the deadly fiend inside him.

To his credit, the naval officer didn't flinch. In fact, Jack caught the flash of recognition in the other man's eyes. One monster appreciating another.

Hermann Schmidt was proving a formidable foe.

"Very well, *Kapitän*. Ask me whatever you wish."

No matter what question Schmidt threw at him, Jack already had the answer.

Chapter Thirteen

By midafternoon, a bone-chilling wind whipped through the Hamburg streets. Moments earlier, Jack had left Kerensky with her companions in the restaurant and then headed south toward the edge of town.

Friedrich Reiter had an unscheduled appointment to keep. One Jack Anderson had put off long enough.

Knowing his prey well, he took a direct route along the intricate network of canals that had inspired the city's nickname, Venice of the North. Every step he surveyed his surroundings with a well trained eye.

So far, the city had been untouched by war. Modern buildings stood shoulder to shoulder with the historic Baroque and Renaissance architecture that drew thousands of tourists to Hamburg every year. The city would not remain intact for long. The British were that determined.

Ignoring a twinge of remorse over the destruction to come, Jack put his mind back on his duty. Traffic was light at this hour, which made his surveillance of the area simple enough. He had chosen this specific route for a purpose. The SS needed to believe they had found him, rather than the other way around.

Enjoying the solitude while it lasted, he lifted his face

to the sky and sniffed. Winter was nearly here; he smelled it on the harsh wind.

Barely ten minutes into his walk, Jack found himself in front of the St. Nikolai Church. While his mind had worked on the mission, his feet had brought him to this bold reminder of God's holy presence in a fallen world. But rather than feeling hope at the sight of the magnificent structure, a wave of regret washed over Jack.

As much as he wanted to walk inside St. Nikolai, maybe get down on his knees and pray, he could not. Like all SS officers, Friedrich Reiter had renounced his church membership years ago. Jack could not be seen entering a church building. For any reason.

Another wave of regret flooded his mind. It was only a matter of time before the Nazis rid Germany of Christianity completely. A new religion had already been created for the people, one based on blood, soil, German folklore and the Thousand Year Reich.

Germany was on its way to becoming a godless country. Pastors and priests who dared to preach the one true Gospel were being sent to concentration camps as quickly as the Jews. Soon all the voices of dissent would be silenced.

Lord, what can one man do in the face of such evil?

The cold silence that followed his question was answer enough.

With a heavy heart, Jack started back down the street.

He barely covered a full block when a sleek staff Mercedes pulled alongside the curb. The vehicle slowed to a crawl, keeping perfect pace with Jack's long, easy strides.

The SS had found him.

A block away from the St. Nikolai Church.

Jack turned his head slowly, leisurely, in time to catch a flicker of movement behind the glass. Eyes free of all emotion, he pivoted to face the car directly. From the backseat, a man in the black uniform of the Gestapo motioned him closer.

Jack's fingers curled into fists. Heinrich Himmler had come himself.

The head of the SS had personally contacted Jack only on a handful of occasions, when the situation required secrecy, stealth and Friedrich Reiter's sinister methods of warfare.

Himmler contacting his dark angel of death now, in broad daylight, meant something big was in the works, something that couldn't wait for the cover of night.

At that thought, an increasing weight of responsibility settled onto Jack's shoulders. He was in too deep. And no one would come to get him out.

He was alone.

Or was he? *I am with you… I am your God.*

Himmler rolled down the window with precise slowness and then skimmed his ice-edged gaze over Jack. "Get in the car, Herr Reiter."

Jack's skin grew slick with sweat, the icy sensation slipping deep within his soul as though an arctic wind had swept through him. Dealing with a man like Hermann Schmidt was child's play compared to a confrontation with the head of the SS, second in power only to Hitler himself.

Squaring his shoulders, Jack climbed into the car, into the world of darkness and evil that defined Friedrich Reiter's existence.

"Herr *Reichsführer.*" Jack closed the car door with a snap. "I was on my way to you."

"How fortunate for us both I found you first."

Jack nodded.

The Nazi motioned to his driver to pull away from the curb, then fell into a long, cold silence. Watching. Waiting.

Jack held the other man's stare. In the stark light of day,

Himmler looked more like an accountant than the head of the SS. There was a kind of exacting, almost efficient, strain in the way he held himself erect and unmoving in his seat. The irony that so much power lay in the hands of such a small, nondescript man never ceased to amaze Jack.

Although there was nothing terrifying or demonic in Himmler's general demeanor, Jack had witnessed first-hand a bloodless indifference in the Nazi's character that made the man pure evil.

Jack's stomach pitched and rolled. As Friedrich Reiter, one of Himmler's most vicious secret agents, Jack wore anger and hatred like an ill-fitting skin. Darkness clung to him, its talons reaching all the way to the place he'd once kept his conscience. He was out of his league with such unprecedented evil.

He feared he'd never come back into the light.

Never will I leave you; never will I forsake you.

Jack nearly jolted at the reminder of God's promise racing through his mind. He'd long since turned his back on the Lord. And yet, had God stayed with him all this time? Did God's mercy run that deep?

"Herr Reiter." Himmler cleared his throat. "We are obliged whenever we meet to remind ourselves of our principles—"

"Blood, quality and toughness," Jack finished for him, accepting the verbal test for what it was—a subtle, yet dangerous, interrogation.

At his immediate response Himmler nodded in appreciation. "We weren't expecting your arrival for another three weeks."

With the suspicion sitting thick and heavy in the air between them, Jack shoved his desperation to cling to God into a dark pocket of his mind and donned the ruthlessness of his alter ego.

Friedrich Reiter would show only brutal efficiency, and nothing but absolute loyalty to his revered leader. "The early arrival was driven by my latest mission for the British."

"Which is?"

The British knew that Jack had to reveal certain facts to the Germans while gaining more valuable information for the British. It was a nasty, tricky business that often ended in both sides losing. But the few gains the British did learn were well worth the price. Or so the new head of MI6 had declared at Jack's last briefing.

"I am investigating a German naval secret weapon. One the British believe is responsible for sinking their cargo ships at an unprecedented rate."

Himmler looked sharply at Jack from behind his pince-nez. The man had a sobering capacity for weighing the underlying agenda behind straightforward information. Unnerving, yes, but potentially useful if Jack stayed focused.

"Then it is as I suspected," Himmler said.

Jack lifted a single eyebrow.

"Admiral Doenitz has withheld information from me."

Friedrich Reiter was a mindless killing machine, trained to allow the SS to do his thinking for him. A brainwashing, of sorts. One founded on paranoia. "You don't trust Admiral Doenitz." It was an obvious conclusion Reiter would make.

Himmler released an ugly, twisted laugh. "I trust no one outside of the SS. The admiral, in particular."

And *that,* Jack knew, was true enough. Himmler's paranoia was mind-boggling, yet all too real. Just a few months ago, he had created a state within the state. By law, the SS was now separate from all other German agencies and loyal to Himmler's personal agenda alone. Jack feared this cold-blooded Nazi's reign of terror was only just beginning.

He thought of the motto engraved on Friedrich Reiter's SS belt buckle and ceremonial dagger. *SS man, loyalty is thy honor.* Such blind obedience could only result in unspeakable horrors.

Jack let out a snort of disgust and tapped into the role he was supposed to be playing. "Doenitz is of the old guard. His ways are dying."

"Agreed. But the admiral is claiming those British shipping losses are a result of his superior U-boats. His fleet is not yet that strong." A calculating expression flashed in Himmler's gaze. "This secret weapon the British want you to investigate must be the true hero, not the U-boats."

"It's what MI6 believes. And why I am here."

Silence fell between them.

But then Himmler's eyes narrowed. "The actress you were with at the Schnebel Theater last night, how is she involved?"

Although Jack had expected Himmler to find out about his association with Kerensky, he had to swallow the quick reflex to deny knowing her. The best way to protect the woman from the fanatical Nazi was to give the obvious answer. "No, Herr *Reichsführer.* My involvement with Katarina Kerensky is of a…personal nature."

He let the insinuation settle between them.

"Ah, very wise. A woman with her connections could be useful to you in the future."

"Precisely." But if Jack had his way, her connections would soon be severed, because she would be living far away from Germany. In England. Or, better yet, America. If Jack was correct and she had so much as a drop of Jewish blood, she must leave Germany immediately.

The Führer's "final solution" was an unspeakable horror that must be stopped. Barring that, escape to all those soon to be affected.

For the first time since becoming Friedrich Reiter, Jack's desire to end the Nazi terror went beyond simple revenge.

Perhaps he was growing a conscience once more. Perhaps his earlier thoughts of God were the whisperings of the Holy Spirit. Perhaps everything—the attempted murder, the becoming an agent—had been leading him to this point in time. Not to stop the monster regime for his own personal reasons, but for people like Kerensky.

And what better way to bring down the enemy than from within its ranks? Could good come out of this evil situation? Perhaps, if God was personally involved. This mission was too big for Jack to carry out alone. But maybe he wasn't alone.

Lord, I—

Himmler's voice jerked him back to the matter at hand. "Your visit is indeed timely, my friend." A terrifying display of obsession flashed in the Nazi's eyes.

Here it comes. The reason Himmler had sought him out this morning.

Jack shifted in his seat. "Tell me what you want me to do." He spoke in Reiter's uncompromising tone.

"I want you to find a way into the Krupp-Germaniawerft shipyard in Kiel, where they are outfitting a U-boat with a new weapon, the same one I suspect the British have sent you to investigate."

Jack held his anticipation in check. *This* was the value of his secret life, this gathering of information from both sides so that he could piece together a solution to help the British war effort. "As you wish, Herr *Reichsführer.*"

"One last request, Herr Reiter."

Jack felt a chill run down his neck, but he held Himmler's unblinking stare.

"I want the information in less than twenty-four hours."

Jack released an almost vicious laugh. "You have great faith in my abilities."

"I have great faith in *my* abilities." Himmler set a black leather briefcase on the seat between them. "Open it."

Jack shot a quick glance at the other man, but Himmler's impassive eyes gave nothing away.

Staring straight ahead, Jack placed the case on his lap. With a steady hand, he released the latch and drew out two sets of blueprints. He ran his finger across the outline of the first. "A German U-boat."

"A brand new design for a U-boat, to be precise," Himmler said. "Type XB is the first of its kind. But there are two more on the way."

Jack's gaze flew across the page. His mind raced, absorbing details, memorizing the technical aspects of the submarine's structure that was so different from other U-boats. "I've never seen one like this before. There are only two torpedo tubes at the stern."

"A feature unique to the XB. You will also see a total of thirty shafts along here." Himmler dragged his finger to the other side of the drawing. "And here."

Jack did a quick calculation. "The dimensions are too large for standard torpedoes." Which meant only one thing.

A new weapon. One that had been kept secret from the SS.

Himmler spoke Jack's thoughts aloud. "We believe the shafts were specifically designed to carry another type of weapon. Your job is to find out what that weapon is, exactly."

Jack nodded, scanning the blueprint with the eyes of the naval engineer he'd been before Reiter had come to kill him. He read each notation, then reviewed the overall proportions. "What's her weight, submerged and fully loaded?"

"Top capacity is 2,710 tons."

Jack released a low whistle. "That makes the XB the largest U-boat ever built. She must pay the price in diving speed and agility."

"Which, again, leads us to believe the XB was built for a different function than open warfare."

"And you want me to verify the nature of the secret weapon, nothing more?"

"That's all." Himmler's lips thinned into a tight line. "For now."

Jack flipped to the next set of blueprints. His eyes scanned the outline of the Krupp-Germaniawerft shipyard, focusing on the U-boat pens just north of the yard facing the Bay of Kiel.

"U-116 is in sub bay A-4, which is," Himmler stated as he pointed to a spot in the northeast quadrant of the yard, "here."

Jack held back a grin. With the blueprints of the XB submarine and the Kiel shipyard memorized, the completion of his mission for the British would be easy.

Too easy.

Himmler must have another agenda for sending Friedrich Reiter to the Kiel shipyard.

Was it a trap? Had Jack somehow betrayed himself since his last visit to Germany? No. If that were the case, he would already be under interrogation at Number 8, Prinz Albrecht Strasse.

With one trip to Kiel, Jack could gain the information he needed to help the British formulate a countermeasure for the bombs. Success tonight meant he would not have to involve Kerensky in the mission any further. In that, at least, he could keep her safe.

Thank You, Lord. It was his first prayer in two years. Short, imperfect, but heartfelt.

Returning the blueprints to the briefcase, Jack pulled the top down and clicked the latch in place. For now, he would think only in terms of the offensive. "I will have your information by 2300 tonight."

"You realize, of course, there can be no room for error." Himmler smiled, very slightly and with just enough vicious intent to alert Jack to the Nazi's dark mood.

"There never is, Herr *Reichsführer.*" Jack returned the smile with equal intensity, his mind drumming up an image of Katarina's sparkling eyes as they'd last stared into his. "There never is."

Chapter Fourteen

Katia didn't relish the upcoming confrontation with Friedrich Reiter, especially after their strained lunch. Aside from the tension-filled exchanges he'd shared with Hermann and her mother, the British spy had boldly staked a claim on Katia. Katia, for her part, had played cheerfully along. A little too cheerfully.

She could try to tell herself that her behavior was all part of the cover they'd been building since the first time they'd met at the theater, but she knew better. A very real connection was building between them.

Unfortunately, Katia had not been the only one to notice. The interrogation she'd suffered from both her mother and Hermann had been long and tedious. Worn out from the experience, Katia considered turning around and settling into a hot bath. But this was not about her. She'd stalled long enough. She had to tell Reiter about her mistake in Admiral Doenitz's private chambers.

Resolved to face the worst, she headed up the front steps of the *Vier Jahreszeiten* hotel.

The late-afternoon wind blew bitter and harsh against her exposed cheeks. Katia didn't mind the cold. She found the nasty weather appropriate for the situation.

Entering the lobby with her famous smile in place, she sauntered toward the heavyset clerk standing behind the reception desk. His balding head shone from the reflection of the lights overhead. The poor fellow stared at her with a mixture of shock and interest.

"Fräulein Kerensky." He bowed in a show of deference reminiscent of old Russia. "What may I do for you?"

The clerk's reverence might remind her of all she'd lost, but this was not the time for nostalgia. "I understand Friedrich Reiter is a guest in this hotel."

"That is correct." The clerk spoke with meticulous politeness, but his eyes began filling with questions. Questions his training prevented him from asking.

She pulled a man's leather glove out of her purse, a prop she'd borrowed from the theater this afternoon. With a flourish, she set the article on the counter. "Herr Reiter left this at my home last evening."

The clerk swallowed, his double chin jiggling from the gesture. "I... Yes, I think I understand. Would you like me to deliver it to his room for you?"

The part of a woman without morals was not one of her favorite roles. In fact, the real Katia, the one she hid under all the subterfuge and lies, was appalled by the shamelessness required of the role. But if she could use her talent for nothing else, she could use it to save innocent lives. Ultimately. She had to get past this German first.

She swallowed her apprehension, shoved the real Katia a little deeper in her mind, and went to work.

"I wish to return the item to him personally. You understand." She punctuated her statement with a sly grin. "Perhaps you wouldn't mind telling me his room number?"

"I cannot give out that information, Fräulein." The clerk dropped his gaze to his toes. "It is against hotel policy."

"Come, now, Herr—" she scanned his name tag "—Schroeder. Won't you bend the rule this one time? For me?"

She drew slow, mesmerizing circles along the glossy reception desk as she spoke.

Schroeder swallowed, his gaze riveted on her swirling finger. "Room 312," he said in a choked whisper. "But you didn't hear it from me."

She placed her hand on top of his pudgy fingers and squeezed gently. "Hear what?" Her tone dripped with syrup.

Stuffing the glove back in her purse, she aimed a quick wink at the clerk, and then made her way toward the elevator. His choked gasp was far more rewarding than applause.

Fully aware that all eyes were on her now, she tilted her nose at a regal angle. After pushing the brass button, she lifted her chin another notch. Because this particular role required unprecedented boldness, she didn't fidget, didn't look around, didn't make eye contact with the couple waiting for the elevator with her.

Although she had to share the small space with the gawking duo, she pretended not to notice how they whispered back and forth as she settled in next to them. She thought she heard something about her loose morals. Katia stifled a sigh. They were obviously too polite or perhaps too conventional to make any comment to her directly.

Typical German behavior, she thought with a hint of bitterness. Never make waves, never question authority and always, *always* look the other way. Like so many in the Fatherland, the elderly pair had been too easily "brought into line" by the Nazis.

For one black moment, Katia wanted to turn and scream at the couple, to yell at them to open their eyes and stop the atrocities going on in their own country.

But what would be the point? Most Germans were, well, they were just so *German*. Her own mother included. When bad things happened to them or their loved ones, they turned the other cheek. Literally. Not out of obedience to the pacifism taught by Christ in the Gospel, but out of fear. And maybe even laziness.

How many times must they be slapped down until they rose up and rebelled? A hundred? A thousand? Or would they never rise up?

Would they simply adapt to the horrors around them, as Elena Kerensky seemed to be doing?

Feeling a great burden resting on her shoulders, Katia rushed out of the elevator at the third floor. She held her breath until she heard the soft swoosh of the doors closing behind her.

Alone at last, she took a deep breath and headed down the hallway, toward room 312. After only a few steps, however, she caught sight of her quarry exiting his room.

He ambled along at an easy pace. She wasn't fooled by the lack of urgency in his steps. Even from this distance, Friedrich Reiter radiated absolute power. He was a man in control of everything, and everyone, around him. Yet there was something else that set him apart. It took her a moment to understand what made him different. He carried none of the Nazi intimidation in his manner. At least not with her.

Odd she would notice that about him now.

He stared at her as he approached.

Her face heated in a blush.

A blush? When was the last time Katarina Kerensky blushed? Long before Hitler had risen to power.

Reiter stopped mere inches in front of her and raked his gaze over her in blunt appraisal. Although the gesture was beyond rude, arrogant even, there was something un-mistakably soft in his eyes.

Captivated, she leaned forward but just as quickly pulled back. "We need to talk," she blurted out.

Feet splayed, hands clasped behind his back, the air around him crackled with impatience. He was clearly headed somewhere important.

"Perhaps another time," he said.

Gone were any signs of the cooperative partner in a shared mission. This was a man who worked alone, a man who needed no one's assistance. "But you don't understand. I must—"

"I said another time, Katarina." He linked his arm through hers and began leading her back toward the elevator.

Caught off guard, she allowed him to turn her around but sanity quickly returned and she dug in her heels. "I haven't yet told you why I'm here."

"It will have to wait. As you can see, I'm on my way out." He looked meaningfully at his watch. "And you have other obligations this evening."

"No, the theater is dark tonight. And I don't have any—"

"What of your mother and her fiancé?"

He had a point. A very valid point. Although no specific plans had been made, Hermann and Elena would expect her company later. "This won't take long."

She tossed her hair behind her back and hurried down the hallway toward his room.

Reiter caught up to her in five strides. "Perhaps you didn't hear me correctly." He clamped a hand on her arm, his gentle touch at odds with the frustration in his gaze. "I said I was heading out."

"What's the rush?"

"As I said, I have to attend to some business tonight."

She didn't like the sound of that. "You will want to hear what I have to say first."

She shrugged away from him and continued down the corridor. "Ah, here we are." She tapped the gold numbers on the door in front of her. "Room 312."

He appeared to debate with himself before letting out a frustrated burst of air. "This better be good."

"Actually, it's rather bad."

A thousand words passed between them without a sound. "Another piece of information you forgot to divulge?"

His directness made her hesitate. But she'd come this far. She wouldn't back down now. "Can we at least do this inside?"

He rubbed a hand down his face, muttered something unflattering about obstinate females. "All right. But don't say a word until I tell you it's safe."

"Safe?"

"We won't be the only ones listening."

The Gestapo had wired his room with a listening device? Already? She hadn't expected this. But she should have. Friedrich Reiter, whoever he was, was not a man to go unnoticed in a place like Hamburg for long.

She needed to be careful with him. Very, very careful.

Pushing past the threshold, Katia made a slow, comprehensive sweep of the room. She noted the spotless tabletops, the shining fixtures and the rest of the perfect decor. It struck her as odd that nothing was out of place. Not even a stray newspaper. She opened her mouth to remark on his unusual neatness, but he stopped her with a finger against her lips.

Frozen like that, with him standing so close she could smell his spicy, woodsy scent, she simply stared at him.

He stared back. Another moment passed, and then another. Their breathing fell into a shared rhythm.

Her head grew dangerously light.

All the fear she'd told herself she didn't feel, all the tension she'd denied for days, came crashing into her. For one insane moment she wanted to trust this man. She wanted him to share her burdens for a while. She wanted to tell him about her heritage.

She would not, of course. For one, the deadly secret was not hers alone.

"Katarina, *darling*." As he lowered his hand from her lips, the warning in his gaze cut like a blade. "What a surprise to see you...."

He trailed off, pointed to a table on her left, the telephone on her right and then up to the ceiling.

Three listening devices in this room alone? Someone wanted to keep a close eye on the man.

Nodding her understanding, she settled into her role. "You left your glove at my home last evening."

"And you couldn't wait to get it back to me, is that it?" His voice sounded amused, but his eyes were deadly serious.

"Something like that." For the benefit of the secret police listening to them, she continued talking in a soft, almost coy tone. She might hate this role but she played it well. "Or perhaps I simply missed you."

He gave her a very masculine chuckle in response. "Ah, darling. What fun you are."

He took two long strides toward a table, then fiddled with the dial of a modern-looking radio until the strains of a Wagner opera crackled in the air between them. *Tristan and Isolde.* Another story of star-crossed lovers. How... appropriate.

"Why don't you come over here and show me just how much you missed me."

She knew her duty, knew it was important to be obvious. She also knew she could very well be heading straight to her doom with this man.

"I thought you'd never ask." She forced out a carefree laugh through very tight lips. No one would believe Katarina Kerensky had to work at this, not even Katia herself.

He turned the volume up a notch, and then kissed her on the...

Forehead.

The gesture was so sweet, and so at odds with the routine they performed that Katia's knees nearly gave out.

"Well." He kissed her again. On the forehead. Again. "That's certainly a nice beginning."

She started trembling, but so did he. For different reasons, she supposed. She could all but feel the impatience vibrating out of him, the frustration at being detained.

Or was it something else that made his hands flex and then relax at his side?

A vague sense of hope shot through her at the thought. She was on dangerous ground with this man, potentially life shattering. She had to remember this was an act for them both.

"I can do better," she said.

This time his chuckle came out low and slightly amused. "Please do."

But he didn't move toward her. The kiss, then, was up to her. She released her breath very slowly, very carefully. No one knew the importance of playing this role with practiced skill better than Katia. Swallowing one last time, she set her hands on his shoulders and lifted onto her toes until her lips gently touched his.

She drew quickly away. "Something like that?"

"It's certainly better than the first." His eyes filled with a challenge. "Why not try that again?"

The air knotted in her throat. She could do this. Of course she could do this. Lifting up again, she touched her lips to his for a second pass. Like a clichéd heroine in a Hollywood movie, she had to cling to him to keep from falling backward. "How was that?" she rasped.

"Much better."

His gaze filled with genuine affection. But in the next instant his expression closed, making him look as if nothing had happened out of the ordinary. The man was a rock.

Stone-faced, he gestured for her to follow him out onto the balcony. She wanted to rage at him for his coldness. She wanted to demand he show some emotion, any emotion. But she knew she wouldn't voice any of her thoughts aloud. The man was a professional spy. And so was she.

This was not a time to lose her head over a man, especially a dangerous one like Friedrich Reiter.

This was a time to take control.

Chapter Fifteen

Head high, determination firmly in place, Katia left all weakness in the room behind her and walked past the double doors leading onto the balcony. At the same moment, the big round sun dipped below the flat line of the horizon.

Utter darkness would soon descend over the city.

"Remember to keep your voice down," Reiter said.

She managed a tense nod in response.

Leaning back against the rail, he stretched his long legs out in front of him. The gesture made him look like he had endless time on his hands.

They both knew better.

"What was so important that it couldn't wait until later?"

Now that the time had come, she couldn't find the words. She hadn't expected her dignity to be so difficult to swallow. Glancing past him, she took a moment to gather her thoughts. Katarina Kerensky was not used to making mistakes. Admitting to them came hard.

"Katarina?"

Sighing, she shifted her gaze back to Reiter's. In a rush of whispered words, she told him everything, concluding with the exact angle of the misplaced chair.

He said nothing. Nor did he move. But she could see him pulling back from her, distancing himself mentally.

"Well?" she prompted.

Five long seconds ticked by, and still, he kept silent.

She dug her nails into her palms. "Do you have nothing to say?"

When he continued looking at her, completely unresponsive, with that unreadable glint in his gaze, she had to resist the urge to reach out and shake him.

But then...

Realization dawned. "You knew," she said. "You already knew."

"Not precisely. But from your conduct in the car this morning, I sensed something had occurred."

Hot tears of frustration stung in her eyes. All this time, he'd suspected something had gone awry and yet he hadn't said a word.

Was he that much of a gentleman? Or that much of a fiend? "I'm rendered speechless."

His lids drooped over his eyes. "Indeed."

She wanted to hate him for his casual behavior, but instead she found herself admiring him for his ability to remain calm in spite of his obvious anger.

He tried to push past her, but Katia grabbed his arm before he could leave the balcony. He looked down at her hand. She quickly released him.

"What do we do now?" she asked.

"We?"

"I'll do whatever it takes to put things right."

"You've done enough. Now, if you'll excuse me." He did not leave the balcony right away. Instead, he leaned against the doorjamb and gave her an impatient lift of a single eyebrow.

He was dismissing her.

Understandable, given the circumstances. If their roles were reversed, she'd react the same way. The wise response on her part would be to trust this British spy to finish the job on his own.

But could she trust him? This man she'd only met the night before?

The obvious answer was *no*.

Time was running out, not only for this mission but for everyone, including the British. England had suffered unprecedented losses from the Nazi secret weapon they were investigating, half of which were merchant ships carrying much needed supplies. If the British Isles were cut off from the rest of the world, England would fall to Germany. And if England fell, who would rise up to stop Hitler?

Katia could not put her trust in anyone other than herself. With a man like Hitler at the helm of Germany, the stakes were too high. "We don't know the mission has been compromised," she whispered.

"It doesn't matter. The moment you left that chair out of place was the moment you became a liability."

"Not necessarily. I can find out the extent of the damage tomorrow night, at my mother's party when the admiral arrives."

His jaw tightened. Clearly, he was having a hard time holding on to his patience. "We can't wait that long. Our options are dwindling. But if I leave now I may still be able to salvage this mess."

"Wherever you're going, take me with you." Desperation made her voice come out shrill.

"Katarina." He pushed forward and reached for her hand. "My darling." The endearment, along with compassion in his eyes, cut past her well-laid defenses.

She placed her palm against his.

"Why is this so important to you? Tell me what is driving your resolve. Perhaps I can help."

She trembled at the implication of his words. Did he know what he asked of her? The terrible burden he would take on his shoulders if she answered him truthfully?

Pressing his lips into a grim line, Reiter tugged her against his chest. He held her tightly in his arms, too tightly, as though he feared she would pull away at any moment.

In truth, he had nothing to worry about. She relaxed in his embrace. If only for this one instant, she wanted to rest in this man's strength. He felt real and solid and trustworthy.

"Have faith in me," he whispered into her hair. "Trust me with your secret."

She heard his sincerity. And in that moment, she knew that she could trust him. She *would* trust him. "I have a Jewish ancestor, a maternal grandparent."

Her words were barely audible but she knew he'd heard her because his already tight hold squeezed even more.

She struggled to free herself.

He loosened his embrace and stepped back first. His blue eyes stared at her for a long moment, giving her a glimpse into their unguarded depths. She saw pain. Raw pain.

"Does Schmidt know?"

"*No.* And he can never find out. No one can find out." She grasped his arm. "My mother must not be put in danger."

"I understand."

He took her hand, placed a soft kiss on her palm, and then stepped back again. Although he'd created physical distance, she detected no other withdrawal in him. In fact, with his stiff shoulders and strained gaze, he looked as tortured as she felt.

"Don't look at me that way," she whispered.

He cupped her cheek with his palm, the rough calluses warm against her skin. "You are very brave, Katarina."

She leaned into his hand. "I am no such thing. I... I'm frightened all the time."

"Then why?" He lowered his hand slowly. "Why do you stay in Germany? Why—" He cut off his own words. "Your mother."

"Yes."

He knew everything now.

All the subterfuge between them was gone. There was only honesty left. And truth. The kind of purity of emotion she hadn't known since her childhood.

Unfortunately, she was not a child anymore. She lived in a dangerous world of mean-spirited men with evil agendas. And she'd just laid her secret before a man she'd met only a day ago.

Panic tried to claw to the surface at the realization. Katia shoved the emotion back with a hard swallow. And then she did something she hadn't done since she was nine years old. She prayed.

Heavenly Father, please let this man be worthy of my trust.

What if God still ignored her? What if she'd said the prayer too late?

She knew so little about this man. Nothing, really. Nothing, except the fact that he was a dangerous spy with his own set of personal agendas.

And she'd just admitted the one thing that could get her and her mother killed.

What had she done?

She'd become weak. He'd made her weak with his sincerity and answering pain.

She was vulnerable now, completely at his mercy. If he proved false, who would rescue her? God? The Lord hadn't saved her father. Why would He save her now?

Her hand flew to her throat. She'd made a terrible blunder with her confession. What if—

"No, Katarina. Don't fear me." He pulled her into his arms once again. "I will never hurt you. Never."

She believed him.

Lord, Lord, why bring this man to me now? When there is still so much work to be done in Germany, so many lives to save and so little time left?

Pressed against him, she could feel his heart beating as hard as her own.

"We have much to discuss," Reiter said. "But I cannot put off my…errand any longer."

"Please, take me with you." She couldn't bear to do nothing, not when she'd been the one to compromise the mission.

"It's too dangerous." He released a long breath of air. "Let me take you home. I'll come for you once I've completed my task and we'll talk. Really talk."

The look he gave her was full of promises. He was no longer the jaded spy or hardened skeptic she'd met the night before. He was a man smitten with her, a man she could trust wholeheartedly, a man willing to protect her with his life.

She'd seen a similar look before, in a number of masculine gazes. But this time she knew the same unguarded expression was there in her eyes, as well.

"Trust me, Katarina," he whispered. "I will help you. And your mother."

Her heart softened toward him.

She was lost. Deeply and truly lost.

"All right," she agreed. "You may take me home."

"You'll wait for me there?"

"I'll wait." *For as long as you ask.*

At the yielding look in Katarina's eyes, Jack caught his breath. He wanted to be worthy of such unabashed trust. He had no idea if he was. *Lord, don't let me fail this woman. I need Your strength.*

Would his short prayer be enough? After all the sins he'd committed, would God hear him now when another person's life depended on his actions?

Afraid for them both, Jack lowered his head toward Katarina's and then stopped halfway down.

What was he doing?

He took a step back and shoved a hand through his hair.

Head swimming, muscles tense, he took another step back, away from temptation, away from a woman who had the power to take his mind off his duty. All because she'd had the courage to admit her deadly secret to him.

Katarina Kerensky was the bravest person he knew.

He tried to refocus his thoughts, concentrating his efforts on what must be done to protect her. The first was to complete their mission on his own. Tonight.

The rest they would decide later.

"Once I drop you off at your house, I will return as quickly as possible." He kept his voice just above a whisper. He didn't want to frighten her, but if she had a Jewish relative—no matter how distant—she was in real danger.

And so was her mother, which added layers of unpleasant dimensions to an already precarious situation. At least the silent warnings and contradictions he'd seen in Elena Kerensky's eyes made better sense now.

"Perhaps we should be on our way." She pivoted in the direction of his hotel room.

He saw her hesitate, then visibly take hold of herself. She regretted her confession.

He would not allow her to buckle under fear now.

"No, Katarina, don't let doubt into your heart." He drew up behind her. "You've trusted me this far, trust me a little while longer."

She turned to face him. "Do you really think this can end well?" A silent plea shimmered in her eyes.

The Lord's words washed over him again. *Never will I leave you; never will I forsake you.* The promise came stronger this time, clearer. As did the sense of peace Jack had thought no longer existed for him.

God had never left him. Jack had been the one to turn away. He'd convinced himself he was alone as Friedrich Reiter. But perhaps atonement began with the simple acknowledgment of the Lord's hand in his life, even in this deadly time of war.

Especially in this deadly time of war.

"Maybe we both need a little more faith," he said aloud.

"Faith?" She angled her head in a show of genuine confusion at his choice of words. "Faith in what? Each other?"

"No. That will take time," he admitted. "What I meant," he said as he took a deep breath, "was faith in God."

He saw the light of optimism in her eyes, right before her face crumbled into a look of stark agony. "God turned His back on me a long time ago."

How many times had Jack thought that same thing in the last two years of his life? Too many times to count. An intense wave of sadness passed through him, sadness for her, for him, for them both. "I understand how you feel, Katarina." He pressed his palm against her cheek again. "More than you know."

Her expression wavered, softened, then firmly closed, as his own would have done had someone said those same words to him before this afternoon. He dropped his hand to his side. "Now is not the time for this discussion."

"No. In that we agree."

Putting his mind back on the mission, he led her into the hotel room then directed her to the open suitcase positioned on the table beside the radio. Opening a hidden panel, he pointed to the cabinet key he'd had made from the wax impression.

She lifted her eyes to his, a question lit in their depths.

"In case something happens to me tonight." He left the rest unspoken.

The quick flash of terror in her eyes—terror for him—caught him by surprise and another layer of his hard exterior melted away.

Katarina Kerensky had done what no other woman had done before. She'd nudged her way into his heart with her convictions and sacrifices and genuine concern for his safety.

Would this brave woman be his salvation, or his ultimate doom?

Chapter Sixteen

21 November 1939, Sengwarden, Wilhelmshaven,
1900 Hours

The promise of a long, hard winter roared into the harbor on a fierce wind off the North Sea. Grim faced and resolute, Admiral Karl Doenitz studied the snow whipping past his office window. The blinding winter wonderland only added depth to his growing headache.

Turning away from the view, Doenitz settled a scowl on the young sailor standing at attention on the other side of his desk. Cold fury tried to work free, but he vowed to listen to the boy's excuses before determining his ultimate fate in the *Kriegsmarine*.

Clasping his hands behind his back, Doenitz got straight to the point. "I understand, *Fähnrich* Heintzman, that you had an unusual meeting last evening." He snapped out the statement with a flick of steel in his voice.

Staring straight ahead, Heintzman's face remained blank. But Doenitz saw behind the mask. Just past the layer of shock stood fear, surprise and guilt. It was the guilt that interested Doenitz most. "Well?"

"I… Yes, sir, it was quite unusual."

Doenitz picked up Heintzman's report off his desk. He'd already interviewed five of the six guards on duty last evening. Heintzman was the last. "And yet I see you failed to include any mention of the incident in your report."

A muscle in the boy's cheek jerked. "I didn't think it was worth mentioning, sir."

"You didn't think?" In a fit of uncharacteristic rage, Doenitz slammed down the paper on the desk. "It is not your place to think, *Fähnrich,* but to follow procedure."

"I…" Heintzman wisely trailed off and waited for Doenitz to continue.

"When a sailor is given an order, it doesn't matter whether he *thinks* the order serves any purpose." Outrage made Doenitz's voice low and deadly. "He obeys without question."

"I regret not serving my Fatherland to my utmost ability."

Under normal circumstances, Karl Doenitz considered himself a fair man. Although these were anything but normal circumstances, he hesitated from instituting rough justice just yet. "Perhaps it is not too late to save what is left of your career, *Obermaat.*"

Heintzman choked down a loud gulp. *"Obermaat?"*

"The demotion is the least of your worries. Know that I will issue formal charges if you refuse to cooperate completely from this moment forward."

Heintzman opened his mouth, closed it and then nodded.

Doenitz picked up the report again, skimmed it quickly. Normally, he hated to repeat himself but as he reviewed the incomplete notations, renewed anger clutched around his heart, and he slammed the paper onto the desk a second time. "I want to know the name of this actress, the one you bragged about meeting to your fellow guards but failed to mention in your report."

It was training, or perhaps self-preservation, that had the sailor answering without hesitation. "Katarina Kerensky."

As he let the significance of the boy's revelation sink in, Doenitz came around his desk. "*The* Katarina Kerensky?"

"Yes, sir."

"She is one of the most well-known names in Germany, perhaps in the world. Are you telling me that she came into this obscure fishing village, yet you failed to report the incident?"

"She promised me tickets to her play and a trip backstage if I kept our meeting quiet." His voice shook, as though he'd only just realized how damning his explanation sounded.

"She asked you to keep the incident to yourself?"

"She wasn't alone. She was with a man, they were…" The boy's gaze darted around the room, dropped to the floor, lifted again. "They didn't want stares."

"Katarina Kerensky came here, to Wilhelmshaven of all places, for a tryst?"

"That was my understanding."

It was plausible, Doenitz admitted to himself. A famous woman would certainly want anonymity if she were involved in something so inappropriate. In such a case, leaving the city made perfect sense. Except, of course, that the woman's secret jaunt to Wilhelmshaven was on the exact night as the break-in into the commanding officer's private quarters.

Doenitz thought of the tiny window in his bedroom. The dimensions were far too small for a man to fit through, but perfect for a woman. She would have needed help getting in, however, just as she had needed help—with the use of his chair—to get back out. Hence, the addition of a lover. "You said she was with a man. What was this man's name?"

Heintzman divided a cautious look between Doenitz and the floor, eventually settling on the floor. "I didn't get his name."

"You didn't get it, or he didn't offer it?"

"Both. Neither. I mean—"

"I know what you mean." Doenitz drew himself up. "What did this man look like?"

Heintzman took a deep breath then let it out slowly. "Nordic. Tall, dark blond hair, large frame. Definitely an officer, he had that kind of command about him. But he wasn't in uniform."

"What was he wearing?"

"I don't remember." The seaman's eyebrows slammed together. "It was dark. He blended with the night."

"And he didn't offer his name, or insist you make a report?"

"No, sir. He looked, well, uh, that is, he kissed Fräulein Kerensky like a man in love."

"You saw the two kiss?"

Heintzman gave a clipped affirmative and added, "Under a streetlight."

"They kissed out in the open. But earlier you said they came to Wilhelmshaven to avoid stares."

"Yes, sir, that's what they told me. Which was why they were dressed in black, perhaps?"

"All black? Both of them?"

"Yes. I remember now. I thought it odd at first, until they explained their need for secrecy. Oh, and the fräulein was wearing pants."

Now they were getting somewhere. "Not an evening dress?"

"No, sir."

Another discrepancy. Another step closer to uncovering the identity of the intruder. Every instinct told Doenitz he had found his man. Or rather, *woman*.

But why would Katarina Kerensky break into his private quarters? And who was the man with her? What, exactly, had they been after? Doenitz knew if he found the answer to one question, he would find the answer to the rest.

Ignoring Heintzman for a moment, he advanced to the other end of his desk and rummaged through a stack of personal correspondence. Pulling out a crisp white square of heavy parchment, he studied the invitation's gold-embossed lettering. Elena Kerensky's annual ball hadn't been an event he'd relished attending.

Until now.

Surely the woman's daughter, the famous princess turned stage actress, would be in attendance with all the other important men and women of the Third Reich.

That was it, of course. Instead of waiting for the intruder to come to him a second time, Doenitz would approach him, or rather her, first.

Now that he knew who he was looking for, and where he could find her, time was on his side. He would go to the ball as planned. He would watch. He would assess.

With one small mistake on her part, and cold, clear thinking on his part, the woman would be his in no time.

He simply needed to proceed with patience.

Fortunately, Admiral Karl Doenitz was a *very* patient man.

By the time Jack arrived at Kiel, the cold mist in the air had become a milky-white shroud. The fog all but strangled the meager light from the waxing moon. Testing the depth of visibility, Jack thrust out his hand in front of him. The lower half of his arm disappeared into the thick soup.

He would have to rely on his memory of the shipyard's position and layout from the blueprints he'd studied earlier that morning in Himmler's car.

With slow, cautious steps, Jack approached the complex from the southeast, cloaking himself inside the impenetrable fog. The crack of boot to ground had him freezing in midstep. The noise came again, behind him and off to his left. Loud, precise, unmistakable.

Cocking his head, Jack listened to the cadence of boots hitting gravel. Click, a short pause, another click, pause. Click, pause, click, pause...

One man. Twenty feet away, his footsteps striking the hard, frozen ground in a slow but steady rhythm.

Glad he'd left Kerensky in the safety of her own home, Jack blew into his cupped palms, flexed his fingers, then pulled out his gun. Crouched low, he slipped into the edge of the dense forest, cleared his mind. And waited.

In a matter of seconds, a beam of light arced in a right-to-left pattern on the road.

Jack couldn't make out the exact uniform the guard wore, or the type of rifle he carried. However, he could hear the man muttering to himself, grumbling about the cold weather and the rotten shift he'd pulled three nights in a row.

An amateur. Probably local police.

Jack knew he could avoid detection by letting the guard continue on his way. But if Jack could silence the man now, his exit out of the shipyard would go much smoother.

Decision made, Jack holstered his gun. He wouldn't have to kill the man, just render him temporarily useless.

As the guard passed by, Jack fell into step behind him.

He couldn't actually see his quarry, only the sweeping light on the road at his feet.

Jack stepped forward. He could hear the man's breathing now, *feel* his nervous energy crackling like electricity on the air.

Another step and Jack slipped his left arm around the man's throat, palm over his mouth, and yanked him backward. The flashlight tumbled to the ground, clicked off at the moment of impact.

Using the thumb of his right hand, Jack applied pressure to the guard's wrist until the gun fell onto the gravel with a dull thud.

Flailing hands came up in a wild fight to fend off Jack's attack. Jack tightened his grip, and the hands fell away.

After another moment, the guard started making odd gurgling sounds.

Self-reproach tried to rise inside Jack, guilt tried to blunt his edge and make him quit before he had the man subdued.

Jack turned off his mind, adjusted his hold, let his training take over.

The gurgling sounds morphed into strangled gasps.

Enough was enough.

A quick blow to the temple and the guard went limp.

Silently, Jack laid his prey onto the ground, far enough off the road to avoid detection.

He took an extra moment to check for a pulse at the throat. The beat against his fingertip came slow, steady, but strong enough to tell Jack he'd done no permanent damage to the man.

Working quickly now, Jack emptied the bullets from the guard's gun, stashed them in his pocket, and then tossed the weapon into the dense underbrush lining the road.

Retrieving the flashlight, he flicked the switch. The

shaft of light flickered, then died. Jack flung aside the useless object and listened to the movements of the night.

Somewhere in the distance, a foghorn wailed, deep and low. The sound kicked him into action.

Moving slowly, he proceeded forward, pausing every few steps to listen and recalculate his position.

At an estimated fifteen yards from the front gate of the shipyard he crouched low. Blood pounded loudly in his ears, making it hard to hear. He took several deep breaths until his pulse steadied.

For several more minutes, he simply listened to the movement of the guard at the front gate, or rather lack of movement. The rhythmic breathing indicated a deep sleep.

Another amateur.

Rising, Jack trekked silently through the gate no more than two feet from the slumbering guard.

Simplicity was often very effective.

Veering left, Jack took a moment to gather his bearings.

Halos of golden mist surrounded a large pole light, creating a murky beacon in the center of the complex. As he worked his way to the northeast quadrant of the yard, he continued to gauge his surroundings.

A light breeze kicked up, sending damp fog slithering along the concrete walls of the cavernous submarine bays. Three massive cranes loomed over ships in various stages of completion.

Everywhere he looked, giant rubber hoses crisscrossed over one another along the ground, presenting a perilous walkway. Hammers, saws, rivet guns and grinders sat in neat rows along metal shelves to the left of the dry docks.

The Krupp-Germaniawerft looked like every other shipyard. However, considering the nature of the work commissioned by the *Kriegsmarine,* Jack thought it was odd that he found no guards patrolling the inner perimeter of the complex.

A trap? Or typical German arrogance? Were the owners of the shipyard so consumed with keeping intruders out, that they had left themselves vulnerable to attack from the inside?

Jack stayed hidden in the shadows as he made his way to the U-boat pens. He quickly located U-116 by its size and position facing the Bay of Kiel.

A small loading crane lay just to the left of the sub, but there was no cache of weapons waiting to be hauled up.

Were the mines already inside the U-boat?

Prepared to enter the steel beast, Jack crossed to the wooden walkway leading to the deck. But he froze as a beam of light swung next to his feet.

So. There was a roaming guard, after all.

Wheeling around, Jack slipped behind the tall stack of the U-boat. Heart hammering in his chest, he tapped in to the man he'd once been. He closed his eyes and prayed. *Lord, I need Your courage and protection tonight.*

The light swept past again. Left to right. Right to left. Jack counted off the seconds between each arc. By his calculations, the guard was closing in on him.

Running out of time, Jack considered his options.

He could scramble into the U-boat, but the beam of light was getting closer. Too close. As much as he hated failure, Jack couldn't risk capture now that he was this far into the mission.

He would simply have to wait for the guard to complete his sweep of the complex before climbing into the U-boat.

Resigned, Jack settled into position to wait.

And then the shouting began.

Chapter Seventeen

Jack froze as the individual shouts blended into one long, angry spurt of German.

All at once, several floodlights burst to life, creating a muted halo of light around each pole. The crack and buzz of electricity surging through ice-coated wires overwhelmed the other noises.

But soon the angry shouts prevailed once more.

Crouching low, Jack stayed in position behind the U-boat stack. In spite of the cold air, he started sweating. He considered ducking inside the sub, but the odds of getting out undetected were heavily against him. The U-boat could easily become his coffin.

He opted to wait it out a bit longer.

One voice lifted above the others, and Jack was finally able to make out the individual words.

He didn't like what he heard.

The guard he had hit on the head had recovered. As a result, every man on duty was searching for the intruder.

His primary goal now was to get out of the shipyard as quickly and as quietly as possible.

He began to walk briskly toward the outer rim of the yard, away from the commotion. He had to fight the need to rush his steps. Catching sight of three pale beams of light vibrating through the fog, he changed direction.

Never will I leave you; never will I forsake you.

Fusing with the shadows, Jack clung to God's promise as he moved at an angle perpendicular to the one he'd used to enter the yard.

Lord, be with me now. I can't succeed without Your help.

After a few more steps, he stopped again, listened to the raised voices and scrambling of feet. He guessed five, maybe six men.

Using the fog to blanket his movements, Jack crept to his left, dropped under a beam that swept just over his head.

He rose again. Took three more steps. Dropped under the next beam of light. He repeated the procedure again and again and again, until the last guard had moved to the back of the yard and Jack had moved closer to the front.

Taking slow, even breaths, Jack let his mind work through the alternatives. He knew once they'd searched the immediate grounds, the guards would fan out, covering one mile at a time. As bad as he wanted to study a mine up close, Jack couldn't stay in the area any longer.

His only chance to avoid capture was to get to his car and out of Kiel before the search expanded past the main perimeter of the shipyard.

As he melted into the mist, he could hear the clumsy guards shouting at one another.

Using the voices to pinpoint each man's position, Jack moved in a wide, cautious circle along the outer rim of the chaos. Keeping his eyes and ears open, he quickly slipped free of the yard.

He took a single step, and then his foot slipped. The resulting crunch of gravel was unmistakable.

Jack flung himself into a run.

They hadn't seen him yet, but it wouldn't be long now.

The rapid report of gunfire trailed in his wake. He picked up speed. A bullet whizzed by his head and drove harmlessly into the underbrush.

Another bullet hurled past him. And another. Jack heard a muffled pop, felt a burning sting high on his left arm.

He'd been hit, but he didn't slacken his pace.

Allowing adrenaline to fuel his steps, he continued in the direction of his car. After several minutes of running flat out, the shouts became distant murmurs. His own labored breathing filled his ears, distracting him, but Jack forced his mind to focus, to numb all other thoughts except one—*escape*.

He entered the edge of the forest. Diving into the thick foliage, he pitched around the front of his car, fumbled with the lock.

Throwing the gearshift into Neutral, he wheeled the car silently back onto the road, letting out a gush of air at the pain in his left arm.

With mechanical movements, he slipped behind the wheel, fired the engine and steered the car south toward Hamburg. He checked the mirrors, relieved that no one followed him. *Yet*.

Not taking any chances, he pressed the accelerator hard against the floorboard.

With one whiff, he caught the scent of his own blood. He took his eyes off the road for a split second and looked at his left arm. He was bleeding badly. Unfortunately, he would have to wait until he had more distance between him and Kiel to tend to the wound.

Lord, God, please protect me a little while longer.

A sense of peace fell over him. Breathing slower now, he took stock of the situation.

He was alive. He'd avoided capture. But he hadn't been

able to study an actual mine. He'd also left a witness, alive and talking. Worst of all, he'd been shot.

He tentatively flexed his left bicep, gave a grunt at the burst of pain.

"Lord," Jack prayed out loud as darkness crept along the edges of his vision, "if this is the end of my life, will You welcome me home, or are my sins too great?"

Part of his mother's favorite verse came to mind. *While we were still sinners, Christ died for us...*

"Is that promise for me, too, Lord? My sins are more than most."

But God demonstrates His own love for us in this: While we were still sinners, Christ died for us... Jack heard the words clearly in his mind. In response, God's peace that transcended all understanding flowed through every fiber of his body.

But then the wind picked up, sending one vicious gust after another in a sideswiping pattern against the car. He focused once more on his driving. The effort to ignore the aching in one arm and control the car with the other stole his breath away.

By the time he felt safe enough to pull off the road, Jack had to lean his head against the steering wheel and gulp for air.

He tried to swallow between breaths, but his mouth was dry as dust. A bad sign, indicating he'd lost a considerable amount of blood.

First things first. He needed to stop the bleeding, before he passed out from the pain and loss of blood.

Setting the brake, he pushed away from the steering wheel, shifting until he had enough room to work unhindered.

He tugged aside his sweater, yanked his shirt free, and then ripped off a strip along the bottom seam. Working as quickly as he could with only one good hand, he rolled the material into a makeshift tourniquet. He then tied off the flow of blood to the wound with a pull of his teeth on one end and his free hand on the other.

His efforts were clumsy and inefficient, but he knew the bandage would hold until he made it back to Katia's house.

He pulled his shirt closed, shrugged into the jacket he'd left on the seat then checked his watch. He tried to calm his mind, but no matter how slowly he breathed, he couldn't seem to focus.

Dragging a hand down his face, he fought to keep his mind free of worry. *Fear not:* the most often stated command in the Bible. Worry was nothing more than the absence of faith.

Faith. Yes, he was slowly realizing he still had a little faith left—though he'd surrendered much to the war effort—far too much.

From this point forward, he would manage what he could manage, and surrender the rest to God.

I am in Your hands, Lord. Your power is made perfect in my weakness.

Favoring his left arm, Jack steered the car back onto the road and pressed down on the accelerator.

In spite of his failure at the shipyard, he still had to keep his appointment with Himmler at 2300 hours. He would be ready. Too many innocent lives were at stake to go into the meeting unprepared, including the lives of a certain Russian stage actress and her blue-blooded mother.

Jack frowned at the road ahead.

Katarina Kerensky's involvement in this mission had been problematic from the start. Considering the secret she'd revealed to him earlier, Jack could no longer endanger her life. By rescuing her, perhaps he could begin the process of becoming an agent of protection rather than an agent of death.

His vision blurred again. Oblivion beckoned. But Jack set his jaw at a hard angle. This mission was far from over. He still had much work to do this night.

First order of business: send Katarina Kerensky packing for the next flight out of Germany.

By the time Jack arrived at Katarina's, the pain in his left arm had become a burning throb. His vision blurred, again. How many times was that? He'd lost count after four. He blinked—hard. The smudge of gray in the center of his eyes didn't go away.

His ears started ringing, but he managed to stagger to the bottom of her front steps without incident. There was no outdoor lighting so he could at least stumble along in obscurity. Thankfully, he'd memorized the yard's layout the last time he was here.

Before navigating the first step he took a moment to catch his breath. He was no stranger to pain. He'd been shot other times. However, he *was* human. And he knew his body well enough to know that two important limbs, primarily the ones holding him upright, were about to give out on him.

He needed to get his arm bandaged, deal with his dehydration then be on his way. He could not miss his meeting with Himmler. There was the important matter of damage control now.

Sending up a prayer for strength, he tripped up four of the five steps. He lost his balance, righted himself just as quickly. All he had to do was climb that last one—which seemed to be getting farther away with every blink. Once inside Katarina's house, he would take a moment to clear his head. That's what he would do first. After he had his equilibrium back he would tell her the whole story of his failed trip to Kiel. She deserved the full truth. She…

Lord, I'm tired.

In a final burst of energy, Jack shoved up the final step. And collapsed against the door. He closed his eyes and waited. One more burst of energy. He needed a little help here. No, he needed a lot of help.

He called on an old staple.

The Lord is my shepherd, he prayed, *I shall not want. He maketh me to lie down in green pastures: He leadeth me beside the still waters…*

Perhaps Jack would stay here awhile. Praying felt that good.

Now where was he?

Yea, though I walk through the valley of the shadow of death, I will fear no evil: for Thou art with me…

He couldn't stay here much longer and risk discovery by the wrong person.

Thou preparest a table before me in the presence of mine enemies…

Another moment of rest, he promised himself, just one more moment and he would pull together his strength and knock.

I will dwell in the house of the Lord for ever!

Just one…more…moment…of rest…

Chapter Eighteen

Katia woke with a start.

Disoriented, she pushed to a sitting position and then rubbed the sleep out of her eyes. She couldn't remember what had startled her. Or why she was on the couch in her living room.

She'd been exhausted when Reiter had dropped her off, mentally and physically worn out from the events of the last two days. That much she remembered. But she wasn't usually so slow to regain her focus.

The room had grown dark, with only a few shadows dancing across the wall in front of her.

Still trying to pull her thoughts together, she shifted her gaze to the clock on the far wall—9:00 p.m., 2100 hours.

Her mind cleared at once. Where was Friedrich? He'd said he wouldn't be long. Why wasn't he back yet?

A maelstrom of emotions had her flattening her hand against her stomach. Familiar panic rose up. Only a matter of hours ago, she'd confessed her darkest secret to a man she'd known less than two days.

Would he prove trustworthy?

Yes. Yes, he would. She couldn't put her reasons into

words, but she knew he was the only man she could trust, the first since her father had died.

But why him? Was it because he'd mentioned God with such conviction in his eyes, as though he'd rediscovered his own faith and wanted her to have that same hope?

Even as she pondered such a miracle, a nagging premonition had her shoving her hair off her face.

Something wasn't right.

She tipped her head and listened past the silence in the room. A sound was coming from her front door.

Knocking? No. More like scratching.

She gave herself a little push and stood. Her legs wobbled underneath her. Obviously, she needed more sleep. She didn't have the luxury.

The scratching came again, more insistent this time.

Was it her mother and Hermann, come to get her for a late supper? She'd claimed a headache earlier and had told them she wouldn't be available for the rest of evening. Surely, they would respect her wishes and take her at her word.

Padding across the thick carpet, she tried to gather her various roles around her. Which one would she need tonight?

Unsure what to expect, her skin went cold with dread.

Katia swung open the door.

"Friedrich." She was only dimly aware she'd gasped his name. But he didn't look right. He was swaying. That much she could discern. But his face was curtained in shadows so she couldn't see his eyes.

He stumbled past her, weaving across the entryway of her home. Two more bobbing steps and he reached out to steady himself against the wall on his left.

"Friedrich, what's happened?"

He mumbled an incoherent response in a language that

definitely was not German, and in an accent she'd heard only in the movies.

Why would he break cover so noticeably?

Fearing something had gone dreadfully wrong, Katia shut the door behind him and then flicked on the overhead light in the foyer.

Hissing, he covered his eyes against light. "Have mercy, woman." He growled out his words in slurred German.

What was wrong with him?

She pulled his hand down and stared hard at his scowling face. His pupils were dilated and unfocused. "Are you drunk?"

His scowl deepened. "Of course not."

Katia had her doubts, especially when he kept listing to his left. She took a sniff of the air around him and reared back. He didn't smell of liquor. He smelled of...*blood*.

A thousand questions shot to her lips but something dark and wet on his left sleeve caught her attention. "You're bleeding."

She had no appropriate role for this unexpected development.

He looked down at his arm. His eyes widened, as though he was surprised to find his sleeve coated with his own blood. "Looks like the tourniquet didn't hold."

"Is that all you have to say?" Her concern made her words sound sharper than she'd intended.

"It's just a scratch." He waved his hand with a dismissive flick. The gesture threw him off balance again.

She reached out to steady him, he tripped back a step and she missed.

"You need to sit down," she said.

"I'm fine." He rocked back on his heels and then threw himself forward. "Nothing to worry about."

"I see that."

"Let me take care of this first." He clawed at the bloody tourniquet on his arm. "Then we'll talk before I go to my meeting with Himmler."

"Himmler? Heinrich Himmler? You have a meeting with the head of the SS? Tonight?" Just how deep undercover was this man?

"Don't worry, Katarina." He placed his good hand on her shoulder. "You haven't been compromised. Everything will be fine."

Fine? He used that word rather loosely. Nothing would be fine as long as men like Adolf Hitler and Heinrich Himmler were in power. Nothing would be fine as long as dissenters were silenced and people like Katia's mother were openly targeted for their Jewish heritage.

"Now. If you could direct me to your washroom."

Still in a state of shock, she automatically pointed over his shoulder.

He turned and swiftly lost his footing.

She caught him by the right elbow. "I'll come with you."

He didn't argue. Instead, he looked grateful, and a little lost, as though he wasn't used to being the one in need and didn't know what to do with the change in their roles.

She wasn't altogether sure herself.

Once in the bathroom, she filled a glass with water and handed it to him. "Here. You look like you could use this."

With a trembling hand, he brought the cup to his lips and gulped the entire contents in one taking. A little less shaky now, he filled the glass again and brought it to his mouth a second time.

She stopped him before he could drink. "No. Slow down. Too much will make you sick."

"I…" He looked at her in cautious silence then set the cup on the counter. "You're right."

"Take off your jacket and let me look at your wound."

She spoke calmly, but her heart beat hard against her ribs. What had happened tonight? Where had he gone?

He must have read a portion of her thoughts because she saw the flash of some deep emotion in his eyes—apology, guilt, pain? She shook her head as she turned to the sink and ran warm water over a washcloth.

"It really is just a scratch," he mumbled. "The bullet missed its mark."

"Thank You, Lord," she whispered. It wasn't much of a prayer, but she was a bit out of practice these days.

Taking a deep breath, she left the washcloth in the sink and turned to face him again. "All right, let's have a look."

Grimacing, he shrugged out of his jacket then pulled off the useless tourniquet. Clearly exhausted from the effort, he sank onto the only seat available in the room. "There. I'm all yours."

Ignoring the little jolt of pleasure at his absolute surrender, Katia glanced down at his arm. From elbow to wrist his sleeve was coated with a thick layer of blood. She wanted to sob. And then throw up. But she was too afraid to give in to either impulse right now. Later, she promised herself, when she was alone, she would give in to the sickness. And then maybe the fear.

For now, she had to concentrate.

This man's life was in her hands, the same hands she couldn't keep from shaking. She had no practice for this, no protective barrier to put in front of the real Katia. She cared for him that much, this man who had dug past all her layers of defense. A dark uneasiness crept over her at the thought.

She must have stood there, unmoving, for quite a while, because he went to work on his arm all by himself.

Stone-faced, he ripped apart the sleeve at the shoulder and then peeled the soaked material away from the wound, inch by brutal inch. He made no sound, nor did he wince, but his eyes glazed over with each passing second.

Katia wanted to weep for him. He had such strength, such courage. He would be an easy man to love.

She shut her eyes a moment, shuddered and then swallowed the last of her hesitation. With her fingers still trembling, she took over. Moving his hand out of the way, she wiped at the blood on his arm with the warm, soapy cloth from the sink.

"I can do it myself," he offered, as if he knew how hard this was for her.

A deep affection surged through her. Even in the midst of his own agony, he thought of her first. She felt exposed under such raw concern.

What was she going to do now?

"Right." She gave her words a hard edge to hide her confusion. "Your previous efforts were very efficient."

He smiled a little, a very little. "I made it here in one piece, didn't I?"

"If you say so."

"I say so."

What if he hadn't made it back to her alive? What if the bullet *had* hit its mark? The thought was too awful to contemplate so she cleared her mind and focused only on what she could control—taking care of his wound.

She placed the cloth under the running faucet and rinsed out the blood. So much blood, she thought. Too much.

She slid a quick look at him from under her lashes and felt her stomach flip inside itself. Even with his skin pale and his mouth tight from gritting past the pain, he mesmerized her. It wasn't his masculine beauty alone that got to her. It was his inner strength. She recognized a man of integrity when she saw one.

How would she ever survive knowing such a man?

Sighing, she wrung out the cloth one last time and went back to work.

Chapter Nineteen

Jack shut his eyes the moment the warm cloth touched his skin again. He nearly whimpered from the effort of holding back a sigh of relief. Katarina's touch was so gentle, her eyes filled with such caring that he felt the sharp stab of some foreign emotion rising up inside him.

Sliding a covert glance at her, he found himself struck all over again by her beauty. He closed his eyes to ward off another rush of unexpected emotions, but her scent filled him. She smelled very female, a combination of zesty white flowers and spice.

Perhaps it was safer to keep his eyes opened.

He wondered where the questions were. She must have at least a few. Didn't women always ask questions? "Don't you want to know how this happened?"

Her brows scrunched in consternation. "Oh, I have a good idea."

With unnecessary force, she tossed the bloody rag into the sink, then quickly pressed a clean, dry cloth to the wound. "You messed up, made a mistake or," she amended as she smiled at him with a look meant to subdue his male arrogance, "probably both."

Jack leveled a gaze that had been known to shrink the

toughest of men. "You'll have to work on your gloating, Katarina. It needs a little more hypocrisy in it."

"Is that so?" Her brows lifted slightly. "Then tell me this, am I wrong?"

He broke eye contact. "You're enjoying my failure far too much. It's unbecoming in a woman of your fine breeding, a woman who's had her own share of mistakes during this mission."

"Let's review, shall we?" She pressed the cloth against his wound with a little more efficiency than before. He preferred her more tentative. It hurt less.

Her lips pulled into a frown. "You went somewhere dangerous tonight, alone, without telling me where. And while you were out, doing who knows what, you got yourself shot." The anger was there in her voice, throbbing just below the surface.

"It's not my first bullet wound," he said in his own defense.

"Of course it isn't. You're a man, aren't you?"

"What's that supposed to mean?"

"Hold this steady." She cocked her head at the cloth on his arm.

He did as she requested, flinching when her fingers brushed against his.

Muttering in Russian about foolhardy men who carried guns, she rooted in the cabinet above his head.

He wished she wasn't quite so angry. It was only going to get worse when he told her what happened. For now, he decided to change the subject. "You'll need to work quickly. I have that…meeting I mentioned."

Without looking at him, she pulled out a brown bottle, scissors, bandages and white medical tape. Hands full, she stepped back and then deposited the lot on the counter.

"Right. You want me to patch you up, just like that,

and then send you into a meeting with one of the most dangerous men in Germany. Getting shot is that common for you, is it?"

Although he bristled at her words, something in her expression had him wanting to placate her rather than antagonize. "It's just a scratch, Katarina. A scratch."

Her lips pressed into a hard line. "Put there by a bullet meant to take your life." A shudder passed through her.

"Katarina, I—"

"Here comes the fun part." Looking entirely too cheerful, she swabbed another washcloth with what looked—and smelled—suspiciously like iodine.

"No, you don't." Jack shot up then collapsed back down as a jolt of nausea swept through him. After several deep breaths, he cleared the pain out of his mind. But the effort drew a thick sheen of sweat onto his brow. "That stuff stings," he complained once he had his breath again.

"Of course it does. That's how you know it's doing the job." She smiled, sweetly, then pressed the cloth against his wound.

He bit back a howl of pain. The woman had a mean streak. Pure and simple.

Focus. That's what he needed. Focus. His mind was stronger than his body. It was all a matter of concentration, a matter of single-mindedness.

She applied a second coat of iodine.

"Have you no compassion?" he hissed.

"Of course. When it's warranted."

"You're doing this to punish me. You're angry. You're scared. And this is your way of getting back at me."

"I'm doing this to clean your wound. Your *bullet* wound. But, yes." She sighed. "I am angry. Scared, too. Mostly scared."

Before he could respond she pressed her lips to his forehead. "You're going to be fine, Friedrich Reiter. Just fine."

He wanted to relax inside all that tenderness, just for a moment, but he didn't know how. He'd been on his own too long.

He was only just beginning to realize how alone he'd been.

"Yes, Katarina." He touched her hand. "I will be fine. I always am."

Her hands started shaking again. "You could have died tonight."

"But I didn't. I won't—*I can't*—allow fear of death to keep me from doing what needs to get done."

Very carefully, very slowly, she set the bottle and rag on the counter. "People who don't fear death are nothing but reckless. They take foolish risks."

"Do I strike you as either reckless or foolish?"

Her answer was immediate. "No. But—"

"Worry is useless, Katarina. It's also a clear sign that our faith isn't strong enough. One thing I've learned these last two years, no, these last two *days,* is that it's important to listen to God's voice and guidance, not our own fear and personal agendas."

Like his own personal agenda for revenge. Vengeance was not his. It was God's alone. Jack could no longer in good conscience act without discerning his own motives first. He must be more obedient. He must—

Katarina's sigh broke through his thoughts. "Faith is hard to come by in times such as these."

Who was he to argue? "You're right. Fear, anger and bitterness are always easier. We live in a fallen world. Maybe the question isn't 'why do bad things happen,' rather '*who's* in control when bad things happen.' God will always be bigger than any circumstance."

Her brows squeezed together, but she didn't respond right away. "It's hard not to ask why."

He had no argument to that. "I know."

She let out a shuddering breath. No longer meeting his gaze, she concentrated on wrapping the bandage around his arm and then securing the end with medical tape. "There." She stepped back and eyed her work. "That should do for now."

He rose, took her hand in his.

She tried to turn away. He pulled her closer.

"Thank you, Katarina. Thank you for taking care of my arm." He lifted her chin with his fingertip. "Thank you for taking care of *me*."

She took a shaky breath, but then visibly relaxed. Reaching up, she touched his cheek. "The next time you decide to strike out on your own, don't. Whether you like it or not, you need me."

A strange calm settled over him. "You're right. I do need you." He wasn't talking solely about the mission.

She, apparently, thought he was. "Where did you go tonight?"

Knowing he owed her the truth, he sat back down. "I went to a shipyard in Kiel. To investigate a U-boat, what I believe is the lead submarine in the magnetic mines mission. I was interrupted before I could finish the job, hence the need for a bandage."

"But." She angled her head at him. "How did you know the U-boat was there and that it was the right one?"

He worked to keep from clenching his jaw. "Himmler told me."

Her eyes widened, but she didn't speak.

"I work…as one of his handpicked agents."

Her hand flew to her throat. "Oh."

He understood her shock. "Rest assured, my loyalties

lie with the British. But I also have certain responsibilities to Himmler and his SS."

He expected her to pale at his admission, to show disgust and disbelief, perhaps even terror. But she surprised him. "What a terrible, lonely way to live." Her voice filled with tenderness. "You never know who to trust, do you?"

"I trust you. And I trust God." He spoke the truth from his heart.

Lord, forgive me for relying only on myself. Help me to rely on You more.

With a look of understanding in her eyes, she reached down and touched his face. "Oh, Friedrich."

He stood. Just as he pulled her close she wrapped her arms around his waist and rested her cheek against his chest.

"You are… I don't know how… I wish…" Her words trailed off on a shuddering sigh.

He thought he understood her inability to put her feelings into words. She'd given him the one weapon that could destroy her—information about her heritage—while he'd given her nothing. Not really. Both the British and the Germans knew he worked with the opposing government. He was a traitor one day, a hero the next. It all depended on what day it was and who was sitting on the other side of the desk.

For once, he wanted to share his truth with someone who would look past the spy.

"My name is Jonathon Phillip Anderson," he said in German, but then switched to English to make his point. "I go by Jack, not Jonathon. I'm an American naval engineer on loan to the British from the Office of Naval Intelligence, ONI. I was born in Lincoln, Nebraska, but grew up in Washington, D.C."

With that last bit of information, he'd given her an equally powerful weapon to use against him.

She lifted her head. The awe and respect he saw in her nearly slaughtered him. He wasn't worthy of this courageous woman's loyalty. But he wanted to be.

"That's it, then." She nodded in acknowledgment. "No turning back for either of us. We're in this together, bound by our individual secrets."

"Yes." He thought of the verse from Ecclesiastes. "'Two are better than one,'" he quoted.

She took a deep breath and finished the rest of the verse. "And if one falls the other will pick him—or her—up."

"Precisely." He pulled her close again. He wanted to stay right where he was, holding her tightly to him. Something powerful had just happened between them, a fragile bond that needed nurturing. Unfortunately, they didn't have the liberty to explore their newfound connection. Not tonight.

"I have to meet Himmler in little more than an hour."

"Will he…" She looked up at him. "Are you in danger because you failed tonight?"

He wouldn't lie to her, not now. "I don't know. I have enough information to share that should satisfy him. But no matter what, the SS will not find out about you or your secret. Not from me."

"I know." She lifted her chin. "I trust you completely."

He knew how hard that came for her. In the face of her courage he fell a little in love with her. Maybe more than a little. "Will you do something with me, before I go?"

"Anything."

"I want us to pray, together."

"I… Yes." She gave him a wobbly smile. "I… I think I would like that, too."

He took her hands in his and then knelt on the tile floor at her feet.

After a moment of hesitation, she joined him on the floor.

His arm might still be throbbing. His head might still feel light. Yet with Katarina's hands in his, both of them kneeling before God in total surrender, Jack felt stronger than he had in years.

He closed his eyes.

"Lord, Heavenly Father, we know You are not the author of destruction, but of peace. I pray You guide us in our quest to stop tyranny, tonight and every night to come. Whether we're together or apart." He paused a moment, then recalled a long-forgotten verse from Zechariah. "We will not succeed in our own strength, but by Your spirit alone. In Jesus's name, Amen."

"Amen." Katarina's hands tightened around his.

And with that simple gesture from her, the night turned a whole lot brighter.

Chapter Twenty

Although it was seconds before 2300 hours, Jack didn't rush his steps. He strode purposely up the front walkway of the rambling three-story mansion. It was an imposing structure, nestled on a knuckle of land perched along craggy cliffs.

The house had been confiscated—most likely from a Jewish family—and turned into the heart of Germany's wireless receiving operation. But this was an *Abwehr* facility, used solely by the military intelligence agency. There was no direct connection to the SS here.

Why had Himmler moved their meeting to this house, of all places, instead of keeping it at the Gestapo headquarters as originally planned?

With the question weighing heavily on his mind, Jack entered the building at precisely 2300 hours. An SS corporal rose from a chair situated in the shadows of the main hall and saluted. "*Heil* Hitler."

"*Heil* Hitler."

"The *Reichsführer* is waiting for you, Herr *Sturmban-*

nführer. Please follow me." With a click of his heels, the corporal turned sharply around and led the way down a long corridor.

Jack followed the man along the darkened hallway, through another corridor and then another. As he memorized the route with one part of his brain, he wondered again why Himmler had brought him here of all places.

Was it a test? An intimidation tactic? A reminder that he was being watched closely?

I will never leave you, nor forsake you.

Jack tucked God's promise into his heart, gathering courage from it as he did. Worry was useless. Himmler would reveal his hand when it suited him. And not before.

In the meantime, Jack would do everything in his power to protect Katarina. No harm would come to her because of him. The most effective tool in his arsenal was the cold-hearted shell of Friedrich Reiter.

After yet another turn down another twisting corridor, the corporal ushered Jack into a small room furnished with only a dilapidated desk and two wooden chairs. The air smelled sour, heavy, like a moldy bunker.

Another tactic, designed to throw a man off his guard. Friedrich Reiter was not so easily manipulated.

"Herr Himmler will be with you shortly," the corporal said, then retreated.

Once he was alone, Jack remained standing, shoulders back, head high. He lifted his left arm slightly but did not wince at the resulting pain the small gesture caused. Katarina had cleaned the wound and dressed it properly. But he needed rest in order for his body to complete the healing process.

He would take the time after the war.

Turning at the sound of the door creaking on its hinges,

he presented a stiff-armed salute as Himmler entered the room. "Herr *Reichsführer*," he said. "*Heil* Hitler."

"*Heil* Hitler."

Jack remained at attention, and waited.

Himmler's restless gaze took in the room, then shifted to Jack's face. "Have a seat, Herr Reiter."

As Jack settled into the less appealing of the two chairs, he noted that Himmler was wearing the black uniform of the Gestapo, the Death's Head prominently displayed above the bill of his cap. The uniform sent a bloody warning. And Jack knew it was no empty threat. Himmler was capable of terrible evil.

I will never leave you, nor forsake you. He relaxed in the reminder of God's truth, and then set aside Jack Anderson for the remainder of the meeting.

"You surprise me, Herr Reiter." Himmler's eyes turned colder, and his voice iced over. "I expected you much later."

"This was our agreed time."

"So it was." He made a grand show of taking off his hat and settling into the other chair. "I understand you took your actress home early this evening, before you had to travel to Kiel."

The statement was meant to let Jack know that Himmler had been monitoring him, personally, along with the Gestapo and various other Nazi agencies.

Friedrich Reiter was a popular man.

"I wanted no distractions from my duties to the Fatherland. I will join her once I leave here. We prefer our privacy, you understand." He punctuated his statement with Reiter's sly smile. It was important Himmler got all the wrong ideas, with one exception. The head of the SS needed to know that Jack was fully aware of the listening devices planted in his hotel room.

"So you are continuing your relationship with the woman."

Jack lifted a careless shoulder. "She has her uses. Aside from the obvious, Admiral Doenitz will be attending her mother's ball tomorrow evening. It's long past time I met the admiral in person."

"You always go beyond the call of duty, Herr Reiter," Himmler said with satisfaction in his tone. "Now, for our other matter. You have news for me?"

Pleased Himmler had changed the direction of the conversation on his own, Jack nodded. Although a certain amount of sharing information was expected, he needed to handle the question of the magnetic mines carefully.

With the cold directness that was Reiter's trademark, Jack leaned forward and lowered his voice. "It is delicate information, Herr *Reichsführer*."

Himmler waved his hand. "It is safe to speak freely here. You may proceed without concern."

"As you wish."

Jack sat back, seemingly relaxed, but he chose to stick to the cautious approach as was in character with his alter ego. He'd failed to investigate U-116 properly, but the head of the SS didn't need to know that. The altercation with the guard was of little importance, as well. Heinrich Himmler cared only about the results of a mission as they pertained to him. He cared nothing of Reiter's methods in retrieving the information.

"The weapon we discussed earlier is a magnetic mine designed especially for submarine use." Jack delivered the information without a single qualm, knowing he'd revealed enough to pit Himmler against Doenitz even more than before. "Its explosive charge carries twice the firepower of traditional torpedoes."

Himmler's eyes gleamed with interest. "Did you say *magnetic* mine?"

"Yes. The U-boats lay a succession of these mines on the bottom of the shallow seabed, mainly near ports and military bases along the British coast. The bombs target ships as they pass by."

Digesting the information, Himmler nodded. "Go on."

"The mines are not discriminating," Jack continued. "Military or merchant, British or American, the target is the closest ship in range."

Himmler's lips thinned. "Then what keeps the mines from blowing up the U-boat once they are released?"

Jack didn't know, hence the problem with designing his countermeasures for the British. But he had a theory, one he could use to keep Himmler satisfied without jeopardizing Britain's attempts to stop the destruction. "There is a delayed-action trigger, a time fuse of sorts, which does not activate until the U-boat has cleared the area."

Jack stopped his explanation there, counting on Himmler's mind-set as a former chicken farmer to neither understand the complicated science of the bombs, nor wish to try. How the trigger worked was still the unknown factor. And after tonight's failure, Jack was no closer to finding out. He still might have to return to Wilhelmshaven, and Admiral Doenitz's private quarters.

He would do so without Katarina.

Clearly unaware of Jack's thoughts, Himmler drummed his fingers on his thigh. "From what you've told me, it is obvious Doenitz wishes to use the mines to further increase public sentiment for his U-boats. A noble end, to be sure, but the secrecy must end."

Jack bit back a sigh of relief. Himmler was satisfied, even though Jack had given him very little information. In fact, Admiral Doenitz should have shared all of this with the SS long before now.

Internal rivalry within the German state wasn't Jack's concern. Himmler would deal with the admiral's secret-keeping himself. Let the dogs battle one another for a while, that was Jack's philosophy.

Himmler shifted, his blue eyes almost colorless now, nothing more than a slit of drab gray against the black pupils. "You have given me plenty to work with. The Führer will be pleased."

Jack nodded, then answered with his well-rehearsed line. "It is my honor to be of service to my Führer, and the Fatherland."

"Very good. Now." Rising, Himmler crossed to a small window, and stared out into the black night for several long seconds.

"I have another opportunity for you," he said, spinning back to face Jack. "It would enable you to return to the Fatherland, perhaps permanently. And it would take advantage of the skills you've acquired in the last two years."

Jack sat perfectly still, waiting, swallowing back a mixture of trepidation and excitement. This was it, then. All roads had led to this moment. He had pushed to get himself here, to the one assignment that would take him deep inside the SS.

"I only wish to serve," he said. But not the Fatherland.

In that moment, Jack put his hope in God and surrendered completely to the Lord's will for his life. He would no longer seek revenge for his own purpose. He would have confidence in the Lord's ability to use him as an instrument to defeat the Nazis' evil.

"What I have in mind would utilize your unique skills," Himmler said again. "That is, if you are interested."

Jack leaned forward. By nature, he was a patient man,

but he could feel his heart pounding with anticipation. Or was it fear? He wanted to hear what Himmler had in mind, wanted to see if all the sacrifices of the last two years were about to pay off.

Even if the outcome meant Jack would have to lay down his own life, the price would be worth it if he could save innocent blood. This was no longer about Jack. It was about courageous people like Katarina Kerensky. It was about a higher plan and service to God.

"I'm interested," he said.

"As you know, I do not trust Admiral Canaris any more than I trust Admiral Doenitz."

Keeping his expression blank, Jack nodded. The lack of trust between Himmler and the head of the *Abwehr* was no secret. The fact that they were having this conversation in an *Abwehr* facility revealed Himmler's serpentine mind and deadly arrogance. The choice of meeting places made perfect sense now. The mouse was actually plotting against the cat inside the cat's own den.

"What is it you want me to do?" Jack asked, certain he'd come to the most important moment of his thirty-two years.

Every small, seemingly inconsequential life decision had prepared him to take on this task. He'd memorized countless Scriptures as a boy, which would now become his primary source of God's Word while ensconced in the heart of the Nazi regime. He'd trained as an engineer and joined the Navy at precisely the right time to warrant the German's interest in him.

Perhaps even losing his way for a time had brought him to a deeper conviction to serve the Lord.

"We will put you in a position within the *Abwehr* itself. You will report back to me any suspicious dealings between Canaris and his closest agents." The smile he sent Jack was as hard and cold as an artic blast.

"Admiral Canaris will allow this?"

Himmler released a vicious chuckle. "He has no choice." That arrogant statement proved the unconscionable power Himmler had acquired within the Third Reich. Even men of equal standing now had to fear the head of the SS.

Proceed carefully, Jack. You are dealing with a madman.

"What of my work inside England?" he asked. It was a reasonable question. An expected one. "I've built a solid cover over the last two years."

"At all costs, you will not jeopardize your situation with the Americans, or MI6. I may need you to return to one or both countries in the future."

A ball of dread rolled ice-hot in his belly. Could Jack do this? No, he couldn't. Not on his own. But he could with God's strength. *I can do all things through Christ who strengthens me.*

"I understand, Herr *Reichsführer*. I will not let you down."

"Tie up any loose ends as quickly as possible. I want you in Berlin within the month."

Within the month. Jack had thirty days to get Katarina and her mother out of Germany.

And then he would be completely entrenched inside the identity of Friedrich Reiter. For a moment, all his guilt and rage rose to the surface.

Jack shoved the emotions back down with a hard swallow. He was a changed man, thanks to meeting Katarina. Her courage had inspired him to return to the God-fearing man he'd been before Reiter had attacked him.

This world was filled with wickedness, but Jack would no longer allow his anger over what the Nazis had done to him to block his confidence in God's ability to defeat evil. He would call on God alone for his strength now.

After two long years of preparation, he would have his chance to become an instrument for good. In thirty days he would infiltrate the internal security service of the SS—the *Sicherheitsdienst,* or SD.

This was it. The moment he'd planned for since Friedrich Reiter had come to take his life. Jack was ready.

Chapter Twenty-One

❦

22 November 1939, Sengwarden, Wilhelmshaven
Kriegsmarine headquarters, 0700 hours

Admiral Doenitz spread the set of blueprints across the top of his desk, for the moment ignoring the U-boat captain standing at attention beside him. He took his time studying the drawings. The revolutionary mines were the most powerful naval weapons ever designed. But the bombs would only be effective if they remained secret.

Satisfied he was making the right decision, he turned his attention to the man on his left.

Hermann Schmidt stood unmoving, chest out, shoulders back, his gaze focused on the far wall. Since serving with Schmidt in the last war, Doenitz had trusted his fellow officer completely. Even at fifty, the man's cold blue eyes, chiseled features and close-cropped blond hair defined Aryan perfection. But it was his unwavering loyalty to the Fatherland that made him an asset to the *Kriegsmarine*.

"These are no longer safe in my office." Doenitz stabbed at the blueprints with his index finger. "Although we don't know exactly what the intruder was after, I am not willing to take any chances."

Schmidt lowered his gaze and considered the drawings in silence. His expression remained neutral throughout his inspection. "Is this the only set of blueprints?"

"No. The engineers who developed the bombs have the originals. For the sake of secrecy, however, only a handful of people have been allowed access to either set."

"Very wise."

"Yes." With silent purpose, Doenitz rolled up the pages, inserted the blueprints into a metal tube and then handed the container to Schmidt. "It is now up to you to keep these safe."

Tucking the cylinder under his left arm, Schmidt nodded. "I will guard them with my life."

"I have no doubt." Satisfied the first part of the meeting was going as planned, Doenitz strode to the map covering the entire south wall of his office. "Germany is at her finest hour, *Kapitän zur See*. It is time the rest of the world experiences the magnificence of our capabilities."

Schmidt smiled with what looked like quiet relish. "Agreed."

"As commander of U-116, you are now among the elite of the *Kriegsmarine*." Dragging his finger along the route Schmidt would take through the English Channel, Doenitz continued, "You are solely responsible for the success of this secret mission."

"I am humbled by the magnitude of your trust, Herr Admiral."

A perfect answer.

Hands clasped behind his back, Doenitz walked to the row of windows on the north wall overlooking the harbor. Freezing rain scratched a steady rhythm against the glass. The chilling cold slicked ice into twisting patterns, making visibility all but impossible at this early hour. "I cannot stress the importance of keeping the blueprints from falling into the wrong hands."

"I understand."

Returning to the map, Doenitz eyed the coastline bordering the English Channel. Cold fingers of purpose clutched around his heart. "We must wage total war on the enemy."

Schmidt merely inclined his head, waiting patiently for Doenitz to continue. This was the advantage of working with seasoned sailors, men who had experienced the humiliation of defeat. Their devotion to the Third Reich was a given.

"As with your other missions, do not pick up any survivors along the way."

Schmidt gave a quick nod. "I will strive only to take care of my own boat and crew."

"That is all I expect." Hard determination edged his voice up an octave. "Any events during your patrol which are in direct violation of the international agreement should not be entered in your war log."

Schmidt's blue eyes turned cold and impassive. "I will report those to you personally."

"Very good. Now, what is U-116's status?"

"Everything is on schedule. She will be outfitted and ready to sail on the twenty-fourth as planned."

Doenitz clasped the other man's shoulder in a brief show of confidence. "I realize laying mines is not a popular task, my friend. Since the weapon does not cause immediate damage to the enemy, you and your crew may never see the fruits of your labor."

Schmidt threw his shoulders back, exuding an unshakable iron bearing. "I only wish to do my part for Germany, Herr Admiral."

Satisfied at last, Doenitz returned to the cabinet that

held the rest of his important blueprints and documents. Before shifting them to their new locations, there was one final matter to discuss with Schmidt.

"Your character and your temperament make you a valuable officer, Hermann," he began carefully. "I am honored to have you among my most trusted men."

"It is an honor to serve under you, sir."

"I understand the sacrifice I am asking of you. But you must dedicate yourself completely to the Fatherland."

Schmidt nodded in understanding. "My personal life will not interfere with my duties."

Ah, the perfect opening. "I trust Elena Kerensky will not be a distraction."

"No, sir." Schmidt looked at him directly, his eyes unblinking. "She understands my duty is to Germany first."

"Good. Good." Deciding to keep his suspicions about the daughter to himself, at least until he had further evidence to support his theory, Doenitz went fishing instead. "What about her famous daughter? What do you know of her?"

Schmidt's lip curled in disgust. "She is a silly, spoiled girl with very little on her mind."

Perhaps. Perhaps not. Doenitz had his doubts.

"Yet she is at the height of her profession," he pointed out. Reason enough to take her seriously.

"Her beauty has gotten her far," Schmidt conceded. "But like most women of her type, she is easy prey for unscrupulous men. SS men, especially." His ruthless tone said how he felt about the company Katarina Kerensky kept. "She is not overly discreet."

"Is there an SS man in particular that's been sniffing around the actress lately?" Doenitz asked. One who had made the journey to Wilhelmshaven with her recently?

Schmidt's lip curled. "This week or last?"

So Katarina Kerensky ran through men, not unusual considering her profession. "You say she's silly and likes dangerous men, is that all you know about her?" Doenitz asked.

"That's all there is to know. Either she is exactly as she seems or she is a brilliant actress." Schmidt released a snort. "You may decide for yourself, of course, when you meet her tonight. But in my opinion, no one is that good at pretending."

Doenitz would indeed judge for himself. In the meantime, he had other documents to move.

"Thank you, *Kapitän*. That is all for now."

Schmidt tossed out his own arm in salute. "*Heil* Hitler."

Doenitz returned the gesture with equal enthusiasm. "*Heil* Hitler."

As Schmidt left the room at a stiff, clipped pace, Doenitz allowed a slow, cold smile to touch his lips. After tonight he would have his answers about the famous actress. He would find out who she worked for and then he would uncover her reasons for breaking into his private chambers, assuming she was indeed the culprit.

Ah, yes. The trip to Hamburg this evening, the one he'd dreaded a week ago, could very well prove to be an enlightening experience after all.

Rissen, West Hamburg, 0800 hours

In sharp contrast to Katia's mood, the day dawned crisp and bright. She would have much preferred a dark and rainy morning for answering her mother's summons.

A reasonable person would be snuggled in her bed at this hour, or at the very least checking on her wounded partner. Unfortunately, family obligation had been bred into Katia from birth. And as much as she wanted to worry over Friedrich Reiter's meeting with Heinrich Himmler, or wonder how the British spy's wound was healing, she found herself putting off her trip to the *Vier Jahreszeiten* hotel and stepping into the quiet, tasteful foyer of her mother's home instead.

Looking around her, Katia sighed. The decor was as stylishly equipped as its owner. Lovely and aloof, the pearl-gray marble floor, cream-colored walls and stern-looking antique table suited Princess Elena Dietrich Patrova Kerensky to perfection.

Katia's mother had been given the villa on the Elbe River two years ago, shortly after she'd become a favorite of Adolf Hitler. More showcase than home, the house had everything a Russian princess in exile could want, even if that princess was of German descent with a secret Jewish grandparent in her lineage.

Katia's skin iced over as she stepped farther into the house. Although she had no proof, she imagined this sprawling home had once belonged to a Jewish family taken by the Nazis.

The thought made her sick, made her seem more like an intruder than usual.

How could her mother live with herself? Where was her conscience? Her disgust? Her shame?

Elena's solid position in German society had given her back the life that had been ripped from her during the dark days of the Revolution. She lived in a fairy-tale world again, one similar to that of the Tsars.

Was Elena Kerensky that shallow? Did she not understand the cost others had paid for the opulence she enjoyed now? The same cost she herself would pay if Hermann Schmidt discovered her secret? She had once claimed to be a devout Christian. Her actions said otherwise. Had Elena joined the new German religion, the *Gottglaubig?*

Had she become one of the blind millions who worshipped the romantic notions of a pagan past?

Lord, if that's true, what am I to do? How am I to proceed?

Katia's breath turned cold in her body. A scream clawed at the inside of her throat, but she kept her expression bland as she made her way to the front parlor. She could not help but think that her heels clicking against the marble sounded like nails to coffins.

Strict control prevented Katia from reaching up and smoothing the wind-tangled hair off her face. She was an adult now, not some naughty child who deserved scolding. Shoulders back, chin high, she took note of the countless flowers that spilled out of pots and vases on every available tabletop. The colorful blooms presented an impression that the war had not yet touched this part of the world.

How long would Elena Kerensky lie to herself?

Rounding the corner, Katia noted a fire had been laid in the parlor, but was not yet lit. The illusion of warmth came from several lamps shooting beacons of golden light throughout the pristine room. No doubt, the soft ambience was designed to create a soothing, welcoming atmosphere.

Katia had never felt so alone, so empty. So terrified. She didn't think she could continue playing the role of the dutiful daughter much longer. The lie was taking its toll.

Lord, I… I… I pray for courage. As prayers went it was a pitiful attempt. Well, she was feeling rather pitiful at the moment, especially as she watched her perfect, serene mother rise from her chair.

Elena stretched out her hand to beckon Katia forward. Dressed in a soft tan dress with brown trim, her hair in its trademark upsweep, Elena looked as elegant as always.

"Darling," she greeted. "You are right on time." Her

tone was pleasant enough, but her eyes remained distant, guarded even, as they had been the day before.

"I am always on time, Mother."

"So you are."

Katia didn't like how Elena watched her, with her pale eyes looking as though she could see straight inside her mind. Katia had to swallow back a wave of nervousness. Why did she always feel inadequate in the presence of the woman who had given birth to her?

Shaken more than she thought possible, Katia ignored the familiar clutching of her stomach and moved forward to kiss her mother's cheek. "You look well."

"I am well, quite well. And how are you, my dear?"

"The same as always." Petrified. If Elena Kerensky could ignore what was happening around her, then so could every other decent citizen of the Volk.

"Come, Katia, sit. Have some tea." There was no warmth in the invitation.

Unsure what to make of her mother's mood, Katia did as commanded. "As I said on the telephone, I cannot stay long."

"Nonsense." Elena waved off the objection. "Your first obligation is to your family."

Katia gave in, hoping to end this command performance more quickly with compliance. She sat down in a stiff-back chair, but she couldn't stop her hand from fluttering absently over her hair.

Elena's gaze followed the gesture. Pursing her lips in disapproval, she poured tea into a china cup. "You look tired, darling."

Katia curled her toes inside her shoes and clamped her hands together in her lap. "I've had several long nights at the theater."

Elena treated Katia to one of her long silences. Only

then did she remember the theater had been dark last night and she'd begged off dinner with complaints of a headache. Would Elena point out the obvious inconsistency in Katia's excuse?

This is what comes of living a life of lies.

Katia held perfectly still and waited. A part of her noticed the servants bustling in and out of the room, making preparations for the party later that evening. The other part of her held her breath in trepidation.

"Yes, darling, I'm sure that must be the reason." Elena placed a cup on a saucer and handed both to Katia. "I don't know why you bother with that ridiculous endeavor. You should be focusing on marriage. You aren't getting any younger."

"I am only twenty-six."

"Long past the age I was when I married your father." A sadness crept into Elena's eyes, but she quickly wiped away the emotion with a determined blink.

Katia fought her own wave of melancholy. She'd thought of her father more in the last two days than she had in the last eighteen years.

"Who would I marry, Mother? Someone like Hermann?" She kept her voice cool and distant, afraid if she allowed her emotions to surface there would be no way to stop them from overflowing into a tangle of words that she could never take back.

Elena's gaze narrowed, but there was no real hardness in her eyes, only a look that Katia couldn't quite decipher. Concern maybe? "You cannot deny that my marrying Hermann will have its advantages," she said at last.

Hands shaking, Katia set her cup and saucer aside. She couldn't hold her tongue any longer. She couldn't. "Would your grandfather agree?"

Calmly, without an ounce of self-consciousness, Elena

plucked a linen napkin from the tea service and dabbed at her lips. "Do not be so quick to judge, Katarina. Grandpapa would want me safe. Marriage to Hermann will provide a certain level of protection I cannot achieve otherwise."

Then it was as Katia had suspected. Her mother was hiding in plain sight. With her royal title, Aryan good looks and marriage to a high-ranking Nazi, no one would think to look into Elena Kerensky's past. But what if they did? What if hatred of the Jews increased? What if the Nazi paranoia grew worse?

By marrying Hermann Schmidt, Elena was taking a terrible risk.

A servant dressed in the required uniform of stark black and white swept through the room, moving close to the two of them. Katia waited until she bustled out again.

"Leaving Germany would provide far better protection," she murmured, holding her mother's gaze with unwavering resolve.

Elena blinked. Then blinked again.

Still, Katia held her stare.

For the first time in years, Elena broke their eye contact first.

Katia reached out and squeezed her mother's hand. "It's not impossible."

Elena tugged free. "Don't say such a thing. Don't even think it. The Führer cannot be stopped. Soon, not only Europe but all the world will become a part of the new Germany."

The new Germany? Elena Kerensky's choice of words confounded Katia, especially when there was an unmistakable warning in her eyes. Clearly her mother saw the danger of staying in Germany. Yet she chose to remain.

Why? Did she really believe there was so little hope

left? That Hitler could not be stopped, and would take over the entire world?

Katia would never lose that much faith in good overcoming evil. She must trust in the Lord, even when she couldn't hear His voice. No, especially then. Her father's death had been a horrible thing, but he'd died free in his belief. His faith in God had never wavered, not even in the end. God had not abandoned her father, nor had the Lord abandoned her as she'd once thought.

She had been the one to turn away.

Forgive me, Lord.

As much as she wanted to rejoice in her resurrected faith, she had to finish what she'd started here. Perhaps she still could convince her mother to leave Germany. She couldn't live with herself if she didn't try. Driven by a new-found desperation, she went to her mother and placed her mouth next to her ear.

"I can get us out." The words fell from her lips almost without a sound.

"No." Elena drew away, nearly shoving Katia back into her chair.

"Oh, but I could."

Horror filled her mother's eyes and she looked desperately around her, as though there were as many invisible people as the visible servants listening to their conversation. "You speak too boldly."

Her mother was right, of course. The secret police had ways of knowing things they had no business knowing. It would be foolish to let her guard down, even in her own mother's house—*especially* in her mother's house.

Realizing no good would come from continuing the conversation with so many servants meandering about, Katia let the matter drop. For now. "I'm sorry, Mother, I misspoke."

"You are tired, darling." Elena placed her hand over Katia's and squeezed gently. "That is all."

"Yes, that must be it."

Elena nodded. "You should consider marriage," she said again, more vehemently this time. "You could start a family and stop what you are doing, before it is too late."

What an odd choice of words. Either her mother was simply being a concerned mother or Elena Kerensky knew more than she should.

Which was impossible, of course. How could Elena know of Katia's secret life?

"You want me to leave the stage," she asked for clarification. "Is that what this sudden push for marriage is about?"

"Yes." Elena gave a short shake of her head. "I wish for you to quit the stage as well as your other, shall we call them, pursuits?"

Her other pursuits?

Fear congealed in Katia's throat. She was no longer certain of her mother's meaning. She was no longer certain of herself. "Do you...do you know that I..."

She trailed off and took a moment to think.

Her mother couldn't possibly know about her dealings with the British. Katia had been careful. She'd been *more* than careful. And yet the truth was blazing in her mother's eyes, in the silent accusation hanging heavy in the air between them.

"Mother, do you know that I play unusual...roles, on and off the stage?" Katia kept her words vague, in case a nosy servant thought to listen to their conversation.

"Yes, Katarina." Her mother's confirmation snaked between them like the hissing vapor from a steam engine. "I know all about the dangerous *roles* you play," she spoke, lowering her voice to less than a whisper, "for the enemy."

"I... I... I..." She had no words.

Elena dabbed again at her lips with her napkin. "And now that I know, I demand you stop at once."

Chapter Twenty-Two

The cloud of panic that had been hovering over Katia's head for the last two days crashed over her with a force that nearly threw her from her chair.

"But how?" she gasped. "Mother, how do you know?"

When Elena simply stared her, her expression completely unreadable, Katia forgot to play a role. She forgot to breathe. She was a child again, vulnerable and scared and stripped of all her protective barriers. "Mother?"

Elena's expression never changed, but deep lines of worry cradled her mouth. She cut a quick glance at the servant dusting the mantel and then rose abruptly. "Come, darling, I want to show you the decorations I've added to the backyard for this evening's festivities."

Glad to perform such a simple act, Katia followed her mother onto the outdoor deck. She had no idea what to say or do next. It was already too late to be wary. Her mother knew she was a mole for the British. Silence was her only defense now.

Once outside, Elena pulled Katia close, easing her into the kind of motherly hug she hadn't given her daughter since she was a child.

Katia resisted the urge to cling.

"I have suspected for some time," Elena breathed in her ear. Drawing slowly away, she commanded Katia's stare. "But you confirmed my suspicions yesterday."

Swamped with a fear she'd never known before, not even when the Communists had come for her father, Katia stuttered. "I... I... I did?"

Had she said or done something wrong during lunch, something telling? In so doing had she blown Jack's cover as well as her own?

"It was the roses," Elena whispered.

Katia blinked. The roses. Of course. The hated *white* roses Hermann had given her yesterday morning.

Elena walked to the edge of the deck and placed her hands on the railing. "Your reaction, or rather lack of re-action, was the defining moment for me."

Katia choked in a painful breath of air.

How had this happened? One small mistake, though certainly not her first or even her worst, and now Katia's control of her world was lost forever.

"The roses were your idea," she said softly.

Elena nodded, but she kept her gaze locked on to the horizon. "I couldn't stand living in doubt. I couldn't stand not knowing." She turned to look at Katia, a shadow of an apology filling her eyes. "I had to confirm my suspicions."

Katia could only stand there blinking. The roses had been a trap. Such elemental simplicity.

Katia's throat clenched around a sob. If her own mother could snare her so easily, surely the Nazis would not be far behind. "Does Hermann know?"

"Of course not. Nor will he ever find out."

A spurt of relief came fast. Nevertheless, Katia chased her gaze around the deck, automatically searching for a hidden enemy that couldn't be found so easily. Paranoia was the legacy of her secret life. Would there ever be a time she wouldn't have to look over her shoulder?

"You play a stupid, dangerous game, Katarina." Elena's voice was no less blistering despite its softness. "Especially with men like Friedrich Reiter courting you at the same time. Unless he, too—"

"He is not a part of what I do." For once, a lie came swiftly and easily off her tongue. A lie that sounded altogether true. Even to her own ears she sounded angry and protective. No, she sounded in love.

Elena gripped Katia's shoulders. "Herr Reiter's pursuit of you is genuine, then?"

Was it? Katia had to think for a minute. He'd gone to Kiel alone, claiming it would be too dangerous for her to go with him. Yet he'd come straight to her when he'd been wounded. He'd revealed his darkest secrets in her bathroom, secrets that could get him killed. And then he'd lowered to his knees and prayed with her.

No intelligent spy would take such risks. And Friedrich Reiter was anything but stupid.

"Yes," she said at last. "His feelings for me are real."
As are mine for him.

The thought brought her no comfort. Only fear.

But they that wait upon the Lord shall renew their strength...

Elena released a sigh. "Perhaps Herr Reiter is the one you should marry."

What a wonderful, impossible, *terrible* suggestion. If Katia were to marry such a man, she would spend her life in endless worry.

Would that be any different from now?

She hadn't slept last night, knowing he'd gone alone to meet with Heinrich Himmler, knowing his wound could have begun bleeding again and she wouldn't be there to patch him up a second time.

"Perhaps he is the one," she admitted, then quickly shook her head. "It is too soon to tell."

Looking satisfied, Elena pushed her agenda a little harder. "Then you will consider marriage and stop your other…pursuits?"

If only matters were that simple. Katia was already in too deep with the British. She knew too much. They would never let her quit. But it was a truth her mother must never know.

Lifting her shoulder in a careless shrug, she set out to ease Elena's mind. "Yes, Mother, I will consider marriage."

"Good, now let us return to the parlor and finish our tea."

"Mother, wait."

Elena paused.

Katia rushed to her and hugged her close, close enough to whisper in her ear. "Are you a… *Gottgläubig?*"

"To the world, yes. In my heart, no. I am a true Christian." She pulled away and patted Katia on the cheek, a sad smile spread across her lips. "But I will never speak of this again with you."

"I understand." It was enough. It had to be enough.

Yet still, Katia followed her mother into the front parlor with a sense of defeat trailing her. Now that she understood her mother better, fretted for her less, her mind whisked back to another topic. The idea of marriage had been put in her head and she couldn't get it out. She could not marry the British spy, of course. Not as things stood.

He worked for the SS. And although his loyalties might be with the British, he served Heinrich Himmler and Katia could never abide that.

What a complicated, tangled mess. Nevertheless, Katia

settled into a benign discussion with her mother about the ball later that evening.

The change in Elena, the obvious relief in her voice, was marvelous to witness. Smiling and nodding, Katia allowed her mother the illusion that she'd convinced her daughter to quit working as a mole for the British. Unfortunately, Katia feared this new trail of lies was as twisted and endless as all the others.

When Elena turned the conversation to the extensive guest list, it seemed to Katia that nearly every high-ranking official in the Third Reich would be in attendance. Her ears pricked as her mother mentioned a familiar name.

"Did you say Admiral Doenitz contacted you personally?" she asked, holding her breath for the answer.

"Yes, he telephoned yesterday. He made a point to ask me if my famous daughter would be attending tonight."

Caution had Katia speaking very slowly. Her mother already knew too much. "He asked about me," she repeated as she swallowed back the lump in her throat, "directly?"

"Yes. And then he asked to speak with Hermann, something to do with his next command."

Katia knew she should ask about Hermann's orders, not out of politeness but because she might learn something valuable. But as Elena continued chattering, Katia found it impossible to concentrate on the words. Her ears were ringing too loudly.

And then one thought shoved out all the others. Karl Doenitz suspected she'd been the intruder in his room two nights ago. Why else would he make a point to speak with her mother, personally, just to accept an invitation to a party?

Nausea rose in short, sickening waves.

Struggling for composure, Katia stared at the patchwork of light the sun made on the rug at her feet.

What was she going to do?

Get control of herself, that's what. Then she had to find Jack. No, Friedrich. She had to continue thinking of him as Friedrich. Yes, she had to tell *Friedrich* about this new development.

Most of all, she must pray for protection. *Lord, I—*

Elena clicked her tongue, the gesture regaining Katia's attention. "Did you say something, Mother?"

Glancing at the clock on the mantel, she gave a little gasp. "I hadn't realized it was getting so late. I would like to freshen up before Hermann returns from Wilhelmshaven."

"Of course, Mother, I understand."

Elena rose and kissed Katia on the cheek. "We live in dangerous times, Katarina." Her eyes turned fierce and determined. "Remember what I said about marriage."

Katia nodded.

"You know your way out."

"Yes." Katia rose, as well. "I will see you this evening, after my performance."

Elena sighed in resignation. "Very well."

Katia battled against her own emotions as Elena floated out of the room. Too many thoughts collided with one another. Her mother knew she worked for the British. Doenitz knew—no, he suspected—she'd infiltrated his private chambers. Friedrich Reiter knew her secret. And Hermann was due back at any moment.

In less than two days, Katia had lost all control of her life.

Who was she trying to fool? She'd never had control. She'd been deluding herself all along, and had blamed God when things went wrong because of her own pride and arrogance.

Lord, God, forgive me. I have sought security in my

*own abilities and I have failed. I realize there is no last-
ing security apart from You.*

Almost immediately, she felt the Lord's strength fuse
around her, giving her courage.

*I cannot do this alone. I pray for Your continued pro-
tection and strength.*

Feeling less burdened than she had in years, she left the
parlor and headed toward the foyer.

Determined to find Friedrich as soon as possible, she
picked up her pace. And nearly collided head-on with Hermann Schmidt in the foyer. "Oh."

He steadied her with a firm grip to her arm. "Fräulein.
You are in an unusual hurry this morning."

Almost too late she remembered the role she played
with this man. "I'm, oh, I'm out of breath." She fluttered
her hand in front of her face.

"You should sit." He directed her toward the lone chair
in the entryway and then applied hard pressure to her
shoulder.

Other than fighting against his touch, she had no choice
but to obey. She sat, or rather collapsed, and then looked
into the Nazi's gaze.

There seemed nothing unusual in the way he looked at
her. In fact, he watched her with the same condescending
expression she always saw in his eyes.

"It's rather warm in here." She let out a shaky breath.
"Don't you think, Hermann?"

"I hadn't noticed."

Fanning her face with her splayed fingers, she caught
sight of the items he'd set by the front door. Her gaze
homed in on the metal cylinder propped up against the
wall. It was the kind of tube designed to house blueprints.

But what sort of blueprints would Hermann carry at
this hour of the day?

"You seem tired, Fräulein. Did you and Herr Reiter have a long evening?"

Oh, he was a clever one, this Nazi. He was testing her. They both knew she'd claimed a headache last night. He thought her stupid. She might as well encourage the misconception.

"Oh, we did." She leaned forward. "In fact, we had a very long night. But don't tell Mother."

"I wouldn't dream of ruining Elena's illusions." His lips pulled into a snarl. "She seems to think you are a good girl."

"Oh, but, Hermann." Katia gave him a sultry look, stopping just short of batting her eyes. "I am a good girl."

He reared back in obvious disgust. "So it would seem."

Playing her role with insipid boldness, she pointed to the metal cylinder. Elena's spoiled daughter would never keep her mouth shut in the face of such a shiny new object. "Oh, look at that, did you bring Mother a gift?"

"No." He yanked the metal tube off the floor with practiced agility. "*This* is none of your business."

"Oh." She hid her interest behind a look of mild curiosity. "Is it something…secret?"

Eyes deadly now, he set the tube out of her reach. "You will not touch this or any of my things. Do you understand?"

"Well!" She drew her bottom lip between her teeth and forced a few tears to the edge of her eyelashes. "You don't have to be rude."

He waved his hand in a dismissive gesture but his tone turned chilling. "I am not fooled by your little act, Fräulein."

Shock stole her breath. "Whatever are you talking about?"

Try as she might, she wasn't able to hide the tremble

in her voice. To add to her distress, her heart quit beating then started again at an accelerated rate.

"We both know you are pretending to be upset, trying to get your way as any spoiled child would do."

She sucked in a relieved burst of air, one that sounded exactly like stunned disbelief. "I don't know what you mean."

"Stop it, Katarina. You are not a child. You are a grown woman who has had her share of male company. Your silly games might work on men like Friedrich Reiter, but they will not work on me."

It would seem the deception she'd woven for the benefit of this Nazi had been more than effective. Continuing the ruse, she blinked up at him in hurt confusion. "You are really quite mean, Hermann."

"Go home, Fräulein." He gave her an impatient glare, the kind men threw at women they had no further use for. "I have important matters on my mind."

He opened the door for her.

"Well, I certainly won't stay where I'm not wanted." Rising, she flicked her hair behind her back and moved past him with her chin positioned at a regal angle.

He banged the door shut behind her.

Katia didn't even flinch. The arrogant Nazi had just made a tactical error in judgment. He thought her ridiculous and harmless, a mistake she would use to her advantage.

She mentally sorted through the pieces of new information she'd just gathered. Fact: Hermann Schmidt was a U-boat captain. Fact: he had been called to Wilhelmshaven for a meeting with Admiral Doenitz himself. Fact: he'd returned with a cylinder designed to carry blueprints.

If the admiral suspected an intrusion in his private chambers, his first order of business would be to shift his most important documents to a safer place. Documents, she surmised, that would include the blueprints of a secret weapon laid by a German U-boat.

Perhaps all was not lost.

Perhaps the Lord had just given Katia the break she needed to complete her mission for the British. If she was able to hold the admiral at bay, she just might be able to pull off the rest.

Oh, please, Lord, let me be right.

Chapter Twenty-Three

Katia didn't find Friedrich Reiter until later that afternoon. By then she was feeling less desperate and filled with conviction. She knew what she had to do. She had to confront the admiral directly.

Would Reiter understand? Or would he try to stop her?

She would find out soon enough.

In order to talk freely, they'd agreed to take a walk together. She knew the picture they made as they strolled along hand in hand. They looked like a couple falling in love. It was not a difficult act for her to play. Friedrich appeared equally ensconced in the role.

Feeling her burdens lift just a little, Katia sat beside him on a bench facing the St. Nikolai Church. She'd like to go inside, kneel before the Lord and offer up her prayers in total subjugation. Except for a few milling tourists, they were virtually alone. But not enough to ignore caution completely.

She settled for drawing strength from the church's magnificent exterior.

Sliding her character into place, Katia turned her head slowly and smiled at her companion with the casual intimacy of longtime friends.

He smiled back, then lifted her hand to his lips.

This is a facade, she reminded herself as a tiny flutter swept through her stomach, *it's not real.*

And yet, she knew she would be devastated when he left Germany. Her heart yearned for all that could never be.

How had this happened? How had she come to the point where she belonged so completely to a man she barely knew?

Cold rays of sunlight had broken through the clouds, but they failed to lighten her mood. Restless now, and more than a little frightened, she shifted on the bench until she looked directly into Reiter's eyes.

He was watching her, his gaze both alert and vibrant. She could almost believe he had not been shot the night before. She knew better, of course. She'd seen the blood flowing down his arm.

Now that the initial shock was over, Katia didn't mind admitting to herself just how scared she'd been when she'd first seen the wound. Thankfully, she'd been able to turn her fear into action. But even now, half a day later, she couldn't let go of the realization that he'd almost been killed.

It was true, then.

She'd fallen in love with the British spy. Stupidly, profoundly, permanently in love. It was the one fight she hadn't prepared for. She had no weapon in her arsenal, no ready-made defense, and certainly no role to wrap around her in protection.

Sighing, she shut her eyes and leaned her head against the bench. She was so tired.

Tired of the games. Tired of the pretenses.

"Last night, you said you trusted me," she began, turning her head just enough to look into his face once again.

He cupped her cheek in his hand. She could see that he

was thinking deeply, carefully considering what he would say before he spoke. "I do. I trust you completely."

Oh, how she wanted to enjoy getting to know this man, learning his strengths and weaknesses, what he liked and didn't like. They could grow together in the Lord. But not today. Today, they had serious business looming over them.

"When I was at my mother's this morning, she told me Admiral Doenitz contacted her to personally accept her invitation and to ask if I would be attending the ball tonight."

In a move that spoke of familiarity, he hooked his arm around the back of the bench behind her shoulders and stretched his legs out in front of him. She was not fooled by his outward calm.

He was furious. In fact, the anger vibrating off him was palpable.

"Then he suspects you were the intruder." Aside from anger, there was also worry in his voice. Caring, too.

"I'm sorry," she admitted on a shaky breath. "I went into this mission too arrogant. I should have been more careful from the start."

He was silent for a long time then he squeezed her shoulder gently. "Sometimes setbacks are part of God's plan." His voice sounded thoughtful, as if he was only just coming to his conclusions as he spoke. "Maybe this is the Lord's way of protecting us in a way we cannot fully understand right now."

Rather than shocking her, his suggestion made her want it all. Happiness. Hope. Faith in a sovereign Lord and Savior. She'd lived without God too long, and in many ways she'd done well enough on her own. Until this mission.

In just two days everything had changed.

She still had skills. She still had talent. Her mistake was in thinking she'd ever had control. She knew turning to the Lord for strength was her only answer. But God had let her down so many times.

"I want to, but I don't know if I can trust the Lord completely," she admitted. "How do you stay sure, Friedrich, and confident, especially when you see so much horror all around you?"

There was an uncomfortable moment of silence before he smiled at her. The gesture made his face look so tender, so patient it nearly brought tears to her eyes.

"Make no mistake," he said. "I'm struggling with this, too. In fact, I have spent the last two years angry at God. But I now realize the Lord never abandoned me during those dark days. I abandoned him."

His words were so close to what she'd decided about her own situation. His sincere faith blew past her anger, shoved aside her painful memories and landed straight in her heart. She desperately wanted to believe again.

It was her choice. And she would choose faith.

"Oh, Jack." She gripped his arm, only half-aware she'd used his real name. She would not make that mistake again. Not even in her mind.

"I wish… No." She shook her head vigorously and released her hold on him. Her hope for a future with this man was not a part of the mission. "What I wish isn't important at the moment. Let's get back to our immediate problems," she continued as she shifted on the bench. "What do you suggest we do next?"

For a moment he looked as if he wasn't going to allow her to change the subject, but then he nodded. "First we deal with what we know." He drummed his fingers on her shoulder. "You're absolutely sure you left no physical evidence of your presence in Doenitz's room other than the chair?"

She caught the rhythm of his fingers, tapped her foot

along to it. "I've replayed every second I spent in that room over in my mind. I was careful, until the chair."

"Then Doenitz must have made the connection through the guard."

"It's a reasonable conclusion," she said.

Lifting his hand, he brushed his fingers absently down her hair. Stroke. Stroke. Stroke. So soothing. So comforting. She fought to keep her eyes open.

"I want you to stay away from the admiral tonight." However polite he spoke the request, there was an uncompromising glint in his eyes. She knew he would not relent on this.

"But we have to find out whether the admiral truly suspects me," she argued. "Or if his interest in meeting me is merely coincidence. We still have the key to the cabinet. We may be able to go back to Wilhelmshaven for the plans yet tonight." *If they are still there.*

Reiter spoke her thoughts aloud. "It would be a wasted effort. Doenitz will have moved all the important documents after discovering an intrusion. And, Katarina," he spoke, giving her a look of regret. "We have to go on the assumption that he believes he has not only discovered the intrusion but also the identity of the intruder."

Panic crawled over her, sneaking up her spine. "Maybe not. If I could just talk to him I could—"

"You will take no more risks," he said in a clipped, measured tone. "Not on my watch."

His eyes flashed with anger. The sudden, brilliant force of the emotion turned his face into something tough, and potentially mean. This, she decided, was her first real glimpse of the man who worked as Himmler's personal henchman.

She stifled a shiver.

"Then what do you suggest?"

Releasing a slow breath, he regarded the sky with such interest she found herself looking up. When he continued watching the sky she wondered if he was praying.

Before she could ask, he lowered his gaze back to hers. "You will confront the admiral only if I am with you." His eyes turned icy-blue as he spoke. "He will not dare to hurt you with me by your side."

"Just how deep in the SS are you?" She didn't try to keep the fear out of her voice.

She thought she saw something terrible in his eyes, right before he looked away from her. "I can't tell you that."

She let his words sink in, understood them on an intellectual level, but couldn't prevent the worry from digging deep.

Squeezing her eyes shut, she decided to focus on their conversation and not the danger this man put himself in daily. "There's something else you should know."

He watched her as though he could take her mind apart piece by piece. Fragments of panic swirled up and her fingers twisted in her skirt. It was a telling sign of her nervousness so she stopped.

"Go on," he prompted.

"My mother has discovered my secret life."

He did not react. Nor his body move, not even an inch, but Katia felt the air around him heating. "And Schmidt?" he asked in a low, feral hiss. "Does he know, as well?"

"No." She tangled her hand in her skirt again. This time she couldn't stop the nervous gesture. The gravity of the situation was bearing down on her too hard. "Nor does my mother know about you. She thinks you are merely courting me."

Making a sound deep in his throat, one that was most definitely a growl, he rose from the bench. Without speaking, he tugged her along with him and then steered her toward the harbor.

His gaze locked on the horizon for a long moment. And still he did not speak.

At last, he glanced down at her with genuine pain in his eyes. He was looking at her with Jack's eyes now. *This* was the man she could adore for a lifetime.

"We have to abort the mission," he said.

"I don't think that's necessary." Although her heart ached, her head worked quickly, weaving facts and possibilities together. "I should have told you this first. Hermann had a meeting with the admiral this morning. When he returned he was carrying a set of blueprints. The metal cylinder was unmarked but my gut tells me that he's carrying the plans to the magnetic mines."

Reiter eyed her with his own unique brand of watchfulness. "You're sure of this?"

"Yes."

"I suppose it's worth checking into." His tone gave nothing away.

Urgency had her switching directions. "I must find out where he put the blueprints."

Jack stopped her with a hand on her arm. "No. It's too dangerous."

"Dangerous?" She gave him a throaty laugh. "The man thinks I'm an idiot. It's his greatest weakness, you know, his inability to see beyond the obvious when it comes to me."

"Katarina, do not underestimate the Nazi. He and the admiral could be setting a trap for you." There was more than anger in his eyes as he spoke. There was fear.

"A trap?" She thought of the way Schmidt had glared at her this morning with obvious disgust. He thought her beyond stupid. "He doesn't have any idea of who I really am. I'd stake my life on it."

"Well, I won't stake your life on it."

"You should have more faith in me."

"Stop and think, Katarina." He gave her one of Jack's looks that grabbed at her heart and twisted. "While you are performing tonight, Schmidt will be at your mother's party. That gives me plenty of time to break into his hotel room and discover if he does indeed have a copy of the blueprints."

Accepting the wisdom of his words, she knew this was no time for ego or foolish arguing. "Hermann is staying at the Hotel Atlantic Kempinski."

Smiling gravely, he threaded his fingers through hers. "If you are right, I could finish this in a matter of hours."

Sadness overwhelmed her at the thought. With the mission complete, this wonderful, courageous man could very well leave Germany tonight. She would never see him again.

Tears filled her eyes.

"Come to England with me," he whispered, pressing a finger to her lips when she started to speak. "No, hear me out. Your mother already knows about your secret life. Admiral Doenitz suspects. It won't be long before others find out. It's no longer safe for you to live in Germany."

His words had her stomach churning with fear. But her convictions were stronger. "I can't leave without my mother. You know this already."

"Take her with you."

"She's determined to marry Hermann."

He pulled in a tight breath. "Then quit. Take no more assignments."

He'd just spoken her mother's greatest wish for her. After these last two days, Katia wasn't sure she didn't wish for the same thing. "They won't let me quit. You know this, also. I am too valuable. And I know too much."

"You could be just as valuable in England. You could train our operatives in German idiosyncrasies. You could teach them the unique body language and other nuances only someone who has lived here would know."

"Why can't you do that?"

His expression closed. "For one, I'm an American. I haven't actually lived in Germany for any length of time. Besides, I have a…different assignment ahead of me."

"What?" Fear edged around her voice. "What is this new assignment?"

"I can't tell you."

"So much for trusting me completely."

"I can't tell you for your protection, not mine." He gripped her shoulders gently and twisted her around to face him again. "I want you safe, Katarina. I *need* you safe."

"No one is safe. We are at war."

Instead of arguing, he stepped back and spread his arms in silent invitation. After only a moment of hesitation, she moved into his embrace and settled her head against his chest.

Folding her close, he kissed the top of her head.

She hugged her arms tighter around him. "You better get moving. There isn't much time now."

"Katarina." He pulled away from her. His eyes were free of all subterfuge. In fact, he looked vulnerable, like he was about to make a declaration. "Katarina. I—"

"No." She shook her head at him, afraid he would pronounce his love for her, deathly afraid that he wouldn't. "Now isn't the time for speeches. I have to prepare for my performance and you have important photographs to take."

"We aren't finished. Not by half." The soft, affectionate look in his eyes had her gulping for air.

Reaching up, she touched his face.

"If you get the photographs you need," she said, "please don't come back for me tonight. Let this be the end for us."

He took a step away from her, and then another, all the while shaking his head. "I won't let you face Doenitz alone. And I won't leave you behind." His tone brooked no argument on either subject.

In spite of her desire to run away with him, Katia had to think of her mother. "I won't go with you."

"Yes, you will."

"No. I won't." This was one argument Katia had no intention of losing.

Chapter Twenty-Four

After all the mistakes, all the stops and starts, Jack completed his mission for the British in less than three minutes. With the photographs taken and the blueprints returned to the metal cylinder, all he had to do now was exit Schmidt's hotel room undetected.

Pressing his ear against the door, he listened for activity in the hallway. Breathing slowly, very slowly, he counted two sets of footsteps shuffling past. There was a pause, a soft murmur of voices, another pause, subdued laughter, and then the rattle of the elevator doors opening and shutting.

Patting the ridiculously small spy camera nestled safely in his pocket, Jack nudged the door open. With the hallway clear, he retreated in the same manner in which he'd come. Ten purposeful steps and he slipped into the ancient stairwell.

Five minutes later, he walked out the front door of the hotel.

The early-winter air spit at his face. He found the cold invigorating, as energizing as the adrenaline flowing through his blood.

He crossed at the intersection under the harsh light of

a streetlight. He was the picture of a law-abiding citizen with nothing to hide. It was one of his best lies.

Only after he made it to the other side of the street did he stop and allow himself a moment to savor his triumph.

His trip into Schmidt's room had resulted in unprecedented success. Jack not only had photographs of the blueprints to the magnetic mines, but he also had a picture of Schmidt's exact route through the English Channel. The chart containing the carefully plotted minefield, including precise coordinates of where each bomb would be laid, had been hidden with the blueprints.

An unfamiliar wave of doubt rose up. He shoved it back with a growl. With or without the uniform, Jack Anderson was a soldier. His actions would ultimately save thousands of lives.

Lord God, I pray for discernment. Help me to take only the necessary steps to protect the innocent and not to harm them.

That was it. He needed to hold on to God. Daily. What had his father once said? The safest place to stand in a storm was next to the Lord. It was good advice. The only answer in times of war.

Jack allowed a smile to play at the corners of his mouth as he swept his gaze to his right, to his left, and then he glanced at his watch. Three hours to rendezvous.

He stuck his hands in his pockets and started down the street toward his own hotel. He still had to change into his tuxedo for Elena's party.

Two days ago he wouldn't have hesitated to head straight to the docks and climb aboard a fishing vessel that would take him to meet the British trawler waiting for him in the North Sea.

But that had been before he'd met Katarina Kerensky. Knowing her had changed him. He had no doubt God's hand had been in their meeting from the start. In the end, Katarina had put a face on the German Resistance for him, and she'd brought a renewed hope to Jack's grim future. He may not survive this terrible war, but he would make sure she did.

Although too many lives depended on what he held in his pocket to risk capture for the sake of a single woman, he couldn't bear to leave her behind, either.

At the very least he could protect her tonight. She would not face Admiral Doenitz alone.

An idea began crystallizing. For once, Jack would use his unsavory connections for his own personal use. And Heinrich Himmler need never know why.

Katia knew her role tonight, and Katarina Kerensky never missed a cue. With a deceptively vacant expression in her eyes, she circled her gaze around the perimeter of the ballroom, taking a quick inventory along the way.

Her mother had outdone herself again. The illusion of happier times was complete, all the way down to the flowers, the elegant music, the glittering crystal and the equally glittering guests.

Thanks to Elena Kerensky's efforts, tonight the handpicked Germans of wealth, privilege and perfect lineage would find it easy to pretend greatness had returned to the Fatherland.

But not without a price.

Katia's stomach rolled at the thought.

But they that wait upon the Lord shall renew their strength; they shall mount up with wings as eagles; they shall run, and not be weary....

She nodded at her mother's butler, and then waited while he announced her with unnecessary grandeur. The responding hush was a perfect accompaniment for the entrance of a princess turned famous stage actress. One more illusion to add to the others.

Fully in her role now, Katia allowed the guests to admire her long blue gown and upswept hair before stepping forward.

She slowly turned her head, nodding at the faces she recognized. In each cluster of people, she searched for Friedrich Reiter. She came up empty.

Where was he?

Surely he'd been successful tonight. Or had Hermann caught him in the act of breaking into his hotel room?

No. Friedrich was too careful and too good at his job. Katia had no doubt he had succeeded tonight. He would be here soon. But would it be soon enough?

Just as the thought formed she caught sight of Hermann speaking with another naval officer. Even with his back to her, the other man fit Admiral Doenitz's description perfectly.

Her whole body tingled with tension. Beneath the tension rushed an undertow of doom that built as she glided through the ballroom.

If Friedrich didn't arrive soon she would face the admiral alone. She would do so with the Lord's courage tucked deep inside her.

She repeated her father's favorite verse in her mind. *But they that wait upon the Lord shall renew their strength...*

Even with the Lord's promise nestled within her, she had a sudden urge to turn and run. But then she thought of Jack Anderson and the dangerous role he played as Friedrich Reiter. His sacrifices were far greater than hers. She would not let him down.

As though sensing her eyes on him, the man speaking to Hermann turned to face her. Even at this distance, she could discern the decorations unique to an admiral's uniform. Karl Doenitz. It had to be him. Although shorter than she'd expected, the admiral wore his uniform with terrifying confidence, making him appear far more formidable than Hermann.

Katia continued across the ballroom. Toward the admiral. She found a desperate need to pray. *Oh, Lord, Lord, I need Your courage. I surrender my will to Yours.*

Feeling stronger, she hid the rest of her nerves behind an easy smile. She kept her movements slow and elegant. No one would know her knees were about to buckle under her.

But just as she crossed to the edge of the dance floor, she caught sight of her mother. In spite of a sense of urgency flowing through her, Katia stopped a moment and admired the woman who had given her birth.

How perfect she looked, Katia thought, elegant, refined, with a hint of sadness in her eyes that made her look even more stunning.

A jolt of love came hard and fast, surprising Katia into staring a moment longer. The realization that she wanted to ensure her mother's safety more than her own jumped into her head and convinced her all the more. This was no longer a matter of saving her only surviving parent. This was about saving a woman she loved.

Katia would not allow the war, the Nazis' hatred of Jews, or even Hermann Schmidt to hurt her mother. Even if she died trying, Katia would protect Elena.

Her best option would be to get her out of Germany.

But first, she had to face a suspicious admiral.

It took all her skill as an actress to bury her concerns for her mother and force her mind on the task the lay before her.

Unfortunately, before she could carry on, her mother closed the distance between them and took her hand. "Katia, you look magnificent this evening."

Katia tightened her grip on their linked fingers. "I was thinking the same of you, Mother."

She didn't have the words to tell Elena how much she loved her; too many years had gone by without saying them and too many fresh emotions had been laid bare this morning. Unable to speak, she simply squeezed her mother's hand again.

This time, Elena squeezed back.

They stood still in the moment, mother and daughter connecting on a deeper level than they had in years.

Elena blinked, breaking the spell first, then kissed Katia's cheek. "You are going to be fine, Katarina. Just fine."

"Yes. After tonight everything will change for us both."

They shared a brief, self-conscious hug, then Elena stood back a step and looked around her. "But where is Herr Reiter? I thought he was escorting you this evening."

"An unexpected business matter came up. He will be here shortly." *I hope.*

Katia turned to look around the ballroom. But when she didn't see Friedrich right away her initial confidence turned to worry. He should have completed their mission long before now. "I wonder where he is," she said aloud.

Elena touched her arm. "Not to worry, darling. I'm sure he'll arrive soon enough."

"Yes, he will. He would never let me down." She smiled as she spoke, but she couldn't help wondering what was keeping him. He had seemed so determined to protect her from the admiral.

Please, Lord, please let him be safe.

Short of going in search of him, there wasn't much more she could do at the moment. So she forced her mind to refocus. "Mother, would you mind introducing me to Admiral Doenitz while we wait for Friedrich to arrive?"

"I'd be delighted. He is just over there with Hermann."

Although not especially excited to speak to Elena's fiancé, Katia allowed her mother to maneuver her through the crowd. They were interrupted at least a dozen times, but Elena Kerensky was an expert at charming her guests with a smile and a few words.

All too soon they stopped in front of the admiral. "Herr Admiral," Elena began. "I would like to introduce you to my daughter, Katarina Kerensky."

Doenitz gave her a slight smile, but his eyes remained hard. "Ah, the famous actress. *Kapitän* Schmidt and I were just speaking about you."

Terror threatened to peel the layers of her role away, but Katia forced down the emotion and blinked up at her mother's fiancé. His eyes were sharp on her, weighing and measuring.

Undaunted, she gave him the vacant smile she reserved solely for him. "I trust you said nothing but good things about me, Hermann."

With an ironic twist of his lips, he nodded. "Of course, Katarina. Nothing but good things."

"Well, then, I thank you." She held back from speaking further while her mother continued looking on.

No matter what, Katia would not include Elena in this complicated battle of wills, especially now that her mother knew about her dangerous secret life.

As though sensing Katia's need to speak to the men alone, Elena said, "Well, darling. I'll leave you and Hermann to entertain the admiral while I tend to my other guests."

She gave each of them a brilliant smile before turning to leave. No one but Katia would guess Elena's fear for her daughter. The woman was proving a better actress than Katia herself. She was very proud of her mother.

But now that she was alone with the two Nazis, she felt

like a hen trapped in a den full of foxes. Her best weapon was silence.

When both men simply blinked at her, she decided to play shy, as though she was overcome with awe over the admiral.

Ignoring Hermann, she turned her full attention to Doenitz. "I have never met an admiral before." Her words came out soft and a little shaky.

Doenitz lifted his eyebrows. "No?"

"I am quite overwhelmed."

They stared at one another, neither looking away, neither acknowledging Hermann. Katia held on to her smile, adding just the right amount of famous actress to the gesture. She knew this role well.

Doenitz, for his part, continued holding her gaze. To an outsider, they looked enthralled with one another.

Which was true enough, but not for the obvious reasons.

Hermann cleared his throat. "Yes, well, I better help Elena."

Neither Katia nor the admiral responded. Instead, they continued to stare at one another. And stare and stare and stare.

Giving a quick farewell and a promise to return to speak to the admiral before the night was over, Hermann turned on his heel and left.

Once alone, Doenitz broke the silence first. "Your mother is a lovely woman."

Katia was not sure what was in his voice. It was not truth. And certainly not affection. "Yes, she is."

"It would be a shame if anything were to happen to her."

Pretending to misunderstand, Katia steered the conversation toward the mundane. "Are you enjoying the ball, Herr Admiral?"

He clasped his hands behind his back. "I do not wish

to sound ungracious, but I much prefer the sea to a crowd of people. And I understand, Fräulein, that you enjoy the sea air, as well." The smile he sent her was as tough and cold as his voice.

Sensing where he was heading, she placed a vacuous look in her eyes. "Why, yes, I do. On occasion."

His smile relaxed only a fraction as he turned to a passing waiter and plucked a flute of champagne off the tray. "I was thinking of a specific patch of sea," he said, handing her the glass. "Along the coast west of here."

She lifted the champagne to her lips, but only pretended to take a sip of the wine. She couldn't afford to be lightheaded now that the conversation was steering into unfriendly waters. "Every coastline looks the same to me."

"Ah, but I understand you appreciate our little harbor in Wilhelmshaven more than most."

She lifted a shoulder, even as her breath tightened in her chest. "Perhaps in the summertime."

"I was thinking more in the vicinity of two nights ago."

He knew. The thought echoed in Katia's ears. Round and round, over and over again. *He knew, he knew, he knew.*

Her initial impulse was to inform the admiral she had no idea what he meant, but she decided to stick with the story she and Friedrich Reiter had told the guard that night. "A woman such as myself has to do what she must to find a moment of privacy now and again."

"You don't deny it, then?"

She struggled to keep her tone mild. "Of course not. Why would I?"

"Why, indeed." He spoke evenly, but his gaze turned shrewd and calculating. "If my memory serves, it was very cold that night."

She knew he was leading her down a path, setting a trap. *Be ye therefore wise as serpents, and harmless as doves.* Yes, she would stay one step ahead of this particular snake, by cooperating with him more than he expected. "I think you are correct."

"Perhaps you needed a moment out of the harsh weather?" he said, with just enough menace to send a ripple up her spine.

She twirled the champagne flute in her fingers. "Oh, I had my own ways of staying warm."

Changing tactics, he spun on his heel and offered his arm. "Shall we walk? A bit of exercise is always good for the blood."

Linking her free hand through his, she nodded. "If you like."

They strolled along the edge of the dance floor and then out onto the balcony. She glanced up briefly at the moon. The tiny sliver shone bright against the midnight silk of the sky. Such a lovely evening, she thought, too lovely for the ugly business of war.

"Now that we are completely alone, I will get straight to the point."

She dropped her hand by her side. "I always appreciate honesty."

"There was an intruder in my private quarters two nights ago. I think it was you."

"Me?" She would not panic. "You must be joking."

"I do not joke. And I suggest you don't try my patience. Was it you, or not?"

"Ah," she began, her voice perfectly even, her emotions completely shut down except for one. Anger. She used it to spark indignation in her voice. "What an absurd question."

"Yet, you do not deny you were in Wilhelmshaven two nights ago."

Katia gave a careless shake of her head, lowered her voice to a whisper. "You must understand, Herr Admiral,

I was with a special…friend that evening. Which is not something I wish to share with the world. If you capture my meaning."

"So you came to Wilhelmshaven for privacy."

"Precisely."

"Then you won't mind if I check out your story?"

She gave him a carefree shrug of one shoulder. "Do what you must."

"If you would be so kind as to give me your friend's name, we'll end this conversation now. And thereby avoid bringing your mother into this."

For a hideous moment, her mind froze. "My…my mother?"

"I don't suppose you wish for her to be subjected to questioning, now do you? Especially over a simple lover's tryst. And when I say questioning, I'm sure you capture *my* meaning." He left just enough unsaid, hanging in the air between them, to put terror in her heart.

Katia started to give a name, any name, then remembered that the Gestapo already knew the identity of her "lover." It was possible the admiral did, too. "I was with Friedrich Reiter that night."

"And who is this Friedrich Reiter?"

Another burst of panic had the air clogging in her throat.

But then a familiar voice sounded above the pounding of her heart. "*I* am Friedrich Reiter."

Chapter Twenty-Five

Katia whipped around, her gaze landing on the one man she trusted to protect her above all others.

If he'd been successful tonight, he should not be here. He should be on his way to England. But he was here, just as he'd promised. She'd known he would come to protect her, but was he also here to salvage the mission with what little time they had left? Or had he completed their mission? Adding to her confusion, he didn't look like the man she knew. There was something different about him tonight, something almost sinister in his bearing. His eyes had turned hard and ruthless, while his lips curled into a cold, vicious smile that made him look like a, like a…

Nazi.

"And *who* exactly are you?" Doenitz asked.

Forgetting all about the mission, Katia decided she would like to know the answer to that question herself.

"I am SS-*Sturmbannführer* Friedrich Wilhelm Reiter." He gave the Nazi salute. "*Heil* Hitler."

Doenitz returned the salute, and then angled his head. "You claim you are SS, yet you wear no uniform."

Katia's thoughts ran along similar lines, but for very different reasons.

Who was this man, she wondered? She didn't see any of Jack Anderson in him now. What sort of horrors must he endure for this role? How often had he played it?

As if in answer to her unspoken questions, Reiter narrowed his eyes in cold menace. "If you have any doubts as to my identity, Herr Admiral, you may take it up with my direct superior, *Reichsführer* Himmler."

"You work with the *Reichsführer*, directly?"

"Yes."

The hard lines of Doenitz's mouth flattened. "In what capacity?"

Reiter's cold smile disappeared, replaced with a cruel twist of lips. "A little of this, a little of that."

Doenitz's face contorted as if he was in pain. "Am I to assume, then, that you were in Wilhelmshaven with Fräulein Kerensky two nights ago under the *Reichsführer*'s orders?"

Katia held her breath as she waited for the answer along with Doenitz. She knew there was something going on between these two, but she didn't quite understand. And yet, somehow it all made perfect sense. Friedrich Reiter was SS. Karl Doenitz was old-school navy. They would hate each other on principle alone.

For the first time since his arrival, Reiter looked at Katia directly. For an instant, she saw in his eyes the God-fearing man who had begged her to return with him to England, but then the hard SS officer was back in place.

"Perhaps," he said, turning his ruthless gaze back to the admiral, "you should take that up with the *Reichsführer* himself."

Doenitz visibly stiffened. "An excellent idea. If you will excuse me, I have a telephone call to make."

"That won't be necessary, Herr Admiral." Reiter's tone was viciously polite, and in that moment, Katia could very well imagine the man capable of cruelty beyond imagining. "The *Reichsführer* is waiting for you in the ballroom."

On full alert, feet braced for battle, Jack held his position in front of Katarina until Doenitz turned on his heel and left the balcony. Only then did he turn to her. Trying to gauge her mood, he took his time searching her face.

On the surface, she looked breathtaking in the long column of deep blue silk and sparkling diamond jewelry. But on deeper inspection, he noted her narrowed eyes and quick pants for air. She was distressed, more than a little stunned. And very, very frightened. He hadn't expected that last bit. Had Friedrich Reiter scared her? He hated the thought.

"Katarina?"

She muttered under her breath, choked back a sob and then started muttering all over again.

He didn't catch a single word. "You want to try saying that again?"

Pressing her hand to her heart, she took two fast inhalations and then spoke slower. "He threatened my mother."

Jack knew she was scared. He could feel her fear vibrating between them. But as she fought to maintain her outward calm, he found himself admiring her courage all over again. Katarina Kerensky was an amazing woman. "He won't follow through. Not now."

She spun to glare at him, her eyes wild and just a little unfocused. "He knows it was me. He *knows.*"

"He suspects. It is not the same thing." Jack would make sure no harm came to her now, even if that meant taking her back to England with him.

"He'll be back." She all but growled out her response. "And then what will I do?"

"He won't return tonight."

Fire snapped in her eyes. "Why?"

"Himmler and Doenitz have far more serious matters to discuss than a break-in."

Hands shaking, she smoothed the hair off her face. "I… You… You're really SS."

There was no defense against her accusation, other than the truth. "Yes. When in Germany, I answer only to the *Reichsführer*."

Breathing slower now, she nodded. "I think I understand."

Again, he thought how brave she was—dangerously brave, as was necessary in times such as these.

Needing to comfort her, he reached out.

She shoved his hand away. "I even understand why you couldn't tell me all of it. I just don't like that you're so deeply involved with men like…him."

Jack wanted to defend himself. He wanted to see her look at the man he wanted to be, not the man he was. But there was no reason to argue over something that couldn't be changed. Katarina's ultimate safety depended on getting past this discussion over his identity as an SS officer.

Drawing her deeper into the shadows, he lowered his voice to a whisper. "Just so we're clear, I was successful tonight. Our mission is over."

"I assumed as much." Her tone was filled with relief.

"I leave for England in an hour."

"I understand."

She stepped back into the light, the beacon washing her in its golden glow. With her dignity wrapped around her like a shield, she looked so alone. The reality of her courage tore at him. There was no way he'd be able to walk away from her now. Not without leaving a large part of himself behind. *Lord, fill me with the right words to convince her to leave Germany.*

"Come back with me, Katarina."

Crossing her arms in front of her, she regarded him with blank, patient eyes, giving him the impression that she saw too much of Friedrich Reiter in him now. "I barely know you."

In that she was wrong. Dead wrong. He'd opened his heart to her. Fully. And now he owed her the rest of the truth. His truth. "You know me better than anyone ever has or ever will."

She continued staring at him, her eyes still a little unfocused. But he saw a brief flicker of hope in her gaze, a tiny hint of wavering that gave him the courage to push.

"Come with me," he repeated, pulling her carefully into his arms. "There's still time to make the arrangements. Not much. But enough."

He half expected her to fight him, but she clung to him as tightly as he held her. "You know I can't."

"I'm getting tired of repeating the same argument." Desperation made his voice crack.

"And I'm getting tired of repeating the same answer."

A good military man knew when he'd lost. This battle had been over before it had started. Nevertheless, Jack cared too much to retreat. Even if Katarina ended her work for the British, even if her mother never married Schmidt, Germany was a deadly place for people with Jewish ancestry—no matter how distant.

"You cannot remain much longer." Letting out a breath, he lowered his forehead to hers. "Tonight I've given you a small amount of protection, but it might not be enough over time. They will watch you closer after this."

"Then I lay low for a while." She leaned her head against his shoulder and sighed. "Please. Don't make me explain this to you again. This isn't about you and me. It never was."

"I know."

She laughed, but there was no humor in the sound. "Try to understand. God's will for my life is here in Germany."

Unsure whether to be pleased or suspicious over her reference to God, he took a deep breath. "This, from you?"

She drew away then fixed him with a direct stare. "You've made a difference in my life, more than you know. I want to believe, I want to have confidence in God again. But I fear it's not enough just to want it."

"Wanting is the first step, Katarina. Come with me. We can find our way back to the Lord together."

"Oh, Friedrich." Her voice softened. "Neither of us have the luxury of putting our needs first."

Jack swallowed. Ached for what he couldn't have. Cleared his throat. Then forced a smile. "I can't change your mind, can I?"

"No."

He was going to fail. No, he *had* failed. He knew that now. Accepted it at last. But he also knew he would return to Germany in less than a month, fully ensconced in his alter ego. He would find a way back to her. The thought made their parting easier. "I'll pray for you. Every day."

"I... Thank you. And I'll do the same for you." She came to him again, wrapped her arms around his waist. "It's not our time."

Cloaked in the shadows again, he pressed his lips against her temple. "There will be a day when this war is over. And then—"

"It will be our time to be together."

"Yes." He held her for a moment longer, just held her as a twisted, frightening mixture of hope and loss tangled together in his heart.

He didn't want to leave her.

He didn't have the right to take her with him. Like she said, this wasn't about them.

God had given each of them a calling for their lives, at a time that required them both to think beyond themselves. They'd been blessed to have these three days.

Shifting her weight, she leaned back to look into his eyes again. "You should probably take your leave at this point."

Yes, he would go. But not before he made it perfectly clear that he was her future. And she was his. He lowered his head and kissed her fiercely on the mouth. Gathering control, he set her at arm's length, but kept his hands on her waist. "This isn't the end for us. I won't say goodbye."

"Neither will I." She touched his lips and then kissed him where her fingertip had been. She kissed him again, tenderly, softly, so softly he trembled.

Silent promises passed between them. Jack believed the Lord would bring him back to her. Someday. The thought gave him the necessary strength to turn and leave her behind.

Chapter Twenty-Six

Jack made it halfway through the ballroom before he was stopped by a soft, feminine voice coming from behind him. "Herr Reiter, I would like a word with you before you leave."

He turned, very slowly, and came face-to-face with Elena Kerensky. He could say many things to this woman, demand even more; instead he kept silent and studied her in candid appraisal.

Tonight she wore her hair pinned in some fancy style of the day. She was dressed in a sparkling silver dress adorned with jewels the color of her eyes. All that was missing to complete the picture of a royal princess was the tiara.

But as regal as the woman looked on the surface, her wide blue eyes blinked up at him in… Jack couldn't put a word to the expression. Fear, perhaps? No, something far more complicated than that.

"I am at your disposal, Princess." He gave her a short bow. "What is it you wish to discuss?"

"Not here," she said. "Follow me."

"Of course."

As she led him out of the ballroom, Jack looked around him. He wasn't usually sentimental, or poetic, but Elena

Kerensky had created an old-world charm that caught his imagination. It was as though he'd been transported back in time.

The air shimmered with the golden light of hundreds of candlesticks. Small tables had been arranged in sets of three, the groupings then separated by an assortment of ornamental trees. Flowers of various colors had been strategically placed throughout the room. While a full orchestra played classical music, mostly Austrian waltzes.

The irony was not lost on him. He found himself smiling cynically as she led him to a small alcove just off the front entrance. The spot was not entirely private, but private enough, as long as they kept their voices down.

For a moment she simply gazed into his eyes. He let her.

"You and I, we are alike, I think," she said at last.

Now that was an interesting comment, one that sent the hairs on the back of his neck bristling. "How so?"

"We do what must be done in these difficult times." Her words were strong enough, but her tone lacked edge. "We align ourselves with whom we must."

In that moment, Jack realized Elena Kerensky was not the hard woman he'd once thought. She was simply trying to protect her daughter. His respect for her traveled up a few notches.

"The world is not always as black and white as some would have us believe," he said in response.

"No." She nodded. "It would seem we are of a similar mind."

"Not so much of a shock when one considers our common interest in Katarina."

"No. Not a shock at all." Elena smiled, just a little. A very little. "You realize, of course, I am not completely blind in my daughter's feelings for you."

His protective instinct reared, but he shoved it behind

an easy smile. "Katarina is a brave woman. I admire her greatly."

"Admire her?" Parental outrage hummed between them. "That is all you feel for Katarina, mere admiration?"

"No. That is not all. Far from it." He did not elaborate, but he allowed his feelings to show in his eyes. He would not lie about something so important as his love for Katarina. It was the one truth he could have whether he was Jack Anderson or Friedrich Reiter.

"You are a very careful man, Herr Reiter." She nodded in approval. "It is a fine quality to have in these troubling times."

"It has served me well."

"I find it necessary to ask you to be a little less careful." He waited for the rest.

"Are your feelings strong enough for my daughter to encourage you to do whatever it takes to ensure her safety?"

The desperation in her eyes was at odds with her smooth tone. Clearly, Elena Kerensky was trying to say something more here, something important, but Jack didn't have the time or the inclination to sort through the subtext of her words. "Princess Elena, I am not your enemy. Please, say what you need to say."

She gave him one small nod. "I could not help but notice that you arrived tonight with the *Reichsführer*. Am I to assume you are an officer in the SS, in spite of your lack of uniform?"

Jack inclined his head, wondering why Schmidt had not shared that information with her himself. "You would be correct in your assumption."

"I see." Obvious relief filled her gaze. Jack had not expected that. The woman was proving a surprise, much like her daughter. They were an amazing pair.

"Then perhaps..." Elena trailed off in order to take a

deep breath. "*Perhaps* you will take the final step to ensure Katarina's safety?"

Did she know of her daughter's work with the British? Or was she simply taking an obvious step by aligning her daughter's future with that of an SS officer?

Every cell in his body stood at attention. "What did you have in mind?" Although he sensed her response before she spoke again.

"Will you marry her, Herr Reiter?"

And there it was. The solution to all their problems. So simple. So obvious. Of course it would come from Elena, a woman securing her own future in the same way she'd just suggested for her daughter.

Jack allowed the idea to settle in his mind. *Is this it, Lord? Is this the answer I've been praying for?*

If Katarina would not leave Germany, marriage to a high-ranking Nazi—say, a major in the SS—would give her a level of protection she would not have otherwise.

With Jack's direct ties to Heinrich Himmler, no one would look into her background, or her mother's. Even if they tried they would never get past Jack, or rather, they would never get past SS-*Sturmbannführer* Friedrich Wilhelm Reiter.

"Yes, Princess Elena, when I return to Hamburg I will do everything in my power to marry your daughter."

It was the easiest promise he'd ever made. Unfortunately, he had no idea when he would be able to follow through.

23 November 1939, 0830 hours, The English Channel, three miles off the coast of Harwich

The wind blew in from the north, howling viciously and punching Jack in the face. Amid the eight-foot swells and overcast sky, the low, steady thunder of *HMS Basset's* engine was underscored by the angry pounding of water against the hull.

Facing into the wind, Jack took a deep breath. The heavy scent of diesel fuel overwhelmed the salty smell of the sea air and did nothing to settle his mind.

Where was the relief? Where was the pleasure over a successful mission completed?

Back in Hamburg with Katarina Kerensky, that's where.

He wanted to return to her. He wanted to be with her, always. But he had to be patient. He had to trust the Lord would, indeed, guide Jack back to her.

Unfortunately, there were no guarantees in war.

Lord, he prayed, *protect Katarina in my absence. We've both come a long way in our faith, but we still have far to go. Soften each of our hearts to You so we may know Your love, regardless of these dark times in which we live. Give us strength to make the sacrifices we must make for You and Your people. Thy will be done.*

"We're nearly there, Lieutenant."

Jack whipped around. He'd been so caught up in praying he hadn't heard the captain come up behind him. Unforgivable. No matter how deep his personal anguish, he should have been more alert. A mistake like that in enemy territory could get him killed.

"Would you care to join me at the helm for the completion of our journey?"

Welcoming the distraction, he nodded. "Of course."

Twenty minutes later, Jack jumped out of the trawler and onto the military dock near Harwich, only to find the head of MI6, Stewart Menzies himself, waiting for him on the quay.

Struck by the anxious look on the director's face, Jack's thoughts leaped immediately to Katarina and he closed the distance between them in a split second. "Did something go wrong after I left Germany?"

"I'll explain in the car," Menzies said, turning away before Jack could question him further.

For the first time in years, Jack felt real terror.

And there was nothing he could do to alleviate his fears but wait for the British spymaster to give him more information.

Jack had never felt so powerless. But as Menzies took his time settling into the back of the Bentley, Jack's temper began to burn away his panic. He buried the impulse to strangle the information out of the other man and waited for the Brit to make the next move.

Once the car was in motion, Menzies finally acknowledged him. "You have the photographs with you?"

Straight and to the point. In spite of his frustration, Jack appreciated the frank approach. "Yes. I was also able to obtain the exact coordinates of the minefield that will be laid in the next few days along the Thames Estuary."

"Then the mission was a success."

There was something in Menzies's eyes that put Jack instantly on alert. Looking out the window, he noted that they were traveling directly parallel to the coast, rather than west toward London. "Where are you taking me?"

Menzies leaned back in his seat and gave a careless shrug. "Let's just say I have a surprise for you."

Jack's eyes cut from Menzies to the passing scenery then back to Menzies again. "I beg your pardon, sir, but I've had enough surprises in the past three days to last a lifetime."

"Rest easy, Lieutenant. We are headed to Shoeburyness, where one of the magnetic mines was found imbedded in the mud along the shore."

Jack relaxed his shoulders. "How much of the device is left?"

"It's completely intact."

A wave of disbelief crested, but then gave way to anticipation. What were the odds of finding a magnetic mine in full working condition? A thousand to one? A million to one?

It was incredible.

No. It was a miracle. God had provided the British with a miracle.

Thank You, Lord.

"We have your entire team already in place," Menzies continued. "Lieutenant Commander Ouvry of the Royal Navy has volunteered to diffuse the bomb for us. And if he fails—"

"I'll step in."

Menzies gave him a sly smile. "I thought you might say that. But for Ouvry's sake, let us hope it doesn't come to that."

Jack sent up a prayer for Ouvry's protection, then fell into silence. The mission had come full circle. Just four days ago Jack had stood on the shores of the Isle of Wight surveying the remains of an American cargo ship, one of over a hundred civilian vessels blown up in the last three months.

Now all Jack had to do to prevent further losses was to finalize his countermeasures. And once he did, the *Kriegsmarine's* deadly secret weapon would be rendered useless.

God's will be done!

15 December 1939, war room, Whitehall, London
1400 hours

"I understand your countermeasures are operational."

"Yes, sir." Jack studied the man on the other side of the

desk. Although he'd met with him on several "unofficial" occasions through the years, this was Jack's first official meeting with Winston Churchill.

Churchill lit his cigar then took several short puffs. The resolute expression on his face fit his craggy features to perfection. "Let us pray this will buy us the time we need to stop Hitler's attempt to cut off our islands from the rest of the world."

"If I can speak frankly, sir, Hitler has underestimated the British."

"True enough." Churchill's expression turned intense as he opened the file on his desk. "I see you gave us a detailed and accurate report of the minefield laid by U-116 last month."

Jack nodded. Hermann Schmidt's efforts had been wasted. Jack couldn't think of a more fitting end to the magnetic mine mission.

"And because of that information," Churchill continued as he tapped the top page of the report, "we have successfully rerouted dozens of supply ships in the last two weeks."

"I didn't do it alone," Jack quickly pointed out. "Without Katarina Kerensky's help, the mission would have failed."

"I see she made quite an impression on you."

"Yes." And he desperately wanted to return to her. Three weeks had passed since he'd seen her last. It felt like a lifetime.

Closing the file, Churchill leaned back in his chair. "I have been informed that your next mission is set."

"I leave for Berlin in two days." And as soon as humanly possible he would find Katarina.

Churchill rose. "Be very sure this is what you want to do, Lieutenant." He came around the desk and settled his hand on Jack's shoulder. "Once you're inside the SD, you will be on your own. Jack Anderson will cease to exist."

Jack kept his gaze steady. "I understand." It was the price he'd expected to pay the day he'd become Friedrich Reiter. This was the mission MI6 had trained him for these last two years. There was no turning back now.

"Send what information you can, but your main objective will be to sabotage from within."

Jack nodded. It was a dangerous mission, one that could end in his death.

Never will I leave you; never will I forsake you.

He would not go into Germany alone.

Churchill spoke his thoughts aloud. "Well, then, Lieutenant, may God go with you."

Jack rose and gladly shook hands with a man some called a warmonger but who Jack considered one of the bravest, most steadfast men he had ever met. "I pray we see one another on the other side of this war."

"For both our sakes, I hope it is soon, Lieutenant." Churchill's eyes darkened with worry. "I hope it is very soon."

Chapter Twenty-Seven

For Katia, every night was the same. Perform her role. Take her bows. Greet her fans backstage.

Night after night, the audience came to watch her become a tragic heroine of a masterfully written play. Night after night, she gave them what they wanted.

While taking her bows, she squinted past the floodlights into the audience, looking for the one man she couldn't seem to forget.

She feared he wouldn't be there. But no matter how many days passed, no matter what city she was in, Katia never gave up hope of seeing Friedrich Reiter again.

He was in her mind always, even as she continued her clandestine work for the British. Over the past months, she'd completed four more missions for MI6. She had worked alone each time. Thanks to her part in the success of the magnetic mines mission, the British trusted her again. And thanks to Friedrich's efforts at her mother's ball in November, Admiral Doenitz had given Katia no more troubles.

Small compensation for a broken heart.

At least her relationship with her mother was healed. Although against the union from the start, Katia had stood as Elena's witness at her wedding to Hermann Schmidt. That day, Katia's heart had broken a little more. She only prayed marriage to Hermann would be enough to protect Elena from the death camps.

No. She would not give in to depressing thoughts now. Elena had made her choices and Katia had made hers. Their individual futures were in God's hands now, the safest place to be in these dark times.

If only Katia could meet Friedrich again and see for herself that he was safe. Oh, how she missed him, how she feared for him. How she wished there was no war separating them.

Lord, is he safe? Please, I pray You keep him safe throughout the duration of the war and beyond.

As she joined the rest of the cast backstage, Katia skimmed her gaze across the milling crowd. Elegant women wearing their jewels and furs clung to men dressed in tuxedos and various military uniforms. *Luftwaffe. Waffen. Gestapo.*

SS.

Tonight, Heinrich Himmler himself was among the crowd. He was wearing the black uniform of the Gestapo. Small of stature, unassuming, it was hard to believe he was the architect of Germany's greatest horrors.

Out of habit, she tried to determine the identity of the other Gestapo officer with Himmler, but the man had his back to her. The hard jolt to her heart made her breath catch in her throat. Could it be him?

She tried to think logically, but the pounding in her head made it difficult. There was something painfully familiar about the tall, broad-shouldered officer. And yet, she couldn't allow herself to hope. She'd been through this routine countless times in the last three months.

Too many nights she'd thought she'd seen Friedrich Reiter. Too many nights she'd been wrong. And left with only a prayer for his continued safety.

But, this time, as the man turned slowly around, her whole body relaxed on a sigh.

He'd come back to her.

He took a single step toward her, one step was all, and the shadows fell away from his face. His sharp, serious eyes and tall, lean body reminded her of a big, beautiful cat.

Code name, Cougar.

She remembered it all now. The tension-filled first meeting, the various battles for control, the ultimate agreement to work as a team, the trip to Wilhelmshaven, praying together on her bathroom floor. And, of course, the promise that he would return to her someday.

She didn't particularly like how comfortable he looked in the Gestapo uniform. Nor did she like the fast jolt of fear that pressed against her chest.

What was he thinking, becoming a member of the SD? If caught, he would be tortured, and eventually killed.

The noble fool.

As he began pacing toward her—slowly, deliberately— her heart stopped beating. Then he halted in front of her and she thought her heart just might beat right out of her chest.

"Katarina, you look as lovely as I remember." The words rolled off his tongue in perfect German, the hint of Austria clinging to the edges just as she remembered.

She swallowed back her nerves. "Welcome to Berlin, Herr Reiter."

He took her left hand in his, kissed her knuckles and

then looked at her with Jack Anderson's eyes. "I've missed you, my darling."

Said so simply, she had no doubt he meant every word. For propriety's sake, she knew she should take her hand back. But she badly needed to absorb the contact. "I've missed you more."

He chuckled at her response. "Always so competitive. It's what I love most about you."

Massaging her bare ring finger with his thumb, his face broke into a smile. "I think it is long past time I purchased you a piece of jewelry."

She put her heart in her eyes and reached up to cup his cheek. "I wouldn't refuse anything from you."

Still smiling, he pulled her hand away from his face and placed it against his chest. "I can't live without you, Katarina. I've tried. I've failed."

He did not look like a beaten man. In fact, he looked rather pleased with himself.

"Well, then, perhaps you should quit trying and admit your defeat once and for all," she said.

"My thoughts precisely."

The tenderness in his eyes made his intentions all too clear. Katia's throat swelled. But then she was bumped from behind. Realizing how many people could be watching them, she sighed in frustration. "I think we should finish this conversation in private."

"Your ability to read my mind is quite impressive."

"It's not really so amazing." She gave him the gentle smile of a woman in love. "We merely think alike, Herr Reiter."

"So it would seem," he said, lifting a single eyebrow. "Now, about that privacy you suggested?"

Smiling, she took his hand in hers and led him to her dressing room.

He shut the door behind them with a firm click.

With her heart racing from anticipation, she turned to face him. Leaning slightly forward, her body seemed to have a mind of its own, as though it was answering the powerful pull of her soul mate.

And then…and then…

He tugged her into his arms.

Just like that, her world felt a little less dark. She pressed her cheek against his chest. "Welcome back, my darling."

He pulled away and then kissed her firmly on the mouth. "I love you," he said in a strong voice. "I should have said it before I left you the last time."

She looked into his eyes and saw the godly man that had helped her believe again. "I love you, too." How could she not?

"Marry me, Katarina."

She didn't want to refuse. But she was afraid of the uncertainty that lay ahead of them. "What about your… journeys?" She spoke carefully, taking great pains not to mention England in case the Gestapo was listening to their conversation. "To distant places."

"My traveling days are over. I am to stay in Berlin for the duration of the war." He gave her a grave look, one that left little doubt to the underlying meaning of his words.

Recognizing the danger he was putting himself in, she fought back a wave of panic.

"Don't look at me like that," he begged. "I have every intention of growing old with you."

She nodded, and found she needed to draw in a long breath before she had the ability to speak again. "Growing old together is a lovely ambition."

"Katarina, take a chance on me. Take a chance on us. It would certainly make your mother happy." One corner of his mouth kicked up in an ironic grin.

So her mother *had* talked to him before he'd left Hamburg. Katia did not blame Elena for trying to protect her daughter in the way she thought best.

Even if Katia wasn't in love with the man, the idea of marriage to an SS *Sturmbannführer* would still make sense. To the Nazis, their union would look like the coveted blending of an Aryan elite with Russian royalty. To Katia's mother, their marriage would be an added layer of protection from the concentration camps.

To Katia, marrying Friedrich Reiter would be all about love. "Yes. *Yes*. I will marry you."

For a moment he only watched her, his gaze alight with pleasure. "I pray I prove worthy of you, Princess Katarina."

She thought of the courage he'd displayed on countless occasions. She thought of the way he'd knelt at her feet in her bathroom and taught her how to pray again. "You have already done that, my love. But now I have one small request of you."

He raised her hand to his lips. "Anything."

"Stay alive."

His gaze filled with the conviction of Jack Anderson. "God led us to one another, Katarina." He kept his voice barely above a whisper as he spoke. "We must believe He will lead us through this war, as well."

She loved his confidence in the Lord. It gave her the courage to hope.

As though God Himself reached down and wiped away the last of her fears, Katia felt certainty spread through her. She wouldn't think about the end of the war or all they stood to lose. She would take each day as it came and would fit a lifetime into every moment she had with this man. "Let's get married as soon as possible."

He enfolded her in the shelter of his warm embrace and spoke softly in her ear. Even if someone listened, they wouldn't be able to discern his words. "Our battles are only beginning, but we will never fight them alone. We have each other and we have the Lord."

"Now that's something worth putting our hope in."

* * * * *

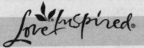

Could this bad-boy newcomer spell trouble for an Amish spinster...or be the answer to her prayers?

Read on for a sneak preview of
An Unlikely Amish Match,
the next book in Vannetta Chapman's miniseries
Indiana Amish Brides.

The sun was low in the western sky by the time Micah Fisher hitched a ride to the edge of town. The driver let him out at a dirt road that led to several Amish farms. He'd never been to visit his grandparents in Indiana before. They always came to Maine. But he had no trouble finding their place.

As he drew close to the lane that led to the farmhouse, he noticed a young woman standing by the mailbox. A little girl was holding her hand and another was hopping up and down. They were all staring at him.

"Howdy," he said.

The woman only nodded, but the two girls whispered, "Hello."

"Can we help you?" the woman asked. "Are you...lost?"

"*Nein.* At least I don't think I am."

"You must be if you're here. This is the end of the road."

Micah pointed to the farm next door. "Abigail and John Fisher live there?"

"They do."

"Then I'm not lost." He snatched off his baseball cap, rubbed the top of his head and then yanked the cap back on.

Micah stepped forward and held out his hand. "I'm Micah—Micah Fisher. Pleased to meet you."

"You're not *Englisch*?"

"Of course I'm not."

"So you're Amish?" She stared pointedly at his clothing—tennis shoes, blue jeans, T-shirt and baseball cap. Pretty much what he wore every day.

"I'm as Plain and simple as they come."

"I somehow doubt that."

"Since we're going to be neighbors, I suppose I should know your name."

"Neighbors?"

"*Ja.* I've come to live with my *daddi* and *mammi*—at least for a few months. My parents think it will straighten me out." He peered down the lane. "I thought the bishop lived next door."

"He does."

"Oh. You're the bishop's *doschder*?"

"We all are," the little girl with freckles cried. "I'm Sharon and that's Shiloh and that is Susannah."

"Nice to meet you, Sharon and Shiloh and Susannah."

Sharon lost interest and squatted to pick up some of the rocks. Shiloh hid behind her *schweschder*'s skirt, and Susannah scowled at him.

"I knew the bishop lived next door, but no one told me he had such pretty *doschdern*."

Susannah's eyes widened even more, but it was Shiloh who said, "He just called you pretty."

"Actually I called you all pretty."

Shiloh ducked back behind Susannah.

Susannah narrowed her eyes as if she was squinting into the sun, only she wasn't. "Do you talk to every girl you meet that way?"

"Not all of them—no."

Don't miss
An Unlikely Amish Match *by Vannetta Chapman,*
available February 2020 wherever
Love Inspired® *books and ebooks are sold.*

LoveInspired.com

LOVE INSPIRED
INSPIRATIONAL ROMANCE

UPLIFTING STORIES OF FAITH, FORGIVENESS AND HOPE.

Join our social communities to connect with other readers who share your love!

Sign up for the Love Inspired newsletter at **LoveInspired.com** to be the first to find out about upcoming titles, special promotions and exclusive content.

CONNECT WITH US AT:

Facebook.com/LoveInspiredBooks

Twitter.com/LoveInspiredBks

Facebook.com/groups/HarlequinConnection